Brognola recognized Sokolov for what he was

The man was a player *and* a pawn. He armed the killers, but he also served them. And above him, shadowing his every move, were men and women who could take him off the board at any time. He lived because they found him useful for the advancement of their agendas.

The big Fed knew that removing Sokolov from circulation was a good thing. Putting him on public trial, revealing some of those he served might also benefit humanity. It wouldn't stop the global arms trade or any of the slaughter that resulted from it, but it might slow the pace of killing. For a while.

If anyone could do the job, Mack B̶e̶l̶a̶ the man.

Don Pendleton's Mack Bolan®

Extraordinary Rendition

A GOLD EAGLE BOOK FROM

WORLDWIDE®

TORONTO • NEW YORK • LONDON
AMSTERDAM • PARIS • SYDNEY • HAMBURG
STOCKHOLM • ATHENS • TOKYO • MILAN
MADRID • WARSAW • BUDAPEST • AUCKLAND

Recycling programs
for this product may
not exist in your area.

First edition October 2010

ISBN-13: 978-0-373-61540-7

Special thanks and acknowledgment to
Mike Newton for his contribution to this work.

EXTRAORDINARY RENDITION

Printed in U.S.A.

It is ironical that in an age when we have prided ourselves on the intelligent care and teaching of children we have at the same time put them at the mercy of new and most terrible weapons of destruction.

—Pearl S. Buck
1892–1973
What America
Means to Me

Gods are born and die, but the atom endures.

—Alexander Chase
1926–
Perspectives

Forget the old line about meddling in God's domain. This time terrorists are meddling in mine. And they'll regret it.

—Mack Bolan

For Private First Class Ross A. McGinnis
1st Platoon, C Company, 1st Battalion, 26th Infantry
God keep

PROLOGUE

Kotlin Island, Gulf of Finland

Special Agent Robert Marx thought it was funny how things seemed to change but actually stayed the same. Staring across the dark, cold water of the gulf before him, he could see the bright lights of Saint Petersburg. Founded under its present name in 1703, the regal city had been renamed Petrograd in 1914, changed to Leningrad in 1924, then had become Saint Petersburg once more in 1991.

The more things changed, the more they stayed the same.

Take *extraordinary rendition,* for instance.

It was a fancy name for kidnapping, dreamed up by some Washington bureaucrat back in the eighties, a means of returning international fugitives to America for trial, even when they were sheltered by a hostile state. After 9/11 the phrase had morphed into a euphemism for shipping terrorist suspects off to friendly nations where "aggressive questioning" was commonplace.

Another euphemism. Why not call it torture?

Regardless, the pendulum had swung again, and the Justice Department was saving rendition for hard-case felons whose wealth and/or political connections placed them effectively beyond the law's reach.

Scumbags like Gennady Sokolov.

For his sake, Special Agent Marx and seven other members of the FBI's elite Hostage Rescue Team were standing in the icy early-morning darkness of Kotlin Island, twenty miles west of Saint Petersburg and a mile west of the Kronstadt seaport.

There were no hostages at risk this night. The mission was a basic find-and-snatch.

Extraordinary rendition.

Their target was a dacha built by Sokolov as a retreat from the daily grind of his murderous business. The team had helicoptered in from the mainland, and their chopper was waiting to take them back again, plus one. A charter jet was also standing by at Pulkovo II International Airport, eleven miles from downtown Saint Petersburg, with its flight plan to London on file.

From there, it was home to the States.

If they lived through the night.

Marx had handpicked his team, choosing only the best. He had two seasoned snipers, one packing a Remington M-40 A-1 .308 sniper rifle fitted with a Unertl target scope, and the other armed with a Barrett M-86 A-1 "light Fifty" in case they had to take out any armored cars. Chuck Osborne carried a Benelli M-4 Super 90 semiauto shotgun, for opening doors and flattening humans. Marx and the other four men on his team were armed with Heckler & Koch MP-5 SD-6 submachine guns, with retractable stocks, integrated suppressor and 3-round-burst trigger groups. As sidearms, all HRT members carried the "Bureau Model" Springfield Armory TRP-PRO in .45 caliber.

Good to go.

They'd waited two hours for Sokolov and his men to fall asleep. Now it was time to make the grab and get the hell off Kotlin, before they ran out of luck.

The snipers were deployed, already covering the grand three-story house, as Marx led his team through the dark toward their selected entry point. It might not be an easy snatch, considering the target, but they'd trained on a scale model of the house, built back at Quantico specially for their mission.

They were as ready as they'd ever be.

Marx led the way, as usual. He was his own point man, never asking any other member of the HRT to do a job he personally shunned. Another thirty yards or so, and they'd have cover from the dacha's seven-car garage while they prepared for entry.

Just a little farther, and—

The night vanished around them in a blaze of metal halide lamps. A deep metallic voice demanded their immediate surrender, first in Russian, then in English.

Marx reacted while the faceless drone was midway through his spiel, raising his SMG and firing at the nearest bank of lights. His team responded instantly, blazing away to either side. Their submachine guns whispered, while the big Benelli shotgun thundered. From a distance, Marx's snipers opened up, but they were short on living targets.

Half the halide lamps were dark and smoking when the muzzle-flashes started winking all around the FBI strike team. Marx staggered as a bullet struck his body armor, bruising his chest underneath the Kevlar vest. He shifted targets, firing at live enemies instead of floodlights now, seeing the mission go to hell and praying that he could still get his team out intact.

But two of them were down already, Jurecki and Zvirbulis—their two Russian-speakers—sprawled on the driveway's pavement, deathly still. Marx didn't want to see the pools of crimson spreading underneath their supine forms, steaming from contact with the frigid air.

Marx felt his magazine run dry and dropped it, reaching for a fresh one. He'd withdrawn the new mag halfway from its pouch on his tactical vest when a slug punched through his armpit, slipping past the armor, tumbling through his rib cage and right lung.

The shock of impact dropped Marx to the pavement. Numb fingers lost their grip on his SMG, and he heard it clatter out of reach. Around him, twitching, jerking, he could see the other members of his team dropping like shattered mannequins.

Maybe the snipers could escape in time and reach the waiting chopper. If they weren't cut off on their retreat and—

Marx blinked as a shadow fell between him and the halide lamps that hadn't been shot out. It took the last of his remaining strength to turn and face the weapon leveled at him.

"Goodbye, American," the gunman said.

CHAPTER ONE

Moscow, Russia

Mack Bolan had the Beatles in his head, Paul and John singing "Back in the USSR" as his Aeroflot Airbus A330-200 circled in a holding pattern over Domodedovo International Airport.

But it wasn't the USSR anymore. Now, it was the Russian Federation, totally divorced from all the cold-war crimes of communism, prosperous and overflowing with democracy for all.

Sure thing.

And if you bought that, there were time-share contracts on the Brooklyn Bridge that ought to make your eyes light up, big-time.

This wasn't Bolan's first visit to Russia, but familiarity didn't relieve the tightening he felt inside, as if someone had found the winding stem to his internal clock and given it a sudden twist. Nerves wouldn't show on Bolan's face or in his mannerisms, but they registered their agitation in his gut and in his head.

Russia had always been the big, bad Bear when he was growing up, serving his country as a Green Beret, and moving on from there to wage a one-man war against the Mafia. Moscow, the Kremlin and the KGB—under its varied names—had lurked behind a number of the plots Bolan had privately unraveled, and had spawned a fair percentage of the threats he'd faced after his government created Stony Man Farm and its off-the-books response to terrorism.

Then, as if by magic, virtually overnight, that "evil empire" had been neutralized. Governments fell, the Berlin Wall came down and the Soviet Union shattered like crockery dropped on concrete.

Threat neutralized?

Hardly.

In some ways, from the global export of its vicious *Mafiya* to home-grown civil wars, continued spying and subversion, and free-floating swarms of ex-government agents peddling the tools of Armageddon, Mother Russia was more dangerous than ever.

And Bolan was going in to face the Bear unarmed.

Well, not the *whole* Bear, if his mission briefing had been accurate. More like a litter of rabid cubs, protecting a rogue wolverine.

Bolan broke that train. His enemies this time—like every other time—were men, not animals.

No other animal on Earth would kill thousands for profit. Or for pleasure.

The pilot's disembodied voice informed him that their flight was cleared for landing. Finally.

Domodedovo was one of three airports serving Moscow, the others being Sheremetyevo International and Vnukovo International. Among them, the three handled forty-odd-million passengers per year. It should be relatively easy, in that crush, for one pseudo-Canadian to pass unnoticed on his way.

Should be.

Bolan had flown from Montreal to London with a Canadian passport in the name of Matthew Cooper. He was carrying sufficient ID to support that cover, including an Ontario driver's license, Social Insurance card and functional platinum plastic. He also came prepared with Canadian currency.

So far, so good.

But Bolan wasn't on the ground yet, hadn't met his contact from the Federal Protective Service—FSB—Russia's equivalent of the FBI.

So, what had changed?

Russian relations with America, perhaps. Depending on the day and hour when you turned on CNN to find out which world leaders were at odds with whom, and why. This week, it seemed, the Russians needed help and weren't afraid to say so.

More or less.

But as for what Bolan would find waiting in Moscow, he would simply have to wait and see.

And not much longer now.

With an ungainly thump and snarl, the Airbus A330-200 touched down.

The Executioner was on the ground in Moscow, one more time.

YURI BAZHOV DISLIKED airports. He didn't care for travel, generally, and he hated flying, but the main reason for his dislike of airports was their fetish for security. They teemed with uniforms and guns that he could see, while other police were undoubtedly lurking in plainclothes or hiding in back rooms and watching the concourse with closed-circuit cameras.

Bazhov stopped short of spitting on the floor, which would have drawn attention to himself. The last thing he needed, standing with a GSh-18 automatic pistol tucked under his belt at the small of his back, was for some cop or militiaman to stop and frisk him on vague suspicion.

The job had to be important, he supposed, although it didn't sound like much. Taras Morozov didn't send a six-man team out to the airport every day, with orders to collect a stranger flying in from Canada.

Not greet him, mind you. Just collect him.

Bazhov had to smile at that, though cautiously. Smiling for

no good reason could draw notice, just the same as spitting on the floor. Most anything out of the ordinary could spell trouble, if you thought about it long enough.

Collect the stranger, he'd been told. Taras had given him a name and flight number, then placed him in charge of the collection team. Which was an honor in itself.

Collect could mean a hundred different things, but Taras had added one crucial proviso. Bazhov had to deliver the stranger alive. Not necessarily undamaged, but breathing and able to speak.

More specifically, to answer questions.

Bazhov wondered if he would be privileged to witness that interrogation. Certainly, he wouldn't be in charge of it. The family had specialists for such occasions, legendary in their way. Kokorinov was probably the best—or worst—a cold man with no concept of remorse or mercy. Bashkirtseva favored power tools, but could be flexible. Nikulin was a savage, plain and simple.

Any one of them could teach Bazhov a thing or two, perhaps speed his advancement up through the ranks. Though, come to think of it, his choice to head up the collection team was quite a vote of confidence.

He needed to be certain that he didn't fuck it up.

Bazhov squinted at the monitor, watching its list of flight arrivals and departures scroll across the screen. He suspected that he would need glasses soon, a damned embarrassment and scandal at his tender age of thirty-five, but he would put off the indignity as long as possible. The first person who made fun of him was dead.

According to the monitor, the flight from Montreal had landed more or less on time, a minor miracle for Domodedovo International. Bazhov couldn't approach the gate where passengers deplaned—another security precaution—and he didn't know whether his target had checked luggage in the belly of the plane. To cover every possibility, he had two men on standby at the baggage carousels, two more positioned where he could observe them from his present station, and his driver, on call, driving incessant loops around the terminal.

If anything went wrong with the collection, it wouldn't be Yuri Bazhov's fault.

But he would pay the price, regardless.

Such was life.

Bazhov saw passengers emerging from the corridor that served the various arrival gates, plodding along with the enthusiasm of dumb cattle entering an abattoir. A few cracked smiles on recognizing relatives or lovers who had come to greet them. Most kept their faces deadpan, as if it would cost them extra to reveal a trace of human feeling.

Bazhov felt his pulse kick up a notch when he picked out his target. He hadn't been shown a photograph, but the description fit, albeit vaguely. More than anything, it was the target's bearing that betrayed him.

Yuri Bazhov recognized a killer when he saw one.

After all, he owned a mirror, didn't he?

SPOTTING A TAIL on foreign turf, particularly in a crowded public place that welcomed strangers by the thousand every hour, could be difficult, to say the least. In airports, where small hordes of people gathered, scanning faces of the new arrivals to pick out their loved ones, partners, rivals, even people they have never met but have been paid to greet, curious staring was routine. The rule, not the exception.

Bolan was on alert before he cleared the jetway fastened to the bulkhead of the Aeroflot Airbus. He had a likeness of his contact memorized, but there was always a chance of some last-minute substitution. People got sick or got dead. They got sidetracked and shuffled around on some bureaucrat's whim. Whole operations got scuttled without any warning to agents at risk on the ground.

Bolan followed the flow of humanity past more arrival

gates, following the multilingual signs directing passengers to immigration and passport control, to customs, baggage claim and ground transportation. His only baggage was a carry-on, and he was expecting a ride at the end of his hike through the concourse, but there was no mistaking the rest.

Bolan showed his passport to an immigration officer whose cropped hair, military uniform and plain face conspired to disguise her sex. She held the passport up beside his face, her eyes flicking back and forth between the photo and its living counterpart, then asked him the obligatory questions. Bolan answered truthfully that he didn't intend to spend more than a week on Russian soil, and that he had no fixed address in mind.

"So, traveling?" she asked.

"That's right."

Frowning, the agent stamped his passport with a vehemence the task scarcely deserved, and passed him on to customs. There, a portly officer with triple chins pawed through the contents of his carry-on, presumably in search of contraband.

"No other bags?" he asked.

"That's it," Bolan replied.

"And if you need more clothes?"

"American Express."

Apparently disgruntled at his failure to discover some incriminating bit of evidence, the agent scowled at Bolan's passport stamp, then nodded him along to clear the station.

Thirty feet ahead of Bolan stood a wall of frosted glass, preventing those who gathered on the other side from seeing what went on at customs. Bits of faces showed each time the exit door opened and closed, but Bolan didn't think his contact would be pushing up to head the line.

He cleared the doorway, with a hefty woman and her two unruly children close behind him. Bolan let them take the lead, converging on a thin, small-headed man whose pale face registered despair at the sight of them.

The joys of coming home.

Bolan was looking for his contact when he saw the skinhead on his left, leaning against a wall there, staring hard at Bolan's face until their eyes met. Caught, be broke contact and made a show of checking out the other passengers, while muttering some comment to the collar of his leather jacket.

Glancing to his right, Bolan picked out another front man of the not-so-welcoming committee, nodding in response to something no one else could hear, hand raised to press an earpiece home.

Clumsy.

But in his present situation, Bolan thought, how good did his opponents really need to be?

"I THINK HE SPOTTED us!" Yuri Bazhov stated.

"So, he has eyes," Evgeny Surikov replied, his voice a tinny sneer through Bazhov's earpiece. "What's the difference?"

Seething with anger yet afraid to make a spectacle in public, Bazhov hissed at the small microphone concealed on his lapel. "What do you think, idiot? That we should take him here, in front of everyone?"

"Why not?" Danil Perov chimed in.

Turning away from customs, Bazhov fell in step a dozen yards behind his target. "I don't want the damned militia coming down on us," he said into the microphone. "Whoever wants to be arrested, do it somewhere else. You can explain to Taras personally, if you don't like following his orders."

That silenced the bellyachers for now. Bazhov followed his man, still unsure where the stranger would lead him. The target carried a bag, but might have other luggage awaiting attention downstairs. Who flew to Moscow with a single bag, even if he was only staying for the night?

Who was this man? Why did he matter to the Family?

Nobody tells me anything, Bazhov thought, frowning to himself.

All right, the bosses didn't owe him any explanation, but he should be told enough to let him do his job effectively and safely. What if this one was some kind of kung fu expert, for example? What if he was carrying a deadly virus in his blood or sputum? Bazhov and his men could wind up beaten to a pulp, infected with some damned thing that would kill them slowly.

Before it came to that, he'd use the GSh-18 and damn the consequences. But it was a last resort, and if he had to kill the stranger, Bazhov might consider saving one round for himself.

The target didn't turn to see if anyone was following his path along the concourse. He played it cool, but Bazhov was convinced that he'd been spotted, maybe Surikov, as well. That made the job more difficult, but not impossible, by any means.

With odds of six to one, how could they lose him?

They took the escalator down toward the baggage claim and ground transportation area, and the other services designed to hasten new arrivals from the airport. Bazhov couldn't help scowling as his target reached the bottom and turned left, away from the long bank of luggage carousels.

"No bags," he told the microphone. "Repeat! No bags. Vasily, Pavel, come rejoin us."

"On my way," Vasily Radko answered.

"Coming," Pavel Malevich replied.

Apparently, their target meant to hire a car. He had no less than half a dozen agencies to choose from, but he might have reservations with a car already standing by. In either case, they had to intercept him, before he vanished into city traffic.

Domodedovo International stood twenty-two miles from downtown Moscow. Call it a half-hour's drive if nobody was speeding, drawing attention from traffic police. In the worst-case scenario, Bazhov could stop the mark's car in transit, stage an accident if need be and lift him before the militia arrived.

Better to take him at the airport, though, perhaps in the garage where the hired cars were kept shiny-clean, with their dents and scratches inventoried for insurance purposes. There would be fewer witnesses, none likely to step forward and defend a stranger in the face of guns.

"Close in," Bazhov commanded. "We will take him when he goes to fetch his car."

ANZHELA PILKIN SMELLED the trap before she saw it closing on the stranger she had come to meet. She seemed to have a sixth sense for such things—so much so, if the truth be told, that fellow agents of the FSB sometimes referred to her as *wed'ma.*

Witch.

Unfortunately, she wasn't a witch, only an FSB lieutenant who couldn't work magic on a whim. She couldn't twirl a wand and make the thugs who had staked out her contact disappear.

But in a pinch, she *could* draw her Yarygin PYa pistol and make them die.

Lieutenant Pilkin hoped it wouldn't come to that. Her mission was covert, and her superiors would frown on gunplay at the airport. It was something they expected from Chicago, New York City—anywhere but Moscow, in the midst of a top-secret operation. Public killing that involved police would spoil the play.

And it would do no good for her career.

She watched the procession pass by, concealed behind a tourist information kiosk, shifting her position to prevent herself from being seen. It was impossible to say if the American now traveling as Matthew Cooper had discovered he was being followed. And while Pilkin hoped so—hoped that he wasn't oblivious to such an obvious approach—she also dreaded what might happen if he tried to ditch the trackers on his own.

Pilkin visualized a free-for-all, fists flying, maybe weapons drawn, and what would happen next? When the militia came, what could she do?

Follow her contact to his holding cell, perhaps, and try to talk him out of custody? She might be able to pull rank on the militia, but to what end? Exposure of the man would automatically abort their mission, and she knew that her superiors likely wouldn't permit a second effort.

So, whatever she attempted, it would have to be unauthorized and hidden from the brass at FSB headquarters.

She was on her own.

Pilkin watched the tall American bypass the sign directing him to the baggage claim and head off toward the bank of kiosks that dispensed hired cars. She knew he was expecting her to pick him up, which meant that his diversion was precisely that: a stall, either to locate her, throw off his enemies, or both.

Before the man she knew as Cooper cleared another thirty yards, Pilkin counted five men trailing him. They might have passed unnoticed in the flow of passengers, airport employees and assorted idlers, if she hadn't been well trained and they had been more skillful.

Enemies came in all shapes, sizes and colors. Some were natural chameleons, while others stood out for their bearing, brutish looks, or quirks that give away their secrets. These five shared a common arrogance most often seen in the associates of the Russian *Mafiya*—and all of them were talking to themselves in turn, revealing to an educated watcher that they kept in touch by means of tiny two-way radios.

And they were armed. The bulges visible beneath some of their jackets told Pilkin that, and she assumed the ones whose weapons weren't evident had simply dressed themselves more carefully. They passed a few militia officers along the way, but were ignored.

So much for tight airport security.

Anzhela Pilkin had a choice to make.

She could keep following her contact and his shadows, wait until they made a move and try to intervene, or she could leave the terminal and fetch her car. Be ready when he needed her.

The second course of action took some faith.

She had to trust that the mobsters were smart enough to bide their time and seek a place with fewer witnesses before they made a move. And she had to trust her contact to remain alive for several minutes on his own, away from Pilkin's observant eyes.

She made her choice, broke off pursuit and started walking swiftly—nearly running—to the closest exit from the airport terminal.

WITH NO SIGN of his contact, Bolan had a choice to make. His basic options were to wait inside the airport terminal or leave it, but both choices had their built-in risks.

Waiting meant somehow dealing with the watchers who were trailing him. He'd counted three, but couldn't tip his hand by dawdling along and sneaking peeks for any others who had joined them. Three was bad enough, with Bolan presently unarmed. A confrontation in the terminal would draw police, and that would be the end of his mission, whether he survived or not.

Leaving the terminal posed different risks. He could obtain a rental car with no great difficulty, but his shadows would most likely make their move when he went to collect it in some nearby parking lot or garage. Bolan assumed that some of them, at least, were armed. Whether their orders were to kill him on the spot or bring him out alive, when he resisted, one or more of them might snap.

And if he managed to survive that showdown, even take their weapons for himself, then what? He'd be adrift in Moscow, with its thirteen million people and no way of reaching his contact.

Who might or might not even be alive.

Bolan couldn't approach the U.S. Embassy, since he was traveling as a Canadian. It wouldn't help to reach the CIA's station chief, since the Company had been frozen out of his mission. He had contacts, but only for potential "cleanup" jobs. Forget the Canadian consulate, too. Even if they agreed to send him "home," his mission would have failed.

On the flip side, he couldn't drop by FSB headquarters in Lubyanka Square and spill his story to a desk sergeant, either. The Russian side was worried about leaks of their own, keeping a tight lid on the operation. It was strictly need-to-know, or so he'd been informed, although the men now stalking him were living evidence that someone had to have spilled the beans.

The good news was that if he managed to clear the airport alive, he knew enough about his target to reach the man's last known address. Bolan supposed that he could arm himself in Moscow, with an estimated 170,000 illegal guns in circulation, but what of it?

His mission didn't call for an assassination. He'd been sent to find, extract and deliver one man to a team that would put him on ice and presumably ship him off somewhere for trial.

That end of it was not Bolan's concern. But he'd been told, with heavy emphasis, that Washington required this guy alive. His showcase trial, apparently, was more important than the man himself or any of his crimes.

A message to the predators: *no matter where you hide, you are within our reach.*

As if they'd care and somehow magically reform.

Unless Bolan could bag his man and summon the extraction unit, none of that was happening.

He made his choice, passed by the car-rental kiosks and kept going, toward the nearest exit from the terminal. He would choose his ground, confront his enemies and see what happened next.

Outside, the sun was going down. The late afternoon was warm and humid, making Bolan's shirt stick to his skin. Across six lanes of airport traffic, opposite his exit door, stood a tall parking garage. Hired cars were picked up and returned on the ground floor. The rest, Bolan supposed, was rented by the space to travelers or those on hand to meet them.

It would be as good a battleground as any.

He had one foot off the curb when a little gray sportster squealed to a stop in front of him, its right-front fender nearly grazing his shoe.

Behind the wheel, the face he had been watching for since his arrival snapped at him, "Get in, will you, while you still can!"

CHAPTER TWO

Washington, D.C., two days earlier

The International Spy Museum was located at 800 F Street Northwest, one block east of Ford's Theater and one block north of FBI Headquarters, directly opposite the Smithsonian American Art Museum and the National Portrait Gallery. It occupied five buildings, renovated at a cost of forty million dollars, and had earned its keep with interest since it opened in July 2002.

The museum had no parking lot of its own, so Bolan left his rental in a commercial garage two blocks over and walked back, still early, enjoying the sunshine. Spring was being kind to Washington, so far.

He doubted that it would be kind to him.

Only a few museums in Washington charged entrance fees. The Spy Museum was one of them, collecting twenty dollars from adults and shaving off a buck for active-duty members of the military. Entry through a "controlled" checkpoint included receipt of cover profiles for each visitor, with instructions to memorize the details in five minutes flat. Fledgling spies received a simple "mission," but weren't required to complete it. Staff "police" stopped visitors at random, grilling them for details of their cover, adding just a hint of spice. For true enthusiasts, the interactive *Operation Spy* pavilion offered simulations that included detection and disarming of a nuclear device.

Bolan went through the motions and moved on, idling

past some of the museum's six hundred exhibits depicting the evolution of espionage from ancient Greece and Rome to the twenty-first century. At any other time, it would have piqued his interest, but he had a real-life mission of his own.

Or would have, very shortly.

Keeping an eye on the time, Bolan drifted toward the museum's Spy City Café, a snack shop for guests whose budgets wouldn't cover dining at the adjacent, upscale Zola Restaurant. He wasn't hungry, but he planned on meeting someone there.

And his contact, as always, was punctual.

"The fish is red," Hal Brognola said as he sidled up to Bolan.

"Guess I'll have the chicken, then," Bolan replied.

Brognola frowned and said, "That's not the counter-sign."

"Sorry. I must've missed the memo."

"Jeez. You kids today."

"If I'm a kid, that makes you—what? A yuppie?"

"God forbid. Let's take a walk."

They walked.

"I thought this place would suit us," the big Fed remarked. "With everybody hyped on spies and role-playing, we ought to fit right in."

"But are we being shadowed?" Bolan asked, half-teasing.

"Hell, who isn't in this crazy town?"

Bolan resisted the impulse to look around for lurking watchers. Paranoia in a spy museum was no way to begin a mission.

"So, what's up?" he asked.

Brognola led him to a room labeled The Secret History of History. A black-garbed ninja figure stood beside the door, arms poised as if to strike, defending upright panels filled with Japanese calligraphy. Beyond the threshold lay exhibits dedicated to some well-known spies, and others who had flown beneath the radar in their day.

Pausing before an exhibit devoted to Harriet Tubman and the Underground Railroad, Brognola asked, "Are you familiar with Gennady Sokolov?"

"By reputation," Bolan said. "Papers call him the Merchant of Death."

"And it fits," said Brognola. "He's ex-KGB, if there is such a thing. Retired as a major when the Soviet Union collapsed and went into private practice, selling anything and everything one group can use to kill another. Absolutely apolitical these days. He's peddled arms, aircraft and military vehicles to everyone from Congo warlords to al Qaeda and the Taliban."

"An equal-opportunity destroyer."

"Anyone who pays can play," Brognola said. "He's supplied both government forces and rebels in fifteen African states that we're sure of, plus others in Afghanistan and Pakistan, Colombia, the Philippines. He gets around."

"And no one's thought to rein him in?"

"Oh, sure. He's got indictments coming out the old wazoo from Justice, Interpol, the Brits and Belgium, where he used to have a clearing house. You know the story, though. Filing a charge is one thing. Making an arrest and bringing him to trial is a whole other ball game."

"I detect a note of bitterness."

"Damn straight, you do. At one time, Sokolov had carte blanche from the Company and State to arm our so-called friends abroad. His cargo planes flew out of Florida, for Christ's sake. Diplomatic cover, when he needed it. Of course, times change. Some of the mopes we armed ten years ago are enemies today. We're taking hits from our own hardware, and it's setting off alarms."

"I'm not surprised," said Bolan.

"Did you know that Sokolov did business with the UN for a while? And NATO? This is *after* his indictment, mind you.

Even on the run, he's still got friends he can tap for contracts in Iraq, Afghanistan and Sudan. Can you imagine that? Son of a bitch sells weapons to our private contractors, for hunting insurgents he's armed to kill them. Talk about the candle burning at both ends."

"Is he that hard to find?" Bolan asked.

"Just the opposite. Not hard at all. He lives in Russia, safe and sound. Their constitution bans extradition of any Russian citizen charged with acts that are legal in Russia itself."

"Which includes selling arms under legal contracts."

"Absolutely. They've done it for decades. So have we, the Brits, the French, Chinese—you name it. Hell, we've sponsored some of Sokolov's transactions. In the Russian view, we're just pissed off today because some of yesterday's allies have jumped ship."

"It doesn't end there," Bolan said.

"You got that right. Call it principle, machismo, whatever you like. The folks I report to aren't letting it go. They've already tried once to extract Sokolov."

"And missed him?" Bolan guessed.

"I wish that's all it was. They lost eight guys from HRT. It damn near took an act of Congress just to get their bodies back."

"So, he's got tight security."

"The best," the big Fed said. "If that's all it was."

"You think someone on this side burned them?"

"I'm not pointing any fingers," Brognola replied. "But any time the Bureau goes off campus, there's a protocol for giving heads-up to the nearest chief of station for the Company. It helps with technical assistance and avoids stepping on any tender toes."

"The whole new era of cooperation."

"Don't you love it? All the stupid backstabbing that came down from the Hoover-Langley feud supposedly got swept away with 9/11. The Company got back into domestic surveillance—assuming they ever got out—and Congress told everyone to play nice. Share the intel both ways, no more hoarding or disinformation between so-called allies."

"Let me guess," Bolan replied. "It isn't working."

"That depends on what you mean by *working*. After all the fretting and reshuffling, look at the twenty-two agencies lumped together in Homeland Security. You've got the Secret Service, Customs, Immigration, the Coast Guard, FEMA, the Border Patrol—even the Plant and Animal Inspection Service, for God's sake. But who's left out?"

"The Bureau and the Company?"

"Bingo! A minor oversight, okay? Leaving our two primary intelligence agencies on the outside, looking in. And if you think the falling towers made them start to love each other, guess again."

"Business as usual," Bolan observed.

"Or worse. Who doesn't want a ton of money to fight terrorism? Spend it any way you like. Just get the job done."

"Well…"

They'd drifted into an exhibit labeled "Spies Among Us," laying out the history of espionage preceding World War II—or, at least, one version of it. Bolan saw no mention of the meeting at FBI Headquarters in November 1941, where J. Edgar Hoover had rejected warnings of an impending attack on Pearl Harbor and threw the informant out of his office.

"The problem arises," Brognola said, "from conflict of interest. Let's imagine Langley has an asset helping arm its clients in the field, while Bureau agents try to lock him up for arming terrorists. One side indicts, the other intervenes. It could get nasty."

"Sokolov's still dealing with the Company?"

"A rumor," Brognola replied. "These things are written on the wind, you know. If there's a document to prove it, I'd be very damned surprised."

Bolan had never given any major thought to how his own

missions were logged at Stony Man. He had assumed some record had to exist, suitably sanitized in the best interest of all concerned.

"And if the Bureau thinks the Company's responsible for eight men down…"

"We're talking cloak-and-dagger civil war," Brognola said. "Aside from which, their boy's still out there, dealing any damned thing he can get his hands on. Which, I'm told, included enough loose nukes to light up all our lives."

"You want him taken out of circulation."

"Not just taken out. Returned alive for trial."

"That could turn out to be embarrassing," Bolan suggested. "Airing all that dirty laundry in a courtroom won't do much for either side's prestige."

"We're the mechanics on this job," Brognola said. "Or, rather, *you* are. Bring him back alive."

"Or?"

"There's no *or* on this one. We could always find a way to smoke him. Drop a smart bomb down his chimney Christmas Eve and claim that Santa farted on the fire. Whatever. Trial is deemed essential, PR-wise."

"Terrific."

"Should you meet our boy's suppliers and customers, however, then the gloves are off. For them, not him. No one will think twice if they go down for the count."

"You mean, no one in Wonderland."

"That's understood. Of course, their friends and family may take offense."

"At least my hands aren't tied."

"Look at it this way," Brognola suggested. "It's an all-you-can-eat buffet, except for one small item in a doggie bag."

"That makes it so much easier."

"I've got the background information that you'll need, and intel on your contact."

"Someone from the Company?" Bolan asked.

"Better. From the FSB."

"Outstanding. All I need now is a Cheshire cat."

"Maybe you'll find one as you go along."

Brognola pulled a CD in its jewel case from an outer pocket of his coat and handed it to Bolan. The soldier palmed the gift, catching a small boy nearby watching from the shelter of his mother's skirt. Wide-eyed and curious.

Bolan gave him a smile, raising a cautionary finger to his lips, and made the jewel case disappear.

"Who's that?" Brognola asked.

"My backup," Bolan said. "He kneecaps anyone who tries to follow me."

"He's built for it."

"So, I'll look over this and book a flight to…where, again?"

"Moscow. Our boy lives near Saint Petersburg, but he's forever back and forth, tending to business."

"With any luck," Bolan said, "I can interrupt his cash flow."

"Interrupt him altogether," Brognola replied. "But gently, if you please."

"My middle name."

"Uh-huh."

"We ought to talk about what happens to the target if it all goes sideways," Bolan said. "How badly do you want him breathing, if I can't deliver him intact?"

Brognola frowned. "The notion of your failing," he replied, "has never crossed my mind."

THAT WAS A LIE, of course. Brognola's job at Justice—and at Stony Man—was to consider all the options anytime he put an asset in the field. Failure was always possible, no matter how much he abhorred the thought of it.

Mistakes were made. Luck turned. Men died.

Sometimes the wrong men died. And women, too.

Brognola didn't like to think about that aspect of his job, but he was paid to think about it, to plan around it. Have another hole card tucked away when best-laid plans went south, sideways, or up the chimney in a puff of smoke.

False modesty aside, Brognola was the best in Washington at what he did, which, on the public record, was a paper-shuffling job at the Justice Building on Pennsylvania Avenue.

He weighed the price of failure in advance. His field agents were also friends, a lapse in strict professionalism occasioned by the circumstances of their meeting. Bolan and the rest had crossed Brognola's path initially while he was with the FBI, assigned to bust the Mafia. He'd played within the rules in those days—to a point, at least, before he'd seen the Executioner in action, scoring wins with the direct, scorched-earth approach.

The rest was history. He'd known who to recruit when Stony Man was organized, and they'd been carrying the fight to human predators around the globe since then.

But not without a cost.

Sunlight enveloped Brognola as he emerged from the International Spy Museum. It stung his eyes and cued his sweat glands to resume their labor. Slipping on a pair of sunglasses, the big Fed focused hard on blocking out the names and faces of lost friends who jockeyed for position in his mind.

Go back to sleep, he warned them. I've got work to do.

And leaks to plug. Maybe.

It wouldn't be the first time that a rivalry between competing federal agencies had drawn blood. In most such cases, wrists were slapped, someone was reassigned or quietly encouraged to retire. Charges were rarely filed. Brognola couldn't think of anyone who'd actually gone to trial during his decades on the job.

Agents were jailed for bribery on rare occasions, or for

selling secrets to a foreign power, but screwing with their rivals in the "sister" services was more or less a given.

Until someone bought the farm.

Brognola made himself a promise. If he found out someone in the Company—or any other branch of government—had sent eight G-men to their deaths in Russia, he would see the guilty parties punished. Off-the-books, if necessary.

Even if he had to do the job himself.

"Homeland security" was nothing but a joke—and a bad one, at that—if the people who'd sworn to uphold it spent all their time looking for ways to hamstring one another. They were worse than useless, in that case.

They were the enemy.

Brognola had spent his professional life negotiating red-tape jungles and negotiating labyrinths of office politics. He played the game as well as anyone in Washington.

But he was sick of it.

In peacetime, it was one thing. Call it busywork or personal amusement. Each department had a reputation and budget to protect—goals that could often be achieved more easily by undercutting so-called friends than going to the mat against real enemies.

But peace, such as it was, had ended when those hijacked planes hit the Twin Towers and the Pentagon. Like it or not, the country was at war, with no end in sight.

And in a war, you either pulled together…or you lost.

In wartime, those who helped the enemy were traitors.

And in Brognola's world, traitors could expect no mercy.

As for Sokolov, the global death merchant, Brognola recognized the man for what he was. A player *and* a pawn. He armed the killers, but he also served them. And above him, shadowing his every move, were men and women who could take him off the board at any time. He lived because they found him useful for advancement of their various agendas.

Brognola, likewise, had masters watching him and

breathing down his neck. Self-interest motivated them, like anybody else, and he could only hope that their needs in this instance coincided with some greater good.

Alive or dead, removing Sokolov from circulation was a good thing. Putting him on public trial, revealing those—or *some* of those—he'd served might also benefit humanity. It wouldn't stop the global trade in arms or any of the slaughter that resulted from it, but it might slow down the pace of killing.

For a day or two.

Small favors, Brognola thought as he neared the entrance to his subway stop.

If anyone could do the job, Mack Bolan was the man.

BOLAN SAT in a drab motel room on I-495, better known as the Capital Beltway. His focus was the laptop humming softly on the smallish writing desk in front of him. Brognola's CD-ROM was giving up its secrets, prepping him for Moscow and beyond.

First up were photos of Gennady Sokolov, with a detailed biography. Bolan surveyed the high points. Born in 1962, in what was now Turkmenistan. No record of his parents had survived, nor any hint of siblings. Sokolov had joined the Russian army at eighteen, had made the cut for Spetznaz— Russia's special forces—eight months later, and had been a captain by the time he mustered out to join the KGB in 1984. Six years later, he had graduated from Moscow's Soviet Military Institute of Foreign Languages, fluent in English, French, Spanish, German and Arabic, besides his native tongue. After the Soviet collapse, he was in business for himself.

And what a business it had been.

Over the past two decades, Sokolov had founded half a dozen cargo airlines, shipping military hardware out of La Paz; Miami; the United Arab Emirates; Liberia and Ostend,

Belgium. From 1992 until the present, Sokolov had armed at least one side in every war of any consequence, and several dozen that had barely rated mention by the talking heads at CNN. He'd left his bloody tracks in Africa and Southeast Asia, in the Middle East, Latin America and Bosnia. In nations theoretically at peace, Sokolov's weapons and explosives found their way to neo-fascists, would-be revolutionaries, ecoterrorists and *mafiosi*.

Sokolov had been arrested once, in Thailand, but had bribed his jailers to go deaf and blind while he escaped and caught a charter flight out of the country. That had been two years ago, and in the meantime Sokolov had spent most of his time in Mother Russia. Recent sightings reported from Damascus and Islamabad remained unconfirmed. No charges had—or would be—filed against him in the death of eight FBI agents who'd died far from home, in a failed bid to end his career.

The next face up on Bolan's laptop monitor belonged to Ruslan Kozlov, a sixty-year-old colonel general in Russia's ground forces. The CIA pegged Kozlov as Gennady Sokolov's primary source of Russian "surplus" military hardware, up to and including stray nuclear warheads. There would be other rogue suppliers scattered far and wide around the globe, but Kozlov was the source closest to home.

The general's face was bland, with full cheeks, gray eyes under snowy brows, and a flat, Slavic nose. He had led troops in Afghanistan, commanded Russian forces in the Chechen wars, and had reportedly given the order for Spetznaz to gas Moscow's House of Culture theater in October 2002, after Chechen separatists seized the building with nine hundred hostages. The gas and subsequent Spetznaz assault had killed the forty-two terrorists and at least 129 hostages, injuring an estimated seven hundred others.

The last face up on Bolan's screen belonged to his contact, Lieutenant Anzhela Pilkin of the FSB. It wouldn't be the first time he'd worked with a Russian agent, when Washington's interests overlapped Moscow's, and while none had betrayed him so far, Bolan always felt as if he was waiting for the other boot to drop.

The lieutenant was thirty years old, auburn-haired, with a grim sort of beauty that might be less rigid in person. Five-seven and 130 pounds, well versed in martial arts and skilled with standard Russian firearms, bilingual in Russian and English. According to Brognola's dossier, she'd joined the FSB five years earlier, after a stint with the military. She'd been promoted to sergeant in that post, after killing a Ukrainian gangster during a drug raid, and had polished off two more sent by the first thug's boss to punish her. The boss, one Mikola Hunczak, had made the next attempt himself and currently resided in Moscow's Mitinskoe Cemetery.

Overall, not bad.

Bolan assumed Lieutenant Pilkin would cooperate with him as ordered by her FSB superiors. But going in, he had no fix on what her orders might entail. When working with Russians—or with anyone outside the normal crew at Stony Man, for that matter—he always kept his guard up, conscious of the fact that while he went about his business, others might be marching in pursuit of separate agendas.

Why, for instance, would the FSB collaborate in Sokolov's extraction, when the government refused to simply extradite him? Was there something to be gained, some face to save, by ordering covert removal? Who was in the know concerning Bolan's mission? Who on the official side might still oppose him?

Colonel General Kozlov could supply an army on short notice to protect his business partner, if he wasn't ordered to stand down. Smart money said that Sokolov would also have his share of allies in the Russian *Mafiya,* who might resent him being snatched and packed off to the States.

And, as the FBI had learned the hard way, Sokolov had to

have his own hardforce of mercenaries, paid to keep him safe
and sound in Moscow, or his dacha near Saint Petersburg.

Against those odds—and the military, whose officers
would do their best to cage or kill him, if and when they
were aware of Bolan's presence in their homeland—he would
pit his own skills and the still-untested talents of his FSB
contact.

Two against how many? Dozens? Hundreds?

Situation normal for the Executioner.

He prepped the files and tapped a button on the laptop's
keyboard to erase Brognola's disk. When that was done, he'd
break it into half a dozen pieces, just in case. There was no
point in taking chances yet, even before he caught his flight
across the polar cap to Moscow.

There'd be time enough to risk his life tomorrow.

Every day beyond that would be icing on the cake.

CHAPTER THREE

Domodedovo International Airport, the present

Bolan slid into the sports car's shotgun seat. Sudden acceleration slammed his door and pushed him backward, made him miss his seat belt on the first try. Bolan's side mirror revealed his shadows spilling from the terminal, one of them speaking into a cell phone as the sportster sped away.

"I hope we're cleared for takeoff," he remarked.

"We are supposed to use the passwords," his auburn-haired savior reminded him.

"Think we can skip it?"

"Under the circumstances," she replied, "I believe that we can. I am Lieutenant Pilkin, FSB."

"Matt Cooper," he replied, without alluding to a rank or government affiliation. Likewise, Bolan didn't mention that he recognized her face from photographs on file.

In these days of cell phone cameras and surveillance equipment, Bolan couldn't be certain that there were no photographs of him.

"I thought we'd have more time," she said.

"For what?"

"Before they broke your cover."

"And 'they' would be…?"

Pilkin shrugged, a good thing, Bolan thought, in the clingy turtleneck she wore. "Who knows? The man you're looking for has many friends. Whether they like him or he buys them, it is all the same."

"That's *we*," he said, correcting her.

"Excuse me?"

"Not the man *I'm* looking for. The man *we're* looking for."

"Of course. Exactly."

"They picked me up first thing, out of the gate," he said. "It's doubtful they have photos, but a name cross-checked against the airline's manifest would do it, if they got a nod from customs or passport control."

"Such things are possible. The man *we* seek—"

"Can we just use his name?" Bolan asked, interrupting.

"Certainly." A note of irritation was in her voice, tugging the corner of her mouth down on the side Bolan could see. "Gennady Sokolov is, as you know, a smuggler. It would not be unexpected for him to have contacts at our major airports."

"You could sweat the officers who passed me through and find out if they're dirty. Crack one of them, and you'll find out who he's dealing with."

"And if they're innocent?"

"No harm done," Bolan said. "I'll send word back to triple-check whoever knew about my travel plans on our side. One way or another, something had to leak."

"And I'm afraid that it's still leaking," Pilkin replied.

Another glance at Bolan's mirror showed him headlights following their car. That wasn't any kind of shocking revelation at a busy airport, but the vehicle in question was performing risky moves to keep Pilkin's car in sight and close the gap between them.

"That was quick," he said.

"They must have had a driver waiting."

"Too bad they're so organized."

"Too bad for them," she said, and flashed a wicked little smile before she shifted, then floored the gas pedal, giving

Bolan another taste of Newton's third law of motion in action.

"If you don't mind me asking, what's the plan?" Bolan inquired.

"Evade them, if we can. If not…eliminate them."

"I'd be more help on the last bit if I wasn't naked."

"What?" Pilkin shot a sidelong glance at Bolan, making sure.

"Unarmed," he said. "Airline security, you know?"

"Of course," she answered. "Try the glove box."

Bolan opened it and found what he presumed to be her backup duty gun, an MP-443 Grach semiauto pistol, also known as the Yarygin PYa for its inventor. The Grach was a double-action piece with polymer grips, chambered for 9 mm Parabellum rounds and packing ten or eighteen in detachable box magazines. Its resemblance to the more famous Glock ended with a partially exposed hammer and an external ambidextrous safety.

Bolan pulled the magazine, relieved to find that it was one of the high-capacity staggered-box models. A nineteenth cartridge nestled in the firing chamber.

He was good to go.

"GET AFTER THEM!" Yuri Bazhov snapped.

"On it," Osip Bek replied, before he whipped their BMW sedan around a slower car and stamped on the accelerator.

"Who's the woman?" Danil Perov asked from the backseat.

"How should I know?" Bazhov replied. "Someone sent to pick him up."

"We nearly had him," Vasily Radko said.

"We *still* have him," Bazhov answered, as he drew his pistol, eased off its safety and held it ready in his lap.

He'd left two men behind to fetch the second car and follow up as best they could. Evgeny Surikov and Pavel Malevich together in the UAZ-469 SUV. They'd have to get directions via cell phone and would likely miss the action, but at least Bazhov had backup if he needed it.

Against two people?

How could they match Bazhov and the four men riding with him now?

As if reading his thoughts, Radko chimed in from the back, saying, "He won't be armed. You can't take anything on planes these days. They even catch the plastic knives."

"Suppose the woman brought him guns?" Bazhov replied. "You didn't think of that?"

He saw Radko grimace in the rearview mirror.

"Are we still required to take the target back alive?"

"Our orders haven't changed," Bazhov reminded all of them. "Whoever kills this guy has to deal with Taras on his own."

Radko muttered something, but he kept his voice low-pitched, allowing Bazhov to pretend he hadn't heard. The fear of Taras Morozov would curb his temper to a point, but if their quarry started shooting at them, or seemed likely to escape, what could they do?

Go back to Taras empty-handed, with excuses?

How would that improve their situation?

"What's that she's driving?" Bazhov asked his wheel-man.

"It's the VAZ 2112," Bek answered, staying focused on the traffic that surrounded them. "Zero to sixty-two in twelve seconds. One hundred fifteen miles per hour at the top end. Doing fifty, she will need 120 feet to stop."

Bek knew cars.

"Don't run them off the road, then, eh?" Bazhov instructed. "I'm not handing Taras a bucket of strawberry jam."

"I won't ram them," Bek said. "But I can't promise you that the woman knows how to drive."

"She's doing all right, so far," Bazhov said. "Be damned sure you don't lose her."

"No problem," Bek answered, and put on more speed.

"You be ready," Bazhov said, half-turned toward his men in the rear. "When we stop them, be careful. The woman can die. Not the man."

"Not to worry," Perov said.

"We're ready," Radko stated.

Bazhov heard them cocking their weapons behind him and hoped neither one of them blew out his brains by mistake. They were pros, yes, but accidents happened.

If he had to die this night, Bazhov could only hope it would be like a man, and not some poor bastard slaughtered by mistake.

BOLAN COULDN'T READ the street signs written in Cyrillic, but he knew that they were heading north, toward central Moscow. That meant crowds, more traffic, innocent bystanders.

And police.

"You have someplace in mind to ditch them, I suppose?" he asked.

"I'm working on it," Pilkin replied. "I did not come expecting you to have a tail.

"There is a park off Chertanovskaya Street," she said. "They have a lake there. Little innocent civilian traffic after dark, because of crime."

"Just muggers and what have you?" Bolan asked.

"No one likely to trouble us, as long as you have that." She nodded toward the pistol in his hand. "Unless you're dead, of course."

"Won't matter then."

"So, we agree," she said. "Five minutes more, if all goes well."

And if it didn't, Bolan knew the drill from prior experience. They'd stand and fight as necessary, if and when they had no other choice.

He shied away from small talk, letting Pilkin drive the car, and concentrated on their tail. Still just one vehicle, as far as he could tell, gaining by fits and starts. Headlights behind it showed him three heads, maybe four.

Assume the worst, and you won't be surprised.

The worst would be more cars, more guns closing in. With a single chase car there were options. A crash could disable the hunters inside without shooting, and even if guns were required, killing three or four men would be quicker, easier, than taking out eight or a dozen.

Bolan didn't mind the wet work, but it grated on his nerves that he'd been burned even before he set foot in the country. He considered that a past trip to Russia, or his past collaboration with the FSB, might have some kind of boomerang effect this day, but none of it made sense.

The enemies he'd faced when Moscow was the global capital of communism were no more than faded memories, long dead and gone. More recently, he had enjoyed cautious collaboration with the FSB. Bolan could think of no reason for them to plot his death, much less kill eight G-men to bait the trap.

Anzhela Pilkin could have shot him at the airport terminal, or simply missed their date and left disposal to the thugs who were pursuing them. The whole rescue charade was pointless, if she and her masters wanted Bolan dead.

What if they simply *wanted* him?

Interrogation was another possibility, but once again, Bolan collided with the brick wall of impracticality. To dress the stage, go through the diplomatic motions, lay the trail—it only clicked if someone in the FSB knew Bolan's true identity. Or, at the very least, the role he played for Stony Man.

And that, he told himself, was next door to impossible.

So, wait and see, he thought.

And from the chase car's progress overhauling them, he wouldn't have to wait much longer.

"WHERE ARE THEY going?" Yuri Bazhov asked no one, thinking aloud.

"Can't say," Bek responded from the driver's seat.

"Just drive!"

Bazhov hit speed-dial on his cell phone, waiting through four anxious rings before he got an answer.

"Who's that?" Pavel Malevich demanded.

"Idiot! Who do you think it is?" Bazhov snapped.

"Yuri! Where are you?"

"Heading north on Chertanovskaya Street. Looks like she's taking us downtown."

"Why would she do that?"

"Depends on who she is," Bazhov replied. "Catch up with us, soon as you can. We need to cut her off."

He broke the link, muttering curses to himself.

This was what came from working in the dark, when everything was need-to-know and no one told him shit. He couldn't second-guess the bitch who'd plucked their pigeon from the snare, because he didn't know who she was or why she'd intervened. Bazhov had no idea why he'd been sent to snatch a stranger from the airport, with instructions that the mark had to be alive upon delivery.

It could be anything. A rival syndicate invading local turf. Perhaps a businessman who'd balked at paying tribute to the Family and now required an object lesson in security. It might be something personal for Taras or the man on top, Leonid Bezmel.

Yuri Bazhov hated puzzles, riddles, anything that taxed his brain unnecessarily. He understood connect-the-dots and liked to skip ahead whenever possible, surprise his adversaries and destroy them with brute force.

He couldn't do that in the present case, because his hands

were tied. His orders barred disposing of this Matthew Cooper, while the woman was a wild card, trouble from the first time he'd laid eyes on her.

Bazhov *could* kill the woman.

But he'd have to catch her first.

And if she had some destination fixed in mind as she was fleeing, what did that mean to Bazhov, his men and his plan? Was she leading them onto another gang's patch? If she was mixed up with the law, somehow, it could be even worse.

Bazhov would ask her, if he had the chance.

Before he put a bullet in her brain.

Somewhere behind him, Malevich and Surikov were racing to catch up and join the chase. Two cars might box the woman's vehicle. Better than one, in any case. With one, all he could do was ram her, sideswipe her, or try to shoot her off the road.

And if Bazhov should kill his sacred target in the process, it would be his ass. He couldn't blame his men for the mistake, when he gave them their orders.

"Osip!" he barked. "Can you catch her, or not?"

"I can!"

"You're sure it isn't too much trouble?"

"No, Yuri!"

"All right, then. Will you *do* it, for Christ's sake?"

Bek's cheeks flushed crimson at the insult, but he offered no response. Instead, he let the BMW do his talking for him, surging forward as he found more power somehow, somewhere underneath its hood.

Clutching his pistol in a fierce, white-knuckled grip, Bazhov prepared himself for battle.

"ALMOST THERE," Anzhela Pilkin told her silent passenger.

"The park there, on the left?" he asked.

"That's it."

Despite its grim-faced reputation, Moscow was a "green"

city. It boasted ninety-six parks and eighteen public gardens, comprising 174 square miles of green zones and thirty-nine square miles of forest. Each citizen of Moscow was blessed with 290 square feet of parkland, versus nine in New York, seven in London and six in Paris. Thousands enjoyed the parks each day.

But few by night.

Pilkin counted on the fear of crime that kept most of her fellow Muscovites away from dark, secluded places after nightfall. There was risk enough of being mugged, robbed, raped, or shot by accident in daylight, without tempting Fate.

She found the side street she was looking for and swung her VAZ sportster off Chertanovskaya Street, leaving the main flow of traffic behind. She lost the rest turning in to the park, killing her lights at once and watching for the chase car in her rearview mirror.

Was there any chance that her pursuers would be fooled and drive past?

No. There they were, making the left-hand turn, and then the right.

"So much for losing them," she said. "We'll have to fight the bastards."

"Ready when you are," he replied.

Pilkin sped along a narrow drive that ran halfway around the park, dead-ending in a parking lot located at the north end of a man-made lake. Arriving in the lot, she put the VAZ through a squealing one-eighty, then killed its engine.

"I'd rather meet them on foot," she told Bolan.

"Sounds good," he replied, and was out of his door in a flash.

They ran into darkness, away from her car, which she knew the pursuers would make their first target. Pilkin hoped it wouldn't be destroyed. She was dreading the paperwork required to explain any damage to state property. There'd be enough just for the shooting, without car repairs on top of it.

She thumbed off her pistol's safety, crouching next to Bolan in the shadow of a hedge, watching the headlights of the enemy's vehicle sweep across the parking lot and focus on her VAZ.

"Now!" she told Bolan, squeezing off three rounds in rapid fire, aimed at the driver's deeply tinted window.

Pilkin heard glass smash as she fired, then Bolan's borrowed pistol barked in unison with hers. The chase car's driver hit his brakes, then switched to the accelerator in a heartbeat, revving past her VAZ, on toward the lake.

Go in! Go in, she urged them silently.

But it stopped just short of splashdown, and the engine died.

YURI BAZHOV FLINCHED from the first crash of gunfire, cursing as something wet and warm spattered the left side of his face. Bek was gagging, choking in the driver's seat, still clinging to the steering wheel as dark blood spurted from his neck, streaking the windshield and dashboard.

The BMW jerked, then powered forward as Bek slumped in his seat, his right foot jammed on the accelerator. Bazhov saw that they were headed for the lake, and he envisioned sinking with the car into its strangling depths.

He cursed the dead or dying man beside him, who was once a friend of sorts. When a hard slap had no effect on Bek, Bazhov bent to grab his right leg, slammed his head against the steering wheel and cursed again, then wrenched Bek's foot sideways and off the gas pedal.

The BMW slowed, stuttered and stalled. Peering across the hood, Bazhov could see that they had stopped with yards to spare before taking the final plunge.

More bullets struck the car, cracking its rear window, drumming against the trunk and left-rear fender. Perov and

Radko shouted from the backseat, angling to return fire, finding no immediate targets.

"Get out!" Bazhov ordered. Feeling absurd, he added, "And remember! Do not kill the man!"

Bazhov nearly dropped his cell phone, stumbling from the car, while Perov and Radko unlimbered their guns. He speed-dialed Pavel Malevich, and this time got an answer on the second ring.

"What's happening?" Malevich asked.

Bazhov raised his phone and let the man hear staccato gunfire.

"That's what's happening, idiot! Do you hear it? Osip's dead, and where in hell are you?"

"On Chertanovskaya Street. You said—"

"Look for a park," Bazhov said, interrupting him. "I don't know what they call it. On your left, somewhere. It has a lake. Listen for gunfire. Move your ass!"

A bullet struck the car within a foot of Bazhov's head and ricocheted into the darkness with a sound that nearly made him wet himself. He had been under fire before, of course, and more than once. But this, somehow, felt different.

It felt like his last moments of life.

In which case, what did he have to lose?

Morozov could hardly punish him if he was dead. There was no pain beyond the final moment of oblivion...unless the priests were right about hellfire.

Bazhov could only face one peril at a time, on one plane of existence. If the fires of hell were waiting for him, by God, let them wait.

Edging around the BMW's right-rear fender, Bazhov risked a peek in search of targets. He saw muzzle-flashes, moving closer, and heard more rounds strike the car.

Thankfully, the BMW had been stolen. It was no great loss, nothing for Morozov to be angry about, he thought. Letting the stranger from the airport slip away, however, was another story altogether.

Bazhov saw his targets now—a man and woman, racing through the night, advancing as if totally devoid of fear. They used the shadows as a cloak, but still came on to meet their enemies.

Bazhov admired that, in his way, but admiration wouldn't interfere with duty. Aiming at the woman, he fired two quick shots, then ducked back under cover as a bullet struck the BMW's taillight inches from his face.

FOUR SHOTS GONE, and Bolan wasn't sure that he'd hit anyone. He'd definitely hit the BMW, and it wasn't armored, but that didn't mean he'd scored on any of its occupants.

Time to get serious.

Pilkin dodged two hasty shots from someone crouching at the Beemer's rear, and Bolan drove the shooter under cover with a round that blew out the right-hand taillight. Almost simultaneously, two guys popped up to fire across the sedan's sleek hood.

One had a pistol, the other one some kind of stubby submachine gun. Possibly a Bizon, with its 64-round magazine, or the smaller PP-2000. As he hit the dirt and rolled, his ears told Bolan that the stuttergun was no Kalashnikov. It was 9 mm, tops, but no less deadly for its caliber.

He came up firing, two quick rounds to make the shooters duck, then rushed them. It was the only option available, since Bolan couldn't linger where he was, and a retreat would only let them shoot him in the back.

Off to his right somewhere, he heard Pilkin firing on the run, another pistol answering. Bolan could only fight one battle at a time, and left her to it, with a silent supplication to the Universe.

The shooters he was looking for had made a critical mistake, both emptying their magazines together. It was easy, in the heat of battle, to forget coordination with the troops around you, but there was no "little" error on the firing line. One slip could get you killed.

Like now.

Instead of wasting precious time and energy to run *around* the front end of the Beemer, Bolan launched himself across its hood, sliding to meet his enemies. He had a flash impression of their faces, gaping at him, then their guns were coming up, ready or not, to meet his charge.

Chaos took over then, with Bolan rapid-firing at the startled faces, blowing them apart at point-blank range where it was strictly personal. The Russians died as Bolan guessed they had to have lived, with brutish violence. They jerked, danced, stumbled, fell together in a twitching heap.

The slide on Bolan's pistol locked open on an empty chamber. He dropped it, claimed the nearest dead man's SMG—it *was* a Bizon, after all—and snugged its unique cylindrical magazine into place.

In front of him, with his back turned, a final shooter blazed away at Pilkin, somewhere beyond the BMW. Bolan shot him in the back without the *High Noon* drama of asking him to turn around and make it "fair."

In Bolan's world, the fair fights were those that he won. No holds barred. There were some lines he wouldn't cross, but none of them applied to adult predators in battle.

"Clear!" he called to Pilkin, and gave her time to chill before he rose from cover.

She approached him, frowning.

"You got all of them yourself," she said.

"I wouldn't claim the driver."

"What are you, exactly, Mr. Cooper?"

"Just a public servant, like yourself."

"I don't think so," Pilkin replied.

"I think we should be leaving, if your car's all right."

"It's fine."

"And before we throw any more parties," he added, "I've got some shopping to do."

CHAPTER FOUR

Kotlin Island

Gennady Sokolov sipped black-cherry vodka from a crystal glass, letting it linger on his tongue before he swallowed and felt the welcome heat begin to spread throughout his body. He hadn't decided, yet, if it would be his last drink of the old day or his first of the new one.

That, he reckoned, would depend upon the news from Moscow.

Sokolov wasn't a patient man by nature. He had learned patience as other men learned carpentry, mechanics or book-keeping—through determination and practice. Much of his time with Spetznaz had been spent waiting or getting ready for some crisis that might never come to pass. Later, when he was serving with the KGB, the typical pace had been slower still. Espionage by committee. Murder by decree, with orders handed down through bureaucratic buffer layers until the deed was executed in New York, Bangkok, Madrid or Rome.

The patience he'd acquired while serving Russia's govern-ment had been of great value to Sokolov once he went private. Those who came to him for weapons always wanted them today—or yesterday, as the Americans were fond of saying—but negotiation of a price and terms for the delivery took time. Oddly, it seemed to Sokolov that those who wished to kill their enemies most urgently were also those who dithered over dimes.

This night he needed patience on his own account, waiting

for word that would relieve him of a burden that was tainting every aspect of his life. The Americans were breathing down his neck, determined that he should be extradited in defiance of his homeland's sacred law.

Whatever happened to their passion for democracy?

So far, they hadn't laid a glove on Sokolov, though he resented the restrictions on his foreign travel. Documents weren't a problem, under any name he chose, and Sokolov was self-taught in the art of personal disguise, but covert travel meant that he couldn't enjoy the luxury to which he had become accustomed.

What, in God's name, was the point of being filthy rich if he could only flaunt it where he lived?

How was a world-class death merchant supposed to awe new clients when he had to scurry through the shadows wearing a trench coat and an artificial beard?

He'd taught a lesson to the damned Americans when they came sniffing at his dacha, but they hadn't learned it well enough. Now, sources told him, there was yet another plan afoot to snatch him, this time with collaboration from the FSB.

That hurt.

And when he hurt, Sokolov liked to share the pain.

The latest lesson for his enemies would start in Moscow, where a certain agent from the States was scheduled to arrive that very night. In fact, a stylish wall clock and Sokolov's Rolex GMT Master II wristwatch agreed that the job should be finished by now. His friends in Moscow should be acquiring the information that Sokolov needed in order to—

He smiled when the telephone rang. Not his cell, but the gold-plated one on his desk, which he rubbed with a chamois after each and every use. Gold smudged with fingerprints was strictly déclassé.

"Hello?"

There was a heartbeat's silence on the other end, before the gruff, familiar voice replied, "Gennady?"

"Who else would it be?"

"No one, of course," said Leonid Bezmel, the boss of bosses for the Moscow *Mafiya*.

"What news?" Sokolov prompted him.

"It's not good, I'm afraid."

"Not good."

"Unfortunately, no."

"Tell me."

"These incompetents Taras sent out to the airport missed their man. They're dead, in fact, which cheats me of the pleasure I'd derive from their chastisement."

Sokolov drained off his vodka in one swallow and commanded, "Tell me everything."

CROSSING THE MOSCOW RIVER on Mokhovaya Street, with the Kremlin complex on their right, Bolan told Pilkin, "We're not off to the best of starts."

"I see only three choices," she replied. "We can give up, press on, or waste time trying to determine which side has the leak."

"It could be both sides," Bolan said. "I've got someone on my end who can try to run it down, but I won't guarantee results."

Pilkin hesitated, then said, "Even asking, with the FSB today, may cause some difficulty."

Bolan heard that, loud and clear.

"Another way to do it," he suggested, "is to cut the apron strings and carry out the mission as assigned, before it started going off the rails."

"The kind of thing that ends careers," she said.

"Depends on how you finish, I suppose. Or whether you were really meant to do it in the first place."

"You suspect corruption?"

"Always. I trust the friends I've had forever," Bolan said, "but I can count them on my fingers. And I still look out for number one."

"I understand this. Here, it is the same. Before the change, we always knew the party leaders placed themselves above the people, but at least they feared exposure and the discipline to follow. Now, when there is so much money to be had, and no one left to draw the line...it's hard to know the rules, sometimes."

"When I run into that, I make my own," Bolan replied.

"We have a handicap," she said. "You were expected, at the airport. So your name, at least, is known in Moscow. If they also know your face—"

"That isn't likely," Bolan interrupted. "And the guys we met tonight aren't handing out descriptions."

"You must not use any credit cards, in that case. Or a driver's license. No cell phone that can be traced."

"I've got cash," Bolan said. "If we run short, I'll pick up more. My phone's secure as it can be."

His Inmarsat satellite phone had a built-in scrambler coded to coordinate with gear at Stony Man and on Brognola's desk in Washington. If necessary, it could store a message for transmission as a high-speed data squirt, in lieu of real-time conversation. In the time the FSB would need to crack the code, assuming that his calls were intercepted in the first place, Bolan hoped to have his mission finished and be back in the States.

"You have assistance waiting, if we are successful?"

"*When* we are successful, transportation's covered," Bolan said. "But first, I need to soften up the other side a little."

"Soften up?" Pilkin frowned.

"Shake up their world and start them finger-pointing," he explained. "Put a few cracks in their united front."

"They'll be surprised already, with tonight's failure," she said. "Whoever *they* are."

"It's a start," Bolan said. "And it doesn't matter much who sent the welcoming committee. As I see it, there are only two or three real possibilities."

"And they are…?"

"Sokolov himself, for starters," Bolan answered, ticking off the options on his fingers. "Second, someone from the *Mafiya* who's working with him. Third, somebody in authority."

"Those men were not militia or FSB," Pilkin said.

"But maybe working under contract."

"Yes," she said reluctantly. "It's possible."

"We'll find out more when I start rattling cages," Bolan told her. "Are you up for it?"

"You're asking me?"

"Seems only fair. If you don't want to ride the tiger, now's the time to bail."

"I have a job to do," she said. "My orders don't include surrender."

"Right, then," Bolan said. "Our first stop needs to be an all-night hardware store."

MAKSIM CHALIAPIN HATED late-night phone calls. None had ever brought him good news, and they typically required him to take action that posed some risk to his standing and career, if not his life.

Such risk and aggravation came with service to the FSB, in which Chaliapin held the rank of First Assistant to the Director of the Economic Security Service. Chaliapin's duties included supervising campaigns against organized crime of all kinds within Moscow Oblast—the city proper and its surrounding federal district—as well as liaison with Interpol and other foreign law enforcement or security agencies.

As Chaliapin left his bed and lumbered toward the shrilling telephone, he knew that he was lucky to have *any* job in government, much less a post with so much personal authority. At fifty-eight, he was a thirty-four-year veteran of what passed in Russia for a civil service. Chaliapin had joined the KGB as a fledgling strong-arm man in 1976 and worked his way up through the ranks to major with a combination of fancy footwork and apparent slavish obedience to his superiors of the moment. When President Boris Yeltsin dissolved the KGB in August 1991, Chaliapin had pulled every string within reach to secure a post with the new Federal Counterintelligence Service, or FSK, which, in turn, was magically transformed into the FSB in April 1995.

He was, if nothing else, a survivor.

Lifting the telephone receiver as if it weighed fifty pounds, Chaliapin spoke into the night.

"Hello?"

"It's me."

Of course it was. Chaliapin grimaced at the sound of Gennady Sokolov's voice. Double-edged steel sheathed in moldy velvet.

"Good evening," he said, careful not to use names. "How may I help you?"

"I assume you've heard about the difficulty at the airport?"

"No." Lying was second nature to a lifelong member of the KGB.

"Nothing?"

"Is this about—?"

"It is."

"And what went wrong, exactly?"

"You were not informed?"

"I've told you—"

"Then, by all means let me break the news. Our package went astray tonight. Four of my men attempted to retrieve it."

"And…?"

"You'll get an invitation to their funerals."

"All four?"

Now Chaliapin *was* surprised. He had supplied a name to Sokolov, a flight number, and then had washed his hands of it. He'd wanted to know nothing more about the problem unless Sokolov discovered something that affected Chaliapin personally. He had regarded that as an unlikely circumstance.

But now…

"All four," Sokolov said, confirming it.

That meant more paperwork for Chaliapin, poring over field reports of four deaths presumed to be *Mafiya*-bound in some way. It would be busywork, at best.

Chaliapin could play stupid with the best of them.

But he was curious. "How did this happen?" he inquired.

"Another person claimed the package," Sokolov replied. "Ran off with it, in fact. My men…protested. They were unsuccessful in asserting ownership."

"Apparently. This other person—"

"Was a woman."

"That is most unusual," he granted.

"It's unheard of," Sokolov corrected him. "Unless she was official."

"What? You can't mean—"

"Do you not have female agents?" Sokolov demanded.

"Certainly. But—"

"And it's possible that some other department might be operating at cross-purposes to yours?"

It was entirely possible. Within the FSB, he constantly competed with the Military Counterintelligence Directorate and the Service for Protection of the Constitutional System and the Fight against Terrorism. Beyond that lay competing agencies—the Federal Protective Service and the militia. Both employed women as agents.

"I will look into it," Chaliapin said.

"I know you will, Maksim. And find the bitch that I need to kill."

THE "HARDWARE STORE" that Bolan needed didn't carry saws, hammers or nails. It wouldn't keep the hours of a normal Moscow shop, and definitely wouldn't advertise in print, or through the broadcast media. Its reputation—its existence— would be carried on the whisper stream that underlaid so-called police society in every nation of the world.

The hardware store he sought carried the tools of death.

"In Moscow," Pilkin informed him, "there are several outlets for the merchandise you seek."

"There always are," Bolan replied. "Take me to one that offers quality as well as quantity. I don't want rusty junk from Chechnya, much less Afghanistan."

"Perhaps Iraq would suit you better?" she replied.

"Nothing immediately traceable," he added, carefully ignoring her remark.

"Such dealers are…how do you say it in America? Connected? They won't hesitate to sell you out if anyone with influence comes knocking."

"Sell *who* out?" he countered. "The only introduction I'm supplying is a roll of cash. Unless the guy you have in mind knows *you*…."

"No," Pilkin replied. "We've never met."

"Sounds good, then," Bolan said, and settled back to wait.

They found the dealer's shop west of downtown, a block north of Povarskaya Street. A stylish jewelry store filled the ground floor, with living quarters upstairs.

A wise man kept an eye on his investments.

Lights were on in the apartment windows when Pilkin rang the bell downstairs. A voice responded on the scratchy intercom, bantering back and forth with the woman for something like a minute, then switched off.

"He's coming down," she told Bolan.

"No problems?"

"None so far."

The man who finally arrived to let them in was forty-something, stocky, with slicked-down hair and bushy eyebrows that resembled Leonid Brezhnev's. Unlike Brezhnev, he smiled—albeit cautiously—for paying customers he'd never met and likely wouldn't see again.

When they were safely locked inside the shop, its owner introduced himself as Fedor Tsereteli. He spoke fluent English without asking why it was required, and Bolan saw him file that fact away for future reference.

So be it.

"You have need of special merchandise," he said.

"That's right," Bolan replied.

"Please follow me."

He led them from the main showroom into an office, where a bank of filing cabinets stood against one wall. At Tsereteli's touch, two of them swung aside, revealing a smallish door secured by a locking keypad. Tsereteli blocked their view with his bulk while he punched in the code, then opened the door. Beyond it, stairs descended to a darkened cellar.

Tsereteli found a light switch, and fluorescent fixtures came alive downstairs. Bolan ducked his head, going through the doorway, and made his way down to the gun vault.

The place had something for everyone: assault rifles and submachine guns, light machine guns and squad automatic weapons, shotguns and pistols, RPGs and rockets, crates of ammunition and grenades. Bolan browsed, taking his time.

His final selections included a Steyr AUG assault rifle, a familiar Beretta 93-R selective-fire pistol with sound suppressor, a Mikor MGL 40 mm grenade launcher, plus spare magazines, ammunition and a selection of hand grenades from Tsereteli's stockpile. Accessories included a shoulder rig for the Beretta, a tactical vest and a Cold Steel Recon Tanto dagger with a black epoxy finish on its seven-inch blade.

"All this?" Pilkin asked him, surveying his selections with a raised eyebrow.

"You're traveling a little light yourself," Bolan replied. "Want something for the road, on me?"

Or, rather, on the two Colombians he had relieved of half a million dollars when he punched their tickets outside Baltimore, two days before his meeting with Brognola in D.C.

With visible reluctance, Pilkin checked Tsereteli's wares and chose a Vityaz submachine gun, model PP-19-01. It resembled an AKS-74U compact assault rifle, but the Vityaz was chambered in 9 mm Parabellum, fed from 30-round box magazines, with a cyclic rate of 750 rounds per minute. Its stock folded against the gun's left side when not in use, and special clips held a spare mag in place beside the one in use.

"That's it?" Bolan asked.

"Everything my heart desires," Pilkin told him, frowning.

"Then," he said, "we're good to go."

LEONID BEZMEL wasn't woken by the purring telephone. A nocturnal creature by disposition and necessity, he rarely went to bed before sunrise, and then didn't wake until noon, unless some dire emergency compelled it.

"Hello," he said without enthusiasm.

"Have you found out any more yet?" Gennady Sokolov asked.

"Nothing beyond what we discussed," Bezmel said.

"How can that be possible?" Sokolov asked.

"Nothing from the police beyond the basics," Bezmel said. "When they know something more, I'll pass it on to you, of course."

"And in the meantime, he's still out there. With this woman. Doing who knows what."

"Perhaps they're having sex," Bezmel suggested.

"I don't find that amusing," Sokolov replied.

"You're asking me to read this stranger's mind and tell you

where he's gone with yet another stranger. I can't do that. I'm investigating, but I will not feed you bullshit just to pacify you. Okay?"

"Four of your men are dead."

"While helping *you*," Bezmel reminded Sokolov. "And still I do not understand how this applies to me."

"Permit me to enlighten you," Sokolov said. "If the Americans take me, they will be taking those associated with me—or, at least, delivering their evidence to prosecutors here. Director Bortnikov would love to mount your head in his Lubyanka trophy room. So would General Nurgaliyev, at the Ministry of Internal Affairs. Perhaps they'll fight over the scraps."

"Is that supposed to frighten me, Gennady?"

"I make no threats," Sokolov replied.

"That's very wise. Because you know I've seen policemen come and go. Some are dismissed, others retired in luxury. A few…have accidents."

"Now *you* would threaten *me?*"

"By no means. We are friends, Gennady. Better yet, we're partners. I would hate to see that ruined by a moment's panic over nothing."

"Nothing? With your men dead and this man running loose?"

"I'll find him. Don't you worry. No one hides from me in Moscow. He'll be gone before you know it."

"I already know it, Leonid."

"Then, by all means, endeavor to forget him. He's the next best thing to dead."

"Make him the *best* thing, eh? And then we'll celebrate."

"Concerning that," Bezmel digressed, "is everything prepared?"

"It will be, when you've solved our problem."

"IT SEEMS we are about to start a war," Anzhela Pilkin said when they were on the road again.

"A small one, if we're lucky," Bolan said. "But I'll be ready, either way it goes."

"I thought this was supposed to be a simple thing. Extract one man. Deal with his guards if necessary and move on."

"Eight men already tried the 'simple' route," Bolan replied. "They're dead. I don't intend to join them if it isn't absolutely necessary."

"You would die to catch Gennady Sokolov?"

"It isn't on my list of things to do," Bolan said, "but the risk is there on any mission. Same with you, I'd guess."

"Sometimes," she granted. "But I do more paperwork than shooting. This night is unusual."

"It's bound to get worse," Bolan said. "You can still pull the plug."

"Pull the…?"

"Hit the silk. Call it off."

"I have orders," she said.

"To meet me and serve as my guide, am I right? Some translation? I'm betting that no one told you to go out and get killed."

"I'm not planning on it."

"No one plans it, except suicides," Bolan said. "Here's the deal. I intend to flush Sokolov out of his hole, whatever it takes. I'll be starting with those who support him, his partners and friends. They'll be loyal to a point, but beyond that, self-preservation kicks in. When he's flushed out of cover, I'll grab him and pass him along to the transporters."

"You make it sound easy."

"That's just my point," Bolan replied. "It isn't. It gets harder, bloodier, with every step we take from this point onward. You don't have to make that trip. I do."

"I won't go back to headquarters and say you've talked me out of my assignment. That is unacceptable."

"If you go, there'll be a point where you *can't* change your mind," said Bolan.

"Is this chivalry?" Pilkin asked. "Or are you looking out for number one again?"

"What difference does it make?"

"I'm curious."

Red Square was passing on their left. Somewhere inside its walls, Vladimir Lenin lay entombed, preserved since 1924 with semiannual baths in potassium acetate, alcohol, glycerol, distilled water and, as a disinfectant, quinine. Others were almost equally revered but buried more conventionally, barred from public viewing—Mikhail Kalinin, titular head of the Supreme Soviet from 1919 to 1946. Felix Dzerzhinksy, founder of the Soviet secret police and Gulag. Konstantin Chernenko, known as "Brezhnev's Shadow," who engineered Russia's boycott of the 1984 Olympic games.

"I have no wish to see you killed or maimed," Bolan replied at last. "If that's what you call chivalry, I guess I'm guilty. On the other hand, self-preservation means I won't have time to coddle you if you go forward."

"You believe that is what happened tonight?" she challenged, sparking anger.

"Not at all. You jumped right in and pulled your weight, no doubt about it."

"Well, then—"

"It gets worse," Bolan repeated. "If you come along for this ride, be prepared to go through hell. Beyond the point of no return, it's do or die."

"I'm ready."

"Be damned sure."

"I am," Pilkin said, "damned sure."

"Okay, then. I understand that Sokolov works closely with a General Kozlov?"

"Colonel General," Pilkin corrected him. "One of his arms suppliers, we believe. Untouchable, politically. He's not the only leak in Russia's arsenal, but probably the single largest."

"And at some point, there's a linkup with the *Mafiya?*"

"Of course. Sokolov deals extensively with Leonid Bezmel. He is what you might call the 'godfather' of the Solntsevskaya Brotherhood, Moscow's most powerful crime Family. His leading competition is the Obshina, the Chechen group led by Aldo Shishani. They hate each other bitterly, and so Shishani hates Gennady Sokolov."

"Sounds like a place to start," Bolan replied.

CHAPTER FIVE

Kotlin Island

Some nights, when sleep deserted him, Gennady Sokolov amused himself by trying to surprise his sentries, catch them napping, as it were, although he'd never actually found one sleeping on the job. Such an infraction would have earned a penalty far worse than mere dismissal, and his soldiers knew it.

Sokolov wasn't a man to trifle with.

He'd made that point with each of those he had disturbed that night, reminding all of them in no uncertain terms that they relied upon him for some measure of their affluence, and that their fates were linked to his. That was a risky game, since any one of them, if pushed too far, might turn against him.

But Sokolov knew people. He could read them—almost read their minds, it seemed—and use his knowledge to control them. How else had he survived four years in Russia's army, seven in the Kremlin's secret service, and nearly two decades of personal dealings with volatile dictators, warlords and rebels? If Sokolov wasn't the best at what he did, he would be rotting in a jungle grave or desert trench by now.

Or worse yet, he'd just be ordinary, some pathetic drone punching a time clock, slaving for his daily borscht.

No, thank you very much.

Better to die than be deflated to the status of a peasant, groveling before the powers that be.

Sokolov took a vodka bottle and a shot glass from the wet bar in his office and retreated to his massive teakwood desk. He pressed a button on the desktop intercom but didn't speak. Only one person in the household would answer that summons.

Less than a minute passed before Sokolov heard the rapping on his office door.

"Come!"

Sergei Efros entered, closed the door behind him and crossed the room to stand at attention before Sokolov's desk. He didn't move again until Sokolov ordered him to sit.

Sokolov spent a moment staring at his chief of security, framing his thoughts before speaking. Efros had spent eleven years with Spetznaz, in the "Alfa" unit, whose main duty was suppressing terrorism. He'd done time in Chechnya and was among the troops who'd stormed the House of Culture in Moscow's Dubrovka district, during the theater siege of October 2002. As one of those cashiered to satisfy public outrage, he had left the service embittered and never thought twice about serving the Merchant of Death in return for a general's salary.

"Still no word from Moscow," Sokolov told him at last.

"I don't trust the militia or FSB," Efros replied. "Let me go there myself, sir. I'll get the information you require within a day."

"It's tempting," Sokolov admitted. "But you may be needed here."

"As you require, sir."

Compliance normally pleased Sokolov. This night, it irritated him. "There's something on your mind, Sergei," he said. "Out with it."

"Sir, it isn't only the police and FSB that I distrust. The Solntsevskaya Brotherhood are scum."

"But useful scum," Sokolov said. "Most profitable scum, as you'll no doubt agree."

"And then, there's General Kozlov."

"Ah. A personal acquaintance, is he not?"

"We never met, sir, but I had the misfortune of serving in his command, as you know."

"The Nord-Ost siege."

"Which he coordinated with the FSB, attempting to impress his own superiors and thus advance himself."

"It's the way of the world, Sergei."

"Yes, sir. But when his plan failed—disastrously—a real man would have claimed responsibility, instead of sacrificing those who simply carried out his foolish orders."

"You believe the Colonel General may betray us?"

"It's a nasty habit of his," Efros said.

"Perhaps you should go down to Moscow, after all. To keep an eye on friends and enemies alike."

"Yes, sir."

"Providing that you leave me in good hands, of course."

"Of course, sir. Ivan has my every confidence. I will instruct him personally, prior to leaving."

Ivan Fet was second in command to Efros, concerning Sokolov's home security. He had dealt with one of the FBI snipers himself when the kidnappers came.

"In which case," the Merchant of Death told Efros, "make me proud."

Moscow

No one at Lubyanka Square was pleased when Maksim Chaliapin worked a night shift. His presence after normal quitting time for officers in charge meant tension, aggravation and a risk of collateral damage.

The Lubyanka was erected in 1898, as headquarters for the All-Russia Insurance Company. Following the Bolshevik Revolution, it was claimed by the Communist Party as headquarters for the new secret police—the *Chrezvychaynaya*

Komissiya, or Extraordinary Commission, shortened to Cheka. That agency had changed names many times over the next seven decades, eventually becoming the home of the FSB.

A prison on the Lubyanka's ground floor had witnessed the detention, torture and death of thousands. Some of its celebrated inmates included British spy Sidney Reilly, Swedish humanitarian Raoul Wallenberg, Czechoslovakian Count János Esterházy, Polish Jesuit Father Walter Ciszek, and Nobel Prize-winning author Aleksandr Solzhenitsyn.

They were among the survivors.

When Maksim Chaliapin found out who had spoiled his evening, he vowed that the persons or persons responsible would not be so lucky.

The FSB no longer had a government license to torture and kill on a whim, but there were exceptions to every rule. Its primary raison d'être was maintenance of national security, and that was clearly at risk when foreigners appeared in Moscow and involved themselves in gunplay as if they had time-traveled from the American Wild West.

Moscow suffered far too much mayhem already from homegrown thugs and mercenaries. Importation of more gunmen to make matters worse was unthinkable. Intolerable.

And it could prove costly to Chaliapin.

While his rank brought him a measure of respect—and fear—from fellow Muscovites, a civil servant's salary in Russia allowed for few luxuries. Maksim Chaliapin, like nearly all of those around him in the present government, supplemented his normal income with gratuities from affluent citizens whom he had helped in one way or another. He resolved their problems, shifted obstacles out of their path, and they were naturally grateful.

What was wrong with that?

None of his private clients was more grateful—or more generous—than Gennady Sokolov. Of course, that gratitude and generosity depended on his satisfaction. Payment for services rendered, not for excuses delivered with failure.

Loss of such a friend, and his money, would gravely affect Chaliapin's lifestyle. Worse yet, if Sokolov was extradited and tried, the proceedings might reveal his ties to Chaliapin. Which, in turn, could force Chaliapin's superiors to protect themselves by sacrificing him.

This night, Chaliapin was doubly worried, fearing that the problem that vexed him might have originated under his own roof, at the Lubyanka. Like any other intelligence agency or large police department, the FSB was split into sections: Counterintelligence, Economic Security, Operational Information and International Relations, Control, Investigation, Science and Engineering, International Relations, and Chaliapin's own Service for Protection of the Constitutional System and the Fight against Terrorism. Within such a system—even within a specific department—there were times when the left hand didn't know what the right hand was doing.

There could be rogues at work under his very nose, following orders Chaliapin hadn't issued and of which he had no knowledge. Orders which, for all he knew, might include his destruction.

But he would soon find out if that was true. And he would put a stop to it, oh, yes.

No matter who fell by the wayside in the process.

"EVERY TARGET on the list is dangerous," Anzhela Pilkin said as they drove past Gorky Park, southwest of downtown.

"Targets always are," Bolan replied.

"Before we start," Pilkin said, "you need to understand that crime and politics are not distinct and separate in Russia."

"That's been my experience around the world," Bolan observed.

"But it is not the same. In your country, a *mafioso* bribes the politicians secretly. To pass a law or to ignore one, grant some favor, close the eyes to this or that transaction. Yes?"

"That's right."

"And when those dealings are exposed, you have a scandal."

"True," said Bolan. "But it seldom changes anything, in the long term."

"In my country, the *Mafiya* and politicians make no secret of their friendship. They appear in public, shaking hands, attending balls and banquets. Reporters for the tabloid press observe, but rarely publish. Do you know of Dak Safronov?"

"It doesn't ring a bell," Bolan admitted.

"He covered military affairs for the *Kommersant,* a daily newspaper in Moscow. In 2007 he reported on an army plan for selling arms to Iran and Syria through Belarus. First, he was 'cautioned' by the FSB. When that did not dissuade him, he fell from a fifth-story window. Four months before that, it was Anna Politkovskaya, shot by contract killers after she criticized Russian policy toward Chechnya. The president denounced the crime, of course, but added that her influence was 'very minor.' Others got the message."

"So, I'm up against a monolith," Bolan said.

"*We* are up against it," Pilkin corrected him. "And it won't help that I am part of it. You know the Bible saying about many mansions?"

"Vaguely."

"It refers to heaven." She surprised him yet again. "But it applies to Earth, as well. Maybe to hell, for all I know."

"Meaning, your own people could wind up hunting us?"

"I guarantee it."

"One more reason why you should consider backing off. It's your life *and* career on the line."

"I've thought about it," she replied. "It makes me angry to consider that I cannot trust my own superiors. If they were hoping that I would be frightened, they've made a mistake."

"Anger's not the best emotion for a soldier going into battle," Bolan counseled. "It can breed mistakes and get you killed."

"I understand this."

"You've heard of General Patton?"

"Blood and Guts," she said. "I know of him."

"He once said, 'No poor bastard ever won a war by dying for his country. He won it by making *other* bastards die for *their* country.'"

"Or for their cause."

"That's it."

"So, Mr. Cooper, which poor bastards shall we visit first?"

KIRIL ASTAPKOVICH DREW deeply on his cigar, then waved away his aide with the gold-plated lighter. "Leave us now," he commanded, and heard the door close seconds later.

"Major Chaliapin," he said, through a light veil of smoke, "you are aware of why I summoned you?"

Leaving no doubt as to their relative position in the pecking order—or the food chain.

"I am, sir," Chaliapin replied.

Some might consider it an honor to be summoned by one of Moscow Oblast's two senators on the Federation Council of Russia. At the present hour, though, most would be wise enough to know that it was not a social call. The senator had to want something, and he wasn't accustomed to refusal.

"Perhaps you will explain, in that case," Astapkovich said.

At forty-eight, he was a rising power in United Russia, the Federation's strongest political party. In the last parliamentary election, United Russia had won 305 seats out of 450 in the State Duma, and eighty-eight out of 178 in the Federation

Council. Its centrist message steamrolled special-interest opposition from competitors including Yabloko, Right Cause, Just Russia, Patriots of Russia and the misnamed Liberal Democratic Party of Russia, whose right-wing ultranationalism bore little resemblance to liberal democracy.

"Our friend in Saint Petersburg cannot have instant results on his latest demands," Chaliapin replied. "So he calls you to draw me away from my work and delay me with threats."

"You have it, precisely," Astapkovich said. "There is no need for any hard feelings, however."

"No, sir. If I gave that impression—"

Astapkovich waved off the budding apology. "Not a bit of it, Major. I simply wish to hear your insight on the matter, which was not, perhaps, explained to me in full."

"Quite simply, Senator, we received word yesterday that a second attempt would be made to remove Gennady Sokolov from Russian soil."

"Another G-man melodrama?" Astapkovich said with a sneer.

"No, sir. According to our information, one man was expected to arrive at Domodedovo this evening and proceed from there."

"One man, in place of…what was it, last time?"

"Eight, sir."

"That's confidence for you. But proceed where? To what end? Surely, Saint Petersburg would be a better starting point?"

"That would depend, I must suppose, on what he meant to do."

"I see," Astapkovich said, though he saw nothing. "This stranger, then. Is he American?"

"He's traveling on a Canadian passport, for whatever that's worth. Flying from Montreal to Moscow, via London. Which proves nothing, as you know, sir."

"Do we know this pilgrim?"

Chaliapin shook his head. "No, sir. He's traveling—or *was*—as Matthew Cooper. We assume it is a cover. Immigration at the airport failed to make a photocopy of his passport, although we requested it."

"An oversight, you think? Or sabotage?"

This time, Chaliapin shrugged. "Most likely, simple negligence. Failure to pass the order on, perhaps."

"This Cooper was expected, though. You had his flight number?"

"Yes, Senator."

"So, he was met?"

Chaliapin cleared his throat. His nervous eyes made a quick circuit of the room, as if seeking escape.

"Sir, I was told… That is, our friend *requested* that the interception be left to private parties."

Meaning the *Mafiya,* presumably the Solntsevskaya Brotherhood. At least they were fairly efficient when it came to killing.

"And?" Astapkovich prodded his anxious guest.

"Sir, I regret to tell you that they failed."

"Failed to do what, exactly, Major?"

"To detain the subject, sir."

"Meaning that he escaped."

"Yes, sir. That's true."

"Did they pursue him?"

"To their sorrow, Senator. Four men are dead tonight."

"And greatly missed, I'm sure. This Cooper killed them?"

"With the possible assistance of a woman."

"What?"

"Two members of the interception team were spared, sir. Something about separate cars. They were together at the airport, though, and saw a woman give the man a ride. The chase began from there. They were delayed, but followed from directions they were telephoned. When they arrived, the rest were dead, sir."

"Most unfortunate."

"Indeed."

"But you, of course, are doing everything within your power to redeem the situation?"

"Absolutely, Senator."

"I would expect no less. What progress, then?"

"So far, sir, none."

"An unknown man and woman, lost somewhere in Moscow," Astapkovich said. "Two out of millions."

"If they're still inside the city, sir."

"Again, why fly to Moscow, if your target is Saint Petersburg?"

"Some kind of misdirection, possibly."

"If so, Major, it's working."

"Not for long, sir."

"Do I have your word on that?"

"You do!"

"Then I shall leave you to it. Thank you for your time. By all means, hurry back to work."

TARAS MOROZOV kept his rugged face deadpan, emotionless, while Leonid Bezmel glowered across his desk. If looks could kill, he thought.

"I've just had Sokolov back on the line," Bezmel declared. "Third time tonight, so far. The bastard never sleeps."

"He's worried," Morozov replied.

"With reason, I suppose."

"After that business with the FBI, I'd say so."

"He bloodied them last time."

"And they'll be hungry for revenge."

"We should have stopped this agent at the airport, Taras."

"Yes."

"Instead, he killed four of our men and made us look like idiots."

"We would have had him," Morozov said, "if the woman hadn't intervened."

"*Would have* is just another word for failure."

It was *two* words, but Morozov didn't think it wise to interrupt his boss with grammar lessons.

"I will find them," he declared.

"Personally?" Bezmel asked.

"If that is what it takes."

"Then, I'd suggest you do it soon. We're to be graced with Sergei Efros helping us, first thing tomorrow. Gennady thinks that Spetznaz reject can accomplish something we cannot. In Moscow!"

"Maybe he intends to gas us," Morozov said.

"I wouldn't put it past him. I want someone covering him every minute he's in town. If he breaks wind or eats a bag of pretzels, I expect to hear about it as it happens."

"That's no problem," Morozov replied with utmost confidence.

Gennady Sokolov insulted him and all the Brotherhood by sending a man of his own to hunt the targets they were seeking. What could one damned Special Forces failure do that Morozov's own army could not?

"We profit from Gennady's business. There's no doubt about it," Bezmel said. "But in his agitation, he forgets about respect. I cannot reason with him in his present state. You must prevent Efros from running roughshod over any of our friends, especially official ones."

"I will," Morozov promised.

"I've been thinking that we might divert him toward Shishani and the Obshina. It does no harm to us, if he harasses them. And who knows? We might even benefit."

If the damned Chechens killed him, for example.

"Won't that agitate Gennady even more?"

"Perhaps. But he can't blame us for whatever happens, and he'll be in a forgiving mood when you produce this Cooper for him."

"And the woman," Morozov said.

"I'm not forgetting her," Bezmel replied. "After we find out who she's working for, maybe I'll let her work for us. Pick out the worst whorehouse in town and make a reservation."

"It's my pleasure," Morozov agreed.

And smiled, for the first time that night.

THE MEN'S CLUB known as Paris Nights stood eight blocks northeast of the Kremlin, on Nikolskaya Street. Its conservative marquee headlined singers whose names meant nothing to Bolan.

"So, this is the place?" he asked.

"Shishani's primary casino," Pilkin replied.

"It doesn't look like much."

"Just wait until you get inside."

She'd given him the rundown on Russia's gambling situation while they drove across town to their target. In the heady days after communism's collapse, in the early 1990s, wide-open casino gambling was only one aspect of capitalism eagerly adopted by the former Soviet Union. The industry grew by leaps and bounds—an estimated thirty-five percent each year, with no federal laws to control it. Reported income from gambling topped six billion dollars in 2005, with few observers publicly willing to speculate on the extent of skimming.

Then, a reaction set in from the Russian Orthodox Church, conservative politicians and reformers outraged by rising crime rates coupled with reports of families left destitute by compulsive gamblers. In October 2006 the Russian Parliament had taken the first step toward strict limitation of legalized gambling, dictating that any licensed casino owner had to hold at least thirty million in liquid assets. Minimum sizes were decreed for gambling halls—eight hundred square meters for a full-fledged casino, one hundred for a slot-machine joint.

If that wasn't enough to torque the shorts of big-time gamblers, a new law also mandated removal of all gambling facilities to one of four designated "uninhabited" areas by July 2009. Henceforth, players would have to seek their pleasure in Kaliningrad, in Krasnodar's Azov City, in Siberia's Sibirskaya Moneta, or on Russky Island in the Kara Sea, offshore from Vladivostok.

Faced with those restrictions, mobsters did what they had always done throughout recorded history. They went underground.

Granted, they didn't burrow very deep. Club names were changed. Some neon signs came down. Proprietors dismissed the sidewalk barkers they had used to virtually drag new players off the streets in better days.

But play continued, at a price.

The same police who took bribes to ignore drug trafficking and prostitution willingly accepted more to let casinos operate with near impunity. On rare occasions when a raid was forced by public pressure, ample warning would be given to permit removal of incriminating evidence. The overzealous beat cop who had walked into a Mob casino unannounced and caught two judges shooting craps was reassigned, then fired and prosecuted after kiddy porn was found inside his locker at the station house.

"Do you have any specs on club security?" Bolan asked.

"All the usual," she said. "Alarms inside and out. Full video surveillance on the players and employees. There will certainly be guards, but I can't say how many, or how heavily they may be armed."

"Shishani won't send two or three to guard his gold mine with slingshots," Bolan said.

"It may be too risky."

"I didn't say that. Those alarms you mentioned. Do they sound for an unannounced raid?"

"I assume so," Pilkin said.

"So, there'll be exits for players and staff, besides coming out through the front door."

"I've heard rumors of tunnels," she said.

"Should be doable," Bolan declared. "While the players and dealers bail out, I can handle the watchdogs."

"*We* handle them," Pilkin quickly corrected.

"You know we're not making arrests?"

"Understood."

"So, we smoke the place."

"And blame Bezmel, yes?"

"That's the plan," Bolan confirmed. "If we can't leave a message here with one of his lookouts, we'll phone it in and spoil his beauty sleep."

"Too bad," Pilkin said. "Aldo needs all that he can get."

CHAPTER SIX

Nothing that Bolan saw on Nikolskaya Street reminded him of Paris. Least of all Aldo Shishani's club that bore the name, although a tiny Eiffel Tower was featured in its understated neon sign.

Some people, Bolan thought, and let it go.

Leaving Pilkin's car a block from the casino, Bolan took a beat to hide his Steyr AUG under the lightweight knee-length raincoat he had packed in Montreal. His backup, snug in armpit leather, was the sleek Beretta 93-R, minus its suppressor.

There'd be no disguising his intentions once he entered Paris Nights, so he had ditched the extra weight. If it came down to pistol dueling in the *Mafiya* casino, he'd let the Beretta speak in full voice, loud and clear. Whether the punks who heard it lived to pass the message on was something else entirely.

But there *was* a message to be passed, and he'd agreed with Pilkin to make delivery job one. She had her game face on as they stood waiting for a break in traffic, poised to cross the street.

It was a busy neighborhood despite the hour, which was creeping up on 1:15 a.m. A weeknight, yet, but Russians obviously liked to party hearty when they had a chance. If those he saw leaving the club were any indication, hangovers would be the order of the day come morning. Some employers wouldn't get their money's worth from bleary-eyed, dull-witted workers.

None of which was Bolan's problem.

He was no reformer, didn't generally give a damn if other people gambled, drank themselves into oblivion, or spent their hard-earned pay on hookers. Bolan was a libertarian of sorts, with no great interest in the foibles of humankind, unless those foibles financed networks of sadistic predators who looted, raped and murdered with impunity.

At least, until they met the Executioner.

He'd never been a Bible-thumper, but private tragedy had driven home a verse or two.

Vengeance is mine; I will repay.

Whoso sheddeth man's blood, by man shall his blood be shed.

Amen and hallelujah.

Bolan saw his opening and took it, double-timing across Nikolskaya Street with Anzhela Pilkin beside him. She matched his pace, clutching the Vityaz submachine gun underneath her jacket, pressed against her ribs.

The two of them were dressed to kill, and no one else in Paris Nights suspected that they were about to crash the party.

Bolan marked the moment when the club's doorman-cum-bouncer noticed them. He stood six-three or -four and kept his scalp shaved, while a padlock beard-and-mustache combination made his lower face look vaguely sinister. He stood with arms crossed, showcasing high-maintenance biceps.

"Ready?" Bolan asked.

"Ready," Pilkin confirmed.

When they were close enough for the doorman to hit them for the cover charge, Pilkin hit him with a burst of rapid-fire Russian. Bolan knew the gist of it, heard Maksim Chaliapin's name in the midst of gibberish, before Pilkin showed him the Vityaz.

The doorman had a chance to recognize it, was considering a fast-draw of his pistol holstered on his right hip, when she whipped the SMG's muzzle into his groin and took the fight out of him in a hurry. She finished it with a short chop into the midst of his agonized grimace, and Bolan hauled the guy's deadweight behind him as they barged into the club.

One of the singers whom he'd never heard of had some kind of heavy-metal number going, wailing like a Russian Axl Rose. The higher octaves knifed at Bolan's ears, making him wince, but he could stand it for another minute while he dumped the doorman off to one side, brought the Steyr out from under cover and prepared to make some racket of his own.

OLEG BILIBIN HEARD the first gunshot and wondered which drunken fool had brought a cherry bomb into the nightclub. Was there anyone in his—or her—right mind who really thought it would be funny?

Bilibin was halfway to the doorway of his second-floor office when the sharp sound was repeated, multiplying faster than his dazed brain could accommodate, compelling him against his will to recognize the truth.

Gunfire? Inside Paris Nights?

Regrettably, considering his clientele, the climate of the times and who he worked for, it wasn't entirely unexpected. Now he simply had to deal with it.

With what? a voice inside his head demanded.

Bilibin delayed a moment at his office threshold, backtracked to a cabinet where banks of television monitors displayed multiple views of the main nightclub, its backstage area, and the "secret" casino tucked away in back. Before he barged into a killing situation, Bilibin had to find out who he was dealing with.

Police? Unlikely, since they hadn't phoned ahead to warn him of a raid.

Bandits? Always a possibility, if they were too stupid or

too strung out on drugs to fear Aldo Shishani and the wrath of the Obshina.

Or could it be raiders from the Solntsevskaya Brotherhood come to wreak some havoc for the hell of it?

Two monitors winked back at Bilibin with muzzle-flashes while the sound of blaring music died beneath his feet and gunfire echoed in its place. Some of the shooters were his own men, finally getting a chance to defend Paris Nights after months of sitting around on their asses with nothing to do.

But the others…

He bent forward, his nose almost pressed to a monitor screen. Yes! It *was* a woman, firing bursts from a submachine gun!

Bilibin knew his duty, as a loyal employee and an oath-bound, tattooed member of the Obshina. Without another moment's hesitation, he opened an adjoining cabinet and chose an AK-105 assault rifle from the rack of weapons waiting there. It was already loaded with a 30-round curved magazine of 5.45 mm M-74 ammunition, ready to shred human flesh at a stroke of its trigger.

Bilibin hadn't killed a man in nearly five years, since his promotion to midlevel management, but homicide was like talking young women out of their panties. Once you had the knack, it never left you.

He hit the stairs at a gallop, his ears ringing with the sounds of combat now that he no longer had four insulated walls around him to deaden the racket. The sharp smell of cordite reached his flaring nostrils, mixed with the odors of cigarette smoke, sweat, some weed and expensive perfume.

No sex tonight for this lot of customers, he thought, unless, of course, a brush with death got some of them aroused.

He reached the bottom of the stairs and risked a sweeping look around the main room of the club. Two bodies were sprawled nearby, a couple of his men cut down before they had a chance to take out the invaders.

There were always more where they came from.

It seemed his customers had managed to escape intact, and Bilibin knew the casino should be emptied by now. He needed to contain the threat and neutralize it before any of his frightened guests did something stupid.

Like alerting the militia.

Investigation of a killing would entitle them to roam at will through Paris Nights. Bilibin wasn't convinced that he could bribe them all into blindness when they found the casino. Not with blood on the floor, and the damned newspapers jabbering about "reform."

He had to stop these outside shooters. Stop them hard, whatever that required, and get the nightclub back in shape before someone in uniform arrived.

And if that meant he'd have to kill some crazy person armed with a machine gun, bent on shooting him, Bilibin wouldn't mind at all.

BOLAN HAD COUNTED seven shooters, two of whom were down and out already, but he knew that didn't mean they'd seen them all. A place the size of Paris Nights, with a backroom casino and a larger syndicate in town, ready to pick the competition's bones, might rate a dozen guns or more to keep it up and running in a combat zone.

He hoped the doorman wouldn't wake while they were bringing down the house—or wake up later and forget the message Pilkin had fed to him before she cracked his walnuts for him. If they had to kill him on their way out, it would be a waste. Ditto if he was too dazed or too stupid to relay the warning.

A staccato burst of autofire helped Bolan focus on the task at hand. Five shooters that he knew of, more or less, had collected in the southeast corner of the nightclub proper, standing fast around a doorway that could only open into the casino. Bolan knew he couldn't let that human barrier defeat him as he palmed a Russian RGN fragmentation grenade and pulled the safety pin, then glanced around to locate Pilkin.

He found her crouched behind an upturned table, twenty paces to his left, exchanging short bursts with the cluster of defenders ranged before her. Slugs were chipping at the table, which had never been designed for personal protection in a firefight, and he knew she'd have to move soon, as her shield got whittled down.

Or maybe not.

He made the pitch without a showy windup, dropped the sizzling egg almost precisely where he wanted it, and counted down the four remaining seconds while his adversaries tried to scramble out of range.

Too late.

The blast and shrapnel killed two of them outright and reduced the other three to lurching zombies, stunned and bloody, barely mobile. Pilkin dropped one of them while Bolan stitched the other two with 5.56 mm bursts and watched them fall.

He waited where he was, still unconvinced that it could be so easy—and a long burst from behind him proved the point. Bolan spun, dropped and rolled away from the chattering stream of Kalashnikov fire. He saw his snarling opposition charging from the general direction of a stairwell they had passed on their way in, sweeping the room with reckless fire and shouting what could only be a stream of Russian curses.

Words couldn't hurt him, but the rounds from that AK could chew him into hamburger. Bolan kept moving, lizard-style, while he returned fire with his Steyr AUG. It was an awkward business, but he caught a break when one slug grazed his adversary's ankle, tripped him and brought him crashing down. Before the Russian could recover, twin streams of fire from the Steyr and Pilkin's Vityaz pinned him to the floor forever, facedown in a spreading pool of crimson.

Once again, Bolan waited to see if any other gunmen popped out of the woodwork. This time, there was none.

He rose at last and approached the padded door to the backroom casino, weighing the odds that more shooters were hunkered behind it, ready to blaze away as it opened.

Bolan chose not to give them that option.

He hit the doorknob with an autoburst that tore it into shiny scrap and punched the door half-open. Only silence greeted him, but Bolan didn't trust it. He pulled the green metal cap from a ZDP white phosphorus grenade and lobbed the bomb into the casino, standing back while it popped and sizzled.

Waiting for screams. Hearing none.

No matter. He'd already sealed the club's fate. Whatever wasn't devoured by chemical fire would have to be scrapped and rebuilt or replaced. Aldo Shishani wouldn't get the death stench out of Paris Nights.

Not even if he lived to try.

THE CALL CAME through at 2:08 a.m. Aldo Shishani wasn't sleeping. On the contrary, in fact. It was the middle of his working day, with gamblers, drug addicts and sex perverts all clamoring for services he was happy to provide, if they had ready cash in hand. He would retire and sleep when sunlight drove the denizens of Moscow's grim nocturnal world back into hiding for the day.

Or, rather, would have slept, if he hadn't received the call from Paris Nights.

That wasn't true, of course. Shishani didn't get a call from Paris Nights, because the club was gone, for all intents and purposes. It had no solid standing walls, no roof or furnishings, much less a working telephone. Say, rather, that he had received a call *about* his former premier club and gambling den, describing its demise.

The caller was a nobody who'd drawn a paycheck at the club and obviously hadn't earned it, if the tale he told was true. A man and woman armed with automatic weapons came out of nowhere, clubbing him unconscious after the woman left a message for Shishani.

Leonid Bezmel sends his condolences to Aldo Shishani. He is running out of time.

Just that, and what more did she need to say?

It came as no surprise that Bezmel would attack Shishani's prize establishment. Shishani had expected something of the sort for months, since their last spate of skirmishes concluded indecisively. The strange part of the deal was Bezmel's choice of raiders. Where in hell had he found a woman tough and cold enough to stand against Shishani's soldiers?

He'd known some crazy hookers in his time, including one who carried a straight razor tucked in her thong and another who had shot her pimp's manhood to tatters, but none who were bona fide soldiers.

There were some, of course. Shishani had seen photos from the annual Miss Russian Army beauty contest, lookers in their tailored uniforms, lined up and smiling. They presumably were trained to fight, not just as pinup girls.

And the Israelis, now. From what Shishani understood, nearly half of their soldiers were women conscripted for duty, including front-line combat and high-risk border patrols, even fighter jet pilots.

Shishani paced his study, scowling at the carpet underneath his feet, trying to reason out the problem. If he took the woman's threat at face value, he was required to retaliate against Bezmel or lose face forever, among both his rivals and Obshina members.

But what if the threat was a ruse?

Who might wish to ignite a war between his Family and the Solntsevskaya Brotherhood? For what purpose?

What he desperately needed was more information, something he could trust to help him plot his critical next move. But who, in all of Moscow, was trustworthy?

Someone who was bought and paid for.

Huffing with impatience now, Shishani turned and reached out for the telephone.

"THAT WAS…" Anzhela Pilkin hesitated, searching for the proper word, drawing a blank.

"Uncivilized?" Bolan suggested from the seat beside her as she drove without clear direction, southbound on Vetoshnyy Pereulok, east of the Kremlin. "Insane?"

"Exciting," she proposed as an alternative. "You can't know how long I have wanted to do that. Walk in and give the bastards what they deserve."

"It's not the best prescription for longevity in law enforcement," Bolan pointed out.

"But satisfying, eh?" she said.

"It can be," he admitted. "But I wouldn't recommend you getting hooked on it."

"Are you aware of how corrupt things are in Russia?" she asked, warming to her subject as she turned east onto Il'inka Street.

"I have a fair idea," Bolan replied.

"Of course, you're here about Gennady Sokolov. You know something about the *Mafiya*, I understand. But do you grasp the depth of it? How it pervades all aspects of our lives?"

"Well…"

"In the West, I understand your leaders spoke of communism as corrupt. And so it was, of course. The leaders had their privileges, as leaders do in all societies. Some literally got away with murder, as you'd say. But now is much, *much* worse."

"I don't pretend to speak for anyone in Russia," Bolan said.

"Then let me," Pilkin replied. "Who leads us? Our first president, after the change, an alcoholic who can barely walk today. He resigns after a televised confession of 'errors' in his rule, begging Russia's forgiveness for 'dreams that never came true.' He's replaced by a man who resembles a house elf from your *Harry Potter* films, ex-KGB, whose critics in the media wear bull's-eye targets on their backs. Now he's prime minister, appointed by his former chief of staff, who has become the president. Next thing you know, a Moscow journalist who writes about corruption in the Kremlin gets a package. Donkey's ears, pinned to a note that reads 'From the Presidential Administration.'"

"Donkey's ears?" Bolan asked.

"It's a Russian thing, okay? You try for something—play a game, seduce a lover, take your pick—and when you lose, we say you got the donkey's ears. It's like your goose egg, understand? A zero. Nothing. You're a loser."

"Okay."

"Now, the *Mafiya,* if they send donkey's ears, it may be something more. You've seen *The Godfather?*"

"Is this about a fish?" Bolan asked.

"Yes! You see it! That's a *threat,* not just a joke or commentary."

"And the journalist who got the ears? What happened there?"

"Nothing, yet," Pilkin said. "She lives in hiding. Wears disguises. Changes cars as soon as one is recognized. The usual."

"You understand," he said, "that none of what we've done tonight will change that, right? We're not starting some kind of revolution."

"I know that," she answered, feeling sudden anger and unable to explain it. "Still, there's no reason why I should not enjoy it, is there?"

Bolan didn't answer that, leaving Pilkin to devise her own response.

And yes, she realized how strange—even perverse—it sounded, saying she derived enjoyment from killing.

"That isn't what I mean, you know? The shooting. I'm not *sad* about it, but I'm not some kind of crazy person, either."

"Never crossed my mind," Bolan said.

"But still, it feels like justice. It's the act of doing something, in a place where nearly everyone you meet drifts with the tide, and those who don't are swept away."

"Well, then, I've got good news, if you can call it that," Bolan replied.

"Which is?"

"We're nowhere close to finished."

TARAS MOROZOV WAITED while the houseman went to tell Bezmel that he'd arrived. Another hectic drive across the city, jumping traffic lights and dodging the police, only to stand and wait.

Some new emergency, no doubt. As if they didn't have enough to cope with now.

Morozov clenched his teeth around a yawn and swallowed it as the houseman returned. A moment later, he was in the usual padded chair, leather upholstery sliding under him, as he faced Leonid Bezmel across a wide, uncluttered desk.

"You've heard about Shishani's place?" Bezmel asked him without preamble.

Morozov could only shrug and shake his head. In modern Moscow, that was multitasking. "No," he said. "Which place?"

"The big one," Bezmel answered. "Paris Nights."

"What about it?"

"Someone raided it tonight."

"Police?"

Morozov couldn't understand why this was worth discussing, much less racing across Moscow to receive the news in person.

"Hardly," Bezmel said, chewing a crooked smile. "Whoever did it shot the place to hell, killed Aldo's men and torched the place. Some kind of chemicals. It may be burning as we speak."

"Is that bad news?"

"I don't like mysteries."

"You want to find out who's responsible."

"I want *you* to find out. We can't tolerate this kind of anarchy. Consider the publicity. It's bad for business in the long run."

"And the media may blame us."

"Not only the media," Bezmel replied.

Of course. If Aldo Shishani didn't know who had attacked his club, he would suspect the Solntsevskaya Brotherhood. They were mortal enemies. Who else would seek to harm him so aggressively?

"Some other syndicate," Morozov said, answering his unspoken question.

"That's no answer," Bezmel told him. "And it's still bad news. If there's a group we never heard of operating in the city, and it's strong enough to pull something like this… You see the problem, Taras?"

"There's been no indication of a new gang moving in," Morozov said. "I have surveillance on the Japanese."

"Not Yakuza," Bezmel replied. "Not triads. The attackers were observed. There is a witness."

"And…?"

"Our man with the militia says the shooters were a couple, man and woman. White, well dressed, well armed. The bitch spoke Russian."

"That's unusual," Morozov said.

"What? A Russian-speaking woman?"

"Someone sending out a woman for a job like that."

"You wouldn't do it?" Bezmel didn't wait for a reply. "Nor me."

"Where would I even find one?" Morozov asked.

"Another riddle to be solved, without delay."

"Of course, there is one. And she's here, in Moscow."

"What? Who?" Bezmel hesitated, then expelled the obscenity. "Son of a bitch!"

"Exactly."

"The woman from the airport! With your stranger!"

Now he's my stranger, Morozov thought, but kept it to himself.

Instead, he said, "A man and woman. Proved killers. She's most likely Russian."

"First they kill my men, and now Shishani's? Why? Can you explain that to me, Taras?"

"Not yet," Morozov replied. "But I intend to."

"It seems that I was premature. We do not have two riddles. Only one."

"Will you relay this information to Saint Petersburg?"

"Why bother?" Bezmel countered. "He's upset enough as it is. And don't forget, his man will soon be joining us."

It was Morozov's turn to swear, putting a smile on Bezmel's face.

"Play nice," Bezmel commanded. "To a point, at least. Don't let him interfere with anything important, but if he's so keen to watch…"

"Suppose he wants to go off on his own and play detective?"

"Let him. What harm could it do?"

"And if he interferes with Family business?"

"Use your own best judgment," Bezmel answered. "With so many killers on the loose in Moscow, accidents can happen."

CHAPTER SEVEN

Maksim Chaliapin felt his cell phone vibrating and recognized the number displayed in its LED window. He cursed under his breath, but could hardly refuse to answer.

"Hello."

"I notice you don't say good morning, Major," Aldo Shishani said.

"Is it good? I hadn't noticed."

"You are wise to doubt it," the Obshina's leader replied.

"So, how may I help you?"

He was careful not to mention names, since cell phone calls could be snatched from thin air, recorded, analyzed.

"I thought perhaps you'd like to earn your money," Shishani said.

"By doing what, precisely?" Chaliapin asked.

"You've heard about the fire at Paris Nights, I take it?"

"That is a militia matter, I'm afraid."

"And FSB investigations never overlap? Is that your story?"

"If there was some explanation…"

"Think of one," Shishani said. "It's what you cloak-and-dagger types live for."

"The present atmosphere is not amenable to fabricated claims."

Shishani laughed aloud at that.

"Since when?" he challenged. "There is always room within the corridors of power for another lie."

Chaliapin thought about the call he'd just received from

Leonid Bezmel. A wild theory, perhaps, linking the stranger from the airport and his unknown female savior to the raid on Shishani's illegal casino. It made no sense to Chaliapin, this elusive "Matthew Cooper" and his lady friend attacking both of Moscow's largest gangs at once.

"I can likely think of something," he informed Shishani.

"I have every confidence."

"If challenged, though—"

"Assert your natural authority."

The mobster's tone was mocking. It set Chaliapin's teeth on edge. His fingers tightened on the cell phone, then relaxed as he regained control.

"I'll be in touch, if any information surfaces."

"Without delay, I trust."

"Without delay. Of course. Goodbye."

Chaliapin broke the link before Shishani could say more, admitting to himself that he derived a certain petty satisfaction from that small act of defiance. At the same time, he was embarrassed by a pang of fear that he may have enraged the mobster.

Even majors in the FSB weren't invulnerable. They could be gunned down like anybody else.

And who would care?

His death would be a two-day wonder in the newspapers, perhaps. The chief of his department would swear vengeance on the unknown killers, might even appear to follow through for a short time, but then new crises would present themselves and Chaliapin's short obituary would be used to line bird cages and wrap fish.

His first mistake—well, not the first, but very possibly his worst—had been accepting bribes from both the boss of the Solntsevskaya Brotherhood and his deadly rival at the helm of the Obshina. Chaliapin wasn't sure what he'd been thinking at the time, beyond visions of rubles dancing in his head, but it was too late for historical revisionism now.

Both syndicates had rightful, albeit illegal, claims to his loyalty and service. Neither was likely to forgive or forget his duplicity if it should be revealed to them.

The only question, in that case, would be who killed him first.

Chaliapin almost laughed at that, since no one had the power to kill him twice, but the harsh croak of sardonic humor died in his throat.

He could make a good case that he hadn't betrayed either gang, as long as he simply protected their interests in Moscow from troublesome raids. A conflict arose when the two stood at odds, each demanding some action that threatened the other. In such a case, Chaliapin could find himself drawn and quartered.

Now that day had arrived.

Or had it?

Gennady Sokolov and Leonid Bezmel still wanted him to find and stop the stranger who'd slain their gunmen after the bungled ambush at Domodedovo International. Aldo Shishani wanted retribution for the deadly raid on Paris Nights. But if the same unlikely duo—male and female, equally adept at killing—was responsible for both events, then Chaliapin saw no conflict of interest.

He could serve both masters by simply doing his job.

Which left him with the same problem: finding the shooters in question.

This day, Chaliapin wondered if he'd been looking in all the wrong places. Could it be that treachery—like charity—began closer to home?

SUNRISE OVER MOSCOW found Bolan and Pilkin sipping strong coffee, waiting for their bargain breakfasts in a small all-night café on Delegatskaya Street. Most of the sparse traffic abroad on gray streets at that hour consisted of delivery vans and the occasional police car. Bolan made a point of smiling when the cops rolled past, and got one back from Pilkin, in turn.

She had ordered their meals in Russian, but they spoke in English, almost whispering across their narrow table, as dawn broke beyond the glass at Bolan's elbow. Silence fell as the waitress brought their steaming plates, and then brief thanks from them both as she retreated toward the vacant counter.

"I wish we could eavesdrop on Shishani this morning," Pilkin said, cutting a plump sausage link with her fork.

"We can do better than that," Bolan said. "We can call him directly."

She blinked at him, chewed and swallowed.

"To say what? 'Hope you're sad that we blew up your nightclub'?"

"That's one possibility," Bolan replied. "But it could have more impact if we showed a little sympathy."

"You've lost me, Matthew."

"It's a simple, basic plan. Divide and conquer, right? Of course, Shishani and Bezmel are already divided, so the trick is pushing them out of an armed truce, into active conflict."

"With a phone call?"

"Make it plural," he suggested. "We can call them both, switch up the warning messages. Turn up the heat and let them simmer. Add some spice out on the street, with visits here and there."

"More raids," she said.

"That's how it works."

"To start a gang war?"

Bolan nodded silently.

"And you've done this before?"

"A time or two."

"Successfully?"

"So far."

"Your strategy is flawed, I think," Pilkin said.

"How so?"

She cut a quick glance toward the waitress, thirty feet away, then leaned closer and said, "These raids you speak of. We control them. Shoot the right men. Torch a gangster's enterprise. No problem. All illegal, mind you, but controlled."

"Exactly."

"*Da*. But we cannot predict what happens when the Solntsevskaya Brotherhood and Obshina take their war into the streets. Their triggermen aren't microsurgeons. They will spray a shopping mall with bullets, sacrifice a dozen bystanders to kill one man—and maybe he's the wrong man, even then. I won't unleash that kind of hell in Moscow."

"Nor will I," Bolan replied. "My goal is a controlled burn. Light the fuse, direct it to specific targets, watch them blow. The shock waves force our man to surface, and we've got him."

"Sokolov?"

"He's what it's all about."

"But still, only one man."

"One man who's made a fortune peddling death and misery around the world," Bolan reminded her. "Think of the thousands he's killed without pulling a trigger himself. Is it millions, by now? Put loose nukes in the mix, and it will be. Who triggers the first mushroom cloud? Does it even matter? Religious fanatics or atheist rebels, ethnic cleansers or some nut who's getting his orders from Alpha Centauri by e-mail. It plays out the same. Cut-rate Armageddon."

"Go after the nukes, then. Go after the buyers."

"I will, when I know where they are. Who they are. First, we have to flush Sokolov out of his hole."

"In Saint Petersburg."

"But his connections are here, in Moscow. Not only the *Mafiya*. Government, too. You know that, Anzhela. You know that every time he makes another sale, most of the world is blaming Russia, not Gennady Sokolov."

She frowned at Bolan for another moment, then seemed to relax. "I need more coffee," Pilkin declared. "We have a long and tiring day ahead of us."

Vnukovo International Airport, Moscow

SERGEI EFROS ENTERED Terminal D of Moscow's oldest airport at 6:05 a.m. His nostrils twitched at the odors of new renovation—fresh paint, sawdust, rubber and sweat.

Terminal D at Vnukovo International was reserved for domestic flights, like the one that had brought him from Saint Petersburg. Because a private Learjet had delivered him, Efros wasn't required to dawdle in a mob of sluggish drones who seemed to think they owned the concourse. He strode past and around them, jostling none too gently those who blocked his path.

The private jet had other benefits, as well. It meant that neither Efros nor his carry-on had been screened by security agents at Pulkovo Airport in Saint Petersburg. His ALFA Combat .45-caliber pistol was safe in its shoulder rig beneath his left armpit, with two spare 10-round magazines in pouches on the right. Inside his duffel bag, Efros carried a KBP A-91 assault rifle, the bullpup design in 5.56 mm NATO, with an integrated 40 mm grenade launcher mounted beneath its short barrel.

If Efros needed any other weapons, he could pick them up in Moscow as he went along. After all, he was representing the world's foremost Merchant of Death.

He spotted Taras Morozov almost immediately, standing off to one side of the concourse by himself, his arms folded, his face deadpan. The underboss of the Solntsevskaya Brotherhood clearly wasn't glad to see Efros, which troubled the former Spetznaz commando no more than a slight pang of gas. Morozov would follow the instructions he'd received from Leonid Bezmel, which would include accommodating Efros in any way possible.

Efros didn't shake hands with Morozov. No sign of friendship was expected. Morozov would have a car waiting outside, and they were eighteen miles from downtown Moscow. Time enough, in transit, to discuss whatever progress had been made in tracking down the enemies who stalked Gennady Sokolov.

In fact, Efros wasn't expecting any progress. He regarded members of the Solntsevskaya Brotherhood and their rival syndicates as little more than apes who'd learned to dress themselves. Granted, they could be cunning—and most definitely dangerous—but none of them were soldiers, even though some claimed that honorable title for themselves. Given the choice, Efros would cheerfully have fed them all into a blast furnace, but it wasn't his call.

Like Taras Morozov, he had his orders, his place in the chain of command. Efros didn't aspire to lead a syndicate or corporation. He was reasonably happy in his present role of troubleshooter and enforcer, using talents that he had possessed since childhood or developed during military service to the Motherland.

This day, with any luck at all, he could apply those talents toward eradication of two pesky insects that had flown into a world they didn't understand, annoying giants. He would crush them both without a moment's hesitation or remorse.

But first, he would discover who had sent them.

Then, the real fun could begin.

MAKSIM CHALIAPIN HAD a cup of mediocre coffee poised against his lips when a shadow fell over his small cafeteria table, the plate with his fried eggs and smoked sturgeon. He glanced from his poor breakfast to behold a pale and nervous face.

"Excuse me, Major?"

"Are you asking whether you may be excused, or whether I'm a major?"

"Yes. I mean, yes, sir!"

"Well, then, which is it?"

Chaliapin watched the nervousness bleed into fear, compounded by befuddlement. He obviously wasn't dealing with a genius, here. The man was fortyish and heavyset, below average height and nearly bald. His rheumy eyes were framed by steel-rimmed bifocals. The teeth that showed between his parted lips were beige and crooked.

"Sir, you are Major Maksim Chaliapin, I believe," the man replied at last.

"You are correct. Thank you for clarifying that. I've been in doubt of it for some time now."

A blink behind the bifocals. No vestige of a smile.

"Sir, I am Feofan Kolkoutine."

"Now both of us know who we are. What do you want, that supersedes this gourmet fare you see before me?"

Irony was clearly wasted on this slug. Kolkoutine swallowed hard as he prepared his next non sequitur.

"Sir, I'm employed here as an analyst for the Counterintelligence Service."

"An analyst of what?" Chaliapin asked through a mouthful of egg yolk and fish.

"Of many varied things, sir. Why I have sought you out like this—"

"A question that I've asked myself," Chaliapin said.

"—is because of your request for information."

"Now we're getting somewhere."

"Yes, sir. Thank you, sir!"

Chaliapin waited for another moment, then asked, "Will I soon be privileged to learn what information you're referring to? Is it a state secret, perhaps?"

"Sir! With regard to last night's events at Domodedovo

International Airport, I may know…that is, I may have…
information concerning identity."

"Whose identity?"

"The woman, sir. You asked if anyone—"

"Sit down, my friend. Would you enjoy a cup of coffee? It
was fresh sometime this week, I'm fairly certain."

"No. I mean, no, thank you, sir. My bladder is—"

"A subject for another time, perhaps. As to this
female…?"

Leaning close enough for Chaliapin to smell his foul
breath, Kolkoutine said, "Sir, I believe she is, er, may be,
one of ours."

"When you say 'ours,' you mean—"

"The FSB. Yes, sir."

Chaliapin felt his stomach churn. He set down his fork,
pushed his plate back another few inches. "What leads you
to believe this?" he inquired.

"Sir, just this morning I quite accidentally heard Comrade
Protazanov—"

"We are not comrades here," Chaliapin interrupted. "Perhaps you saw the memo?"

"Sir, I'm sorry. It's—"

"Move on."

"Yes, sir. Assistant Deputy Director Protazanov was
speaking on the telephone. I did not mean to eavesdrop, truly,
but—"

"Your point!"

"Sir, what he said was, 'No, she made the contact. At the
airport, yes. I don't know anything about the shooting. No,
no further contact.' Then he noticed me and walked away. It
was a cell phone conversation, and—"

"You claim to quote his words verbatim?" Chaliapin
asked.

"Oh, yes, sir. I am blessed with total recall. An eidetic
memory. Some call it 'photographic,' but—"

"A fascinating subject, I've no doubt. As to this conversation, have you any notion who the most elusive *she* might be?"

"No, sir. I'm sorry, sir."

"But this—what was his name? Petronovich?"

"Protazanov, sir. Assistant Deputy Director of Counterintelligence Elem Protazanov, sir."

"He'll know the name?"

"Most certainly, sir."

"In that case," Chaliapin said, "I think we're finished here."

"Sir?"

"Try this," said the major as he shoved his breakfast plate toward Kolkoutine. "It's almost better than it looks. Don't thank me. I have other fish to fry."

"HE'LL BE HERE any moment," Chaliapin told his visitor.

"I still don't like this," Kiril Astapkovich said, exhaling smoke with every syllable, as if he were a talking dragon. He had lit a fresh cigar on entering Chaliapin's office, less than ten minutes earlier, and it was nearly half-gone.

"Liking doesn't enter into it," Chaliapin said. "If the FSB has set this thing in motion and I didn't even know it, think what else may still be waiting to surprise us."

"Thank you, no. I'd rather not," Astapkovich replied.

"Sir, as I have explained, I cannot simply order a release of information from the Counterintelligence Service to my own branch. They are separated for a reason. Even asking for the name, through channels, would require—"

"I understand the problem, Major. I don't like it, but I'm here to help you solve it if I can. Without exposing either one of us to repercussions. Do *you* understand?" Astapkovich queried.

"Of course, sir."

Chaliapin understood that Senator Astapkovich would stab

him in the back without a second thought if it served his personal needs.

"Perhaps, in the time we have left to ourselves, you'd explain how you plan to prevent any comebacks? Will not this man who's coming simply turn around and squawk to his superiors?"

"Not if he thinks I have authority to ask the questions, sir. Not if his job—indeed, his very life—depends on it."

"And that's where I come in?"

"Yes, sir."

"All right, then, damn it! If you're sure—"

A rapping on the office door cut short Astapkovich's complaint. Chaliapin's lieutenant poked his head into the office, announcing their guest's arrival.

Make that "Judas goat," the major thought.

Assistant Deputy Director of Counterintelligence Elem Protazanov entered Chaliapin's office a moment later, closing the door behind him. He was a husky, athletic-looking man with dirty blond hair, in need of a shave. The stubble, bleary eyes and rumpled suit suggested that he'd spent the night at headquarters, trying to resolve some problem that still troubled him.

Chaliapin made the introductions, noting the way Protazanov's nostrils flared at mention of the senator's title. Protazanov took the seat that Chaliapin offered to him, but he sat down gingerly, as if he feared its cushion might be spiked with razor blades.

"Thank you for making time to see us," Chaliapin said. "A matter of concern has come to my attention, and I hope you may be able to resolve it."

"Sir?"

"Last night, a passenger from Canada arrived in Moscow via Domodedovo International. His name, according to the passport he displayed, was Matthew Cooper."

Protazanov said nothing, but he shifted in his chair, crossing his legs.

"This person is a subject of concern for my department. Surveillance was in place, but he evaded it with the assistance of a woman yet to be identified. I now have reason to believe that you may know the woman's name, and where she can be found."

"What reason, sir?" Protazanov inquired.

"This is the Lubyanka," Chaliapin said. "Have you forgotten that the walls have ears?"

"Am *I* under surveillance, Major?"

"For the moment, just be thankful that you're not under arrest. Four men are dead, assassinated by this Cooper person and, perhaps, the woman. At the very least, she's his accomplice. Now, there may be reason to suspect they are involved in arson and mass murder at a nightclub in the city."

"What?"

"If you have knowledge of their whereabouts and hold it back, thereby assisting them in the commission of more crimes, you may face trial as an accessory. Perhaps, it could be said, as a conspirator. As you're no doubt aware, the Russian Penal Code provides for execution for murder with aggravating circumstances, or attempted murder of a law-enforcement officer."

"I have done nothing of the kind!"

"But someone has," Chaliapin said. "Someone must pay. If not you, sir…then who?"

PILKIN CLOSED her cell phone, frowning.

"No one home?" Bolan asked.

"Voice mail. That's unusual."

"Your boss always picks up?"

"I've never failed to reach him. Even in a meeting, he will answer, say he has to call back later."

Bolan had no answer for the small dilemma, but he said, "It may be better this way."

"Better? How?"

"Deniability. Someone may hook him to a polygraph, or whatever the FSB's using these days, and he won't want a lie on the record."

"He'd still be held responsible for what I've done," Pilkin said. "How do you say it in America? The buck stops here?"

"That's how we used to say it," Bolan answered. "But it's been a while since anyone in office practiced it. There's more buck-passing in the government than any crap game."

"Here it is the same," she said. "Responsibility is something to be delegated. Only credit is desired."

"I'm feeling like a broken record," Bolan told her, "but you still have time to cut your losses. Go in now and tell your boss I dragged you into this against your will. The first skirmish was self-defense. Feel free to blame the rest on me."

"And send you after Sokolov alone?"

"Don't get me wrong," Bolan replied. "You've done a bang-up job, so far. But where we're headed, honestly, it won't make that much difference. One gun or two against the home-team odds, it's pretty much the same."

"You think so, eh?" Pilkin's tone, together with the angry color in her cheeks, told Bolan that he'd struck a nerve.

"I didn't mean—"

"Would you say to another man, 'Your help means nothing'?"

"First," Bolan replied, "that isn't what I said to you. But a fact's a fact. Two guns against a hundred, or a thousand, don't improve the odds significantly. I don't care whose finger's on the trigger."

"You expect to fail, then? Is that what you're telling me?"

"No, ma'am. In fact, the odds look fine. For me, that is.

But when the smoke clears, I'll be out of here. I don't have any roots in Moscow. I don't punch a time clock for the FSB. You're hauling baggage that can pull you down and drown you, even if we win."

"I'll risk it," Pilkin replied.

"Okay. It's still your call. But if it worries you, not making contact with your boss right now, you need to sniff the breeze and see if you smell bridges burning. Think about what happens if you can't go home again."

"If that's the case," she answered, "then it's already too late. Whatever happens, even with support from my superiors, I'll still be sacrificed."

She had a point. It was depressing, but he couldn't contradict the lady, based on past experience.

"Well, if that's how it is," Bolan said, "all we have to think about is where we drop in next."

"We've called on the Obshina. We should give the Solntsevskaya Brotherhood equal time."

"Sounds fair," Bolan replied.

"But first," she said, "I need a shower and a change of clothes."

"Home's risky."

"No one's had the time to trace me, yet," Pilkin said. "I promise you, we won't be long."

Against his better judgment, Bolan said, "All right, then. Home it is."

CHAPTER EIGHT

The block of apartments stood on a dog-leg street connecting Vorontsovo Pole Street and the main artery of Sadovoye Koltso, three miles due east of the Kremlin. Like most such buildings in the Russian capital, it was a gray box whose designers had no time or inclination to add decorative frills.

"Sixth floor, around that northeast corner," Sergei Efros told the others, pointing.

None of them had anything to say. They were a stoic trio, out on loan to him from Taras Morozov, and it was obvious that none of them appreciated taking orders from a stranger who wasn't a member of their precious Family. Efros cared no more for their feelings than he would if stepping on a cockroach.

"You—" he pointed to the bullet-headed man who called himself Agniya "—go around back and see to it she doesn't slip out that way."

Muttering, the thug departed, plodding over asphalt and a patchy bit of lawn with the enthusiasm of a man on his way to an hour-long prostate exam.

"You two will come with me," he told the others, known to him simply as Gavril and Rassul. Gavril was fat, with black curly hair and a matching beard. Rassul could have passed unnoticed in most crowds, if not for the V-shaped scar that depressed the bridge of his nose.

Efros had made an educated guess about the sixth-floor apartment's location. He had the number—6022—and presumed that it represented some "clever" counting scheme, since the blockhouse before him clearly didn't have a thousand flats per floor.

It hadn't taken long to trace the woman, after all, and while Efros had played no part in the discovery, rather arriving serendipitously as it was revealed, he would feel free to claim the credit when he spoke to Sokolov again.

Which, if his luck held, might be very soon.

Efros couldn't lay odds on whether they would find the FSB agent at home, but it was obviously worth a try. Even if she was gone—a fifty-fifty proposition, in his mind—they might find something to suggest a destination, or revealing her companion's true identity.

Whatever name the gunman had been born with, Efros didn't think that it was Matthew Cooper.

All of them were armed for the invasion of the woman's flat. Efros had both his ALFA Combat pistol and the A-91 assault rifle concealed beneath his raincoat, prepared for any level of violence he might encounter. Gavril carried a .44 Magnum Desert Eagle autoloader beneath his left arm, while Rassul had an Armsel Striker 12-round revolving shotgun stuffed under his pea coat, stock folded to fit.

It felt like overkill, going in, but Efros reminded himself that this Anzhela Pilkin was a trained FSB agent who had helped kill four men only yesterday—and perhaps eleven, if she and her boyfriend had pulled off the Paris Nights raid, as Morozov suspected.

Efros wasn't sold on that scenario, although he wouldn't rule it out. There'd been a time when women ranked among the top terrorist killers in Europe and the Middle East— Leila Khaled, Gudrun Ensslin, Ulrike Meinhof—but those days were gone now. The stupid Taliban mentality required submission, silence and averted eyes, not heroism on the firing line.

Which didn't mean the Russians might not have a ball-breaker or two on tap.

The elevator creaked and squealed, lurching as if it might stall out between the fourth and fifth floors, but it finally delivered them to six. Efros was first out of the car, noting a wall placard with numbered arrows that directed him off to his left. Gavril and Rassul trailed behind him as he quick-stepped down the drab and musty corridor.

He found 6022 and rang the bell, trying the obvious. No answer from within left him a choice of kicking in the door or picking its cheap lock. He opted for the quiet choice.

"Keep watch," he told the borrowed goons. "And don't shoot me by accident."

"I don't shoot anyone by accident," Gavril replied, flashing a gap-toothed smile.

Efros knelt on the threadbare carpet and began to probe the lock.

ELEM PROTAZANOV SWALLOWED his second glass of pepper vodka in a single gulp and felt it scorching through his system, giving him an extra jolt of courage for what had to be done. No matter how he searched his mind and heart, there was no viable alternative.

He cursed himself for crumbling in the major's office, told himself that it had been the age-old Russian weakness for authority. Confronted by a superior officer and a well-known member of the Federation Council, there had been no way Protazanov could refuse their demand for information. Compliance was nearly genetic.

But that was all bullshit.

Protazanov had broken because he was weak. They hadn't threatened him with much beyond loss of his job—which he expected now, despite his sniveling cooperation—and he had spilled what he knew—a plan by the powers that be to quietly rid Russia of Gennady Sokolov, remove an embarrassing blemish from the body politic and reap rewards in the form of increased American investments.

But none of that mattered.

The sin that would damn him to hell everlasting was giving up Anzhela Pilkin's name.

Protazanov could have accepted full responsibility for the move against Sokolov, even named his superiors in a bid to frighten Major Chaliapin and Senator Astapkovich, without feeding Lieutenant Pilkin to the wolves. He had chosen the route of dishonor, and now loathed the sight of his own ugly face in the mirror.

He could warn her, though it might already be too late, and so he'd made the call. Voice mail. Whether she checked the messages in time to save herself, or was already screaming in a Lubyanka cell, it was beyond Protazanov's control.

The only thing remaining now for him to do was carry out the final expiation of his crime. He might have borne it, if there'd been some prospect for arrest and torture, but it seemed to Protazanov that he would simply be cut adrift, left to wallow in an alcoholic haze until his heart or liver failed.

Too slow and unreliable. He might drag on for years that way, in misery.

The Makarov PM would deal with that.

Even with pepper vodka churning in his stomach, Protazanov couldn't miss his own head if he fired at skin-touch range. Could he?

Best to make sure, he thought, and placed the pistol's muzzle underneath his chin. A straight shot to the brain from there, but what would happen if he flinched at the last second? Would he simply end up blind, perhaps defaced in the literal sense?

Protazanov didn't feel like gambling today.

A shot into the mouth was best, aimed well back toward the brain stem. There was no surviving such a wound. Death would be instantaneous, or close enough to it for government work.

Protazanov opened his mouth, inserted the pistol, then realized that he couldn't speak around a 9 mm tongue depressor. Withdrawing the Makarov, he fumbled for coherent words and finally settled for "Anzhela, forgive me."

The handgun tasted oily as he forced it back into his mouth.

"THAT'S DONE IT, then," Pilkin said, closing her cell phone. "They know who I am."

Bolan knew there were half a dozen ways it could have happened, but he asked the question anyway.

"Who spilled it?"

"The assistant deputy director of my branch," she answered dully. "He left me a voice-mail warning."

"That was big of him."

"It's not his fault," she said, her eyes focused on the road in front of them.

"How do you figure that?" Bolan asked.

"Russians have been taking orders since Rurik of Novgorod became our first king, back in the ninth century. Through all the czars and commissars, it's been one thing we're good at."

"That's a lot of crap," Bolan replied. "It hasn't stopped you from writing your own rules."

"I'm not so different," Pilkin insisted. "Anyway, Elem is part of the last generation. He has nothing outside of the FSB."

"We need to see him, if it's safe," Bolan said. "Find out what he spilled, and who he gave it to."

"I have the names already. Major Maksim Chaliapin and a senator from Moscow Oblast, Kiril Astapkovich."

"You know them?" Bolan asked.

"Major Chaliapin is first assistant to the director of the Economic Security Service, concerned with corruption and organized crime. I work for the Counterintelligence Service."

"No overlap there?"

"Officially, no. He outranks me, of course, but it's not customary for one department to meddle with another."

"And the senator?"

"A wealthy, prominent man. He represents the majority party in power."

"Any link to Sokolov, by chance?"

Pilkin hesitated. "None that I'm aware of, but it's possible. In any case, he has nothing to fear."

"Why's that?" Bolan asked.

"Members of the Federation Council are immune from prosecution in most cases," Pilkin explained. "It is the same in your country, I think."

"While Congress is in session, members can't be jailed except for treason or commission of a felony," Bolan recalled from high-school civics courses.

"Here, unless they kill or rape someone in front of witnesses, they're safe."

"From prosecution, maybe," Bolan told her. "Not from me."

They were halfway to Pilkin's apartment when she asked him, "Do you think they will be waiting for us?"

"It's a safe bet. Skip the shower," he suggested. "You can buy fresh clothes, if you're concerned about it. I've got cash to spare. No plastic trail that way."

"You're right," she said. "But first, I need to check on Elem."

"Who?"

"My boss. He called from home. He sounded…bad."

"Anzhela—"

She cut him off. "He's been a friend to me. If you prefer, I'll drop you somewhere safe and come back when I've seen him."

"No, thanks," Bolan said. "I'll keep you company."

"It won't take long," she said, sounding a bit less tense. "Perhaps there's something more that he can tell us."

Their destination was a block of apartments off Sadovoye Koltso, near Moscow's Aquarium Garden. From what Bolan could see, driving past, there was no aquarium and precious little garden. The place looked more like a park boxed by buildings that needed a fresh coat of paint.

They were a block from their target when Bolan saw the emergency flashers. There were three marked militia cars, two unmarked sedans bearing government plates, and an ambulance standing with its rear doors agape.

"This can't be good," he offered as they slow-crawled past the scene with other gawkers.

"There!" Pilkin said, pointing. "That's Chaliapin, talking to an officer of the militia."

Bolan picked out the man she'd indicated, memorized his craggy face, then lost him as they rolled out of range.

"I need to see—"

"You've seen it," Bolan interrupted, wise enough not to touch her. "Whatever was going to happen, it's done."

"But he may be alive!"

"You can check that by phone, from a safer distance. What you can't do is barge in, back there, or keep cruising the block until somebody spots you."

Pilkin turned left at the next intersection, but she didn't double back as Bolan had feared she might. Her cheeks were blotched with crimson as she drove, but it began to fade by slow degrees.

At last, she dabbed her eyes and said, "You're right. There's nothing I can do for Elem now but to find out if he's still alive. And then, whatever has been done, I can avenge him."

Kotlin Island

"I'M MAKING PROGRESS," Sergei Efros said. His voice in Gennady Sokolov's ear, while familiar, seemed distant and small.

"What do you mean by progress?" Sokolov demanded.

"I've identified the woman who met this Matthew Cooper at the airport. She's an FSB agent, apparently assigned to help him by her supervisor in the Counterintelligence Service."

"Counterintelligence? They treat me like a foreign spy now? They've forgotten all the business that we've done together?"

"You know the FSB," Efros replied. "No one keeps track of what the rest are doing, and they stab one another in the back without a second thought. You still have good friends there, in spite of everything."

"I hope so," Sokolov replied. "If they have turned against me, I'll have more work for you soon."

He could imagine Efros smiling as the mercenary told him, "One's already gone. I didn't have to lift a finger, either. Stupid bastard did himself in, after a certain major—"

"No names on the phone!"

"I know that. Anyway, this man couldn't take it, so he ate a bullet. Problem solved."

"Is it? I do not hear you say you've found the woman, or this Cooper. I do not hear anything about the people who put all of this in motion."

"It takes time. You know that. I'm still working."

"Well, work faster! One of us is running out of time!"

Sokolov slammed down the receiver, then stood fuming, doing mental exercises to control his fury and his blood pressure. The last thing that he needed was a heart attack or stroke to finish off the job his enemies had started on him.

How they'd celebrate, if he dropped dead right now.

But Sokolov didn't intend to make it easy for them. They would have to fight for anything and everything they tried to take away from him. He'd worked too long and hard to simply shrug and let the bastards have it all.

If he was driven out of Russia, there were other countries that would shelter him. Iran, perhaps, or Syria. The Saudis were selective in their grants of sanctuary, but he'd done some favors for the royal family. Worldwide, there were fifty-odd nations without U.S. extradition treaties, nearly half of them in Africa, where Sokolov had done extensive business.

The problem with a Third World hideaway was that a person couldn't read the mood from one day to the next without a soothsayer. This day's friends might wake up tomorrow hating you, for no good reason other than the way you combed your hair or stirred your coffee.

All in all, he hated the idea of leaving Mother Russia, but survival trumped homesickness every time.

As always, Sokolov would do whatever was required for personal security. If that meant weeding out the false friends in his garden, then so be it.

What was a little more blood to the Merchant of Death?

ALDO SHISHANI ANSWERED on the second ring and recognized Maksim Chaliapin's voice despite its seeming weariness.

"What word?" he asked.

"The woman has eluded us so far," Chaliapin said. "The assistant deputy director of her branch has killed himself. I lack authority to touch the men above him, or to question them."

"You think it goes that high, then?"

"How should I know?" Chaliapin sounded testy. "I, a major, am not privileged to know such things. I am supposed to wait until they blow up in my face."

"It's not your face at risk," Shishani said. "No one's harmed you yet, or even made a move in your direction. On the other hand, my men are dying."

"So are Bezmel's," Chaliapin said. "I don't know what to make of that."

"Make nothing of it. Leave that part to me, Major. Your task is to locate this woman—Pritkin, is it?"

"Pilkin."

"Yes. Whatever. Find her, and this Cooper person. I will take them off your hands. It shall be as if they never existed."

"Bezmel wants them, too," Chaliapin replied.

"Does he, now?"

"There's a bonus involved."

"I can top it!"

"But what I should do is hang on to them. Use them to clean house at the FSB. When I find out who put this all in motion—"

"Maybe they will crush you. Make you have an accident, perhaps, or simply put an end to your career. Remember that you're hunting whales, not minnows."

"I can go over their heads," Chaliapin said.

"But to whom? Who can you really trust?"

Chaliapin didn't answer for a moment, then asked, "How much?"

"For live delivery of both," Shishani said, "alive and fit for questioning, four million rubles."

"Make it five."

"If you deliver them before the day is out."

"In which case, I am wasting time. We have a deal," Chaliapin said, and cut the link.

Five million rubles.

Shishani did the math. It came to a bit over ninety-seven thousand dollars per head, for the people who'd murdered his men and destroyed Paris Nights. Call it five thousand for each day he would keep them alive and screaming, after they'd told him who was behind the attack on his family.

Worth every penny, in the end.

When he knew everything *they* knew, Shishani could retaliate against his enemies, both known and presently obscure. Then blood would flow in Moscow's streets.

Shishani was a Chechen patriot of sorts. He'd taken no part in his country's two wars against Russia, except where he was able to profit from contraband sales, but there was a bit of pride involved in the Obshina's long campaign against the Solntsevskaya Brotherhood. Maybe all of them were Russians, in some abstract sense, but Aldo Shishani was no anthropologist. Barely one generation removed from mountain bandits, he lived by the feud and expected to die by it, when his time came.

"Not today," he muttered to himself, and reached out for the vodka bottle standing on his desk.

This day, it would be someone else's turn.

And if the ax should fall on Leonid Bezmel, so much the better.

Fifteen years and more, Shishani had known and despised the Brotherhood's leader. Long before he'd worn the tattooed stars of a boss, Bezmel had been an arrogant, obnoxious shit.

Some might have said the same about Shishani, and he couldn't argue with them. He could kill them for their insolence, but rising to the top of any ruthless syndicate required a certain arrogance. A willingness to trample on the bones of others who had literally failed to make the cut.

But two such men, such Families, within a single city—even one as large as Moscow—made the urban landscape overcrowded. Neither side had room to breathe, much less expand.

Shishani had heard the line spoken in various old Western movies from Hollywood. Gunfighters glowering over a bottle of whiskey, one or the other saying, "This town ain't big enough for the two of us."

It always meant a showdown, and Aldo Shishani could feel one coming. Any day now. Any hour.

He could hardly wait.

"No one's heard anything," Pilkin told Bolan as she slid into the driver's seat and closed her door. "At least, they won't admit it."

She'd insisted on calling FSB headquarters, using a land line instead of her cell phone. They'd stopped at a gas station south of the river, with traffic rushing past like there was no tomorrow.

And for some, there wouldn't be.

Bolan assumed that Pilkin's boss and friend was among that number, but it wasn't his place to direct or dictate how she grieved. He understood that she'd feel set adrift without her lifeline to the FSB, hunted by those who signed her paycheck, and he knew exactly how that felt from personal experience. Bolan would not have wished it on his own worst enemies.

Assuming that he'd let them live.

"It's my fault that he's hurt…or worse," she said, when they were moving once again, lost in the stream of cars.

"There's no point going down that road," Bolan replied. "Put any moment of your life under a microscope, and you can find some way to blame a dozen different people for whatever might go wrong. Your boss—"

"Elem Protazanov," she interrupted him. "He has a name."

They all have names, Bolan thought. What he said was, "Elem, then. He made a judgment call—or, likely, someone higher up the ladder made it for him, and he passed the order down to you. 'Meet so-and-so, at such-and-such a time.' None of us knew there'd be a hunting party at the airport, or that any of the rest would flow from that."

A half lie, anyway. Bolan had known he would be spilling blood before he caught his flight in Montreal. He hadn't known exactly who would die, or how, but Stony Man had never sent him on a mission that involved diplomacy or hand-holding. Nothing that ended happily for all concerned.

"You make it easy for me," Pilkin replied.

"It's never easy," he corrected her. "It's not supposed to be. You play the game and take your chances. Everybody at the table knows they could be busted out on the next deal. They take that chance because it matters to them. Motives vary, but the hard-core players stay until the last card's turned."

"Elem was never married," Pilkin informed him. "He believed that it was incompatible with his career. I always told him it was silly, but he wouldn't budge. Apparently, I am the same. We live and die alone."

"You're not dead yet," Bolan replied. "And anyone who could mistake you for an old maid is an idiot."

"You try to cheer me up, now."

"Not my style," Bolan assured her. "But I can't afford to have you in the dumps, either. If we're continuing with this, I need you focused. If you're pulling out, you still need to stay on top of your game."

"I am not pulling out," she told him. "Someone still has much to answer for."

"Right, then," he said. "Let's start collecting tabs."

CHAPTER NINE

"The bastard shot himself," Gavril reported when he returned from talking to one of the younger militia grunts. "He must have known we'd be coming to see him."

"How could he?" Rassul asked. "We didn't even know it, when we started out."

"Not us," Gavril tried to explain. "*Someone,* all right? He must have known *someone* was coming for him."

"Ah."

"He won't be talking, anyway," Sergei Efros observed, hoping that it would end the lesson in semantics. "We still need someone who can help us find the woman."

"Someone else from work," Rassul suggested. "Like a friend."

"A bosom friend, I hope," Agniya said, grinning.

"It's worth a try," Efros admitted, thinking that he could have Morozov reach out to someone at the FSB. The Solntsevskaya Brotherhood would have contacts, as did Sokolov. If all else failed in Moscow, he could have Gennady make a call. It went against the grain, but with survival riding on the line…

"I'll check and see if there's been any progress on hotels," Gavril declared, fishing a cell phone from one of his pockets, punching in a speed-dial number.

Efros reckoned that would be a washout. The Web site that he'd used to book his own room—still unoccupied—had listed 162 Moscow hotels, and Efros knew that list was incomplete. Besides, he didn't think the couple he was seeking would check in somewhere and rent a room. Most definitely not under a name he'd recognize.

"We're being followed," Agniya said, reaching up to make a slight adjustment to his rearview mirror.

"Are you sure?" Efros asked.

"Almost. Let's see."

Agniya took them through a series of erratic turns. Efros watched for a shadow in his side mirror and thought he'd found it.

"Gray Mercedes?"

"That's the one," Agniya said. "Still with us."

"Not militia," Gavril advised. "They only drive shit cars."

"It will be hard to lose him," Agniya said.

Rassul, half-turned in his seat, piped up. "I know that driver. Semyon something. Alferov, Antonov—something with an *A*. He's with the Obshina."

Aldo Shishani's men.

Efros made up his mind within a second, flat.

"Stop in the middle of the next block," he told Agniya. "We'll find out what they want."

"They may not want to talk," Gavril suggested.

"That's all right," Efros replied. "Neither do I."

Agniya drove another half block, hit the brakes, and Efros was out of the car in an instant, clutching his A-91, while Gavril and Rassul piled out with pistols in hand. The Obshina soldiers scrambled for their own guns, nowhere close to being fast enough.

Efros triggered a burst of 5.56 mm manglers through the Mercedes's windshield, shredding the faces behind it at twelve rounds per second. His sidekicks were unloading, too, in what passed for rapid-fire from their sidearms, while gawkers on the sidewalk wailed and broke for cover. Four bodies twitched, then jerked, finally collapsing on upholstery turned crimson.

Instantly rejuvenated by the sounds and smell of battle, Sergei Efros gave the Mercedes a parting shot—one of his 40 mm rounds from the A-91 bullpup's integrated grenade launcher. It was an antipersonnel round, HE fragmentation, that would have the crime-scene people sifting remains with a strainer. Its shock wave rocked Efros back on his heels and put a tight smile on his face.

"There, that's better," he said, turning back toward their idling sedan.

When they were on the move again, Agniya said, "Taras may not be happy that you did that."

"You mean *we,*" Efros corrected him. "Don't let it worry you. I call it self-defense."

"Or maybe it was done by them we're looking for," Rassul suggested. "They hit Shishani once, already."

"Food for thought," Efros replied. "But it won't matter who we drop along the way, as long as we collect the woman. Focus, now. Ideas!"

THE RIVERFRONT warehouse stood with others on Push-kinskaya naberezhnaya, facing northwestward across the water. Normally, Bolan would have approached it at night, but a drive-by revealed no barges or trucks being loaded, no workers in sight.

Too easy.

Three cars in the parking lot told him the place would be guarded, on top of whatever security systems Gennady Sokolov had installed to protect its contents. Bolan didn't think there'd be any direct alarm to the militia, since most or all of what was stored inside the warehouse violated Russian law. That didn't mean there wouldn't be alarms to summon reinforcements, though, if anything went wrong.

"It's one of three arms caches that I'm certain of," Pilkin told him on their first pass. "There's another farther down the river, and the third is on the north side, on a rail line near the city limits."

"He can move guns day and night," Bolan observed.

"And does," Pilkin said. "We've tracked and photographed a number of his shipments, but a photo doesn't show what's in a wooden crate. No search warrants allowed without more better evidence."

Bolan smiled, finding it quaint when her English hiccupped. "Is it true that he also moves vehicles? Aircraft?"

"Oh, yes," she replied. "But those travel direct from the bases where they are stationed. Some are sidelined as surplus or slated for training. Others simply disappear. The GRU investigates, of course. Sometimes they prosecute a sergeant or a private. No one ever mentions Sokolov."

The *Glavnoje Razvedyvatel'noje Upravlenije*—GRU—or Main Intelligence Directorate of the Russian Armed Forces General Staff, was the Russian Federation's single largest foreign intelligence agency, with a staff six times larger than the civilian Foreign Intelligence Service. One of its branches also dealt with crimes committed by active-duty Russian military personnel, including theft, desertion and war crimes.

It stood to reason that Sokolov had to have greased someone in the GRU to keep his death machine up and running smoothly through the years. He'd never meet the small-fry who were sacrificed from time to time for the sake of appearances, and those who faced trial by court-martiàl wouldn't know that the arms and vehicles they diverted wound up in Gennady Sokolov's hands.

Suspicion counted for nothing.

"The best daylight approach is a direct," he said when they were parked a half block from the warehouse. "If there's a problem getting in, show your ID, and I'll take it from there."

"We'll take it," she corrected him.

The walk back seemed to drag, but that was an illusion.

Moments later, Bolan was trying a doorknob, then ringing the bell when he found it was locked. Footsteps echoed from inside, and a peephole opened in the steel door, revealing a lone bloodshot eye.

The doorman growled something in Russian. Pilkin replied in kind and held her ID up to the peephole. More muttering, before the door was finally unlocked and opened.

Bolan took the lead, dropping the doorman with a silenced Parabellum round between the eyes and sweeping on along a narrow corridor to reach the warehouse proper. Pilkin was at his elbow when he got there, facing ranks of wooden crates stacked six and seven high.

Nearby, three men stood grouped around a forklift, with a fourth man in the driver's seat. It took a moment for the swiftest of them to discover that they had an audience. A heartbeat later, eight eyes locked on Bolan, Pilkin and the guns in their hands.

In Maksim Chaliapin's personal experience, most people made at least one friend at work. Some went the other way, befriending everyone they met, but those were generally stupid people, desperate for some kind of companionship.

Lieutenant Anzhela Pilkin hadn't been desperate.

It helped Chaliapin to think of her in the past tense, as a problem he'd already solved. That made him feel as if he'd made some progress since the interview with Elem Protazanov—as, in fact, he had.

Chaliapin didn't know where the lieutenant was—not at home; not at the militia-infested flat where Protazanov had blown out his brains—but he had found one of her friends inside the FSB. Perhaps the only one, based on reports he had received.

Lieutenant Pilkin was a cautious woman, as befitted her rank. She kept most of her coworkers at arm's length, making acquaintances in lieu of intimate associations. Her file revealed no lovers, male or female, indicating either that she was adept at covering her tracks, or she was one of those rare individuals who found their whole raison d'être in work.

Not likely, Chaliapin thought, after he'd seen her photographs on file. But his interest in her private life was strictly professional. He needed some means to locate her, reel her in for debriefing, dissection, disposal.

And now, Chaliapin thought he might have it.

He faced the young woman seated at attention, in the chair planted before his desk. According to her dossier, the slender blonde was twenty-eight years old, unmarried, with no reprimands on her record so far.

"Sergeant Maria Boguslavskaya?"

"Yes, sir."

He liked the worry lines around her eyes. They were a decent start.

"You joined the FSB five years ago, from military service, yes?"

"That is correct, sir."

"How do you enjoy the work?"

She blinked at that, surprised. "I find it most fulfilling, Major."

"And you have friends among your fellow workers?"

"Yes. A few, sir." Back to worried, now.

"Lieutenant Anzhela Pilkin, for instance." Not a question. Chaliapin glanced down at her open file, to make the point.

"Yes, sir. We're friendly."

"More than that, I think." He let a knowing smile tug at the corners of his mouth.

"Sir, I don't understand."

"It's very simple, Sergeant. Your good friend is missing. I am—*we* are—gravely concerned for her safety."

"Has something happened, sir? Is Lieutenant Pilkin in trouble?"

"There have been inconsistencies in her behavior,"

Chaliapin said. "Reports of an erratic nature. We're concerned that she may be acting under coercion."

"Sir, whatever may have happened, she is loyal to Russia and the FSB."

"Of course, Sergeant. But questions must be answered, all the same. And if we cannot find her, if she will not answer calls or pages, well…"

"Sir, do you have her cell phone number?"

"Certainly. If she still has the phone, she's either turned it off or screens the calls. None are returned."

"She'll recognize the office prefix, sir. I mean, if she had some reason to think she was at risk…"

"How could I reach her, then?"

"With all respect, you couldn't, sir."

"But if she had a friend who cared enough to bring her safely home, perhaps?"

"It might work, sir."

"I hope so," Chaliapin said. "For the lieutenant's sake. Some hereabouts suggest that she has turned against us."

"Oh, no, sir! I promise you, that can't be true!"

"But if she won't present herself, you understand the ultimate result? It can't go well for her."

"How may I help, sir?"

"Sergeant, since you ask…"

SERGEI EFROS DREADED his next phone call. He stood well back from the demolished warehouse, watching firefighters at work trying to douse the stubborn flames. That would be thermite, he supposed. And Semtex could explain the blown-out walls, twisted and pocked with countless bullet holes from ammunition cooking off.

The stock would be a write-off. Efros didn't want to think about the money lost, all up in smoke and flames. They would be bringing bodies out before much longer, what was left of them, but flunkies didn't count for much. Profit would always be the bottom line.

So far, the damned militia had found no witnesses. Broad daylight on the waterfront, and Efros had no doubt someone had seen the killers coming or going. Someone could describe them. A man and a woman, perhaps?

Or was it someone else?

Efros still found it hard to believe that two people alone would tackle Gennady Sokolov *and* the Moscow syndicates. If Sokolov was their primary target, why not go for him directly, in Saint Petersburg?

The FBI had failed at that, quite recently, but they were bound by rules of law that clearly didn't trouble Matthew Cooper and his lady friend.

Gavril had phoned Taras Morozov to report their killing of the four Obshina gunmen, so that Morozov and Bezmel's people could brace themselves for any retaliation. They would blame him, of course, but Efros cared nothing for their "Families," secret oaths or prison tattoos. To him, they were like children playing pirates.

Dumb, but deadly. He would definitely have to watch his back.

And, once again, what else was new?

He heard the distant phone ring in Saint Petersburg, and in his mind's eye saw Gennady pacing, waiting for the latest news.

"Hello?"

"It's me," Efros said.

"Yes?"

"So far it seems our friend in the FSB is fumbling in the dark. Can't seem to tell if this was an assignment or somebody's whim. One idiot's already killed himself."

"Can you accomplish anything down there?"

"I'm working on it," Efros answered. "By the way, we've had some trouble with the old Chechen crowd."

"What kind of trouble?"

"They were stepping on our heels. I brushed them off."

"Damn it!"

"Don't worry," Efros said. "They started it. In case you haven't heard, this Cooper and the woman have been running wild. After they dusted Bezmel's men, they shot up an Obshina club and burned it down. Sounds like they're hoping for a war between the Families."

"I don't want to be caught up in that shit!" Sokolov snapped.

"You won't be. I've got one job, here. I'm doing it."

"I have a feeling that we're running out of time."

"Well, someone is," Efros replied, hoping he sounded confident.

"I'll reach out to the major. He has much to answer for."

"Good luck with that. He sounds like an idiot."

"Don't underestimate him. He's survived this long when some of those around him would be glad to stab him in the back, and most would look the other way."

"It's made him sloppy," Efros said. "He's getting old."

"Whoever said that dying young was something to admire?"

The line went dead and left Efros wondering if he had just offended Sokolov. He thought of calling back, for all of half a second, then dismissed the notion as pathetic. He wasn't some teenage Romeo courting a pimply Juliet. Sokolov paid him to speak bluntly, analyze whatever threats confronted them and make them go away.

Sergei Efros would earn his pay in Moscow.

And he didn't care who suffered in the process.

THE BROTHEL STOOD a quarter mile northeast of the Lubyanka, on Myasnitskaya Street. At some point during Moscow's history, it had to have been a stately private home. Its grand exterior had been maintained without surrendering to the trend that required all things to look "modern," sacrificing taste to fashion, and the grounds were well maintained.

A stone wall hedged the property, but no gate barred the

driveway to obstruct arriving customers. It wouldn't do to keep them waiting at the curb, and stationing a full-time gateman on the street would have been deemed too ostentatious.

The establishment desired no rude attention from its neighbors. It required no advertising beyond word of mouth. Its clientele was affluent, and never indiscreet.

"So, this is Bezmel's place?" Bolan asked as they turned in to the mansion's driveway, rolling toward the house.

"His best brothel, but not the only one, by any means. This is reserved for customers with influence and lots of rubles."

"And they'll be open at this hour?"

"Service guaranteed around the clock," Pilkin said, making no attempt to conceal her disgust.

"Okay. Same drill as at the nightclub, then. Take out the muscle if they try to stop us. Boot the rest and shut the place down for remodeling."

"With pleasure," Pilkin replied.

They drove straight to the house, past broad green lawns, and parked the car in front. The tall front doors opened as they began to mount the front porch steps, meaning there had to be surveillance cameras, maybe with motion sensors on the driveway as a backup.

They were greeted by a woman in her sixties, stylish, doubtless something of a beauty in her youth, whose smile and practiced patter faded when she saw their guns. She turned, bolted and tried to slam the door behind her, but she wasn't fast enough.

Bolan was half a step in front of Pilkin, kicking the door before it had a chance to close. It caught the whorehouse madam turning, reaching out to shut it, and the impact dumped her on her backside, snorting fear and outrage.

Pilkin snapped something at the woman, gestured with her SMG and got the woman hustling toward the exit. Bolan assumed she'd call for reinforcements at her first opportunity, and he planned to be gone before they arrived.

From the foyer, they barged into a parlor where a half-dozen working girls sprawled in next to nothing, putting their wares on display for the next customer through the door. A couple of them perked up at first sight of Bolan, then squealed when they noticed his rifle and Pilkin close on his heels, with her SMG leveled.

It made a cute stampede, Bolan thought, bare bottoms jiggling as the ladies ran for cover. Pilkin called after them in Russian, warning them that nowhere in the house was safe for hiding, and about that time, two goons appeared at the top of a staircase to Bolan's left, pulling sidearms from shoulder rigs worn over skintight T-shirts.

His Steyr was up and locking into target acquisition as the first thug raised his pistol. Bolan nailed him with a 3-round burst, performing fatal coronary bypass surgery from thirty feet. The dead man took a nosedive down the stairs, while his companion fired a wild and wasted shot, then turned to run.

Three 5.56 mm shockers caught him midway through his second stride, punching him forward through a clumsy dead-end somersault that left him sprawled out on the landing, faceup toward the ceiling, blind eyes staring at infinity.

By then, most of the parlor girls had changed their minds about remaining in the house, trailing their madam toward the door and grounds beyond. Upstairs, more frightened voices called out, working girls and guests alike emerging in a stumbling rush of coitus interruptus.

And they weren't alone.

Among them, bulling through the gaggle, came more shooters, scowling over gunsights as they ran along the second-story balcony to join the bash.

PILKIN MET THE LEADING soldier with a short burst from her Vityaz submachine gun, gutting him with 9 mm Parabellum rounds that bounced him off the nearest wall and left him twitching on the carpet, an obstruction that his friends were forced to hurdle as they charged the stairs.

Her partner was firing then, as well, and it was tricky to avoid the stumbling, screaming hookers and their tricks at first, before the unarmed sheep got wise and hit the deck. That left three shooters standing on their own, exposed, with no choice but to fight or die.

In fact, the three did both.

They went down firing, Pilkin would give them that much credit, but their aim was rotten. Bullets from their weapons gouged the walls and ceiling, shattered pieces of a massive chandelier that overhung the parlor and demolished hanging artwork without coming close to Cooper or herself. Perhaps the downward angle spoiled their aim, or maybe they were frightened to the point of jerking triggers when they should have squeezed. Pilkin didn't care.

It was enough to find herself still standing and unscathed while her opponents soaked the upstairs carpet with their blood.

Another moment passed before the echoes faded and she understood that there were no more gunmen coming. Taking the stairs three steps at a time, she routed the survivors with commands and curses, driving them ahead of her.

One of the johns was in a mood to argue. He was paunchy, balding, and his face seemed vaguely familiar. From television, perhaps, or from photos in *Izvestia?* It didn't matter when he started railing at her, forgetting his state of undress and demanding that Pilkin explain herself.

She sent his dentures flying with a buttstroke from her SMG and kicked him downstairs.

By that time, Cooper was roving the ground floor, opening doors and shouting in English, issuing warnings to large empty rooms. Pilkin ranged along the second-story hallway, checking bedrooms, finding no one concealed in closets, under beds, in lavatories.

Time to go.

The first incendiary canister popped while she was descending the stairs, white smoke billowing out of a party room below her, on the left. Pilkin wondered if the thermite could demolish stone, thought that it might be worth remaining at the scene to watch, but she and Cooper still had work to do.

In fact, it seemed, they were just getting started.

She felt her cell phone vibrate as she reached the bottom of the staircase, but ignored it. Cooper was retreating, pausing to pitch a second grenade underhand toward the rear of the house. It tumbled out of sight along a corridor that may have served the dining room and kitchen, then exploded with a hissing sound.

More white smoke, filling up the house, pursuing Pilkin and her partner toward the porch. She didn't know how long the ancient house would take to burn—if it would burn at all—but they were in the car and moving moments later, powering along the driveway toward Myasnitskaya Street.

When they were safely back in traffic, Pilkin retrieved her phone and glanced at its display. She frowned at what she saw and told Cooper, "I need to answer this."

CHAPTER TEN

Pilkin pulled into a restaurant's parking lot and sat with the car's engine idling while she read a short text message on the cell phone for the second time.

"It's from a friend," she told Bolan. "A sergeant with the FSB. She's heard about our trouble, about Elem, and she wants to help."

"I'd tell her, 'Thanks, but no thanks.' Keep it short and keep it moving."

"You believe they'll trace the call?"

He countered with a question of his own. "Is there some reason why they wouldn't?"

"I've already told you. She's a friend."

"So was your boss," Bolan replied.

"What are you saying?" Pilkin was angry now.

"He was your friend, but when the crunch came down, he dropped your name. Whatever happened next, whether he couldn't live with it or someone took him out to break the link, it doesn't change the basic fact. He gave you up."

"I told you once before, it's—"

"Not his fault," he interrupted. "Yeah, I heard you. But no matter what you say, he made a choice. I'm asking you to stop and think before you trust another friend inside the FSB right now and stick your head into a noose."

"Maria won't betray me. We're like sisters. You don't understand."

"Sisters betray each other all the time," Bolan reminded her. "You must know that as well as I do."

"Not Maria," she said stubbornly.

Bolan switched strategies. "So, what's the plan? If you plan to call her, I suggest we do it on the move."

"Yes, right. That's good."

A moment later, they were back in traffic, going with the cross-town flow in a southwesterly direction, no destination in mind. Pilkin had her friend's number on speed-dial. Someone answered on the second ring.

Bolan listened to the Russian agent's side of the short conversation, for what it was worth. She spoke Russian— some obvious questions, some snappish replies to whatever her friend may have said—then her tone veered toward sadness. He guessed they were talking about her ex-boss, who was probably tucked in a drawer at the morgue by that time. At three minutes and counting, long enough for any trace he'd ever heard of, Pilkin broke off the call and closed her phone.

"Elem is dead," she told him.

"It figures."

"They're calling it suicide."

"Anything's possible."

"Yes. Now the major has questioned Maria."

"That's Chaliapin?"

"The same man who called in Elem with the senator watching."

"So, what did she tell him?"

"Maria has nothing to tell. She works in the Department for Activity Provision. I don't tell her what we do in my department, and she wouldn't ask."

"No office gossip?"

"But of course. Who's drinking on the job, screwing his secretary, taking home office supplies. All serious offenses. There's a filing clerk in Science and Engineering who stores pornography on his computer. Very racy stuff."

"But work's off-limits?"

"Absolutely. With Maria and myself, at least."

"So, she just called to find out how you're doing?"

"No. She wants to meet me."

"Ah."

"You think it is a trap?"

"Don't you?"

"I have considered it," she said.

"And you'll have told her that it's not a good idea."

"I said I'd meet her in an hour, at the Park Kultury Metro Station, just across from Gorky Park."

"Okay, then. Did you want to wear the bull's-eye on your back, or on your forehead?"

"I have told you, she *will not* betray me!"

"Great. Suppose you're right about that. Do you trust the major? Do you think he might be smart enough to tap her line or have somebody tail her, just in case the two of you hook up?"

"I think it's very likely," Pilkin replied.

"So, why in hell—"

"To find out," she cut in. "To send a message back, if that's the case. Maybe to catch one of the henchmen and question him myself."

"You're sure about this?" Bolan asked.

"If you'd prefer," she told him, "you can sit it out."

"No, thanks," the Executioner replied. "I'm in."

Kotlin Island

GENNADY SOKOLOV loved weapons. In his younger days, a fellow Spetznaz officer had once remarked that Sokolov had gun oil flowing through his veins. It was a compliment, and he'd accepted it with pleasure.

On this endless day, to calm himself, the Merchant of Death was fieldstripping a Kedr PP-91 machine pistol, breaking the small weapon down into seven constituent parts for inspection and cleaning. It hadn't been fired in some time, but the mindless activity soothed Sokolov, calmed his mind and allowed him to think without pacing his office.

The news from Moscow wasn't good. Sergei Efros had made no significant progress beyond obtaining the name of a woman he couldn't locate. What good was that to anyone? And what was he to make of the attacks on gangsters in the capital?

Sokolov understood the first killings. Bezmel had sent a team to lift the stranger known as Matthew Cooper on arrival at Domodedovo International. They'd blown it and were killed. That kind of error happened every day in Gennady Sokolov's world.

But the rest—the attack on an Obshina gambling house, and now a brothel owned by Bezmel's family—it made no sense. This Cooper had been sent for Sokolov, presumably to bring him in dead or alive. Why was he playing games in Moscow with a woman from the FSB?

Sokolov was accustomed to uncertainty. Most of his customers around the world were volatile, erratic types whose violent lives conditioned them to shun routines, act on a whim when planning would be preferable, and unleash their psychopathic tempers at the strangest times. The Merchant of Death stayed alive by expecting the unexpected.

He'd been prepared, for instance, when the FBI kidnap squad came to his home unannounced. Sokolov had treated them like any other criminal trespassers who might threaten his well-being. They were dead because of simple-minded arrogance.

But this was different.

It had intrigued Sokolov to learn that his latest opponent was landing in Moscow rather than Saint Petersburg or even Novgorod. He had considered it a piece of misdirection, to deceive and lull him, understanding that the stranger would be met by someone local to provide the services of an interpreter and guide.

But why remain in Moscow to harass the *Mafiya?* It seemed insane, unless…

No. He could make no sense of it.

Sokolov reassembled the machine pistol, taking his time, no race against the clock as if he were in boot camp. He did it with his eyes shut, strictly by touch, first locating each part on his desktop, then returning it to its proper place, listening for the metallic *snick* of a proper fitting before he moved on to the next.

It was a shame, Sokolov thought, that he wouldn't have the pleasure of meeting Matthew Cooper himself. He would have enjoyed staring into the man's frightened eyes before blasting the brain from his skull. And the woman… Well, surely he could have devised some amusement for her.

But Sergei would deal with the pair of them soon. In the meantime, his gun reassembled, the Merchant of Death decided it was time to turn up the heat on a comrade whose recent performance was not worth the checks he received every month.

Sokolov dialed the number from memory, waited through four rings then heard the old familiar voice.

"Major Chaliapin," he said. "We need to talk."

SERGEANT MARIA Boguslavskaya considered stopping after one stiff shot of vodka, but decided on a second, just for balance. It was a cliché, she realized, swilling the liquor that ranked among her homeland's foremost national pastimes, but she couldn't help herself.

Without false courage flowing through her veins and burning in her stomach, she was worried that she couldn't leave her office, much less cross the city for a meeting with her best—perhaps her *only*—friend.

Sergeant Boguslavskaya wasn't beautiful. In fact, she thought of herself as plain on her good days. She wasn't at all like Anzhela Pilkin, vivacious and lively. It seemed miraculous to her—almost bizarre, in fact—that they had ever spoken in the first place, much less become intimate friends.

She had the borscht to thank for that. They had met while standing in line in the FSB staff cafeteria, waiting for service. Boguslavskaya had risked a comment on the soup's appearance, and Pilkin had answered with a joke that made her laugh out loud. From there, they'd wound up sharing a corner table for two, and somehow lunches had become a habit. After that…well, she could hardly count the times they had gone out together, to the theater and the ballet, to films and lectures. Never on a double date, of course, since no man cared enough to ask Boguslavskaya out.

Or, rather, no man who was after anything except a sweaty one-night stand.

Boguslavskaya had no time for such men. For *any* men, in fact. She hadn't spoken of the longing that she felt for Pilkin, was waiting for the perfect moment that had yet to come along, when she'd be brave enough to risk a word, a touch, a kiss.

And now, she thought, it never will.

She had to see Pilkin one last time. To warn her of the danger she was facing and, perhaps, to say what had remained unspoken far too long.

If she could only find the courage.

If it wasn't already too late.

The Park Kultury Metro Station seemed a perfect meeting place. There would be passengers and passersby aplenty at this time of day, providing cover and a crowd of witnesses that would dissuade the FSB and anybody else from making any overt hostile moves. A few brief words of warning, a

profession of her love, and if they never met again, at least
Maria would not suffer the eternal pain of knowing that she
should have spoken but didn't.

She wouldn't have to brand herself a coward.

What would the decision mean to her career? Nothing,
unless they were discovered. In which case, she might be
prosecuted, though she wasn't clear as to what charges would
apply.

Major Chaliapin had said that Pilkin was in trouble, that
she'd been misled somehow by Elem Protazanov. Chaliapin
simply wanted to speak with her, straighten things out and
prevent any scandal.

It all seemed very reasonable, as she listened to him. But
Maria reckoned there was more still left unsaid. She'd spent
enough time at FSB headquarters to realize that most staffers
had some ulterior motive for everything they said and did.

Most, except Anzhela Pilkin.

She had her secrets, of course, working as she did for
Counterintelligence. Maria didn't ask about such things, because it would be prying, and because they didn't interest her,
in fact.

She worried, now, about the safety of their meeting, but
she couldn't call it off. She had no weapon she could carry
to the Metro Station, since her job didn't require the issuance
of firearms. She could only hope for the best.

With a backward glance at her small, tidy office, Sergeant
Maria Boguslavskaya closed the door and locked it. Moving
toward the elevators, she wondered when—or if—she'd ever
see the place again.

ALDO SHISHANI SLAMMED an open palm against his office
wall, then followed it with two swift kicks, cursing a blue
streak while he hammered the teak paneling.

It was a way to vent his rage, though he avoided swinging
closed fists at the wall. He'd cracked two knuckles that way

eighteen months earlier, and they still pained him in cold weather, a reminder to control himself whenever possible.

Or punch a slightly softer target.

Like a human face.

Shishani's underboss, Magen Manaev, stood beside his boss's great desk, his eyes downcast, the sacrificial bearer of bad tidings. Manaev couldn't be held responsible for the report he had delivered, logically, but common sense sometimes went out the window when Shishani was enraged.

"Four more?" the godfather demanded, as if asking might erase the number he'd already heard.

"Yes, four," Manaev said. "They're at the morgue now."

"Shot for nothing! In broad daylight!"

"Well—"

"For nothing!"

"They were tracking one of Bezmel's crews. Dziga checked in by cell phone just before the shooting."

"Did they start it?"

"Witnesses and the militia say no. The car in front of them stopped short, and Bezmel's people came out blasting. Our men never fired a shot."

"I'll make that bastard Bezmel wish he was never born."

"There's something else," Manaev said.

"What, *more* bad news?"

"Odd news. The crew that Dziga and the rest were following went into an apartment house, then came out empty-handed. No reports of anybody injured there. Dziga took pictures of them with his phone. Three faces I already know—"

"I want them dead!" Shishani interrupted.

"I already gave the order. They'll be taken down on sight. The fourth man, though... I feel that I should know his face, but I can't place it."

"Did you save the pictures?" Shishani asked. He still

marveled at the countless things a simple pocket telephone could do.

"Right here."

Manaev palmed his cell phone, switched it on and pushed some buttons before handing it to Shishani.

"That's the best one," he declared.

Shishani squinted at the small photo and felt his anger swelling up inside him like a jet of lava rising.

"Son of a bitch!" he snarled. "I know that man. Sergei Efros. He's Gennady Sokolov's chief of security."

"The Spetznaz guy? So, Sokolov is part of this."

"He sends his pit bull here, to challenge us? The worst fucking mistake he ever made!"

"He's still up in Saint Petersburg, I think. After that business with the FBI, he won't stray far from home."

"I don't care if he's in a bunker in Siberia. The stupid bastard will not get away with this!"

"I'll put a team together. They can fly up there this afternoon and—"

"Wait! I want to see this Efros first. Put out the word I want him alive."

"If he resists?"

"I didn't say he has to be intact. Just breathing, with a tongue, so he can talk."

And plead for his miserable, worthless life.

"I'll do it now," Manaev said. "About the men we lost… Three had no families, but Tikhon Volkov has—or had—a pregnant girlfriend."

"Give her something. Maybe send her to the country, eh?"

"I'll see to it."

Alone once more, Shishani gave the nearest wall another vicious kick, snarling between clenched teeth.

So, Sokolov saw fit to pick a quarrel with the Obshina, who had never troubled him? The choice was his.

Aldo Shishani had a consignment of pain prepared for the Merchant of Death.

ANZHELA PILKIN'S MIND was swirling as she prepared for her meeting with Maria Boguslavskaya. A crowded public place, by daylight, should be safe. But this was Moscow, with its soaring murder rate and criminals who thought nothing of fighting pitched battles in rush-hour traffic.

Secretly, she was relieved that Matt Cooper insisted on following her to the Park Kultury Metro Station. He wouldn't be obvious about it—and Maria hadn't seen him, anyway—but it was still a comfort to know that he would be nearby. Prepared to help her if it was, in fact, a trap.

Pilkin didn't doubt Maria's loyalty. She recognized the other woman's loneliness, the gratitude that seemed to ride her friendship piggyback. There had been moments when Pilkin thought Maria might feel more for her than simple friendship, and she'd taken extra care to offer nothing in the way of sexual enticement.

Still…

Within the FSB, conspiratorial thoughts were the rule, not the exception. Pilkin's whole working life revolved around ferreting out one criminal scheme after another. She knew from personal experience that everyone had secrets, some of them worth killing to protect.

Maria wouldn't willingly betray her. She was reasonably sure of that, although there were no iron-clad guarantees of anything in life. More likely, Pilkin supposed, Maria might be shadowed by a spy or team of spies dispatched by Major Chaliapin.

For what purpose? To arrest her? Find Matt Cooper? Or, perhaps, destroy them both?

She knew their tricks, if not all of their faces. Pilkin's field experience rivaled that of most men that she knew from headquarters, and she'd definitely seen more action in the past twelve hours than most of them had seen in their entire careers.

She recognized the possibility that Major Chaliapin might send members of the *Mafiya* to deal with her. Whether he picked the Solntsevskaya Brotherhood or Obshina, both would have a killing grudge to settle with her and Matt Cooper. It would be a handy way for Chaliapin to clean house, all the while claiming that he had done his best to bring her in out of the cold.

And she could see the tabloid headline now: Rogue FSB Agent Gunned Down At Gorky Park. Mysterious Foreigner Dies with Woman Spy.

No, thank you, very much.

Pilkin double-checked her weapons, topping off their magazines, putting spares in her pockets, and making sure both guns had live rounds in their chambers, with their safeties off. Whatever happened at the Metro Station, she would not go down without a fight.

"Still time to change your mind," Bolan said when they were off and rolling toward the rendezvous.

"I need to find out what Maria wants."

"That she can't tell you on the phone."

"Exactly."

"Okay. If there's a place to park within sight of the station, I'll stay with the car," he said. "If not, I'll find someplace to set up shop and cover you. We'll have to run for it and fetch the car, if anything goes wrong."

"Thank you," she said, "for coming with me."

It was hard to say.

"You're welcome," Bolan said. "I just hope we come out of it alive and kicking."

So do I, Pilkin thought. So I can deal with Sokolov. And then, maybe, come back and put a bullet in the major's head.

THE CALL SURPRISED Sergei Efros. He knew that Sokolov wouldn't phone him in Moscow, except in the case of some crisis at home, and they had spoken within the past half hour. No one else in town had his cell number except—

"Where are you?" Taras Morozov demanded without any of the usual preliminary salutations.

"Eastbound, nearing the Lubyanka," Efros answered.

"Well, get over to the Park Kultury Metro Station, next to Gorky Park, as fast as you can," Morozov ordered.

"What's the hurry?"

"We just got a call about Pilkin. She'll be meeting someone from the FSB outside the station in another…twenty-seven minutes."

"Shit! You've left it late enough!"

"I just found out myself," Morozov said.

Efros gave the directions to Agniya, in the driver's seat. A heartbeat later, they were screeching through a U-turn in the middle of the block, while angry horns blared all around them.

"Christ!" Efros snapped. "Keep it on the road, and don't attract the damned police, eh?"

"Okay, okay," his driver said.

"What's up with the meeting?" Efros asked.

"Our contact didn't say," Morozov replied. "Just be there. And Bezmel wants the bitch breathing when you bring her in. Breathing and fit to talk. Remember that."

"You don't ask much."

"I don't *ask* anything."

Efros smiled at that, declining to accept Morozov's challenge—for the moment. If his luck held, there would be another time when they could talk about the gangster's arrogance in private, and the better man would be the one who walked away.

Agniya had the car under control now, while Gavril and Rassul were busy in the backseat with their weapons. Efros didn't have to check his A-91 to know that the rifle had a full 30-round magazine and a 40 mm antipersonnel grenade loaded in its integrated under-barrel launcher.

All of which would be overkill, if Bezmel and Morozov wanted the FSB woman alive. Breathing, Morozov had said, which didn't mean she had to be in perfect shape, of course. She might not miss an arm or leg, if it came down to that. Tie off the stump and toss her in the trunk.

Efros might have defied Bezmel and killed the woman for the hell of it, but he was curious himself. Why would the FSB—or part of it—collaborate with the Americans to extradite Gennady Sokolov? And who was Matthew Cooper, flying in from Canada to help with the abduction?

Sergei Efros hated mysteries. Each time he faced an enemy there were imponderables to consider, questions that remained unanswered until one side or the other had prevailed and slain their enemies. Whenever Efros had a chance to solve those riddles in advance, he grasped it eagerly.

With any luck, he might be able to eliminate the latest threat to Sokolov in Moscow, and prevent a recurrence of the FBI's abortive raid on Kotlin Island. It would likely mean a bonus for him, if he pulled it off, together with the private satisfaction of a job well done.

And killing. That was always sweet.

"How long?" he asked Agniya.

"Eight, nine minutes, if we don't catch any lights," the driver said.

"So, don't catch any lights."

"Don't catch the lights. Don't draw attention from the damned police. You can have it one way or the other."

Efros turned on his borrowed wheelman, smiling grimly.

"If we miss this setup, I'll let you explain it to Morozov. Does that suit you?"

"We won't miss it," Agniya replied, tight-lipped.

"I hope not," Efros answered. "For your sake."

CHAPTER ELEVEN

The West knew Gorky Park primarily from fiction and film. Martin Cruz Smith set the tone with his bestselling novel of the same title, in 1981, backed up by a film that struck box-office gold two years later.

Few in the West knew any more about the Park of Culture and Recreation, sprawling over three hundred acres along the Moscow River, created in 1928 from the gardens of the old Golitsyn Hospital and the Neskuchny Palace, expanding over time to become the capital's outdoor social center.

Anzhela Pilkin's visit on this afternoon wasn't a social call. She may have come to meet a friend, but it was deadly serious. In fact, she found herself frightened as she approached the Park Kultury Metro Station, moving eastward on foot along Krimskiy Val Street.

It wasn't danger that unnerved her, as much as the thought of betrayal. If Maria Boguslavskaya had turned against her, for whatever motive, it could spell the final death of trust for Pilkin. Always a skeptic—sometimes even cynical—in her approach to others and their motives, she'd found a true friend in Maria, at the FSB of all places.

Or, rather, she thought she had.

If Maria turned against her now, led her into a trap, Pilkin thought that it would be the final insult. It would leave her with no one to trust except Matt Cooper, an American she'd never see again once their mission was finished.

Assuming both of them survived that long.

Speaking of Cooper, he had tried in vain to park Pilkin's

car within sight of the Metro Station, so they'd left it in a parking garage four long blocks northwest of the station and on the wrong side of Krimskiy Val Street.

If they were ambushed, it would be a long run back.

More likely, they'd be dead before they had a chance to run.

Still, Pilkin felt better knowing she was covered, even if she didn't know where Cooper was. He'd told her that he would be close enough to help, but what did that mean? How could anyone help her if she went down with the initial shot from hiding?

She immediately banished such defeatist thoughts and focused on Maria, on what she believed to be their solid friendship. It was possible that she had learned something at headquarters, some information that she thought would be of use to Pilkin, and feared to share it on the telephone. In Moscow, even with the KGB "defunct," you never knew who might be listening and taking notes for future reference.

On the flip side of betrayal lay another dark scenario. Major Chaliapin might have persuaded Maria that Pilkin had lost her mind, sold out her country and betrayed her oath of office—or, in the alternative, that Pilkin herself was in some danger and required a friend to pull her chestnuts from the flames. In that case, no guilt would accrue to Maria's account, but the net result would be equally grim.

A third possibility—and by far the most likely, to Pilkin's mind—was that Chaliapin had learned of her bond with Maria and summoned the woman to his office for the kind of interview that was a Lubyanka specialty. Whether he went with charm or threats or innuendo, possibly a mixture of all three, Chaliapin wouldn't try to break Maria. He'd simply frighten her senseless, release her...and see where she ran.

In this case, straight to Pilkin.

She saw the Metro Station, still a block ahead, and drew

her coat more tightly around her, clamping the three-kilo Vityaz submachine gun between her left arm and her ribs.

Pilkin hoped she wouldn't need it, but she had switched off the weapon's safety.

Just in case.

"HERE! LET ME OUT here!"

"There's traffic," Agniya replied.

"Just stop the car!"

Agniya hit the brakes with no attempt to curb the vehicle, letting the blare of horns wash over him while he stared straight ahead.

Before he left the car, Efros told Gavril and Rassul, "You two come with me. Keep those guns out of sight until you need them!"

Then, he turned to Agniya. "Keep circling. Make it figure eights, whatever, but be ready in a hurry if we need you. Got it?"

"*Da.*"

Then they were out and jogging toward Gorky Park, Agniya pulling off without them in the southward flow of traffic along Bol'shaia Yakimanka Street. Efros could see the mammoth Ferris wheel in front of him, one of the city's leading landmarks, but he focused on the Park Kultury Metro Station, still more than a block away.

His targets would be waiting there. Efros would recognize the women from two ID photographs that Taras Morozov had forwarded to his cell phone while they raced through traffic. He had only a brief verbal description of this Matthew Cooper, passport stats, but Efros reckoned that he would be easy enough to pick out from the crowd.

He'd be the only one trying to help the women stay alive.

Despite the season, it was cool in Moscow, so the coat he wore to hide his automatic rifle wasn't out of place. Rassul still had the Armsel Striker hidden underneath his pea coat, while Gavril had decided to back up his .44 Magnum Desert Eagle with a folding-stock AK-108 assault rifle. Scanning the parkside crowd for familiar faces, Efros wondered how many of those ranged before him would finish the day in a hospital bed or the morgue.

In fact, he didn't give a damn.

He had three targets, one of whom had to be delivered more or less alive to Taras Morozov. Efros wasn't afraid of Morozov, per se, although it wasn't wise to buck the Solntsevskaya Brotherhood in Moscow. More to the point, he stood to benefit if Bezmel's men could make the FSB lieutenant spill her guts before she…well, *spilled* her guts.

Even if he got lucky and killed Matthew Cooper in the next few minutes, there was still the matter of the men who'd sent him to retrieve Gennady Sokolov. That was the threat Efros had to guard against, in preservation of his nice fat salary.

It was a threat that would exist as long as Sokolov himself survived. A sinecure for Efros, if he played his cards correctly, kept his wits about him and gave Sokolov no reason to complain about the service he provided. Killing Matthew Cooper and his lady friend would help, in that regard. But learning who had sent them, reaching out to punish those long-distance enemies, could leave him set for life.

Or, the attempt could get him killed.

All in a day's work for a mercenary, after all.

They reached the intersection, waited for the light to change, then crossed Krimskiy Val Street with a hundred or more fellow Russians, roughly equal numbers of them moving to and from the park.

Those leaving were the lucky ones.

They were about to miss a bloodbath.

SERGEANT MARIA Boguslavskaya lit a cigarette, took half a dozen nervous puffs, then dropped it to the pavement and ground it beneath her heel. The nicotine failed to soothe her. If anything, it seemed to leave her more on edge and anxious than before.

What am I doing here? she asked herself.

She owed it to Anzhela, any help she could offer in exchange for unselfish friendship. And she owed it to herself, as well. The chance to make a selfless gesture in defense of someone who was being persecuted. Not just anyone. A person that she loved.

How rare that was, these days.

Boguslavskaya had been waiting at the entrance to the Park Kultury Metro Station now for fifteen minutes, half-expecting someone to mistake her for a prostitute. Granted, she hadn't worn any alluring garments, but her pacing had to have seemed suspicious. She'd kept a sharp eye out for any faces she might recognize from work, but thus far no one recognizable from headquarters had crossed her path.

Which proved precisely nothing.

She was on the verge of going home again, calling the whole thing off and missing Anzhela, when she decided that would make things even worse. When Anzhela arrived—*if* she arrived—she wouldn't simply turn and leave. No, she would wait to find out if Maria had been unavoidably delayed.

And in the process, she would make a perfect target for her enemies.

Who were they? Why would Anzhela be hunted through the city as described by Major Chaliapin? Why could he not contact her directly? Why had Elem Protazanov killed himself?

Too many questions, and she couldn't answer any of them. She suspected that Protazanov had gone bad, somehow, and sent Anzhela to do some kind of dirty work without a warning of the risks involved. He'd been exposed and took the coward's exit, leaving Anzhela to face the wrath of Protazanov's enemies, whomever they might be. Now she was on the run, afraid to take a call from headquarters.

Why would she trust Maria?

Because they were more than coworkers. They were *friends*.

When Boguslavskaya finally saw Anzhela approaching, she thought it had to be her imagination. Only when she'd blinked and looked again did she allow the faintest flare of hope, immediately stifled by another rush of fear. She nearly raised a hand to wave, then reconsidered. Smiling weakly, she moved to greet Anzhela, clutching her purse in one hand and the front of her coat with the other.

Pilkin saw her, and corrected her course to meet her friend halfway. A stout man jostled Boguslavskaya, brushing against her left shoulder, and muttered something that may have been an apology. She ignored him, pressed on toward Anzhela, searching for words in her mind.

What should she say first? Should they hurry off to someplace safer, someplace more private, before she tried to explain anything?

They were still fifteen to twenty feet apart when something struck Boguslavskaya above her left breast, slamming her over and back to the pavement with irresistible force. She lay stunned for a heartbeat, mind spinning, before she heard the gunshot. When she tried to stand, or even sit upright, her muscles refused to obey the mental command.

She was drowning, it seemed, something warm and wet in her throat, choking her. When she coughed, it tasted salty and metallic all at once.

She looked for Anzhela, but she could barely make out trees and the facades of nearby buildings looming over her. Too late, she realized that it *had* been a trap, in fact. And she had been the bait.

The fool.

BOLAN HEARD the first shot from his post south of the Park Kultury Metro Station. He'd seen a woman stepping forward, as if to greet Anzhela Pilkin, then saw her go down with a bright puff of crimson at her back.

An exit wound. And the shooter was—where?

The target had been facing north, toward Pilkin, which placed the shot's source farther back, in the direction of Krimskiy Val Street. That put the gun—or one of them, at least—*behind* Pilkin, cutting off her retreat toward the parking garage where her car stood waiting.

Bolan broke in that direction, running against the flow of foot traffic, jostling and dodging pedestrians who had guessed the sniper's location and were now intent on running in the opposite direction. It made perfect sense.

Unless you were the Executioner.

Bolan veered off into the park, running past frightened Muscovites and buildings marked with signs he couldn't read. Museums, amusements; none of it had any meaning for him now. His single-minded purpose was elimination of the shooter who was likely bent on making Pilkin his next target.

He'd seen her hit a crouch and draw her weapon as her friend went down, then she was lost to sight among the fleeing bystanders. Now his new position let him glimpse her, sheltered by the Metro Station's southeast corner, cutting glances back and forth between her fallen friend and the direction of the fatal shot.

She didn't see the second shooter, slinking toward her on her blind side. He was porky and bearded, with a mop of curly hair, packing one of the several dozen Kalashnikov models produced by Russia's Izhevsk Mechanical Works. When Bolan spotted him, he was already close enough to make the shot but didn't take it, moving nearer for a guarantee.

Or something else?

As Bolan turned to intercept, the creeper made his

move—not firing, but charging at Pilkin's back, as if planning to tackle or club her. It struck Bolan, then, that the hunters might want her alive for some reason, but there was no time to consider their motives.

From twenty yards out, Bolan triggered a round from his Steyr AUG and placed his shot between the stalker's shoulder blades. The fat man fell facedown and shivered once in passing, then lay still. Pilkin turned, surprised, to find him lying there, then she caught Bolan's eye and flashed a nervous-grateful smile.

Almost before that pleasantry could register, a bullet hissed past Bolan's face. He was already ducking, dodging, when he heard the shot, immediately followed by two more. He made the weapon as a 5.56 mm rifle, firing at him from the north and slightly to the east, but couldn't pin down its precise location without pausing for a look.

Which would be tantamount to suicide.

The sharp report of a 9 mm round from Pilkin's position told Bolan that she was in the game, opting for semiauto fire to minimize the danger of civilian casualties. Using the opportunity she had provided, Bolan ducked behind the nearest structure facing onto Leninskiy Avenue and ran with Olympian speed toward the building's north end. From there, with any luck, he might have a shot at the enemy rifleman, a chance to cover Pilkin's retreat toward her car.

Whatever her friend had planned to tell Pilkin, she'd never hear it. They'd taken the bait and walked into the trap. The best that they could hope for, now, was getting out alive, then carrying the battle to their adversaries on some other front.

Revenge could wait.

Survival was the top priority right now.

And it was far from guaranteed.

SERGEI EFROS hated going into battle with his hands tied. Rules and regulations were for weaklings who were worried about losing, fearful of their treatment by opponents who were strong enough to conquer them. No torture. No reprisals. No mistreatment of civilians.

Whining bids for mercy.

Efros fired another 3-round burst in the direction of a target whom he knew had to be the tricky and elusive Matthew Cooper, missed and cursed under his breath. Before he had a chance to try again, a bullet whispered past him from the general direction of the Metro station, making Efros duck between cars parked along the curb. Next time he looked, the man was gone.

Running away, or flanking Efros? He'd already killed Gavril, which only left Rassul and his shotgun for backup. Agniya, circling the scene and awaiting instructions, was next to useless.

It would be so much simpler, Efros thought, if he could simply kill the woman and be done with it. Granted, he shared Leonid Bezmel's interest in whatever she might have to say about Sokolov's enemies, but playing tag with two accomplished killers in a public place, in broad daylight, was a fool's game.

He was free to kill the man, but couldn't spot him. He could see the woman, but was not supposed to kill her.

It was madness.

Taras Morozov's words still echoed in his head. *Bezmel wants the woman breathing when you bring her in. Breathing, and fit to talk.*

But if he had to wound her in the process, nothing he'd been told forbade it.

All he needed was a clean shot.

Efros risked a look around the ZIL sedan that sheltered him and saw the woman moving, breaking toward the park proper. He tracked her with his bullpup rifle, leading her and aiming low to cut her legs from under her. A 3- or 4-round burst should do it, drop her on the run and shock her into immobility with pain while Efros closed the gap between them and disarmed her.

As for Cooper—

Bullets struck the ZIL's fender and hood, caroming off in ricochet, one of them nearly parting Efros's hair. He tumbled over backward, wincing as his skull struck pavement, then he rebounded in a livid rage.

"Rassul, you idiot!" he snapped into the combination microphone and earpiece that he wore. "Where are you?"

"Waiting for the woman, like you told me," Rassul answered, a tinny voice in Sergei's ear. "I'll have her for you in a minute."

Fuming at the gunman's insult, Efros tried another look across the field, cleared now by most of the civilians who'd been loitering around him when the shooting started. There she was, sprinting back the way she'd come, toward Krimskiy Val Street.

Efros snapped the A-91 to his shoulder, lining up the aperture and front post sights as best he could in haste. Precision shooting wasn't necessary. All he had to do was aim low, stroke the trigger lightly and remember not to keep on shooting as she fell into his line of fire.

Another second, and—

With a crack and clang, the rifle was whipped from his grasp, its butt slamming Efros's cheek on the fly-by and slamming him back against the ZIL's bumper. He groaned a curse, rolled over on his side and spit blood onto the sidewalk's pavement.

What in hell was that? Had someone actually shot the rifle from his hands?

Efros looked for the A-91, glimpsed it in time to see a passing runner aim a kick at it and send the weapon flying.

Furious, he drew his pistol, lurched upright and turned to seek his fleeing prey.

ANZHELA PILKIN RAN for her life. A part of her cried out to stand and fight, but common sense replied, Fight who? For what?

Maria was already dead, cut down before she even had a chance to speak, proof positive—to Pilkin, at least—that she'd known nothing of the ambush in advance. Maria would no more participate in such a suicidal act than she would run naked around Red Square.

Pilkin ran because her friend was dead, gunmen were in pursuit and Matt Cooper had placed his life at risk to cover her retreat. She might be dead already if he hadn't shot the fat man who was creeping up behind her at the Metro station.

Now, at least, she owed him an attempt to live.

She ran full tilt toward Krimskiy Val Street, hoping that she could find a way on foot through traffic without being crushed or crippled in the process. If she fell, if she was lamed, then she was finished.

And the keys to her sedan were in her purse. Without her, Cooper would be stranded there, in Gorky Park, when it was swarmed by the militia.

How long before they came, lights flashing, sirens blaring? Not much longer, in the heart of Moscow, where there were as many cell phones now as ancient women wearing babushkas.

She ran, and had the highway in her view when someone suddenly leaped out in front of her. Not quite from nowhere, as she saw that he'd been hiding in the recessed doorway of a public restroom. When he grinned at her, it emphasized a V-shaped scar on the bridge of his nose, but Pilkin was more concerned about the weapon in his hands.

Some kind of combat shotgun, she supposed, before she

shot him with her Vityaz SMG from six or seven paces. Knowing the first goon shot by Cooper wasn't wearing body armor, Pilkin aimed for the center of mass and tattooed Scarface's chest with a lethal 4-round burst.

Game over—for the shotgun man, at least.

A low wall separated Pilkin from Krimskiy Val Street, where strollers were ducking, dodging and fleeing as fast as they could. She hurdled it, barely breaking stride, holdover from her early FSB training.

Glad that she'd stayed in a semblance of shape, Pilkin hit the sidewalk running, plunged across it and immediately headed into traffic, angling toward the north side of the busy street and beyond it, four punishing blocks to where the car waited.

Behind her, more shots made Pilkin hunch in reflex action, waiting for the bullet that would end her life, but none came close enough for her to mark their passage. She was in the midst of traffic now, more likely to be killed by speeding Muscovites than hurtling bits of lead and copper.

Horns blared at her, drivers shook their fists and shouted unintelligible curses from their open windows. Some were mute, cursing behind a wall of glass. Others were quick enough to see Pilkin's gun and recoil in surprise, veering away from her at the risk of striking other cars.

Somehow she got across the avenue without any damage. She was turning, glancing back in search of Cooper, when he suddenly appeared beside her, barely winded from the look of him, and gripped her arm.

"No time for sightseeing," he said. "Let's move!"

"Smart-ass!" she snapped at him—and moved.

They ran the whole way back to the garage where Pilkin had parked her car, hiding their guns only when they were within sight of their goal. They slowed a little then, as well, to catch their breath and cast off the appearance of fugitives in flight.

"There's still at least one shooter back there," Bolan told her as they entered the garage on foot and started climbing concrete stairs to reach the fourth level.

"He'll want us more than ever now," she said.

"I hope so," the American replied. "I'm dying to meet him."

CHAPTER TWELVE

Sergei Efros reached the sidewalk, ALFA Combat .45 in hand, blood streaming from his open cheek, and bellowed at the passing cars, "Where are you, damn it?"

Any passing driver could have been forgiven for believing him a madman, shouting at himself in the midst of a psychotic break.

All but one.

"I'm here," Agniya's voice replied, through Efros's earpiece. "Coming up behind you on your left."

Efros faced westward along Krimskiy Val Street and spotted the car almost instantly, veering across lanes to run at curbside, slowing into the final approach despite horns bleating fury behind it.

Efros was ready and threw himself into the empty shotgun seat without forcing Agniya to stop completely. The driver saw his blood-streaked face and asked, "What happened to you? Where's Gavril and Rassul?"

"They're not coming," Efros told him. "And we're heading in the wrong direction."

"What?"

"The wrong direction! We need to turn around!"

"What, here?"

"Unless you'd like to drive a few more miles and let the marks get away. I'll let you break the news to Taras."

Agniya whipped the car out of its curb lane, veering toward the central concrete island that divided Krimskiy Val Street's eastbound lanes from westbound traffic.

Other vehicles were swerving madly, raising a chorus of blats, squeals and screeches. A tanker truck loomed like a mountain on wheels to their left, air horn moaning, but Agniya beat it by inches before the collision that would have destroyed them. In another heartbeat, they were bouncing over the divider island, scraping metal underneath and doubtless doing major damage to their ride, before they nosed back into traffic traveling the opposite direction.

There, Agniya did it all again, charging across the lanes from south to north this time. A small car clipped their left-rear bumper, snapping Efros's teeth together painfully, but otherwise they managed to complete the strange maneuver without injury.

As to how many little rats were calling the militia already, Efros couldn't guess and didn't give a damn. He pointed toward an intersecting street, a block ahead of them, and told Agniya, "There! I saw them run up that way, just before you got here!"

Agniya was silent at the wheel, as grim-faced as ever, following directions like a skinhead robot. Efros couldn't name the street where he had glimpsed the woman and her savior turning north on foot, but as they reached it, he made out the sign.

Maronovskiy Avenue.

They made the turn on two wheels, maybe three, then leveled off. Agniya slowed a bit, scanning the street with narrowed eyes, asking, "Where are they?"

"I'm not a mind reader," Efros replied. "They had a fair head start on foot. Just keep your eyes open."

"They're open. I see nothing."

"And your mouth shut, while you're at it."

Agniya muttered some unintelligible comment, then shut up. Efros ignored him, scanning every shop and doorway as they passed. He'd seen the woman clearly and would recognize her in an instant. As for Cooper...

"There!"

"What? Where?"

"They must have left their car in the garage," Efros explained, pointing to the street entrance with its sign, a half block farther north.

"Or parked along the street," Agniya said. "Or ducked into a shop. Or run off down—"

"Shut up!" Efros barked. "We're checking the garage."

"Yes, *sir!* Just as you say, *sir!*"

Efros felt a sudden, almost overwhelming urge to blow the driver's brains out, push his body from the moving car and carry on alone. He might have done so, if he hadn't thought he'd need a wheelman sometime in the next few minutes, while his hands were occupied with dealing death.

To Matthew Cooper. Not the woman.

Not unless she made it absolutely unavoidable.

Which, Efros thought, now seemed more likely by the moment.

PILKIN DROVE, as usual. Bolan was happy to be riding shotgun, if the shooters who had missed them at the Metro Station showed up on their tail again. She took the high-rise garage's zigzag turns at twenty miles per hour, obviously anxious to be on the street and gone.

"Thanks for the save back there," she said, turning her vehicle onto the third level, heading down. "I never saw him coming."

"Everybody has a blind side," Bolan said. "It's why we watch each other's backs."

"No one was there to watch Maria's."

"No."

"I wonder who'll watch mine, when this is done?"

He half expected her to add, *If we're alive,* but if it crossed her mind, she kept the pessimistic notion to herself.

They reached the second level, tires whining lightly on

pavement as Pilkin cranked through another tight turn. The garage was full, but the hour was wrong for departures, it seemed, so they had the run all to themselves.

Until they reached ground level, anyway.

A black sedan was nosing into the garage, its driver leaning from his open window, lunging for the ticket that would raise the wooden arm and clear his path for entry. Bolan didn't recognize the shaved scalp or the face beneath it, but he saw Pilkin stiffen in the driver's seat, eyeing the other vehicle.

"It's Sergei Efros," she informed him. "Not the driver. There, beside him."

"Who's that?" Bolan asked her.

"Sokolov's chief of security."

"That can't be a coincidence," Bolan said.

"No."

The incoming sedan had passed its automated checkpoint and the wooden arm was lowering behind it, by the time its passenger saw Pilkin and did a double take that would've done an old vaudevillian proud. The man she'd labeled Sergei Efros raised a pistol from his lap and leaned across his driver's line of sight to aim.

"Hit it!" Bolan snapped, but the FSB lieutenant had already seen the threat and moved to counter it. She floored her gas pedal, a squeal of tires announcing their acceleration, then their ride crashed through the wooden rocker arm on their side of the two-lane passage and they left a shocked cashier calling for Pilkin to stop.

A heartbeat later, pistol shots rang out inside the cavernous garage, and Bolan heard no more from the cashier. That could've been because they'd cleared the exit, turning hard right onto Maronovskiy Avenue and roaring out of earshot.

Anyway, he hoped it was.

The chase car would be forced to turn around, no simple task within the narrow confines of the entryway to the garage. Call it a three-point turn, if their intended killers caught a break and didn't hit one of the concrete posts or parked cars lining both sides of the passageway. Ideally, they would trash their ride and wind up stranded, but it didn't feel that way to Bolan.

It was too much to expect. Too much to hope for.

They'd cleared one block, were starting on another, when he saw the black sedan emerge from the garage and turn to follow them. The front-seat faces were amorphous blobs, but he could sense the malice radiating from both.

Two down, that he was sure of, and the pair behind him made it four. A standard ambush set, but why had their first shot been wasted on Pilkin's friend? Why hadn't they dropped their main target—one of them, anyway—when a clean shot was provided?

"Lead them somewhere," he said. "Let them catch us, as long as we're clear of civilians."

"Have you lost your mind?" she demanded.

"Maybe," he admitted. "But I've got a hunch that they want you alive. If I'm right, we can use it against them."

"All right," she replied. "But I warn you. *I* don't want *them* living at all."

"IT'S HER!" Sergei Efros spit, raising his pistol as he recognized the driver of the car about to pass them.

She saw Efros at the same moment and gunned her car past the cashier's booth, snapping the wooden rocker arm at its base and spinning it off to one side. Efros fired after her, no longer caring who he wounded, but his shot missed by yards, while Agniya flinched and recoiled from the blast.

"Get after them!" Efros commanded.

Agniya grimaced at him, right hand rising to his ear. "Say what?"

"I said, get after them!"

"All right! Chill out!"

"I'll chill out when we've caught them. Drive!"

Agniya couldn't simply make a U-turn in the space available. He did his best, but still lost precious moments while their quarry gained a lead. At last, when they were able to escape from the garage, Efros saw the woman's VAZ 2112 sedan turning right on a side street, two blocks ahead.

"Hurry! If they escape, I'm going to feed you your balls."

"I'm not the one who let them get away the first time," Agniya said. "You're not even Solntsevskaya Brotherhood."

Efros jammed his pistol hard against Agniya's skull. "Fuck you and your so-called Family," he snarled. "If you have a brain in there, you'll drive as if your life depends on it."

Agniya took him at his word, flooring the accelerator and roaring after the car that had already vanished from sight. They cleared the two blocks rapidly and swung into a screeching turn eastward. The street led them into some kind of industrial park, the kind of maze where warehouses shared space with light industry, office blocks and trucking companies.

It seemed to Efros that there were a thousand places where his prey could disappear. But then he saw Pilkin's car just turning on another, smaller side street, this time to the left.

"See it?" he barked. "Close up! Get on them!"

"This is a BMW, not a rocket sled," the driver answered, but he still milked more speed from the big sedan's engine and reached their side street in time to see the VAZ turn right.

"They're trying to lose us," Efros said.

"You think so? What genius!"

"Just drive, idiot!"

"Go to hell," Agniya spit back, but even after wishing Efros into hell, he drove the Beemer like a pro.

Pilkin was leading them in circles, hoping that they would become confused, get lost somehow, but Efros wouldn't let himself be shaken off so easily. He almost had her in his sights, now. She'd escaped him for the last time, come what may.

A sudden, horrifying thought struck Efros, and he asked Agniya, "How's the fuel tank?"

"What?"

"The fuel tank! After all this driving—"

"Half-empty," Agniya said. "You want to stop somewhere and top it off, right now?"

"Just drive!"

This time, Agniya laughed at him. Efros decided he would kill this one for mocking him, as soon as he'd outlived his usefulness. It would be simple, then, to blame the woman or her comrade.

Any moment now—

Agniya hit the brakes, and Efros felt the BMW swerving, sliding, to avoid collision with the VAZ sedan that sat in front of them, both doors open, without a living soul in sight.

BOLAN HAD GONE to ground behind a large sign sculpted out of stone, irregular in form, which advertised some kind of nearby factory. He didn't have a clue what it produced and couldn't have cared less. Cover was all that mattered at the moment, and he hoped that Pilkin had found some.

Quite by accident, they'd turned in to a cul-de-sac with no escape except reversing back the way they'd come. Bolan had seen the chase car closing in behind them, and he knew they'd have a squeaker on their hands, assuming that the gunmen didn't riddle both of them on sight.

So, he had improvised.

Ditching the car was risky. It was possible the BMW chasing them would slam into Pilkin's smaller sedan, crippling it, or that the shooters would blaze away at the VAZ on sight, with identical results. Either way, win or lose, it would be bad news for Bolan and his partner. Gunned down or stranded afoot—which was worse?

No contest.

With a bit of moxie and a gun, Bolan could always get another car. If need be, they could drive off in the BMW and replace it at their leisure.

Barring some event where endless torture was the only other option, dead was never best.

Bolan had no iron-clad plan in mind, beyond surprising Sergei Efros and his pal with the abandoned car. That guaranteed a moment's hesitation, pondering the riddle, even while the hunters kept their guard up. And while they were gaping, wondering, the Executioner could do what he did best.

In the fraction of a minute still remaining to him, Bolan wondered why Gennady Sokolov had sent his chief of security to Moscow. Was the Merchant of Death getting nervous? Did he honestly believe one man could move the hunt for Pilkin and Bolan forward to its culmination?

And if so, was he correct?

A squeal of tires told Bolan that his adversaries had arrived. First, rubber crying on the turn, then scorching as the driver slammed his brakes and swerved. The BMW missed Pilkin's car and came to rest midway between it and the sculpted block of stone where Bolan lay, clutching his Steyr AUG.

How long before employees from the several surrounding firms emerged to find out what was happening? And how long after that before they summoned the militia?

Not long.

Two angry voices reached his ears. One sounded almost accusatory, the other caught somewhere between defiance and apology. He couldn't understand a word of it, but knew the squabbling men would never pass for friends.

One of them had to be Efros. If he had a chance to grill the man, it could be useful, but a seasoned pro could tough it out through most interrogations, short of using drugs Bolan didn't possess. The cruder methods—which the Executioner detested but had used on rare occasions when he had no other choice—would likely fail.

Torture was always problematic. Most victims would happily confess to anything while fabricating mythical offenses to relieve their suffering. Professionals, by contrast, could survive for weeks or months by dropping crumbs of information here and there, most of them false, but all requiring independent research while the inquisition stalled.

Bolan had never heard of Sergei Efros, but he knew that Sokolov would hire only the best to supervise his personal security. Most likely Spetznaz, on a par with Green Berets or Navy SEALs, but lacking any notion of restraint where dealing with civilians was concerned.

Forget interrogation, then. Go for the kill.

Drawing a breath to hold him through the next few moments, Bolan made his move.

IN RETROSPECT, Pilkin knew that she had blown it. Anger and adrenaline were working on her nerves. Maria's murder and her own two brushes—as she'd thought—with sudden death, had left her with a feeling that her personal motor was revving on high, while she was stuck in neutral gear.

It didn't help for Cooper to surmise that Efros and his gunmen hoped to capture her alive. Instead of adding to her confidence, it forced her mind to dwell on what would happen to her if the snatch team was successful. Hideous vistas of pain yawned before her, until she'd regained control of her mind and focused on stopping Efros, bagging Sokolov and shipping his ass to the States.

Alive or dead? Right now, she didn't care.

So, she was anxious, and didn't wait for Cooper's signal that the trap was closing. She rose from where a massive brick gatepost concealed her, at the mouth of an office block's parking lot. The other man—not Efros—saw her, swung around in Pilkin's direction, bringing up a pistol.

And she fired too soon. Second mistake. She missed her target, scarred the BMW's jet-black paint job, and was forced to duck again as her adversary returned fire, spraying her face with brick dust.

She cursed her own impulsiveness, imagining what Cooper had to be thinking, now that she'd spoiled their surprise. His Steyr barked a second later, with a heavy pistol answering.

The best that she could do, for penance, was to end the skirmish quickly. Get it done, kill Efros and his man before police arrived to make things worse. And in that instant, Pilkin was forced to ponder what she'd do if faced with imminent arrest.

There was no question of her being safe in jail. Even if the militia should place her in a solitary cell with padded walls and floor, in maximum security, with guards outside her door around the clock, she would be easy prey. The only question left was whether she'd be killed by someone from the FSB, the *Mafiya,* or someone sent by Sokolov. And finally, what difference did it make?

Kill them and get it over with!

Suiting her action to her thoughts, Pilkin tried again and got another face full of brick dust for her effort. The driver was a fairly decent shot, who didn't hesitate as some are prone to do in mortal combat. Nothing he had done so far suggested any pressing need to capture Pilkin alive.

Which gave her an idea.

"Sergei!" she called out. "Sergei Efros! Hear me!"

On the far side of the cul-de-sac, Matt Cooper heard and held his fire.

"What do you want, Lieutenant Pilkin?" Efros challenged her. She'd used his name, now hers was known to any witnesses in hiding at the scene.

"One question?"

"Ask it!"

"When you could have killed me in the park, why didn't you?"

"Some think you might be useful, if persuaded to discuss your present mission. As for me, I'll take what I can get."

"Thanks for your honesty," she called to him, hoping Cooper had used the intervening time to mark a target, find a better vantage point—do *something.*

"Now," she added, taunting Efros, "I believe it's time for you to die."

Pilkin came up firing, peppering the BMW with her submachine gun, missing Efros by an eyelash as he dived for cover, out of sight.

BOLAN HAD LISTENED to the brief exchange between Anzhela Pilkin and Sokolov's chief of security. She'd drawn out an admission that his boss and others wanted her alive, which might have left some agents gripped by fear, but she was bearing up and fighting back, taking the battle to her enemies.

Now it was Bolan's turn.

It was a risk, but the soldier knew he had to take it, giving up his cover for a better field of fire. He didn't bolt out carelessly, but rather rolled away from the tall slab of sculpted stone that sheltered him, buying a few more heartbeats while his ducking, dodging adversaries tried to figure out if they were looking at a target or a shadow.

Pilkin was helping, squeezing off short bursts from her side of the cul-de-sac to keep them hopping, forcing them to worry about being shot from one side if they tried to watch the other. She was careful not to place herself directly opposite Bolan's position, to avoid the risk of hitting him or taking rounds from his spot in return.

It couldn't last much longer, Bolan realized. Somewhere, in one of the surrounding offices or factories, someone had placed a call to the police or was about to. Either way, the first squad car to reach the scene would seal the cul-de-sac.

Which might not trouble Bolan's enemies, but would wreak havoc on his plans.

He wouldn't shoot a cop. It was a pledge made to himself at the beginning of his one-man war against the Mafia, and he had kept it faithfully, despite confronting cases of brutality, corruption, even murderous behavior by a small minority of officers who sold their honor cheaply and thereby dishonored every hero who had stayed the course, defending law and order in chaotic times.

As for the two thugs now before him...

Bolan caught the chunky skinhead driver lumbering around the back side of the BMW, his teeth bared in a peculiar snarling grimace that made him look more simian than human. Still, that wasn't a banana in his hand. It looked more like some variant of the Czech Skorpion machine pistol.

Bolan squeezed off a double-tap before the skinhead knew he was in danger, drilled him through the lungs and dropped him like a load of dirty laundry on the pavement. Reflex made the driver's trigger finger clench, spraying a hail of aimless automatic fire across the nearest lawn and driveway. From the sound of it, he had the .380-caliber model.

The Skorpion spit itself empty while gunfire continued from Pilkin's side of the street. She was dueling with Sergei Efros, pinning him down. Bolan took advantage of the moment, rising from his prone position, charging toward the BMW to do his part.

When he was halfway there, Efros came scrambling from behind the car, his scalp bloodied by a graze that clearly left him shaken. He was fumbling to reload a semiauto pistol, nearly had it done when he saw Bolan and the Steyr leveled at his chest.

"Idi na xuy husesos," he said, half-smiling. *"Kooshi govno ee oomree!"*

"Back at you," Bolan said, and killed him where he stood. The 5.56 mm tumblers slashing through his chest slammed

Efros back against the Beemer and pinned him there for something like two seconds, then let gravity drag him to rest in a heap.

Bolan called out to Pilkin, "All clear!" A moment later, she was there beside him, staring down at Efros in the street.

"We should have questioned him," she said.

"I didn't like his attitude," Bolan replied.

"I'm thinking of the man who sent him."

Bolan nodded. "So am I."

CHAPTER THIRTEEN

Kotlin Island

Gennady Sokolov cradled the telephone receiver with a trembling hand. He tried to recall the last time he'd been on the verge of panic, fearing that his life had reached its end.

Had it been in Sudan, when a cocaine-addicted warlord pressed an automatic pistol to his head, accusing Sokolov of shorting him on ammunition shipments and deflowering the warlord's thirteen-year-old daughter?

Or the time he'd watched two thugs from the Medellín cartel give a suspected informer a Colombian necktie, slitting his throat and pulling his tongue through the gash, while their boss harangued Sokolov on the virtue of loyalty?

Neither of those compared to this.

Sokolov keyed the intercom and waited for Ivan Fet to enter his office, closing the door behind him. A trim, athletic thirty-something, Fet was six feet tall and might have weighed one hundred ninety pounds, without an ounce of fat in sight.

"Yes, sir?"

"I've just been on the line to Moscow," Sokolov informed him. The rest stuck in his throat.

"Yes, sir?" Fet said again, politely prodding him.

"It's Sergei. He's been killed."

The left corner of Fet's mouth twitched, but Sokolov couldn't have said whether it marked a grimace or a fleeting smile. He chose to think that it was shock.

"Who did it, sir?"

"Apparently, the same pair who've been raising hell down there since yesterday."

"So, the Canadian and that bitch from the FSB."

"The same. And if this Cooper is Canadian, I'm second cousin to Rasputin."

"It's been said, sir," Fet replied, trying to lighten up his mood.

"Has it?" Sokolov nearly smiled. "It would appear that you're my new chief of security, assuming that you want the job."

"Yes, sir! And thank you, sir!"

"You may be cursing me, this time tomorrow," Sokolov replied.

"Shall I pack for Moscow, sir?"

"No!" Sokolov physically recoiled from the idea. "I never should have sent Sergei, to start with. Let Bezmel and Chaliapin earn their pay, for once. I wash my hands of them."

"A wise decision, sir. May I suggest a doubling of the guard, in case—"

"No need for that," Sokolov interrupted him. "We're leaving Kotlin."

"Sir?" The news seemed to surprise Fet more than Sokolov's report of Efros's death. "Are you quite sure that's wise?"

"Why not?" Sokolov asked. "The FBI already dropped a kidnap team onto my doorstep. Now, we have this pair who seem to be untouchable, blazing their way through Moscow high and low. How long before they turn up here?"

"Sir, I can—"

"Stop them?"

"Yes, sir!"

"Possibly. But we've already drawn enough attention to ourselves on Kotlin. I intended this to be my sanctuary, not a free-fire zone. You know the neighbors have been getting restless."

"I can deal with them, as well."

"In this case, I prefer withdrawal to a brave last stand. You'll humor me, of course." Not making it a question.

"Yes, sir. I mean, as you wish, sir!"

"As I wish. Exactly. Since we know my tormentors will be stuck in Moscow for at least a short while longer, we still have the luxury of time. Alert the house staff that we shall be leaving in three hours."

"Going where, sir?" Fet asked.

"That's my secret."

"Of course, sir. But if I'm expected to defend a place effectively, I must know the location."

"All will be revealed," Sokolov said. "As to defenses, they have been prepared. I've no doubt that you'll wish to make refinements, but I'm confident that you'll be pleasantly surprised."

Fet kept his face deadpan as he replied, "I'm looking forward to it, sir."

MAJOR MAKSIM CHALIAPIN read the note a fourth time, scowling at it, straining hard to find some hidden meaning tucked between the lines.

Nothing.

It was a pink rectangle from a standard office notepad, lined for tidy penmanship. His secretary's handwriting was crisp and clear as ever. It concealed nothing that he could find, and yet it vexed him terribly.

The message was succinct and unequivocal: Report to Gen. Bakunin's office at 11:00 a.m.

Just that, and nothing more.

General Dmitri Bakunin was a sixty-year-old veteran of the KBG who had remained on board and salvaged his career when the Soviet Union collapsed. Rumor had it that he knew too many secrets to be pensioned off against his will. He knew where the bodies were buried—and, it was said by those in position to know, he had planted some of them himself.

Chaliapin checked his watch and saw that he had half an hour to prepare for his meeting with General Bakunin. But how? A tranquilizer might be useful, but the major had none in his office.

Never mind.

He spent five minutes in front of a mirror, trying his best to look wise and alert, then rode the elevator up to the fourth floor of the Lubyanka, where the top brass had their offices. Bakunin was third in command, below Director Bortnikov and his chief deputy, for all intents and purposes the FSB's chief hatchet man.

And would Chaliapin get the ax this day?

Bakunin kept him waiting in the anteroom, under the cool gaze of his secretary—a willowy captain whose blond hair bristled in spikes like a porcupine's quills. She studied Chaliapin with the fine disdain of one who knew that her position rendered her invulnerable to attack by anyone outside the rarefied levels of supreme authority.

Chaliapin wondered what services she performed for General Bakunin, but before the fantasy could run its course, she jarred him back to grim reality.

"The general will see you now, Major."

Chaliapin had never faced a court-martial, but he imagined how a defendant had to feel in the dock, facing judges who held his life in their hands.

General Bakunin was a fireplug of a man, no more than five foot six, but he exuded power. His gray hair, streaked with white, was oiled and combed back, flat against his skull. Eyes of the same gray, more or less, bored into Chaliapin like twin augers.

Bakunin returned Chaliapin's salute without much conviction, then gestured toward a straight-backed wooden chair that stood before his desk. Chaliapin sat, bolt upright at attention, swallowing an urge to clear his throat.

"Major, you can imagine why I've called you here today."

"No, sir."

"No?" Bakunin's eyes held Chaliapin's in a grip that he couldn't escape.

"No, sir."

"In that case, I'll enlighten you. You are, I take it, cognizant of certain violent disturbances in Moscow, occurring since yesterday evening?"

"Yes, sir. I am."

"Including the suicide of an FSB officer?"

"Yes, sir."

"In fact, you visited the scene of that event, although the officer in question was not from your own department."

"Sir, in such a case, I'm sure that all of us are equally concerned."

"Some more than others, possibly," Bakunin said.

"I'm not sure that I—"

"Now, it seems another FSB member has been dispatched by violence. A Sergeant Boguslavskaya. You recognize the name?"

"Yes, sir."

"In fact, you spoke to her a short time prior to the events that claimed her life. Is that not so?"

"As to the time, sir—"

"Yes, or no?"

"Yes, sir."

Bakunin frowned. "Major," he said, "kindly explain yourself."

Izmailovsky Park, Moscow

BOLAN AND PILKIN were hiding in plain sight. They needed to regroup, and she'd suggested one of Moscow's favorite parks—once a separate village, then a commune built by Czar Aleksei Mikhailovich in the early seventeenth century, now a tourist attraction including birch forests and a lovingly restored palace once occupied by Aleksei's grandson, Czar Peter the Great.

They weren't strolling the woods, or paddling a rowboat out to Silver Island for a look at Pokhorovoskiy Cathedral, of course. They were content to sit in Pilkin's car, in the park's spacious lot, and converse in low tones while foot traffic surrounded them, screening them from prying eyes.

"So, you were right," she said. "They do want me alive."

"Or did," Bolan replied. "I have a feeling they'll be less concerned about it now."

"Chaliapin killed Maria," she said. "As surely as if he pulled the trigger himself."

"I'd definitely like to visit him," Bolan said. "But we need to keep our eye on the ball. That's still Sokolov. He's job one."

"So, we're off to Saint Petersburg now? As if nothing has happened in Moscow?"

"I said he's job one, not the *only* job. Prioritize. We've got the stew pot simmering. Nobody needs to watch it, for a while. I want the target bagged and tagged before we get around to mopping up."

"You won't forget Maria, then?"

"Not likely."

Bolan didn't feel like telling Pilkin that he'd forgotten no one who had fallen in his long and often lonely war. Beginning with his own lost family, that ever-growing list was a reminder of those times he'd slipped or dropped the ball—and of his own mortality.

The ghosts were his alone. Bolan wasn't inclined to share.

"All right, then," Pilkin conceded. "It will take too long to drive, and Chaliapin will be watching all commercial flights. We'll have to charter something private."

"Even better," Bolan answered, thinking of their weapons. "Money's not a problem, if you have someone in mind."

"We normally use military planes, but I've become acquainted with some pilots who don't ask a lot of questions about passengers or cargo, if the price is right."

"Sounds good," he said, "as long as they won't sell you out to Chaliapin."

"They are not informers," Pilkin explained. "Just businessmen who find themselves encumbered by the law from time to time."

"Who doesn't, when you think about it? Can you reach them now?"

"Unless they're flying. Let's find out."

Pilkin found her cell phone and tapped out a number from memory. Bolan didn't have to think about eavesdropping, since she spoke in Russian. The conversation was brief, but she seemed satisfied as she broke the connection.

"Good luck," she told Bolan, half smiling. "My first choice can see us within the hour. We must hurry."

"Which airport does he fly from?"

"Vnukovo, the city's oldest. Chaliapin may be watching all of them, but since we won't be checking through the terminal, we have a decent chance of missing anyone he sends to watch for us."

"There's still your car," Bolan reminded her. "Someone could find it while we're gone."

"I have a plan for that," she said. "We won't be coming back to Vnukovo, but to Sheremetyevo International. From there, we rent a car, go back to Vnukovo, and find out if anyone has taken mine. So, either way, we're mobile."

"Sounds good," Bolan said. She didn't need reminding that they might not be returning from Saint Petersburg. That part was understood.

"We go, then, yes?"

"We go," the Executioner agreed.

"THREE MORE of our men dead! For what?" Leonid Bezmel raged.

"It's what we get for working with the FSB," Taras Morozov answered. "Chaliapin needs to pay for this in blood."

"He'll pay, all right," the boss of the Solntsevskaya Brotherhood declared. "Before all this is done, that prick certainly will pay."

"I'd like to do it personally," Morozov said.

"All in good time, Taras. First, we need to think of what's best for the Family."

"Revenge is always best. Reminding Aldo Shishani and the other scum of who's in charge."

"We won't accomplish that by waging war against the FSB. In fact, it could destroy us," Bezmel said.

"One man," Morozov said. "Make an example of the major, and whoever's chosen to replace him will think twice before he fucks us."

"First things first," Bezmel replied, surprised to feel a measure of his rage subsiding. "I must speak to Sokolov and find out what he means to do about Efros."

"I'd send him back to Kotlin in a garbage bag."

"Your anger does you credit, Taras—to a point. Beyond that, it becomes an obstacle to logic."

"Leonid, it's one thing, helping Sokolov sell weapons. When we stand between him and the government, we suffer. You can see it all around you."

"And I *also* see the profit waiting to be made from one last shipment. Don't forget the Arabs, Taras."

"I've forgotten nothing."

"They are paying millions for their special item. I'm convinced that Sokolov will see the wisdom of increasing our share, as a form of reparation for the losses we've incurred on his behalf."

"And if he doesn't?"

"In that case," Bezmel said, "I would propose we take it all. His business, everything. It doesn't take a washed-up spy to peddle guns around the world. The market's ready-made. Our army's damn near giving them away."

"Cut out the middleman," Morozov said, smiling at last.

"See how the logic works?"

"And when it's time to cut him out…"

"I can't let you have all the fun," Bezmel said. "Sokolov or Chaliapin? We can always flip a coin."

"Or we could let them kill each other," Taras offered. "Put them in a shed with hatchets. Last man standing gets a prize."

"Between the eyes?" Bezmel asked.

Morozov shrugged. "We can't leave any witnesses."

Bezmel laughed heartily—and made a mental note to watch his underboss more closely in the future. Morozov was absolutely ruthless, as required of one in his position, but it struck Bezmel that his ambition might be getting out of hand. When it came time to settle Family accounts, perhaps another name should be appended to the list.

And in the meantime…

"You've been checking on Shishani's people, right?"

"That's right. We're watching those who matter, keeping loose track of the rest."

"Perhaps the present situation may be turned to our advantage," Bezmel said. "Aldo already thinks we've gone to war with him, thanks to the antics of this Cooper person and his bitch from the FSB. Why not proceed as if it were a fact?"

"Hit the Obshina?"

"Just hard enough to keep them in their place," Bezmel replied. "And to acquire some of their better properties, if you should see the opportunity."

"I'll *make* the opportunity."

"I thought you might. Be careful, though. We don't need any more surprises at the moment."

"Aldo is the one who needs to worry about being taken by surprise."

"See to it, then," Bezmel instructed. "While I deal with Sokolov."

"If you need any help…"

"I'm not a virgin, Taras. It's like stealing a bicycle."

"Don't you mean *riding* a bicycle?"

Bezmel smiled and replied, "I mean what I say."

MAKSIM CHALIAPIN FELT as if he'd just been spanked and sent to bed without his supper. Still, he thought, it could have been much worse.

He wasn't facing any charges, yet. General Bakunin hadn't threatened any sort of formal inquiry, although it still might happen if he couldn't put the mess to rights, and do it soon.

Bakunin was, above all else, a trained survivor. He had outlived most of his contemporaries in the KGB, avoided exile or worse during various purges, and had emerged with rank and status intact after communism's collapse. He never asked a question without purpose—or without knowing the answer beforehand. If he felt that Chaliapin threatened him in any way, even by implication or through simple negligence, the general would cut him down without a second thought.

But if Bakunin was untouchable, he still might be placated. His remarks, though veiled and cryptic, had suggested that Chaliapin still might salvage his career. Indeed, the very fact that they had spoken, when Bakunin could have simply placed a call and flushed Chaliapin's life down the shitter, offered some hope of redemption.

What Chaliapin did with that opportunity remained to be seen. But he clearly had no time to waste.

To save himself, Chaliapin knew that he had to stop

Anzhela Pilkin, silence her forever, while avoiding any blowback that would point to him or to the FSB. Above all, he could not disgrace the agency in any way, if he hoped to appease the general and thus ensure his own survival.

Elem Protazanov's suicide was a step in the right direction, and Chaliapin knew he could downplay Maria Boguslavskaya's murder. The FSB had thousands of employees, any one of whom might be caught up in a gangland shooting by coincidence. A hero's funeral and a pension payoff to her family should cover it, as long as Leonid Bezmel kept his mouth shut.

And what choice did he have? Could he complain of joining in a criminal conspiracy that cost the lives of three cheap thugs?

As for the death of Sergei Efros, Chaliapin could prepare a press release describing him as a rogue ex-soldier, involved with hoodlums in some as-yet-unidentified crime. No one would miss him. None would mourn his passing.

Which left only Gennady Sokolov.

He was a problem that could still blow up in Chaliapin's face, and take Colonel General Ruslan Kozlov down with them. No amount of fancy footwork would cover *that* scandal, if Sokolov spilled what he knew.

But why would he? Only the good graces of the Russian government prevented his extradition to America, where he faced trial, a guaranteed conviction and imprisonment for life without parole. Sokolov couldn't think that he would benefit by fouling his own nest.

If, on the other hand, he should be lifted out of Russia and delivered to the CIA for transport through some backdoor process, Sokolov might well decide to sing in self-defense. Those in the States who hated Russia would be thrilled to put him on display, explaining how the trade in military surplus arms was run, the threat it posed to stable governments—and not-so-stable ones—throughout the world.

Maksim Chaliapin wouldn't suffer alone, if that happened, but he *would* suffer. Shit always rolled downhill, and he was in a prime position to be buried in it, when accomplices with higher ranks and richer friends scrambled to save themselves.

In this case, he would take a lesson from America itself, the Western films of Hollywood. They taught him that a man did what he had to do to survive.

And so he would.

Beginning now.

Vnukovo International Airport

VNUKOVO INTERNATIONAL, located eighteen miles southwest of downtown Moscow, was built during World War II as a military airfield. Converted to civilian use after the war, it launched its first civilian flight in April 1956 and saw Russia's first jet airliner lift off five months later. It is still best known for the November 1957 crash that killed Russia's Minister of Foreign Affairs, Grigore Preoteasa, and most of his flight crew. Romanian dictator Nicolae Ceausescu survived that accident to keep his date with a firing squad, three decades later.

The airport had been modernized and expanded since those days, but its age still showed. Bolan was spared a tour of its concourse when Pilkin bypassed the domestic terminal and drove out to a row of hangars leased to private charter companies.

They approached the fourth hangar in line. He couldn't read the sign mounted above the hangar's doors, and didn't bother asking what it said. Outside the hangar sat a single-engine Technoavia SM92 Finist, painted some version of electric-blue.

Bolan stayed current on the basics of civilian aircraft, as he did on military vehicles. He knew the Finist operated with a single pilot and could haul eight passengers or twelve hundred pounds of cargo. Its STOL capability—short takeoff or landing—made it the aircraft of choice for Russia's Border Guard. Its maximum range was eight hundred miles, with a ceiling of ten thousand feet and a top speed of 170 miles per hour. The flight to Saint Petersburg, roughly four hundred miles from where they stood, would take two hours and thirty minutes, barring any unforeseen difficulties.

Such as being blown out of the sky.

A man dressed in mechanic's overalls approached them from the hangar, smiling at Pilkin, letting it slip as he studied Bolan. He spoke briefly to the FSB agent in Russian, then offered Bolan a strong hand with permanently stained fingernails.

"Valeri Utkin," he said. "I'll be flying you north."

"Glad to meet you. Matt Cooper."

"We're gassed up and ready to go," Utkin said. "I'll just change while you stow any luggage you're taking along for the flight."

Utkin was pulling down the zipper on his jumpsuit as he left them, showing off a muscle shirt beneath it. Bolan brought their weapons from the car in duffel bags, while Pilkin shifted his carry-on and a small bag of clothes she'd picked up in a rush, after finding her flat was off-limits. The gear was safely stowed by the time their pilot returned.

Don't ask, don't tell.

"All ready, then?" Utkin asked.

"As we'll ever be," Bolan replied.

The pilot had changed into jeans, a turtleneck and an old bomber jacket with fleece lining. He saw Bolan eyeing it and smiled.

"Don't worry, Matt. It doesn't get that cold upstairs in this baby. I simply like the jacket's look." He winked, adding, "The ladies like it, too."

"Some ladies," Pilkin corrected him. "I like a three-piece Valentino."

"Such a snob, you are," Utkin said, bowing as he ushered Pilkin inside the plane.

It wasn't roomy. Even with seating for eight, the Finist was under thirty feet long from propeller to rudder. Its wingspan was greater, at just under forty-eight feet. Still, as promised, the cabin was warm and the seats no more cramped than the average seating in coach on commercial airlines.

Bolan sat down across the narrow center aisle from Pilkin, strapped in and felt the plane's 360-horsepower engine revving as Utkin prepared for takeoff. Waiting for their clearance from the airport's tower, he began to think about what lay ahead of them.

But all he saw was death.

CHAPTER FOURTEEN

Moscow

Magen Manaev stood on a plastic milk crate and surveyed the faces ranged before him. Every word and footstep echoed in the nearly empty warehouse he had chosen for their meeting place. The sound didn't concern him, though, since Manaev had supervised a sweep for listening devices while he waited for his soldiers to arrive.

They were the best—or worst—of the Obshina, sons of Chechnya hardened by years of war, imprisonment, the lives of crime that they had chosen for themselves. Their families, those still alive, were patriots whose hatred of the Russian empire spanned six generations, dating from the Caucasian War that started for their ancestors in 1817. Nothing had happened since that time to soften any of their attitudes toward Moscow, although they were pleased to pillage and corrupt their enemy's sacred city.

"All here, then?" Manaev asked Zakhar Panin, his chief lieutenant.

"Forty, as you ordered," Panin said.

Manaev recognized them all, could have recited their accomplishments from memory as if reading police files. Every man who stood before him was a tried and tested killer. Some enjoyed it more than others, but they all were experts. None among them had slain fewer than a dozen enemies.

"You all know why you're here," Manaev said, by way of introduction. "The Solntsevskaya Brotherhood have lost its mind again. Not for the first time, the organization reckons it can drive us out of Moscow. With your help, I mean to prove those bastards wrong."

A growl went up from the assembled soldiers. No one seemed to find Manaev's speech melodramatic or amusing. They'd been raised on conspiracy theories and paranoia, conditioned to live in a black-and-white world where Chechnya embodied every virtue and Russia personified foul degradation.

"You all know Leonid Bezmel," Manaev declared, evoking another snarl from his audience. "We have been patient with him long enough. He and the other Russian pigs must learn the price of insulting their natural superiors."

A handful of his men responded with a shout to that, the others quickly joining in. Manaev saw the light of anger and fanaticism in their eyes.

"Zakhar has your assignments. You'll be splitting into four-man teams to carry out your missions. We have city maps for those who need them. Also weapons and ammunition for those who've flown in from Omsk and Novosibirsk. We'll have a local man with each outside team, to make sure no one gets lost."

There were a few chuckles at that, no one taking offense.

"The main thing," Manaev continued, "is to hit the bastards hard and keep them down. We only want to do this one last time. Questions?"

A soldier in the front row, Balin Dudayev, asked, "What about the militia?"

Manaev frowned. "Ignore them, if they show you the same courtesy," he said. "We own some of the pigs, but not as many as the Brotherhood. If any try to stop you, treat them as your enemies."

He didn't have to spell it out. Some of these men had killed police, and none would voluntarily submit to an arrest in

Moscow. Not when they were on a mission to preserve the Family.

"I know you'll make us proud," Manaev told them. "Go, now. Do your work!"

With one more rousing shout, the mobsters broke ranks, some heading for the exit and their waiting cars, while others turned toward a long table laden with weapons and boxes of ammunition. None of the firearms were traceable. All had been stolen or purchased from black-market dealers whose sources were anyone's guess.

Manaev watched them go, feeling every inch a general upon the eve of battle. Only his responsibilities to Aldo Shishani kept him from going along for the ride. Someone, after all, had to hold the fort and safeguard the king.

"I need a drink," he told Zakhar Panin. "Keep me informed when they've made contact, eh?"

TARAS MOROZOV TRIED to remember the last time that he'd killed a man. He recalled the event—the man's bloody face, screaming for mercy—but how long ago had it been? Four years? Five?

His rank as underboss of the Solntsevskaya Brotherhood generally exempted him from personal participation in wet work, but today was an exception. One, moreover, that he welcomed with enthusiasm.

He was on the streets again, eager to prove that he still had the skills and courage to defend his chosen Family against attack. His boss aside, there were no generals this day, just soldiers fighting for their honor and their turf.

It made a nice change, riding out to battle with his men, instead of going to a banquet or a party at some nightclub where the staff were paid to fawn and kiss his ass. From time to time, he thought, even the richest and most powerful of men needed to dirty their hands, remember who they were and where they came from.

That, in Morozov's view, was the problem with most politicians. Craving luxury alone, without the hard work that supported it, they were always for sale to the highest bidder.

Cruising eastward along Sadovaya-Karetnaya Street, surrounded by six soldiers in his ZIL limousine, Morozov stroked the weapon lying in his lap. He'd chosen a certified classic, no-frills AK-47 with a folding metal stock its sole refinement. He preferred the mother of all modern Russian weapons to its later variants of lighter caliber, with their "improvements" that did nothing but detract from the original.

And any moment now, he'd have a chance to use it.

"Two blocks," his driver said while they were waiting for a traffic light to change. "The place is on your left."

Morozov shifted to an empty jump seat by the nearest window, then checked his weapon's safety to make sure he'd switched it off. He reveled in the click-clack sounds of weapons being cocked around him, breathing in the heady scent of gun oil.

Their target was a gay bar owned by Aldo Shishani's Obshina. The Chechens weren't gay—well, *most* of them weren't—but they would sell babies to pedophiles if they could make a few rubles.

And why not?

It wasn't the trade that Morozov despised, but its owners. He wouldn't be happy till all Chechen scum had been run out of Moscow or buried beneath it. Anything that damaged the Obshina helped Morozov's Family.

"Get ready," said their driver as the windows powered down along the left side of the limo. Morozov saw the club called Ramrod looming large over his rifle's sights.

A heartbeat later, he was thankful for the earplugs he'd inserted after entering the limousine. They'd made his idle conversation with the others somewhat awkward, but they saved him a colossal headache now, with weapons hammering away inside the car's confined space. Hot brass spewed from ejectors and bounced all around him, while bullets flayed the club's facade.

Morozov tried to miss the stampeding pedestrians, but saw a couple of them fall and wasn't terribly concerned. The whole damned neighborhood was gay, as far as he knew, and while the militia would certainly investigate the shooting, there were still enough old hands on board—and plenty on the gang's payroll—to minimize any potential damage.

As for howls of outrage from the media, who cared?

Taras Morozov hadn't felt this good in years. He couldn't wait to visit his next target, and the next one after that, until Moscow was purged of foreign trash and safely back in Russian hands.

TURBULENCE GRIPPED the Technoavia SM92 Finist, causing it to heave and shudder. Bolan kept his eyes fixed on the bulkhead straight ahead of him, avoided peering out his window toward the ground nine thousand feet below. There were equations for determining a falling object's speed as it accelerated toward the point of terminal velocity, but Bolan didn't feel like running any of the calculations in his head.

He might turn out to *be* one of those objects, and the only part of any formula that mattered then would be the lone word *terminal*.

He gave Valeri Utkin credit for handling the light aircraft under trying conditions. It could have been worse, but that knowledge didn't stop Bolan's stomach from clenching. A glance across the aisle at Pilkin revealed pinched features, worry lines around her eyes and mouth.

Where would they land if Utkin lost it? Somewhere near Tver, a one-time medieval stronghold later known as Kalinin from 1931 to 1990, when it reverted to its ancestral name. By reputation, Tver's citizens were tough fighters in wartime and fumed over meddling from Moscow when taxes were raised with no increase in service to match. The Patriots of Russia had a solid following in Tver, and sometimes vented their displeasure with the central government in forceful ways.

But Bolan didn't plan on landing there this day. His destination was Saint Petersburg, in Leningrad Oblast, still more than a hundred miles distant by air. He had no reason to believe their flight would be cut short, but in his mind and heart, he seldom made a move without anticipating sudden death.

That was the price a soldier paid for taking on the world.

He hadn't planned that life, of course. Who ever did? It had been simple in his youth: sign up to serve your country and protect the folks at home. Bolan had gone to war unknowing that an older, more insidious enemy threatened his family and everything he loved. Sometimes it took a tragic loss to strip a hero in the making of his illusions.

Bolan was older now, and wiser, but the knowledge he'd accumulated didn't make him any happier. Quite the reverse, in fact. He'd often wished that he could turn back time, recapture something of his former innocence. But he had done things that could never be undone. Witnessed atrocities that couldn't be unseen, once they were burned into his memory.

War changed everyone it touched. Every soul affected bore its scars. Some wounds bled from the heart and through the eyes.

Bolan had never second-guessed his choices, and he wasn't starting now. His course was set by destiny or Fate before he knew there was a journey to be made and, once embarked upon the long, strange trip, there was no turning back.

Saint Petersburg awaited him, hiding a man he'd come to find, extract and ship off to the States for trial. The rest of it—all that he'd done with Pilkin so far, and what would follow if they lived—was an extension of his central mission. He was taking care of business. Making sure that Sokolov's accomplices in slaughter paid their fair share of the tab.

Brognola hadn't spelled it out that way during their meeting at the International Spy Museum in Washington. There'd been no need for him to itemize the butcher's bill.

The big Fed knew how Bolan worked.

He would expect no less.

And when the smoke cleared…then what? Would the Russian Federation be a better, cleaner place?

Bolan didn't believe in miracles.

This day, he was a sanitation worker. Taking out the trash.

MAJOR MAKSIM CHALIAPIN was pulling strings and calling in markers, doing whatever he could to find Anzhela Pilkin and Matthew Cooper before it was too late. Whatever was required to save himself at this point, Chaliapin was prepared to do it.

Why else would he have a GSh-18 pistol tucked into his belt when he normally carried no weapon? His FSB rank precluded personal involvement in fieldwork under normal circumstances, but events over the past day had been anything but normal.

Now it seemed they would have anarchy in Moscow, with Russian and Chechen mobsters at one another's throats. Chaliapin frankly didn't care if they were all exterminated, though his covert income would be whittled down considerably by that loss. Still, there would always be the bribes from individuals such as Gennady Sokolov, practitioners of what the Communists had once opposed, but which was now an ingrained part of Russian life.

Free enterprise.

Chaliapin blamed the politicians for his nation's current state of degradation. When the homeland's soldiers were insulted, when they went unpaid, what could they do but find new ways to make ends meet? If that meant selling off the military hardware that Russia produced in abundance, stockpiling enough to kill every human on the planet a thousand times over, why should anyone feign surprise?

Russia had guns and bombs. The outside world had money.

Do the math.

Chaliapin cared nothing for how Russia's weapons were used in the so-called Third World—or in the West, for that matter. He'd been a covert warrior and a dirty fighter all of his adult life. Now, with nothing to defend except himself— his reputation and his very life—he was prepared to pull out all the stops.

Sadly, Lieutenant Pilkin and her friend were nowhere to be found.

Chaliapin had thought first of family, turned up an uncle, some cousins, and soon satisfied himself that they possessed no useful knowledge. There was no point in holding them, since none had seen Pilkin in more than a year, and in any case, they were more useful as bait, on the streets, than caged in the Lubyanka's dungeon.

Where friends were concerned, Bezmel's gunmen had killed the only one on record. Lieutenant Pilkin had acquaintances at work, not confidants. Chaliapin had unearthed no trace of any lovers since her breakup with a clerk from the Ministry of Energy, some two years earlier. If she was having any sex, it seemed to be a solitary enterprise—or else well covered and concealed from prying eyes.

In short, she was a ghost.

It wasn't difficult to lose a body or a soul in Moscow. Seventh largest city in the world, with some seventeen million registered citizens and who knew how many living off the proverbial grid. Still, when the machinery of State began to grind its way along in search of one or more specific persons, they were generally found sooner or later.

And that, from Chaliapin's point of view, was the problem.

For him, it would have to be *sooner,* rather than later. He couldn't stall General Bakunin for more than a couple of days—and one would be better. If he could wrap the troubling matter up by sundown, with no loose ends remaining, he might still be golden.

Otherwise…

Chaliapin was already planning sudden-exit strategies, but none of them struck him as realistic. Was there anywhere on Earth that he could run, where Bakunin's hunters wouldn't find him? Antarctica, perhaps, or somewhere in the steaming Congo swamps.

Chaliapin paged his driver and prepared to hit the streets in search of salvation.

Lake Ilmen, Novgorod Oblast

GENNADY SOKOLOV stood on the wide veranda of his second home, scanning the placid waters of Lake Ilmen. The lake sprawled over 379 square miles, fed by fifty-two rivers, and supported a fleet of fishing boats. From where he stood, Sokolov could see the hydroelectric dam on the Volkhov River to the north, or turn and watch the lights come on throughout Veliky Novgorod.

His sudden exit from Saint Petersburg had been a matter of survival, but Sokolov wasn't abandoning his links to civilization. Veliky Novgorod was the administrative center of Novgorod Oblast, situated on the M10 federal highway between Saint Petersburg and Moscow. Its name translated from Russia as "the Great New City," although it was hardly new. In fact, surviving records of its settlement date from 859 AD, nearly three hundred years before Moscow's first mention in print, and no other Russian city rivaled Veliky Novgorod's collection of medieval monuments.

That history was comforting to Sokolov, whose life work had erased so much potential history around the world. It pleased him to stand in the shadow of ancient structures and reflect on their longevity.

Of course, if he had lived in ancient times, he might have sold better and bigger catapults and siege engines to barbarian warriors from the east, permitting them to demolish the Novgorod Kremlin and stately Saint Sophia's Cathedral. Veliky Novgorod might not exist today.

Smiling at the whimsical thought, Sokolov turned away from his view and stepped back inside his villa. The house was slightly smaller than his home on Kotlin Island, but it still had all of the luxurious amenities befitting a man of his wealth and position.

Whatever *that* was.

Entrepreneur or fugitive? Hero or villain? Patron of revolution or accomplice to oppression?

Sokolov supposed that he was all of the above.

And he was on the verge of closing his most lucrative, most controversial business deal. The buyers—if they chose to buy, that was—would be arriving soon. If they agreed to Sokolov's terms and had cash or its equivalent on hand, he would be pleased to make the sale.

Whatever happened once the goods changed hands was none of his concern. Clearly, even his worst critics could grasp that logic. Sokolov was no more to blame for hatred, war or death in the world than a used-car salesman was responsible for drunk drivers or children run down in crosswalks.

Sometimes, Sokolov rankled at the injustice of it all. Human beings had been slaughtering one another in wars, rebellions, crusades and inquisitions for thousands of years before he was born. Who fashioned the clubs, forged the swords, strung the bows, fletched the arrows? Did history condemn the armorers who served Alexander the Great, Julius Caesar or Napoleon? Only since Hitler and the Krupp Trial had production of arms been labeled a crime—and Krupp's main offense had been using slave labor, not turning out guns by the thousands.

The hypocrisy rankled, of course. Nations like the United States and Israel made billions of dollars and shekels peddling lethal hardware around the world, to some of Earth's most repressive regimes. Both had used Sokolov as their agent on many occasions—but now they condemned him, and why? Because he refused to discriminate against certain paying customers on grounds of their race or religion?

Preposterous! What could possibly be more unfair?

He recognized their fear, of course, but that wasn't his problem. Sokolov hadn't designed their foreign policy, hadn't forced them to alienate the vast majority of nonwhite peoples on Earth.

He wasn't the disease. But he offered a cure.

Sokolov buzzed for Ivan Fet, preparing a smile for his new chief of security as Fet arrived. "Ivan," he said, "please double-check that everything is ready for our guests."

"Yes, sir."

That was the secret. It was all about respect.

Pulkovo Airport, Saint Petersburg

SAINT PETERSBURG'S airport had no customs or immigration checkpoints for domestic passengers, and Bolan was relieved to see no uniforms loitering around the hangar where Utkin parked his aircraft. Better yet, there was no sign of any goons waiting to spring a trap.

So far.

Pilkin paid Utkin the last installment of his fee while Bolan unloaded their baggage, reminding the pilot that he'd been hired to stick around and fly them back to Moscow on short notice. Utkin was all smiles with cash in hand, explaining how he would refuel and run the standard diagnostic tests on his airplane while they were gone.

Next up, collection of their rented car. Bolan assumed there would be English-speaking clerks on staff, but why draw the unwelcome notice to himself? Pilkin had booked the reservation by phone, before their departure from Moscow, using a false name and credit card number that Bolan provided, backed up by a toll-free "customer service" number that would connect any callers to Stony Man Farm. The card was good, its bills paid up and ID flexible.

The wonders of modern commerce and technology.

Bolan carried their duffel bags to the terminal and waited outside while Pilkin signed off on the car and collected its keys. He had a rough moment as two militiamen passed by, slowing as if they might decide to stop and question him, but a squawk from the radio one of them carried distracted the pair, and they passed on inside to deal with some problem.

Pilkin returned before they did, and Bolan allowed himself a sigh of relief, trailing her to the parking lot where hired cars stood in shiny, polished rows. Their ride was a stylish Geely MK four-door sedan, manufactured in China, which Pilkin said was nicknamed the "King Kong."

"Why's that?" he asked.

She shrugged. "Something about the headlights, I believe. Some people think they are too big, like eyes in a monster face. I don't see it, myself."

Bolan stowed their hardware in the Geely's backseat, while Pilkin settled in behind the wheel and turned the key. The King Kong's engine purred.

"Next stop," she told him, "is the waterfront. You know I didn't call ahead about the boat."

"We'll find something," the Executioner replied, exuding confidence.

The problem, he guessed, wouldn't lie in reaching Kotlin Island. It would be surviving, once they landed.

CHAPTER FIFTEEN

Saint Petersburg was often called the most Western, in terms of its culture and population. Its historic center and surrounding monuments were formally recognized by the United Nations Educational, Scientific and Cultural Organization's World Heritage Committee as one of 878 World Heritage Sites scattered around the globe.

Tourists who viewed the city's marvels benefited from Saint Petersburg's celebrated "white nights"—twilight lasted all night from mid-May through mid-July—but that phenomenon worked against visitors preoccupied with covert tasks best performed in darkness. Neither was the city's weather conducive to night-prowling. Average noonday temperatures of seventy-two degrees Fahrenheit in July drop to a median of minus thirty-one in winter, with an average yearly temperature around forty-two degrees. Bolan and Pilkin would miss the snow that blanketed Saint Petersburg for an average of 123 days each year, but they would still feel the night's chill on Kotlin Island.

If they got that far.

Step one was crossing the seven miles of Neva Bay that separated Saint Petersburg from Kronstadt, on the island. They could ride the public ferry out to Kotlin, but they couldn't take a hostage back to Moscow with a boatload of civilian witnesses, so that was out. They'd also need a set of wheels on Kotlin, which hadn't been booked ahead of time, for fear of tipping Sokolov that company was on its way.

Pilkin drove them to the waterfront, cruising along the

docks past large warehouses and ships lying at anchor, loading cargo for transit through the Gulf of Finland to the Baltic Sea, then through the Kattegat and Skagerrak to reach the North Sea and Atlantic beyond. They rolled past fishing piers and sleazy sailors' dives to reach a section where charter boats sat at their moorings, waiting for clients.

"We need a special kind of captain," Pilkin told Bolan. "One, I think, with the soul of a pirate."

"You have one in mind?" Bolan asked her.

"Perhaps."

"Why am I not surprised?"

"I make all kinds of contacts, working for the FSB," she said.

"And are they known to headquarters?"

"Not this one," she assured him. "We've done business in the past, but nothing on the record. It would be…too much, you know?"

He knew, all right. Some things were best not committed to writing. Hell, some things were best *forgotten,* but that didn't mean their memory could be erased.

"Suppose he's out?" Bolan asked.

"Then, we find another pirate. Or a captain that will trust his boat to customers who pay a premium, perhaps?"

Bolan knew that tune. Pay enough up front, and some people would let you drive away with their firstborn. A boat was easier, but nonetheless expensive. And you couldn't front the marked-down price of a depreciated model, either.

Bolan hoped Pilkin's pirate would be present and accounted for when they came calling. Otherwise, his war chest would be critically depleted, maybe tapped. And there was still a chance that he'd be needing ready cash in quantity before he wrapped the Russian job.

Pilkin found the dockside office she was seeking, though it barely qualified for that description. At first glance, it looked more like a run-down garage with a boat moored behind it, but Bolan knew appearances could be deceiving.

The man who greeted them looked like a pirate, including the black patch that covered his left eye socket. In place of a tricorn hat, however, he wore a stained and faded baseball cap. His denim shirt and pants, rough hands and scuffed work boots bore testimony to the fact that he wasn't a summer sailor.

Pilkin introduced him as Carlo Kasatkin, then spoke rapidly in Russian until the one-eyed captain smiled and shook her hand a second time.

Smiling herself, she told Bolan, "We have a ride."

Ilmen, Novgorod Oblast

"I DO NOT TRUST this man," Faisal Kelani said.

"Nor I," Yazan al-Kami added.

"We are not required to trust him," Ahmed Bajjah replied. "He is a mercenary who cares nothing for our people or our cause. But his possession of the weapons has been verified. Our mission has one purpose only—to negotiate a final price."

"This all could be a trap," Kelani repeated. His objection had been voiced so often that it had become monotonous.

"In which case," Bajjah said, "it is too late for us to save ourselves."

To illustrate his point, Bajjah gestured with open hands, reminding his companions that they occupied a speeding limousine with guards on board, provided by their host. There was nowhere for them to go, nowhere to hide. They spoke Arabic, to preserve a vestige of privacy, but for all Bajjah knew, the guards might be linguists.

Kelani and al-Kami made no further protests. It wasn't their place to argue with Bajjah, though he made a point of welcoming sincere advice. Beyond a certain point, however, protest might be labeled insubordination, and its consequences were severe.

The Sword of Allah, which all three men proudly represented, wasn't a democracy.

Bajjah, highest ranking of the three and rated number four or five within the group at large by Western manhunters, was forty-one years old, a Saudi from a wealthy family who had abandoned luxury and privilege to wage unending war against the state of Israel and its global allies. He was branded a terrorist kingpin in warrants issued by the United States, Great Britain and Interpol, none of which had thus far been able to catch him.

Kelani, Bajjah's friend and second in command for this specific mission, was a thirty-five-year-old Palestinian Arab whose hatred for Israelis knew no limits. When not engaged in errands such as this one, or delivering pep talks to young would-be suicide bombers, Kelani spent his time culling library archives for proof that a vast Jewish conspiracy had dominated Earth from the time of the Crusades into the present century. Being a single-minded scholar, he found evidence no matter where he looked, fueling the rage that sprang from slaughter of his kinfolk by Israeli bombs on the West Bank.

Al-Kami was the youngest of the trio, a twenty-five-year-old Jordanian with four years of service to the Sword of Allah behind him. His name, so far, was unknown in the West, and Bajjah hoped to keep it that way, for a while longer, at least. Al-Kami had already distinguished himself in several actions against the American Crusaders and was being groomed for bigger, better things. If only he could learn to mask his feelings more effectively, to bite his tongue when speaking out was dangerous, he might survive to realize his full potential for the cause.

Their mission was relatively simple. They would negotiate

payment for weapons to punish Israel and the West for their crimes and bring the filthy infidels to their knees.

The Soviet Union had offered covert support to various anti-Israeli and anti-American groups for decades, including gifts or bargain sales of weapons, ammunition and explosives. Despite its godless doctrine, the Russian Communist Party had been generous to the Sword of Allah and similar groups.

But the new, improved Russia was even better. Seemingly lawless and perched on the brink of bankruptcy, the state's "democratic" regime had adopted a pragmatic approach to regaining solvency.

Everything was for sale.

In 2008 Moscow had acknowledged a cache of 5,200 nuclear weapons—the world's largest stockpile of earth-shattering tools. The U.S. State Department questioned that figure in April 2009, claiming that Moscow held a mere 3,909 nuclear warheads, versus America's 5,576. Bajjah's independent sources had verified that Russia's land-based Strategic Rocket Forces possessed 489 missiles with 1,788 warheads, while twelve submarines in the Strategic Fleet carried 609 warheads and the Russian air force boasted 258 bombers packing 924 cruise missiles.

But the specific numbers were irrelevant.

The Sword of Allah didn't need a thousand warheads, or a hundred intercontinental ballistic missiles. What the movement needed was a small, dependable supply of what the Western media had dubbed "loose nukes."

Whatever Russia claimed today, it was a fact that prior to 1991, her arsenal had included more than twenty-seven thousand nuclear warheads, plus enough weapons-grade uranium and plutonium to triple that number. Subtract 5,200 or 3,909 from twenty-seven thousand, and the discrepancy was obvious.

Where had the other nukes gone?

Some, it seemed, had found their way into the hands of one Gennady Sokolov. And he was willing to share.

All that remained was to negotiate a price.

Kotlin Island

CARLO KASATKIN talked nonstop while they were crossing Neva Bay, from cast-off to arrival at the Kronstadt waterfront. Once he had taken Bolan's measure, the captain switched from straight Russian to iffy English, regaling his passengers with tales of smuggling, shipwrecks, sea monsters, storms that strained credulity to the breaking point and beyond.

In short, he was good company. He asked no questions and agreed to await their return with "a friend."

Kronstadt was once considered the world's most fortified seaport, with forty-two military installations lining Kotlin Island's shore. Never captured by an enemy force since Peter the Great seized Kotlin from Sweden in 1703, the island and its primary settlement remain a major staging area for Russia's Baltic fleet, guarding the approaches to Saint Petersburg.

Kasatkin radioed ahead from the midpoint of their seven-mile journey, interrupting his choice anecdotes long enough to arrange for two friends to meet their boat and help with docking. That accomplished, he shook Bolan's hand and planted loud kisses on both of Pilkin's cheeks before bidding them farewell.

"I see you soon," he added as they disembarked.

I hope so, Bolan thought, but kept it to himself.

On shore, Pilkin led him to a storefront office bearing the logo of an international car rental agency. The place wasn't much to look at, but they provided a new Volga Siber four-door sedan with a 2.4-liter GEMA engine, manufactured in South Korea by the unlikely combination of Chrysler, Mitsubishi and Hyundai, joining forces as the Global Engine

Manufacturing Alliance. Its resemblance to the Chrysler Sebring and Dodge Stratus was anything but coincidental.

Once behind the Volga's wheel, Pilkin wasted no time getting out of town. She crossed the Peter and Catherine canals, rolled past the huge Naval Cathedral without a second glance and rolled on to the northwest. She slowed once Kronstadt proper was behind them, since the island was only seven and a half miles long. Rushed as they felt, arriving at their destination without something in the way of preparation could be fatal.

"This is where he killed your FBI agents," Pilkin reminded Bolan.

"Yes."

"And there were many of them," she added.

"Right."

"So, what is our advantage, then?"

"We don't play by the rules," Bolan replied.

PILKIN PARKED off-road, behind a line of trees that had been decorative, once upon a time, but now were growing wild and swathed around their trunks with thorny undergrowth that screened their sedan from the highway. Sokolov's villa lay a quarter mile farther west, across overgrown fields that would cover them most of the way.

They suited up for battle, modesty forgotten in the moment, changing out of stylish street clothes into denims, strapping on their weapons for the hike to Sokolov's hideaway. Despite his air of confidence, Bolan couldn't help thinking of the Hostage Rescue Team that had been shot to ribbons just a few short days earlier, trying to lift their target from the same hardsite. The G-men would've been equipped with body armor, doubtless with at least one sniper covering them from a distance, possibly in radio contact with the authorities.

And they were massacred.

"You know—"

"I'm coming," Pilkin interrupted. "Don't try to talk me out of it."

"Okay."

He had considered waiting for nightfall, going in dark, but it felt too risky, wasting all that extra time on Kotlin Island when they could be moving, putting ground between themselves and any pursuers bent on retrieving Sokolov once they'd snatched him.

If they snatched him.

A team of U.S. Marshals was standing by in Saint Petersburg, warrants in hand, all signed and countersigned in Moscow, to accept delivery of the fugitive. Bolan had their chief's number and had dialed it from the boat, delivering a terse stand-by report. He wouldn't call again until they had collected Sokolov—or if they missed him.

Should worse come to worst, and they found themselves in a trap with no exit, there wouldn't be time—or any need—for a call. The marshals would know that they'd failed when their corpses were found.

And someone else could make the next attempt.

Maybe to punch Sokolov's ticket next time, rather than trying to take him alive.

Bolan knew they had trouble a hundred yards out. The villa was too quiet for a place with tenants at home. Sokolov might not use his fireplace, but an occupied house still made noise. Furnaces or air conditioners obeyed the commands from their thermostats. People talked, laughed, sobbed or sneezed. They watched TV or listened to the radio. They ran water and flushed toilets. Even if housebound, they still moved around behind windows.

But none of that was going on. For all intents and purposes, the place was dead.

They crouched outside for fifteen minutes, watching, listening, waiting for any sign of life. There were no vehicles in evidence, no movement anywhere inside or out, although none of the drapes were drawn.

At last, Bolan and Pilkin approached the house. Not stealthily, but moving in the open, daring anyone in hiding to reveal himself. When nothing happened, Bolan knew they'd come too late.

He broke in, anyway, and moved through rooms that Sokolov had occupied until quite recently. The smell of humans lingered in the house, but it was fading. The previous night's meal was nothing but a whiff of garlic on dead air.

"Where has he gone?" Pilkin asked.

"I don't know," Bolan told her, "but I'm going to find out."

Ekaterininsky Park, Moscow

TARAS MOROZOV'S limousine cruised slowly north on Olimpiyskiy Avenue, taking its time like a great hungry shark, while other traffic flowed around it. As rude as Muscovite drivers normally were, none cursed or blew his or her horn at the limo. All seemed to know it was trouble on wheels.

The limo's passenger compartment smelled like an indoor shooting range, thick with the stench of cordite. Its occupants had opened windows and turned up the air conditioner, but the reek was slow to dissipate. Around their shoes, the carpet glittered with spent cartridge casings.

Morozov loved it.

He hadn't been hunting like this since his early twenties, when a gang war rocked Moscow for long weeks on end. In those days, everyone was fair game for their rivals and for the militia. There'd been no rules to speak of, no treaties setting turf aside for one gang or another. Things were much more peaceful now or, rather, had been until very recently—but if Morozov was honest with himself, he missed the old days.

"I don't see him," he said to the soldiers around him.

"Is this the old Gypsy?" one of them asked.

"Matéo Danko," Morozov said. "They're called Romani, now."

"I know this one," another soldier said. "He claims to be the king of something, but I can't remember what."

"The King of Roma Everywhere," Morozov said. "He is a little man with big ideas."

"The kind that gets stepped on," one of his men said, grinning.

"Not until I hear whatever it is he's wanting to tell me," Morozov replied. "Get that straight."

The call had come in on his cell phone, Danko himself announcing that he could point Morozov toward prime targets in his feud with the Obshina. The imaginary king had mentioned no names, but Morozov hoped he might learn the whereabouts of Aldo Shishani himself. That head would be a prize, indeed, when he delivered it to Leonid Bezmel.

"Is that him?" asked a shooter seated forward, near the divider that screened their driver from view.

Morozov followed his man's pointing finger and saw Matéo Danko's small, slender figure planted on a park bench, forty yards or so back from the street.

"Stop here," he ordered.

His driver started to protest. "Sir, the police—"

"Stop here, I said!"

The limo stopped dead, idling at the curb, still with no bleats of outrage from the cars behind it that had to wait for an opening in traffic on the driver's side. Morozov supposed that Muscovites weren't as stupid as they might appear on casual inspection.

"Out!" he barked, and crowded close behind his soldiers as they piled out of the limousine. They tried to screen Morozov, scanning the park for danger despite his impatience.

The stunted, self-styled king had seen him now and had

his hand raised, waving, like a long-lost kinsman greeting family at a railroad depot. Morozov thought the old man had to be getting senile. If this turned out to be some kind of joke or product of the Gypsy's second childhood, Morozov would be pleased to leave him leaking on the bench for sanitation workers to remove. He would—

Morozov heard the wet splat a microsecond before some kind of warm fluid spattered his cheek and lapel. Blinking, he spun in that direction and beheld one of his guards collapsing, half of his face shot away.

Two of the others grabbed Morozov then, shoving him back toward the limo's open door, as the first echo of gunfire reached their ears. Morozov managed a hasty backward glance and saw Matéo Danko running like a teenage track star for the far side of the park.

"Bastard!" he snarled.

Morozov had one foot inside the limo when another of his men grunted, a barnyard sound, and crumpled to the pavement. Still clutching Morozov's arm, the dead or dying soldier almost dragged him back and down into the gutter, but the others wrenched his hand loose, shoved their boss into the limousine and piled in after him.

"Go! Go!" he shouted at the driver, even as the car began to move. Another bullet struck its armored flank and spurred the limo onward, urging it to greater speed.

"A trap!" Morozov raged. "I want that little bastard! Send the word!"

Kotlin Island

"No COMPANY," Carlo Kasatkin said, frowning, as Bolan and Pilkin climbed the gangplank to board his vessel. It seemed to be an observation, nothing more.

"We'll pay you for the extra passage, anyway," Pilkin said in English.

"Sure, sure. I just wonder if we're waiting."

"No," Bolan replied. "We're heading back."

The captain nodded, let it go and called out to a helper lounging on the dock. Five minutes later, they were under way, retracing their watery path toward Saint Petersburg.

"You think he knew somehow that we were coming?" Pilkin inquired.

Bolan shook his head. "Who was there to tip him? Utkin only knew that we were flying to Saint Petersburg, and Long John Silver didn't know who we were looking for on Kotlin. Even if he had, we know he didn't call ahead."

"What, then?"

"Maybe he guessed, or played the odds. He could be spooked, with what's been going on in Moscow, so soon after HRT came knocking on his door."

"The FBI, that is?" Pilkin asked.

This time, a nod. "He has to know Justice won't let it rest with that. The welcoming committee that was waiting for me at the airport says he's wired in, somehow, and he can't be happy that his men down south keep missing us."

"I should know where he's going," Pilkin said. "There's a flat in Moscow, where he stays when he's in town on business, but he won't go there to hide."

"Someplace with privacy," Bolan suggested. "Someplace he can defend. Maybe ride out a siege."

The FSB agent shook her head. "Nowhere that I can think of. He has friends, of course. And there could easily be properties that have escaped official notice."

"So, we start from scratch," Bolan replied.

"In Moscow?"

"What else have we got?"

"I feel that we have wasted too much time," Pilkin said.

"It wasn't wasted," Bolan said. "The pot's still boiling. All we have to do now is reach in and grab someone who has the intel that we need."

"You have someone in mind?"

"A few," Bolan replied. "I'd like to start off with the *Mafiya,* assuming that he'll stay in touch to close on any deals they might have working. If that busts out, we'll try your major at the FSB."

Pilkin's eyes glinted at Bolan. "I would like that very much."

"Bearing in mind that what we want is information, first."

"Of course. But afterward, perhaps a little justice?"

"I don't see why not."

"It's time for vodka!" Carlo Kasatkin called out from the wheelhouse. Grinning, he added, "Come join me! I tell you of the time a shark ate my first mate!"

"Sounds tasty," Bolan said.

Pilkin frowned and said, "I know exactly how he felt."

CHAPTER SIXTEEN

Lake Ilmen, Novgorod Oblast

Gennady Sokolov was known from Bangkok to Beirut and Belfast as a gracious host. He treated all guests equally, giving them shares of his considerable charm, and did his homework in advance to avoid embarrassing gaffes.

Therefore, being conscious of Islamic law, he didn't offer alcohol to his three visitors. When they sat down to eat, there'd be no pork or any other forbidden items on the menu.

First, however, there was business to discuss.

When his three guests were settled on a long, deep couch with coffee cups in front of them, Sokolov addressed himself to their obvious leader.

"You have, I think, decided to avail yourself of my services?"

"If the price is right," Ahmed Bajjah replied.

"Of course. It goes without saying." Sokolov paused, conjuring a thoughtful frown from his trick bag of expressions for all occasions. "The question, then, is one of value. Warheads and weapons-grade material, as you may be aware, are presently available in varied size and quantity. Some reckon that this means we have a buyer's market, but such objects have intrinsic value and are costly to procure. The risk involved, you understand."

"Of course," Bajjah replied.

"I'm fortunate," Sokolov said, "in having a variety of items presently available or within reach. Some warheads, weighing several hundred kilos, would require a truck for transport. Others may be more convenient for individual transport. As for weapons-grade material, enriched uranium-235 or plutonium-239, I have access to large quantities. You may purchase by the pound, as if shopping for groceries."

"More expensive than goat's cheese, I trust," Bajjah said.

Sokolov laughed at the joke, as expected. Humor was a valuable tool for closing sales. "Unfortunately, true," he said, when the hilarity had waned. "If you have some idea concerning the size of device you may want…"

"Large enough to make a lasting impression," Bajjah replied.

"The basic unit—what is generally called a Hiroshima bomb—ensures total destruction within a one-mile radius of ground zero. Severe damage extends to one mile and a quarter, moderate damage to two miles, light damage to three and a half miles. Of course, that only represents destruction from the blast itself. Thermal radiation comprises thirty percent of the Hiroshima bomb's destructive force, ionizing radiation, while residual radiation—fallout—comprises five to ten percent, depending on the weapon and materials employed."

"And if we wanted something larger?"

"It is almost certainly available," Sokolov said, speaking with every confidence.

"Something Manhattan-size, for instance?"

"Certainly. Manhattan's total area is roughly thirty-four square miles. Ten megaton would flatten the financial district. One hundred would ensure destruction from the Battery to Central Park, plus most of Brooklyn. Also Hoboken, New Jersey, if anyone cares. Five hundred megatons… Well, you get the idea."

"Portability remains an issue," Bajjah said.

"The W72 tactical device, America's smallest, is sixteen inches long, eleven inches in diameter and weighs fifty pounds. It yields six hundred tons of force. I have Russian items on hand with substantially greater power. If three or four were introduced into a city like Manhattan simultaneously, the result would be impressive.

"Assembled and delivered to a neutral country," Sokolov went on, "the cost is two-point-five million dollars, or eight million rubles."

"It's expensive," Bajjah said.

"As the Americans say, you get what you pay for. Component parts without assembly would be slightly cheaper. Cash-and-carry, with your men assuming all the risks of transport, also saves a bit."

"We are not made of money, after all," Bajjah stated. "Despite all Western propaganda, we have no oil wells."

"Perhaps I could discount the rate if you're buying in volume."

When Bajjah smiled, Sokolov saw a bright, prophetic flash of gold.

Moscow

THE FLIGHT BACK from Saint Petersburg seemed twice as long to Bolan as the same trip heading north. That was impossible, of course. They even had a tailwind on the southward journey, helping them along. Still, he was burdened with a sense of wasted time and effort. Every minute he spent searching empty homes or flying between cities was a gift of time to Sokolov and company.

They followed Pilkin's plan, touching down at Sheremetyevo International Airport and renting a car for the drive back to Vnukovo International. Valeri Utkin pocketed his bonus and went off to kill time in the airport's bar, while Pilkin and Bolan made the extra trip.

No one was staking out the car, but they spent some time checking for GPS trackers that might have been added during their absence. Finding none, they stowed their gear and struck off for Moscow proper, eighteen miles to the northeast.

Pilkin had called ahead while they were airborne, speaking to an acquaintance with the militia. She'd started out by probing cautiously, to see if any kind of all-points bulletin in her name had been issued, but there seemed to be no general alarm. Whatever might be happening inside the FSB, her so-called comrades were playing it close to the vest.

Her other questions, couched in professional terms, had elicited news of a near-miss attack on Taras Morozov, second in command of the Solntsevskaya Brotherhood. A couple of Morozov's men were dead, and he was being questioned by militia detectives in regard to those deaths and some others, all occurring recently. If Pilkin desired to speak with Morozov, she should be quick about it. Lawyers were already circling and demanding his release.

At the moment, Morozov was still confined to militia headquarters.

Bolan and Pilkin made it across town in time to find Morozov's limousine still waiting outside the drab police building. The rear driver's side was scarred by bullet strikes, but the armor had done its job. Four guards, one of them wearing a chauffeur's uniform, were clustered by the car, awaiting the return of their lord and master.

Pilkin drove past, boxed the block, and brought them back around to park up range from the stretch with the car's engine idling. Anything they did from that point on would be a deadly gamble, facing both Morozov's men and the militia.

Bolan wasn't concerned about the hardmen. He was focused on the cops, remembering his private pledge that he would never drop the hammer on a lawman, regardless of the circumstances or the provocation.

"Here he comes," Pilkin said.

"Ready?" he asked her.

"As I'll ever be."

"Let's roll."

She eased the car forward, traveling at something close to walking pace along the curb, directly opposite the limousine. Bolan watched Taras Morozov approach the limo, flanked by two sleek lawyers, with another couple—maybe junior partners—bringing up the rear. When they were level with the limousine, Morozov homing on its open door, Bolan went EVA.

One of the guards saw him coming, barked something in Russian and died with the words in his throat. Bolan's 93-R coughed through its suppressor and kept on coughing as the guards dropped in their tracks. Two, three, four down.

The lawyers weren't retained to take a bullet for their client. Scattering, they left Morozov on his own, exposed, as Bolan ran to close the gap. Morozov, to his credit, stood and waited for it, almost standing at attention, snarling in the face of death.

Bolan cracked him across the nose, just hard enough to stun the man, then grabbed his arm and hustled him across the street.

"Don't dawdle," the Executioner said. "You're late for an important date."

"AND IF YOU'RE NOT to blame," Leonid Bezmel asked, "who is?"

His voice rose to the level of a shriek on the last words. Four lawyers cringed before him, their faces white as typing paper.

"Well?" he challenged them, when no one spoke. "Answer!"

The oldest of the four and senior partner of their firm, Orest Koltsov, eventually found his voice. "Mr. Bezmel," he fairly whispered, "you sent bodyguards for Mr. Morozov."

"The guards," Bezmel reminded him, "were wise enough to die without abandoning their master. You four—"

Koltsov dared to interrupt him, saying, "They had guns. We only have our legal papers. We're not fighting men, you understand?"

"I understand the four of you ran off like frightened children, and you can't even describe the man who took Taras, who cut my soldiers down like targets in a shooting gallery. What good are you to me?"

The younger of the two senior attorneys, Stepan Grinin, raised a cautious hand as if he were a boy at school asking to use the lavatory.

"What?" Bezmel demanded.

"Sir, the man was tall and—"

"Had a gun. I heard your useless shit the first time, Grinin. Did none of you see his face? Perhaps his car? I realize that you were busy running, but the color of his hair, at least?"

"Dark hair," one of the cringing flunkies said. "I saw dark hair."

"And nothing else? From anyone?" Bezmel inquired.

The four stood mute, shaking their heads.

"All right." He glowered at the young man who had spoken. "What's your name?"

"Lev Zhukovsky, sir."

"Good. Lev Zhukovsky, since your eyes appear to be the sharpest of the lot, you choose."

"Choose…what, sir?" Frightened now.

"Which of these other slugs I punish for their cowardice. Since they see nothing, one of them will leave his eyes with me today."

Zhukovsky quailed. "Sir, I cannot—"

"Or volunteer yourself. It's all the same to me. You have five minutes to decide."

The other three had Zhukovsky surrounded, jabbering at him in terror, as Bezmel stepped into the anteroom beside his office.

"Well? You heard?" he asked the man who waited there.

"I heard," replied Nikolai Tatlin, Morozov's chief lieutenant and his strong right arm.

"What do *you* think?"

"Shishani," Tatlin said without a moment's hesitation. "He blames us for the attacks he's suffered. He would strike back in this way."

"And snatch Taras, instead of simply killing him?"

"For information," Tatlin said.

"Then he may be alive," Bezmel replied.

"It's possible."

"And I shall never know, unless I ask."

"Talk to Shishani?"

"Why not?" Bezmel asked.

"Sir, your security—"

"I'll use that new invention called the telephone."

Embarrassed, Tatlin dipped his head. "Yes, sir."

"Of course, Aldo will claim he's innocent. And there's a chance it may be true. We still have Mr. Matthew Cooper and the woman from the FSB at large and unaccounted for."

"The lawyers didn't see a woman," Tatlin said.

"Unless it's written in a legal brief or on their paychecks, those four are blind."

"You're right, sir."

"Has it been five minutes yet?" Bezmel inquired.

"Closer to three," Tatlin replied.

"No matter," Bezmel said. "Go and collect my eyes."

ANOTHER WAREHOUSE, on another Moscow waterfront. Pilkin said the place was sometimes used for training exercises by the FSB's SWAT team. At one end of the cavernous interior, folding partitions stood together with a lot of objects that resembled stage sets from a theater.

"The walls and other pieces of the kill house," she told Bolan.

Now his mind put the pieces together. Kill houses were

structures—or sets—used by commandos to simulate various do-or-die operations. Hostage rescue, wrangling barricaded gunmen, searching for ticking bombs. Evacuating wounded from an urban battle zone. The kill house had it all.

Bolan had been there, himself, in his Green Beret days. Blank ammunition was standard, but live-fire exercises weren't uncommon for elite warriors, whether they served civilian law-enforcement agencies or military units such as Special Forces or the U.S. Navy SEALs.

Or Spetznaz, sure. Why not?

From the assorted furniture on hand, he picked a straight-backed wooden chair and carried it back to the midpoint of the warehouse. Pilkin was waiting for him with their hostage and a roll of silver duct tape. Morozov was muttering something to Pilkin as Bolan approached. It prompted her to pistol-whip him, opening one cheek and nearly dropping the man to his knees.

"Don't break his jaw," Bolan advised. "He needs to talk."

"I tell you nothing, bitch," the mobster said with a sneer. "If you have a brain, be smart and kill me now. You're dead already, anyway."

"You want to die, I'll make a note," Bolan replied. "But first, take off your clothes."

"Strip me yourself," Morozov said, and spit toward Bolan's feet.

"One last chance," Bolan said.

"Go fuck yourself!"

"Fair enough," Bolan said. Then he drove a fist into Morozov's gut, putting his weight behind it. While Morozov was vomiting, Bolan ripped off the man's clothes, leaving the mobster naked, huddled on the chilly concrete floor.

"Now, as you see," Bolan pressed on, "you're free to make this difficult or easy on yourself."

"I'm not a fucking rat," Morozov wheezed, still rocking and clutching his gut.

"Right, then. Get in the chair."

Morozov blinked at him and said, "I can't stand up."

Bolan drew the Beretta 93-R as he said, "Then you have no use for your knees."

"Wait!" Morozov raised a hand, as if mere flesh and bones could stop bullets. Slowly, laboriously, he crawled to the chair and hauled himself aboard it.

Bolan plied the duct tape swiftly, expertly, securing Morozov's arms and legs. Then the man was held upright in the chair with more loops wrapped around his hairy chest. Removing it would hurt like hell, if Morozov was breathing.

"No matter what you do," the Russian mobster said, "I will not talk!"

"Then let me tell you what we know already," Bolan said. "You're Taras Morozov, second in command of the Solntsevskaya Brotherhood, heir apparent to the throne when Bezmel buys the farm."

"What is this farm?"

"When he kicks off," Bolan explained. "Steps on a rainbow. Bites the big one. When he dies."

"I say nothing about the Brotherhood. Do your worst to me. I die knowing that others will avenge me and your screams will echo over Moscow."

"I'm not interested in your Family," Bolan said.

Morozov blinked at him and asked, "What, then?"

"Gennady Sokolov."

"That one? What about him?"

"We went up to see him on his island, but he stood us up," Bolan said. "What we need, now, is his forwarding address."

"You lost him, eh?" Morozov chuckled. "That's a good one."

"No address? No pointers?"

Morozov smiled. "I tell you nothing."

"Okay," Bolan replied. "Let's try it the hard way."

ALDO SHISHANI HESITATED before accepting the telephone from his houseman. He was still processing the announcement that Leonid Bezmel wanted to speak with him personally.

"Are you sure?" Shishani asked.

"As sure as I can be, sir."

The rival mobsters hadn't spoken directly in years, and then only to accuse each other of poaching on restricted turf. Otherwise, they passed messages in the form of bodies, bombs and bullets. Now, in the midst of their worst war ever, why would Bezmel phone Shishani, of all people?

Reluctantly, he took the phone, thankful that his hand didn't tremble.

"Hello?"

"Shut up!" the once-familiar voice snapped at him.

Shishani scowled, replying, "How can we talk if I shut the fuck up, you piece of shit?"

"You listen, while I tell you who's a piece of shit," Bezmel raged. "I want Taras returned alive. I want him *now!*"

Shishani's scowl turned to a puzzled frown. "It seems you've lost your senses," he replied. "I do not have your monkey."

"He was taken!" Bezmel raged. "Four of my men were killed! I want him back!"

"I'd gladly send him home in pieces," Shishani said, "if I had the prick."

"You deny it, then?"

"It's not denial, just a fact."

"Who took him, then?" Bezmel demanded.

"It's a pity that you've lost what little mind you ever had," Shishani taunted. "Can you not think of anybody else who might have done this thing?"

"I don't— You mean…?"

"While you were hunting me, someone's been hunting you," Shishani answered. "Hunting both of us."

Bezmel was silent for a moment, then spit back, "You lie, and now you're fucked!"

"*I'm* fucked?" Shishani replied, furious. "Show your face, and we'll find out!"

"You'll see me soon enough," Bezmel assured him. "My face is the last thing you'll *ever* see."

The line went dead before Shishani could respond. He clutched the phone, fighting an urge to slam it on the floor and crush it underfoot. The blind fury passed after a long, white-knuckled moment.

"Fetch Magen. Now!" Shishani told his houseman.

The man hastened to obey. Magen Manaev stood before his master moments later. "What has happened, Aldo?" he inquired.

"I've had a call from Leonid," Shishani said.

"From Leonid? *Bezmel?*"

"The very same. It seems he's lost his second in command."

"Morozov."

"Yes. And he blames us."

"He's wrong. I'd know if any of our men had been so lucky."

"As I told him. But the prick's lost his mind. He's coming after us."

"What else has he been doing, since last night?" Manaev asked.

"I tell you, he's insane. Better to find him first, but if we can't…we must prepare for anything. He might come here himself. Double the guards."

"Aldo, it means pulling more soldiers from the streets."

"Then do it! And have *all* the others searching for Bezmel. We won't have any peace until he's dead."

"The others? Cooper and the woman?"

Shishani made a sour face, as if he'd tasted something rotten. "Never mind them," he replied. "They have a flair for finding us. We must be ready to repel all enemies."

"I'll see to it."

"While you do that," Shishani said, "I'll have a word with some of our associates in the militia. Perhaps they can distract Bezmel—or find him, at the very least, since we're not able to."

"I'll find him, Aldo. Give me time."

"Time is one thing we may not have," Shishani said.

"DO YOU BELIEVE him, then?" Pilkin asked.

"I need to check it out," Bolan replied.

"More traveling, I take it?"

"There's a trick I'd like to try before we hit the road again."

"Oh, yes?"

Veliky Novgorod and its neighboring lake lay roughly 325 miles north of Moscow. Call it a five-hour drive, or a two-hour flight if they went back to Valeri Utkin. Either way, Bolan preferred to take out some insurance if he could.

Taras Morozov had, at last, provided them with the supposed location of Gennady Sokolov's preferred retreat, with numbers for the landline and the weapons dealer's last known cell phone. He'd rolled over, finally, not from a threat of pain, but rather in reliance on a promise that he'd be released once "Matthew Cooper's" business with Sokolov was finished.

"He is not my Family," the mobster had declared, remaining steadfast to his boss and to the Solntsevskaya Brotherhood.

"I need your help," Bolan told Pilkin.

"Of course."

"I want to see if Sokolov is at his home-away-from-home, but without spooking him. A call could do it, but I don't speak Russian."

"Sokolov speaks many languages."

"But I don't plan on speaking to him."

Pilkin was frowning now. "Explain this, please."

"I want to call the house, impersonating Morozov, and *ask* to speak with him. I'll get a flunky first, and if he goes to fetch the boss, that tells me he's at home. No one around him would expect a member of the *Mafiya* to call up speaking English."

"And you hang up before he answers?"

"That's the ticket."

"Don't you think he may be curious?"

"I'm counting on it," Bolan said.

"We should assume that he has caller identification."

"That's why I'll be calling from Morozov's cell phone."

"And if Sokolov returns the call?"

"He'll get voice mail."

"You don't think he'll try calling Leonid Bezmel, in that case?"

Bolan had already considered it. "I grant you, it's a gamble," he replied. "My gut tells me he'll wait to hear from Morozov. But if he calls the boss, what can they tell him? Morozov is off the grid."

"Kidnapped. You don't think hearing *that* will frighten Sokolov?"

"Not if he's safe in Novgorod, three hundred-something miles away."

"He's closer to the action now than in Saint Petersburg."

"But no one's linked him to the new site," Bolan said. "It wasn't in your files, or mine. Which means the CIA and FBI were also clueless."

"But his cell…"

"Goes with him," Bolan said. "It doesn't give a caller his location, just long-distance access. My best guess, if he calls Bezmel and finds out that Morozov's gone missing, Sokolov's more likely to ditch his cell phone than bug out to a new hideaway."

"Perhaps," Pilkin said, then added, "What do you want from me?"

"A bit of scripting. I have a decent understanding of proper Russian. Teach me enough slang to introduce myself and ask for the boss, and listen in to help me through if anything goes wrong."

"You don't ask me to make this call."

"And you know why," Bolan replied.

"Because no gangster lets a woman do his business?"

"Right again."

"Someday a woman will surprise you all."

"It happens every day," Bolan assured her.

"I'll call Valeri now," she said, "and have him standing ready."

"Good idea."

"You're calling Sokolov right now?"

"Not yet." Bolan was looking past her, toward Taras Morozov in his straight-backed chair.

"First," he said, "I have to see if I can arrange to have someone pick up our friend."

CHAPTER SEVENTEEN

It worked.

Using the speaker function on Taras Morozov's cell phone, Bolan dialed the landline number he'd obtained for Sokolov's retreat outside Veliky Novgorod and heard the distant telephone ring twice before one of their target's housemen answered.

They'd rehearsed a brief wrong-number dodge, in case Sokolov picked up the phone, Pilkin confident that she could recognize his voice, but they were golden when a stranger growled, "Hello?"

Closing his eyes and hoping to approximate the proper Muscovite accent, Bolan announced in Russian, "This is Morozov, calling from Moscow. Put Gennady on the line."

The first-name usage made Sokolov's gofer hesitate before he asked, "Who did you say?"

"Taras Morozov," Bolan snarled. "Don't make me say it again, asshole."

He'd thought the *asshole* was over-the-top, but Pilkin had assured him it suited Morozov's personality, and she was right.

"Okay, okay," the flunky muttered. "Hang on while I get him."

Bolan severed the connection then, and switched Morozov's cell to voice mail before he dropped it into an overstuffed chair that was part of the FSB kill house decor. It might sit there for weeks before anyone dropped by and noticed, long after their work was completed.

One way or another.

"So, we're finished here?" Pilkin asked.

"We are."

"Valeri's looking forward to another flight, so soon. He says the way you pay him, he won't have to work again this month."

"As long as he's around to fly us back from Novgorod," Bolan replied. He didn't see the point in adding, *If we're still alive*. Why jinx it, going in?

"He'll wait. What will you do with Sokolov?"

"I need to call the U.S. Marshals in Saint Petersburg and get them down to Novgorod," he said. "I'll do that once we're rolling."

"Are we ready, then?" she asked.

"Let's do it," Bolan said.

It was a fifteen-minute drive from the warehouse to Sheremetyevo International Airport, where Pilkin had caught Utkin idling over a glass of vodka before returning to his normal berth at Vnukovo. It had occurred to Bolan that the pilot might get hinky or decide to sell them out for bigger bucks, but he trusted Pilkin's instincts far enough to wait and see.

Bottom line: it was impossible to plan for every possible failure or act of betrayal. Even when Bolan had waged one-man war without allies, he'd still run afoul of circumstance and coincidence often enough to remind him that nothing in life was ever guaranteed—except its eventual ending.

This time, they'd have a shorter flight from Moscow to Krechevitsy Airport, located seven miles northeast of Veliky Novgorod. It wouldn't have been Bolan's first choice, since Krechevitsy was home to the 110th Military Transport Aviation Regiment of Russia's 61st Air Army, only converted recently to handle civilian flights, but Veliky Novgorod's other airport—Yurievo, situated two miles from the city center—

had closed in 1996, transformed into a weather station whose runways were used for auto racing.

Always something strange in Mother Russia.

Once they were airborne, without any problems, Bolan willed himself to relax. If Sokolov was off and running, spooked by his abortive phone call, there was nothing he could do about it. And in that case, they would still be closer to their man than they had been at any point so far, since Bolan had arrived in Moscow.

If he missed the Merchant of Death at Lake Ilmen, Bolan would find someone who could put him on the runner's track. He wouldn't rest until the job was done, or someone cut him down in the attempt.

The Executioner knew only one way to pursue an enemy.

Full throttle, to the bitter end.

THE SLAUGHTERHOUSE was located beside the Moscow River, on Berezhkovskaya naberezhnaya. In times gone by, its offal had been dumped into the river, fouling waters that were now—at least in theory—protected by more stringent environmental regulations. Which, in most cases, meant more expensive bribes for those who wished to operate as they had always done, poisoning their neighbors for profit.

Leonid Bezmel approached the abattoir after hours, when the bloody work of dismembering cattle, sheep and young horses was done for the day. Bezmel had owned the business for five years, since its owner fell on financial hard times and came begging for money he couldn't repay. This day, aside from turning a consistent profit, the meat works served Bezmel as a convenient place for interrogating and disposing of his enemies.

And if a few stray thugs should find their way into the following day's sausage, where was the harm?

Bezmel sat in his armored limousine and waited for his

bodyguards to double-check the parking lot. When they were satisfied that it was clear, they opened two large umbrellas specially made from Kevlar, holding them aloft as Bezmel left the car and scurried inside the building, shielded from any snipers they may have overlooked.

The slaughterhouse possessed an odor all its own, at once repugnant and enticing. One summer, in his teens, Bezmel had worked in such a place, before he learned that it was easier to steal money than sweat for it. The fact that he was never squeamish helped immeasurably in his new career. These days, from time to time, he joined in the dismantling of an adversary just to keep his hand in, and to let his soldiers know that there was nothing he, their boss, wasn't prepared to do.

This day's work, he thought, might well be a labor of love.

Matéo Danko was waiting when Bezmel arrived, trussed up like a Christmas goose and hanging upside down, six feet off the floor, from chains encircling his ankles. The blood had settled in his swarthy face, making him look as if he were about to have a stroke.

The old Gypsy should be so lucky.

Still, he was full of piss and vinegar. At sight of Bezmel, walking upside down from his perspective, Danko grinned and said, "At last! The king arrives!"

"You're in a good mood, eh?" Bezmel inquired.

"Why not, with all this special attention?"

"You tried to kill my second in command today."

"Not I," Danko replied.

Bezmel allowed himself a shrug. "You did not pull a trigger, it is true. You lack the skill and courage for it. But you served as bait, to draw him in."

"A tasty morsel like myself, who could resist?" the Gypsy asked.

"We butcher tasty morsels here," Bezmel replied. "You

have betrayed me, and the sentence for that crime is death, without exception. You must now decide if that death will be swift and clean, or long and slow, with all the pain I can contrive for you."

"Romani don't fear pain," Danko informed him. "We've been persecuted throughout history. It *is* our history."

"So, you'll appreciate dissection, then. Do you suppose your family might like to come and watch? Perhaps join in? We could prepare a Gypsy stew."

Bezmel turned toward the gunman on his left. "We have the address, Andrei, yes?"

Andrei grunted assent.

"The tender ones are best," Bezmel told Danko. "Older ones like us are tough and stringy, though nutritious. For a sweeter flavor, I am thinking we should add a bit of little Esmerelda, with perhaps a dash of Florica. Is she the little blue-eyed one? I'm told they're most unusual among your people. Very rare."

Danko had lost his smile, and tears were streaming down across his forehead, dampening his oily hair.

"Please spare them!" he rasped out, barely a whisper. "I will tell you anything!"

"Let us begin at the beginning, then. Who hired you to betray the man I've treated as a son?"

MAJOR MAKSIM Chaliapin was disgusted with himself. So far, despite the full resources of his rank and office, coupled with his years of personal experience, he'd been unable to locate Anzhela Pilkin or the man she had collected from the airport—how long ago? Was it twenty-four hours?

To Chaliapin, it felt like ten years.

He or his agents had searched every corner of Moscow, it seemed, although Chaliapin knew that wasn't literally possible. He'd started with known FSB safehouses and contacts, moving on from there to canvass dodgy sources who inhabited the netherworld between Russian officialdom and the realm of criminal enterprise.

So far, they had turned up one Fedor Tsereteli, a jeweler whose shop on Povarskaya Street served double-duty as a black-market arsenal. With only minimal persuasion, Tsereteli recalled selling a small arsenal of weapons to a couple matching the description of Pilkin and Cooper, a short time after the first set of killings in Moscow. Of course, he hadn't asked for names and couldn't say what his customers wanted with so many guns, much less where they might be hiding between skirmishes.

It was something, but not enough to save Chaliapin when General Bakunin's deadline expired. That thought sidetracked Chaliapin into musing on the origins of the term *deadline*— so emphatic, so final—but he caught himself in time to keep from drifting off and wasting precious time.

Time he didn't have to spare.

In something close to desperation, he'd reached out to Gennady Sokolov, seeking to learn if the arms dealer had been approached or threatened since the bloodshed began in Moscow, but there was no answer at Sokolov's home on Kotlin Island. Chaliapin wasn't among those favored with possession of Sokolov's cell phone number, and while he might have obtained it with effort, that also struck him as a waste of precious time.

Protecting Sokolov wasn't his job or primary concern. Despite the payments he'd received for turning a blind eye to Gennady's operations, Chaliapin's first and foremost concern was self-preservation. If he failed to clean up the mess that had sparked General Bakunin's wrath...

Chaliapin saw the irony in his peculiar situation. If he had done nothing, simply stood aside and let Sokolov go down in flames, along with Leonid Bezmel and his damned Solntsevskaya Brotherhood, he would have no problems now. It was the effort to assist his covert paymasters that had placed

Chaliapin in his present position, trapped between the proverbial skillet and flame.

He was feeling the heat, and could think of no way to escape.

Literal flight was hopeless, of course. General Bakunin would have him under surveillance, prepared to arrest him at once if Chaliapin tried to leave Moscow. His only salvation lay in finding and eliminating Anzhela Pilkin, along with her foreign crony. Whoever he was, wherever he came from, the stranger had to die with his rogue FSB accomplice.

Nothing less would do.

Chaliapin knew that it was time to ask Leonid Bezmel for help. He dreaded it—and wasn't sure that it would work, in any case—but he could think of no alternative.

He'd sold whatever passed for his soul long ago. Now Chaliapin hoped he could persuade the boss of Moscow's *Mafiya* to grant him a second mortgage.

Krechevitsy Airport, Novgorod Oblast

IT WAS THE SAME routine on landing, no inspection by customs or immigration, but the conspicuous display of Russian military uniforms and Ilyushin Il-76 strategic airlifters still set Bolan's nerves on edge. Valeri Utkin laughed it off and helped them with their bags this time, slyly remarking on their weight.

"Give me the bag, if it's too much for you," Pilkin said, and got another laugh.

Their rental car, this time, was a four-door Hafei Lobo sedan manufactured in China for export abroad. Bolan stowed their bags in the hatchback and took the driver's seat, sliding it back to gain more legroom. It was tight, but he could handle it. Gennady Sokolov, if they located him, would have the backseat to himself on the return trip, bound and gagged.

Lake Ilmen lay just under four miles due north of Veliky

Novgorod. To get there, with Pilkin reading the road signs and pointing the way, Bolan had to pass two of Russia's oldest monasteries, the triple-domed St. George's and St. Anthony's, designed by local master architects in the eleventh century. The symbols of old-time religion had survived both czars and commissars, remaining solid as the faith they represented into modern times—but Bolan had to wonder how, exactly, they had served the local populace.

Clearly, they hadn't kept a serpent in the person of Gennady Sokolov from settling in the neighborhood, establishing a hideaway and—if he followed the same course of action he'd pursued everywhere else—corrupting local officials to cover his tracks.

Bolan hoped those officials would stay out of his way during the next few hours, while he completed his mission. If not, they could complicate matters and make them worse for all concerned. He wouldn't pull the trigger on a cop in Russia, any more than he would in the States, but other locals who attempted to defend their resident Merchant of Death would have to deal with the Executioner.

And they might not survive the experience.

"You've seen this place we're going to?" he asked Pilkin.

"Photographs only," she told him. "Some aerial views."

"Any details on security?"

"Sokolov never leaves himself unprotected. We must expect concerted opposition."

Fair enough.

"And the police?" he asked.

"A unit of the militia based in Veliky Novgorod. How quickly they respond," she said, "depends on when and how they're notified of a disturbance."

Bolan wasn't sure that Sokolov would welcome a police intrusion on his property, although he might well opt for that in lieu of being extradited for trial and near-certain conviction stateside. And if experience had taught him anything, Bolan knew that when Big Money called, the police arrived as quickly as possible.

"We're on the clock, then," he replied.

"If Sokolov chooses to ask for help," Pilkin said.

"And if he doesn't, all we have to deal with is his private army."

"Simple, yes?" She smiled at him engagingly.

"Are you enjoying this?" he asked.

"It could be worse," she said. "I could be sitting in the Lubyanka basement, talking to Major Chaliapin."

"With any luck," he said, "you'll have that interview on your terms."

"How do you say it? I should keep my fingers crossed?"

"That's how we say it," he confirmed.

But Bolan didn't plan on crossing any of his fingers.

He would need his trigger-finger free.

Lake Ilem, Novgorod Oblast

"WE HAVE A DEAL, then?" Gennady Sokolov asked.

"We have a deal," Ahmed Bajjah agreed.

Sokolov shook hands first with the man in charge, observing proper protocol, then with his two companions in order of their seniority as he surmised it. When none of them grimaced or shied away, Sokolov knew he had guessed correctly.

Four suitcase nukes, nine million U.S. dollars. They had agreed on a one-fifth payment up front, with the same amount upon consecutive delivery of each weapon, spread over four months' time and as many countries, to minimize the risk of interception. Even then, if one or two were lost against all odds, the others should get through.

With what result?

Sokolov gave no more thought to the matter than he did when selling a consignment of rifles or pistols. If he *had* paused to consider it, his first instinct would have told him the nukes were for bluffing, tools for international blackmail that would let the Sword of Allah recoup its expenses a thousand times over, while reaping no end of free publicity.

And if the bombs were detonated...so what?

Despite all the prophets of doom, nuclear blasts at Hiroshima and Nagasaki hadn't destroyed life on Earth. Neither had some 2,100 test explosions since 1946, more than 600 of those above ground and at least four—all Russian—detonated in outer space. Japan—the only nation ever targeted for nuclear bombing—had bounced back swiftly, growing stronger and richer than ever before within a decade. Seen in that light, Sokolov supposed he might be doing the world a favor.

And being well paid for it, in the process.

He had laid on an Arabic feast to celebrate the closing of their deal. The meal began with a choice of soups, meatballs or lentils with beans and rice. His guests had three salads to choose from: mint and parsley, truffles, or chard stems in sesame oil. Entrees included broiled lamb and liver, Circassian chicken, and fish stew with red pepper. Side dishes offered a choice of rice with chickpeas, stuffed grape leaves and eggplant, okra stew, and artichokes in oil.

Nothing but the best for rich fanatics.

In the midst of dining, Sokolov's houseman disturbed him with word of a telephone call from Taras Morozov, in Moscow. Sokolov excused himself with profuse apologies, walked briskly to his study—and found the line dead. His stooge couldn't explain it, and when Sokolov dialed Morozov's cell phone number from memory, it shunted him to voice mail.

Sokolov left a terse message acknowledging the call, stopped short of an apology for missing it and glowered at the houseman as he hastened to rejoin his paying guests.

The interrupted call meant nothing, in itself. Despite

Russian technology, dropped calls were commonplace, especially when using cell phones to communicate across long distances. If Morozov had something urgent to report, he would call back.

But still, it nagged at Sokolov. Since losing Sergei Efros to his enemies in Moscow, he was more inclined than ever to be nervous, worried over threats that might turn out to have no substance. Sokolov supposed the stranger from America was still running around Moscow, harassing members of the *Mafiya* for no apparent reason, which suggested that Sokolov's intelligence concerning Matthew Cooper's mission had been incorrect.

And if that was the case, he needed new sources.

In the present situation, with indictments hanging over him and buyers closing on his first sale of nuclear weapons, Sokolov could afford no mistakes. One misstep could land him in a prison cell for life—or end his life entirely.

Neither choice pleased the Merchant of Death.

"NICE PLACE," Bolan observed.

"He likes to live in style."

The villa on Lake Ilem was smaller than Sokolov's house on Kotlin Island, but its grounds were spacious enough for privacy, surrounded by a chain-link fence with razor wire on top, decorated with signs that warned against trespassing. Behind the fence, thick hedges screened the property from view.

That worked well enough, until Bolan determined that the fence wasn't electrified. Relieved at that, he went to work with wire cutters, creating a flap in the chain link, then burrowed headlong through the hedge. It was juniper, clingy and pungent, but it had no thorns to tear his clothes and flesh.

There were no dogs in evidence, a risk he'd faced and come prepared for with the suppressor-equipped Beretta clutched in his right hand. No sentries, either, at the moment, though he couldn't rule out roving patrols. Bolan waited for Pilkin to burrow through behind him in the lowering dusk, then they spent a moment together, surveying the house and its visible grounds, a black Hummer parked away to the west side, unguarded.

"Expect cameras," Anzhela said.

"I was thinking of land mines," Bolan replied.

"You don't mean…?"

"In his own lawn? I doubt it."

Not that Sokolov would have any trouble obtaining antipersonnel mines, grenades with trip wires, or any other defense tools he desired. He probably had warehouses packed to the rafters with different explosives, detonators, chain guns with infrared triggers—you name it.

But would he want to cause that kind of ruckus here, at his country home-away-from-home, where it would disturb wealthy neighbors and send them rushing to their telephones. Sokolov wouldn't want cops on the scene unless he controlled them. In which case, Bolan would have to fall back on Plan B.

If only it existed.

In and out appeared to be the only game in town—take Sokolov's defenders as they came and drop them on the spot, then snatch the boss and split before any kind of reinforcements arrived, official or otherwise. The U.S. Marshals were already standing by, midway between the villa and Veliky Novgorod, with choppers ready for an airlift north to Pulkovo Airport in Saint Petersburg. From there, he would be someone else's problem, traveling in care of JPATS—the Justice Prisoner and Alien Transportation System often dubbed "Con Air," courtesy of Hollywood.

And good riddance.

But Bolan couldn't wash his hands of Sokolov until he made delivery, and that required physical custody. Which brought him back to square one.

In and out.

"Ready?" he asked Pilkin.

"Ready," she answered.

They started across the broad lawn, side by side, homing in on the house. It was an easy sixty yards from cover, if they passed unchallenged, but Bolan knew that was asking a lot from the gods of battle.

Too much, in fact.

They'd covered half that distance when a pair of sentries rounded the northeast corner of the house, to Bolan's right. They noticed the intruders just as Bolan spotted them, swinging around and leveling his pistol in a firm two-handed grip.

The Beretta coughed twice, sending death to meet the strangers who were fumbling for their own guns, worn on shoulder slings. The taller man caught a Parabellum round between his teeth, but this was no stage magic act. The deadly impact slammed him over backward, head and shoulders touching down before his backside hit the ground.

His shorter, older sidekick took it in the chest, staggered, and still kept grappling with his weapon, even as his ruptured heart pumped blood into his body cavity. To keep the standing corpse from squeezing off a warning shot, Bolan dispatched another round that punched a vent between glazed eyes and put the shooter down for good.

"We hurry now?" Pilkin asked.

"We hurry now," the Executioner confirmed.

CHAPTER EIGHTEEN

Gennady Sokolov held a stuffed grape leaf poised before his open mouth when the first crack of gunfire caused him to drop it, staining the white tablecloth and his slacks. He vaulted to his feet before his three guests had their chairs pushed back to stand.

"Be calm, please," he requested. "This is probably a false alarm. But just in case, Ivan will lead you to a more secure position."

Before he finished speaking, Ivan Fet was in the doorway of the dining room. He showed the three Arabs a somber smile, saying, "Now, gentlemen, if you'd just follow me…"

They did as he requested, albeit scowling after Sokolov as he retreated in the opposite direction, likely thinking he intended to abandon them. In fact, the very opposite was true. Sokolov meant to find out who had fired those shots, and why. If it *had* been an accident, disturbing three important customers, there would be bloody hell to pay.

But then, all hell broke loose.

There was no question of a slipup, after half a dozen automatic weapons opened fire in unison. He recognized the Kalashnikovs by their sound, from long experience, and heard a shotgun added to the chorus as he reached his study, moving swiftly toward the cupboard that concealed his private arsenal.

Sokolov paid his bodyguards extremely well, but in a situation where his life might be at stake, he still trusted himself above all others. He had forgotten none of his Spetznaz training or experience—had bolstered it, in fact, with lessons learned from warlords and assassins all around the world, during the course of trade.

Gennady Sokolov could hold his own against the best. Of that, he had no doubt.

But still, he was afraid.

From the cupboard, he chose an AN-94 assault rifle—the Avtomat Nikonova model chambered in 5.45 mm—adopted by Spetznaz and Russia's Ministry of Internal Affairs to replace the AK-74. His particular model had a GP-30 grenade launcher clamped beneath its barrel, and Sokolov fed the stubby weapon a 40 mm buckshot round before stuffing his pockets with spare magazines for his rifle. Thus armed, he left his study and moved swiftly toward the kitchen, where a side door granted access to the outer grounds.

Sokolov was no wet-behind-the-ears moron, to be caught waltzing out the front door of his villa into some sniper's gunsights. Danger might lie all around him, but he still possessed the skill to gauge a combat situation and react accordingly.

The sounds of battle grew louder as he approached the kitchen, slowing as he reached its doorway. Peering around the jamb, he found the room empty, with pots still simmering on the stove designed for a commercial gourmet restaurant. His serving staff had fled, and who could blame them?

Dinner was adjourned. Now, it was time to kill.

Sokolov wondered who had come for him, this time. He doubted that the FBI would try again so soon after their last embarrassing defeat, but that still left a world of possibilities.

Teeth clenched, his weapon cocked and locked, Gennady Sokolov went out to meet his unknown enemies.

THE THIRD SENTRY was late, lagging behind his comrades, but he reached the yard in time to see them drop. Bolan squeezed off another round from his Beretta, nailed the third man cold, but as he toppled backward, dying muscles made his index finger spasm on the trigger of his folding-stock Kalashnikov. It fired off half a magazine skyward, before the weapon kicked free of the dead man's hand.

And that was all it took.

Whatever happened next, Bolan knew he and Pilkin were on the clock, and it was counting down to zero hour on Doomsday. Sokolov might not call the militia, but when his neighbors had recouped their wits from the initial shock of gunfire, they'd be on the line to headquarters without delay.

And there was still the rest of Sokolov's in-house security to deal with, plus the chore of finding Sokolov himself.

They charged the house together, Pilkin as conscious of the urgency as Bolan was. They reached a spacious patio, complete with a hot tub and massive barbecue, fronted by sliding glass doors with a mirrored finish. Bolan couldn't see inside the house, and didn't care. He stitched the shiny windows with a short burst from his Steyr AUG and brought them crashing down in razored sheets and shards.

And just like that, they were inside.

Security was scrambling to box them in, contain the threat before eliminating it, some of them rushing to the skirmish site outside, while others could be heard advancing through the house, shouting instructions back and forth. Whatever they'd been taught concerning stealth, it was forgotten in the rush to save their boss.

Pilkin took the shooters who were closing in behind them from the yard. Her Vityaz submachine gun stuttered, spewing death and shiny brass, while hardmen scrambled, ducked and sprawled outside. Bolan trusted the lady from the FSB to do her job while he focused on killers closing from inside the house.

He knew the guards would have one mission only: to defend the man who paid their salaries. They would do everything within their power to eradicate intruders. Failing that, they'd fight a rear-guard action while their boss slipped out and made his getaway.

Bolan was heavy-laden in his combat harness, packing ammunition for his rifle, pistol and the Mikor MGL he'd slung across his back, a hedge against extreme emergencies. The launcher weighed twelve pounds with its 6-shot cylinder empty, but Bolan didn't begrudge the extra weight. Better to lug the piece than *wish* he had when the chips were down and he had seconds left to live.

For the moment, though, he'd trust the Steyr and do his best to clear out the defensive line before his quarry had a chance to flee.

The angry-worried voices stilled when they were right on top of Bolan. "We've got company," he cautioned Pilkin, sidestepping toward a massive oaken china cabinet that would provide fair cover in a pinch.

"On both sides," she replied, firing another burst of Parabellum rounds across the flagstone patio.

"I'll see you when it's done," Bolan said.

Hoping it was true.

PILKIN PULLED the empty magazine from her SMG and snapped home its side-by-side twin with thirty fresh rounds. The split-second lull prompted two of Sokolov's men to rush the house, firing from the hip as they came, punching holes in the wide room's plaster walls and ceiling.

Pilkin had her cover, didn't need to rise and find her mark, just let the shooters charge into her line of fire. A three-round burst took out the point man, spattering his backup with a spray of crimson mist before a second burst dropped him beside the other twitching corpse.

Easy.

But they were cornered, and she knew it was the worst

position they could be in. Sokolov could slip away once more, while they were pinned down, fighting for their lives.

More to the point, they might be killed.

Pilkin knew the American saying that the best defense was a good offense. She thought the time had come to test that principle, but she'd need help. And from the sound of it, Matt Cooper faced more guns than she did, rallying to cut off further access to the house.

Pilkin waited for a lull in firing from behind her, then called out to Bolan, "We should finish this!"

"I'm working on it," he replied.

And when she risked a glance in his direction, the big American was hunched behind the china cabinet, unslinging the grenade launcher that vaguely resembled a bloated version of the classic Russian PPSh-41 submachine gun. Instead of firing 7.62 mm Tokarev rounds from a 71-round drum, however, the launcher held six 40 mm grenades primed to explode on impact.

Not enough to level Sokolov's villa, perhaps, but enough to leave it in urgent need of repair—and to scatter his soldiers like so many toys.

If it wasn't already too late.

Pilkin strafed the patio again, keeping her adversaries down and under cover, while her ally readied himself. She waited for the almost comic plop of the grenade launcher firing, huddled in her corner near the window, ducking bullets from outside.

The first plop sounded, and she made herself as small as possible before the first blast rocked Gennady Sokolov's retreat. Another heartbeat, and the air was full of smoke and plaster dust, her ears were ringing. Pilkin heard a distant sound of screams, immediately smothered by a second detonation.

On the patio, one startled face revealed itself, immediately followed by another and another. The FSB agent saw hardened killers grimace as the rapid-fire explosions shook their master's villa. Pilkin gave them another fleeting instant to appreciate the havoc, then began to blast those faces out of frame with her Vityaz, milking the SMG's trigger for 3- and 4-round bursts.

Blood streaked the patio, divided into streams that flowed around the patio and pooled against the near side of the hot tub. Just as Pilkin ran out of living targets, she heard Cooper's voice behind her.

"Are we finished here?"

"I think so," she replied. But kept an eye on the apparent dead as she prepared to follow Cooper deeper into Sokolov's retreat.

GENNADY SOKOLOV grimaced as explosions caused his house to shudder from within. He saw smoke pouring from the shattered sliding doors that faced the patio and scanned the bodies sprawled there. Soldiers who had died in his defense— or, put another way, failures who couldn't do their job.

He turned his back on them, retreating toward the side door he had used to slip out of the house. The rapid crumbling of his defenses frightened Sokolov, a feeling he wasn't accustomed to, and one that sparked a furious response.

He wanted blood—but first, he had to find his guests and see them safely off the property. The interruption of their meal might doom his contract with the Sword of Allah. How much worse would it be, then, if three of the group's ranking members were killed at his home while under Sokolov's protection? Instantly, the terrorists would shift from paying customers to vengeance-crazed fanatics, pursuing a fatwa against Sokolov.

The last thing he needed, just now, was a fresh set of enemies howling for blood.

Retreating toward the doubtful safety of his house, Sokolov

hoped that it wasn't already too late for his three Arab customers. While he had ordered Ivan Fet to guard them, Fet was obviously more concerned about defending the villa and stopping the intruders, a division of his concentration that might prove deadly for Ahmed Bajjah and the others.

Sokolov already had a plan of action forming in his mind. He would collect the Arabs, lead them to his armored Hummer with a handful of guards—or without them, if need be—and escape while the remainder of his men mopped up the enemy. Or were mopped up, themselves.

In either case, he and the Sword of Allah's emissaries would survive. There might even be time and opportunity for Sokolov to turn the incident to his advantage. The attack would demonstrate that he was hunted, too, as they were. He could understand their plight and sympathize. Better, he could provide a means for both the Arabs and himself to seek revenge.

And at a discount, if it took a little extra sweetener to keep the deal in place. Above all else, Gennady Sokolov was a resilient businessman.

He reached the side door's threshold, hesitated for an instant, then swallowed the impulse to flee on his own. Training and grim determination drove him forward through the haze of dust and smoke, beyond the empty kitchen, toward the panic room where he had left Bajjah and his companions.

Only moments now, and they would be away to safety. Sokolov could log one more defeat for his persistent but inept opponents. Every time he managed to elude them, one more chapter was appended to his legend.

No one could capture the Merchant of Death.

Not while he had defenders guarding his retreat, and clutched an AN-94 assault rifle in steady hands. Or, if his hands trembled a bit, no one who faced him down would live to tell the tale.

BEYOND THE SMOKING rubble and the bodies sprawled amid it, Bolan found a hallway leading toward the heart of the house. He followed it instinctively, with Pilkin behind him, covering their flank. It was too much to hope that he'd disabled all of Sokolov's defenders in their first engagement. Every forward step increased the likelihood of an encounter with the enemy.

"He could be out and gone by now," Pilkin said, keeping her voice low-pitched.

"No way to tell, unless we bail without checking the house," Bolan replied.

"I know, damn it!"

And even then, he knew, they couldn't tell by simply counting vehicles outside. Retreat meant giving up their foothold on the villa without gaining anything. It couldn't be much farther. Five more minutes, maybe less.

But the police…

Two gunmen stood before another door, barring the way. They glimpsed Bolan at the same time he saw them, turning their weapons toward him as he hit the floor, clearing a field of fire for Pilkin behind him.

Four guns hammered for a smoky moment in the hallway. Bolan's human targets crumpling under fire, falling together on the threshold of the door they'd guarded with their lives. A wasted effort, but they'd given everything they had for Sokolov.

Bolan was up and moving in another instant, hitting the door with a snap-kick and following through, aware of Pilkin trailing, still covering his advance. He scanned the room for Sokolov, but saw only three men in business suits, with kaffiyehs covering their heads.

It took another beat for recognition to strike home. The flankers meant nothing to Bolan, but his mental mug book instantly produced a slide show for the Arab in the middle of the lineup.

Ahmed Bajjah, a ranking member of the Sword of Allah, sought by law-enforcement agencies worldwide. His presence in Sokolov's villa could only mean dirty work brewing, with profit for some and pain for hundreds, maybe thousands more.

He made the choice at some unconscious level, almost instinct, triggering a burst that raked the cringing terrorists from left to right and back again, painting the beige wall behind them with scarlet before they collapsed.

"I take it that you knew them?"

Something in Pilkin's voice made him turn. She was leaning against a wall to the right of the door, a pained expression on her face. A second glance showed Bolan the bloodstain low down on her side.

"Let me see that," he said.

"It's nothing," she insisted. "We need to find Sokolov first, and get out of this place before—"

"What have you done!" a voice bellowed behind her, as Sokolov crossed the threshold, an automatic weapon clutched against his chest.

The arms dealer saw his late customers heaped on the floor, read the death of some lucrative deal in their posture and snarled as he swung his rifle toward Bolan. Pilkin gasped in pain as she whipped her SMG up and across Sokolov's face, slamming him backward to the floor.

"I think he'll come along now, eh?" she asked, forcing a smile.

PILKIN COVERED Bolan as he bound Sokolov's hands at his back with thin plastic restraints at the wrists and elbows, then heaved the still-unconscious form across his shoulder in a fireman's carry. Sokolov was neither small nor scrawny, but the extra weight didn't appear to faze the Executioner.

"Ready?" he asked her.

"*Da*. I'm ready."

"If you can't walk—"

"What?" she challenged him, trying another smile for size. "You carry both of us *and* fight Gennady's men? I don't think so."

"Okay, then." His voice was reluctant.

"The fence is a long way from here, I admit."

"We're not going that way," he replied with a smile of his own.

A key dangled from his left hand. Pilkin saw the Hummer logo on its fob—the minitank that she had glimpsed, parked on the west side of the house as they approached it from the large backyard.

"Better," she said.

"Now, all we have to do is get there and pile in, without getting wasted," Bolan advised her.

She straightened, trying not to grimace from the pain. "Piece of cake," she said.

"Anytime, then."

"Now is best," she told him.

"Right."

Bolan led the way, burdened with Sokolov and weapons, turning to his left beyond the open doorway, obviously looking for an exit that would place them close to the Hummer without requiring them to circle the house without cover. Pilkin followed, breathing through clenched teeth as she jogged behind him, feeling every step through the leaking wound in her side.

She stumbled at one point, dropping to one knee, and couldn't stop herself from crying out as something seemed to rip inside her. Bolan stopped and turned, retreating to crouch beside Pilkin, seemingly heedless of Sokolov's weight on his back.

"Can you stand?" he asked.

"Yes! I'll make it."

A sudden sound behind her brought Bolan lurching to

his feet, firing his Steyr AUG one-handed. Pilkin twisted, slumped against the nearest wall for support and triggered a burst from her submachine gun toward the three men who had nearly overtaken them.

All three were down a moment later, when Bolan helped her stand, then turned away with visible reluctance, trusting her to follow him. Somehow, they made it to a spacious kitchen without meeting any further opposition, found a side door to the villa standing open, and stepped through it to behold the jet-black Hummer parked a few yards distant.

They were so close now, Pilkin thought the world had to fall away beneath their feet. Something *had* to go wrong. They'd come so far, and—

"Are you with me?"

Bolan's voice surprised her, roused her from a kind of waking dream.

"With you," she told him as he slammed the Hummer's right-rear door on Sokolov, stretched out on the backseat, and held the right-front door open for her. "You watch the package," he suggested, "while I drive."

"A good idea," she said, and dragged herself into the passenger's seat.

Her pain was fading now, it seemed, as her ally slid behind the Hummer's steering wheel, locked all of their doors with the touch of a button, and fired up the engine. Pilkin turned in her seat to watch Sokolov, wishing the bastard would wake and try something, give her a reason to shoot him.

They were moving, then, hail pinging on the Hummer's armored body, while a small voice in Pilkin's head crooned, *Hold on. Just hold on.*

IT WAS A LONG RUN to the gates of Sokolov's estate—or felt that way, at least, while they were under fire. At least a dozen shooters Bolan hadn't seen before turned up from somewhere, blasting at the minitank with everything they had, but that was strictly small arms, with no heavy guns or rocket launchers built for stopping armored vehicles.

One guy appeared to think that he could stop the speeding Hummer with his body, maybe hoping that the unknown driver who had killed so many of his friends that night would have a change of heart and swerve at the last second. Leaping into Bolan's path, the soldier fired an AK at the Hummer's windshield, scratching it but having no real impact.

And he looked surprised when Bolan ran him down.

"That had to sting," Pilkin said, and laughed. A brittle sound.

Nobody else tried that approach, but there were three men waiting at the gate with automatic weapons, laying down a screen of fire before him.

"Brace for ramming," he warned his companion, and held the pedal down, charging the gates at close to seventy.

It was no contest. Even though the impact jarred them, dumped Sokolov to the floorboards in back, and likely damaged the Hummer's alignment, the gates were thrown wide, dragging sharp metal claws down both sides of the car as they crashed through, but failing to trap them. Another moment, and the highway's pavement was beneath their fat tires, Bolan racing back toward where they'd left the rental car.

"Hang on," he said to no one in particular. "We're getting there."

"You woke him up," Pilkin said.

"It's just as well," Bolan replied. "I'm tired of hauling him around."

Sokolov spoke up, in English. "Who are you? Where are you taking me?"

"To justice," Pilkin informed him.

Two minutes and counting from the gate, they reached the rental car and Bolan stopped the Hummer. He got out, opened the right-rear door and dragged Sokolov out by his collar, manhandling him until he was upright. From there, the Executioner marched him around to the rental, ignoring the arms dealer's protests, and shoved him into the Hafei Lobo's backseat. Another thin restraint secured his ankles before Bolan shut the door.

He turned to find Pilkin still in her seat, one leg dangling out of the Hummer, her face as pale as chalk. Bolan reached her in two strides, pressed fingertips to the side of her throat and detected a faint, thready pulse.

She tried to smile and missed it as she said, "It may be slightly worse than I let on."

"We'll get some help."

"Too late, I think," she said, and spilled into his arms, a flaccid rag doll, weighing next to nothing.

Bolan tried the pulse again and couldn't find it. Cursing underneath his breath, he carried Pilkin around the Hafei Lobo, belting her into the shotgun seat.

"Now only one of you," Sokolov said.

He had no time for any further comments, as the sound suppressor of Bolan's pistol rammed between his lips, snapping off two teeth at the gum line.

"One more word," the Executioner advised his wide-eyed prisoner, "and you're as dead as dead can be."

CHAPTER NINETEEN

Moscow

The old Gypsy had told them everything. Once he'd begun, Matéo Danko couldn't spill the story fast enough. His tongue kept tripping over words, forcing Bezmel to slap his face and order him to start again, speak clearly and leave out the damned Romani gibberish.

At last, it was a simple story, simply told. Aldo Shishani was acquainted with the Gypsies and their business, both in Moscow Oblast and surrounding areas. He had reached out to Danko, used the old man's lust for power to his own advantage, promising control of all Romani rackets in the city if Danko could help Shishani rid himself of Taras Morozov. Danko had dealt with the Brotherhood mobster in the past, but readily agreed.

There had been other questions, but not many. When the cutting started, it was more for Bezmel's pleasure than an effort to extract more information. At the point of death, when Danko's eyes had already begun to glaze, Bezmel had leaned in close to him and whispered in the Gypsy's ear.

"Your children, next."

Whether he followed up on that or not, it had been good to see the panic flare in Danko's dying eyes and know that he was weeping on his way to hell.

Assuming hell existed.

Bezmel rarely thought about it, and on those occasions when he did, it didn't worry him. With all that he had suffered as a child, all of the bloody butchery emblazoned on his memory, what was eternity in flames? It would require a very special hell to take him by surprise, much less to make him plead for mercy.

In the meantime, he had enemies to kill. Beginning with Shishani, if the little prick dared to show his face in Moscow.

And he would. At least, Bezmel hoped so.

Before he cut Matéo Danko's throat and watched him die with panic in his eyes, Bezmel had let the old man make a phone call. Ordered it, in fact. Encouraged by a pistol at his head, Danko had played his part to sheer perfection, alerting Shishani to a golden opportunity the Chechen wouldn't wish to miss.

A chance to end his war against the Solntsevskaya Brotherhood once and for all, by cutting off the viper's head. Leonid Bezmel on a silver platter, offered to secure Shishani's promise to Danko.

Shishani was suspicious, naturally, but he'd agreed to meet Danko in person, swallowed the old Gypsy's claim of being too harried and frightened to impart his information on the telephone. Bezmel congratulated himself for the neat reversal of Shishani's original scheme, but he took nothing for granted.

Aldo Shishani might be Chechen scum, but he wasn't a fool. He might change his mind and beg off, sending a snatch team after Danko. And even if he kept the rendezvous, he'd bring his soldiers with him. Bezmel was counting on that.

He would meet the Obshina with overwhelming superior force, crushing the Chechen threat in Moscow once and for all. Any who slipped through the net would be marked for execution on sight, thus encouraging them to leave Russia for good. Come what may as a result, no twinge of weakness would prevent Bezmel from killing each and every one of his rivals.

Afterward, of course, there would be hell to pay—or, rather, politicians and police. Bezmel would have to part with massive bribes, but he could well afford it. Few administrators in the vast Russian bureaucracy were strong or ethical enough to turn their backs on ready cash.

There would be trouble, but he would survive it, as he always had before. Survival was a talent cultivated from his infancy that always served him well. Aldo Shishani shared that trait, but he was running out of time.

The Chechen was as good as dead.

He simply didn't know it yet.

Veliky Novgorod

THE U.S. MARSHALS WERE on time. Bolan expected nothing less. He'd called them from the road, watching his rearview mirror all the way for tails and hoping any pursuers would be distracted by the burning hulk of the Hummer that he'd left behind. It should be worth a look, at least, and could delay them while they tried to see if anybody was inside.

Nobody was.

He'd driven from the lake with Pilkin beside him, slumped against her door as if she was asleep. Gennady Sokolov was as silent as the grave behind him, on the rear floorboard, keeping his comments to himself as if his life depended on it—which it did. They made the trip in silence, Bolan slowing as he reached the outskirts of Veliky Novgorod.

The last thing that he needed was a traffic stop by the police, with a corpse in the shotgun seat, a kidnap victim in back, and his own scruples forbidding an easy solution.

Scruples.

Bolan wondered how much they were worth, sometimes. He'd launched his early war against the Mafia to punish criminals the law had found untouchable, and in the process he had broken every statute in the books, aside from sexual offenses.

He'd become a murderer, kidnapper, thief and terrorist—to some, at least. He couldn't count the lies he'd told along the way, could barely keep track of the lives he'd damaged by association. He'd lost track of the bodies, too, though none were ever really forgotten.

All for what? To make the world a "better place"?

If so, it wasn't working.

What had really changed since Bolan first embarked upon his long crusade, except the names and faces of the predators he hunted? Criminals still robbed, raped, murdered, tortured innocents in every city, every state and every nation on the planet. If someone had asked him, Bolan would've guessed that there were more today than when he'd started his one-man cleanup campaign.

He caught himself there, glanced at Pilkin's pale face in profile, and reminded himself that it *did* make a difference.

Every scumbag he took off the board had a ripple effect, lives that wouldn't be ruined or ended because that particular predator ceased to exist. In Sokolov's case, tens of thousands might see one more dawn because he, in particular, stopped selling small arms and weapons of mass destruction.

Would someone else step in to fill the void? Of course. And when he—or she—did, the Executioner would be waiting. Thinning the predators, one at a time.

He met the marshals at a warehouse north of town. They had three carbon-copy SUVs and dressed enough alike to pass for cast members on a reality show called *Strong Silent Types.* Their leader approached Bolan cautiously, checked out his two passengers, then introduced himself as Deputy Marshal Jeff Coleman.

"You had a rough time, I guess," Coleman observed.

"Worse than some," Bolan granted.

"Looks like our boy took a couple of hits."

"Rough times, like you said."

"Well, you're out of it now, anyway. We'll get some shots

of that mug, for the record, then load his ass up. Leave all your hardware here, and we can tip the locals to your partner once we're airborne."

"I'm not going with you," Bolan said.

"Excuse me?" The deputy's face had gone grim.

"I'm not done yet."

"Mister, what you've done here is poke one giant hornet's nest. They're going to swarm you like nobody's business, and they won't quit stinging till you're dead."

"Thanks for the advice."

"But you're not taking it?"

"I have a few stings to deliver of my own," the Executioner replied.

The Lubyanka, Moscow

MAJOR MAKSIM Chaliapin let the telephone receiver slip from numb fingers into its cradle, slumping backward into his desk chair. The news he'd received left him stricken, torn between panic and despair.

It had happened.

Gennady Sokolov had been snatched, after all.

Chaliapin couldn't say who was responsible, although the damned Americans were first *and* second on his list of suspects. And he would have bet his pension that Anzhela Pilkin was somehow involved, with the foreigner known as Matthew Cooper.

Profanity poured from the major's lips almost unconsciously, venting his fury and frustration in a torrent of abuse directed at...whom? His rogue lieutenant? Sokolov? Himself?

What difference did it make?

A sharp pain in his chest distracted Chaliapin for a moment, then passed when he shifted positions. No heart attack, then. He wasn't that lucky.

General Bakunin would destroy him now, beyond the shadow of a doubt. Chaliapin would have no pension to bet on Lieutenant Pilkin's guilt or on anything else. He'd soon be penniless, stripped of rank and disgraced—but at least he wouldn't starve. Whether Bakunin had him shot or packed him off to prison for life, Chaliapin never had to worry about where his next meal would come from.

Unless…

One man might still be able to protect him, if Chaliapin could plead his case convincingly enough. It would mean self-abasement, certainly, no end to personal humiliation. But at least he might survive. Assuming that his friend agreed to help *and* had sufficient influence to block whatever moves Bakunin made.

Chaliapin reached out for the telephone once more, speed-dialed a number, waited through two rings, then heard it answered in the Khamovniki District of southwestern Moscow.

"Ministry of Defense," the sexless operator said.

"Major Maksim Chaliapin, FSB, calling for Colonel General Ruslan Kozlov, if he is available."

Please, please be in!

"One moment, sir."

"Thank you." The last words almost choked him.

The seconds dragged, before a buzzing filled his ear and Chaliapin heard a receptionist—this one certainly female—say, "Colonel General Kozlov's office."

Chaliapin repeated his self-introduction and spent another thirty seconds on hold before Kozlov came on the line.

"Major Chaliapin," he said. "A surprise."

Not a *pleasant* surprise, Chaliapin noted.

"Have you heard?" he inquired.

"Heard what?" Kozlov asked.

"Our friend from Petrograd has been abducted."

Silence on the line, stretching as taut as a garrote, before

Kozlov asked, "Are you certain of this? How good is your source?"

"His own chief of security."

More silence. Then, "Do you suppose he'll talk?"

Chaliapin considered the matter of telephone taps, then decided to answer, regardless.

"To save himself? Certainly."

"I think so, too."

"In the meantime, I'm fucked with Bakunin."

"Would *you* talk?" Kozlov asked.

He knew the right answer. "Of course not!"

Did Kozlov believe him? One way or another, he said, "Let me deal with the general."

"Yes, sir." Too soon for relief, but he managed a near-breathless "Thank you."

"Our friend is now a liability," Kozlov said. "It would be a boon to all concerned if we could silence him."

"Yes, sir."

"That falls within your purview, does it not, Maksim?"

"It might. Yes, sir."

"If you had contacts who could reach him, far away."

"Such people certainly exist, sir."

"Then, for all our sakes," Kozlov directed, "call them! Call them *now!*"

Vnukovo International Airport, Moscow

BOLAN PAID OFF Valeri Utkin, listened to one last expression of condolence over the loss of Anzhela Pilkin, and left the pilot counting his money. Driving off, he supposed that the Veliky Novgorod militia had to have collected Pilkin's remains by now and started their investigation of her death.

Remains.

It was a fitting term, if you believed in souls and such, the disembodied essence of humanity that left its fleshy envelope when Death served an eviction notice, winging off to…where, exactly?

Bolan didn't claim to know if "God" existed, or if there was more than one in play at any given time. He bought the notion of a "higher power," but had no spare time for pondering its nature.

One thing he could say, with perfect certainty. Whoever—or *whatever*—might be watching over humankind on Earth, he'd seen no evidence of intervention, good or bad. The thing called Life seemed more like an experiment in progress, launched and then observed without any apparent effort to direct its course. Whatever strategy emerged was left to the devices of the sentient bacteria called Homo sapiens.

And Bolan had his strategy in place, for the remainder of his Moscow mission. He'd delivered Sokolov and put him out of mind, leaving his fate to courts, attorneys, jurors—and, with any luck, jailers.

But there was still work to be done.

And payback was a bitch.

He had a list of targets and, perhaps, sufficient time to visit each of them in turn. Some took priority over the rest. They might be scrambling for cover even now, as word of Sokolov's abduction spread. Or maybe he would find them spoiling for a fight.

In either case, he meant to teach them that nobody was untouchable. Nobody had a free pass from the Executioner.

The seeds of chaos and dissension that he'd sown in Moscow would be helpful. Even now, the Solntsevskaya Brotherhood and Obshina were at each other's throats. Bolan could help with that, and at the same time visit wrath on some of the officials who had sold Anzhela Pilkin down the river.

Starting with a certain Major Chaliapin at the FSB.

Spies weren't police, in Bolan's estimation. Hence, they weren't covered by his private ban on the use of deadly force against lawmen. He'd fought the KGB in bygone days, and wouldn't give the spooks safe passage just because they'd changed their name.

An uphill fight still lay before him. Bolan knew that and acknowledged it. He might not make it out of Moscow, but the same was true of every battlefield he'd ever trod. And if his enemies got lucky, if they took him out, Bolan could promise them one thing.

He wasn't going down alone.

Bolan couldn't vindicate Anzhela Pilkin in official eyes, but he could damned sure avenge her.

Starting now.

Vidnoye, Moscow Oblast

IN 2007 A REPORT aired by the British Broadcasting Company claimed that one-quarter of Russia's modern economy was controlled by a tiny group of thirty-six billionaires. True or not, most of the men—and they were all men—named in that story resided in Moscow's southwestern suburb, the Leninsky District, with Vidnoye serving as its administrative center.

The filthy rich—a term employed advisedly, considering their business practices and contacts—occupied palatial homes on grand estates that rivaled royal dwellings from the czarist era. Many behaved like minor gods, immune to law, dismissive of public opinion.

One such was Leonid Bezmel, whose estate in Vidnoye was a symbol of his triumph in a world where he had faced and vanquished every rival who opposed him. None had ever forced him to retreat or seriously threatened his supremacy.

Until this day.

It seemed, now, that his world was under siege by forces he couldn't identify, much less eradicate. He could, if given time enough, destroy the Chechen Obshina, but what of

Sokolov's abductors and the chaos they had sown in Moscow, slaughtering his men with evident impunity?

It was all bad for business, a slap in his face that stung his outlaw soul.

Bezmel acknowledged satisfaction, therefore, when he had received a call from Colonel General Ruslan Kozlov of the Russian army. They were well acquainted, but the soldier usually kept his distance from Bezmel, fearing that any documented contact with the Brotherhood might end his career.

But now, he sought an audience. Not merely conversation, but an interview at Bezmel's estate, where he could be certain of security—at least, inside the walls. Bezmel couldn't ensure that Kozlov reached Vidnoye without being seen or followed, and the general had refused his offer of a lift with guards and driver trained to spot such things.

Oh, well.

It wouldn't bother Bezmel to be seen with Kozlov. Quite the opposite, in fact. As for the general, he was a grown man of some influence, who made his own choices. If they came back to bite him in the ass someday, Bezmel thought, whose fault was that?

The general should be arriving any moment now. In fact… yes, from his study window, Bezmel saw a limousine nose up against his gate, where soldiers of another kind—*his* soldiers—were on hand to greet the officer whose rank meant less than nothing to them.

Everything was relative.

Bezmel waited until Kozlov's limousine had covered half the distance from the gate to his front porch, then went to greet his guest. He was prepared to listen, hear whatever Kozlov had to say, and judge the presentation on its merits.

A matter of some mutual concern, Kozlov had said, rightly declining to elaborate when who knew how many unseen ears were eavesdropping. The only way to talk real business was in person, face-to-face, watching the other person's eyes. To hell with e-mail, Skype, and all the other gadgets invented for the sole purpose of minimizing human contact.

Bezmel liked to meet his friends—and enemies—in the flesh. That way, he could judge their intentions along with their words. And if need be, he could wrap his hands around their necks, squeezing until their lying faces turned a lovely shade of blue.

Which nearly matched the stylish suit that Colonel General Kozlov wore, emerging from his limousine. He'd left his army uniform at home, whether to separate one occupation from another or to indicate that he was presently off-duty, Bezmel didn't know and didn't care.

He had Kozlov within his clutches, now. And if the general displeased him, well, there was no guarantee that he'd be seen again, by anyone on Earth.

"STOP HERE. I'm getting out," Aldo Shishani ordered.

His chauffeur and soldiers didn't argue. Instantly, his limousine swung to the curb on Golovacheva Street and sat with its engine idling while Shishani stepped out of the car, surrounded by gunmen.

"You and you," he said, pointing to two of the largest, "will stay here with me. The rest, go on and keep our date with Bezmel, if he has guts enough to show up."

The others piled back into the car, and Shishani watched it roll away toward the rendezvous point, near the Triumphal Gates.

Kuzminsky Park was part of a former noble estate, occupied by the Golitsyn princes from 1820 to 1917. Their vast wealth and influence hadn't spared them from the Russian Revolution, and while some of their ancestral buildings lay in ruins, much had been preserved on 375 hectares of beautifully landscaped terrain. From where he stood, Shishani could see the Egyptian pavilion, the bathhouse, the musical pavilion and the Church of the Vlakhernskaya Icon of the Mother of God.

None of it mattered to him in the least.

Shishani was focused solely on the park's Triumphal Gates, copied from those of another palace at Pavlovsk, outside Saint Petersburg, designed by architect Carlo Rossi. Again, the artistry meant nothing to the Chechen mobster. He was tracking his car and his men toward Leonid Bezmel, fingered for an ambush via telephone by Shishani's occasional friend, Matéo Danko.

Not that Shishani would ever trust a Gypsy.

He had used Danko in the past—quite recently, in fact—but knew the little ferret would sell his soul to the highest bidder on any given occasion. Danko *might* know where Bezmel was meeting with allies to plot Shishani's death, or he might have switched sides in return for a payoff, using his wiles to sucker Shishani. If that was the case, he would fail.

And he'd suffer a slow, screaming death at Shishani's convenience.

The limousine was closing on its target. Watching through a pair of opera glasses, Shishani scanned the surrounding park for any sign of Bezmel, his armed entourage, of the luxury cars in which he habitually traveled. Several expensive vehicles were parked near the Triumphal Gates, but Shishani couldn't read their license tags and would have needed his laptop to check them, in any case.

Shishani watched his limo roll up to the car park, slowing to a crawl on the approach. He could picture his men hunched inside, gripping weapons, scanning the pavement and parkland for targets. All of them knew Leonid Bezmel by sight, and most would recognize at least a few of his soldiers. If nothing else, the *type* stood out: low-brow, no-neck thugs with simian faces, sneering at a world they barely understood.

If any such were present, Shishani thought, he should be

able to see them from where he was watching. And if none were there…

The rocket came from somewhere to his left, streaking across Shishani's narrowed field of vision, detonating when it struck the left-rear quadrant of his limousine. Another followed almost instantly—an RPG, no doubt about it—smashing through a window on the driver's side and peeling back the car's armored roof like the lid of a cheap sardine can.

One of his soldiers was cursing behind him, reeling off a long list of obscenities.

"Shut up!" Shishani snapped. "We're leaving. Call the backup car!"

It was too late to save his soldiers now. But there was ample time to plot revenge.

CHAPTER TWENTY

Major Maksim Chaliapin's small but well-appointed house was situated on Moscow's north side, off Ostankinskaya Street, within easy walking distance of Ostankino Park. It was a single home—detached, as they would say in London—and therefore bespoke a certain level of achievement in the present-day bureaucracy.

Watching the house, Bolan decided Chaliapin wasn't filthy rich, unless he hid it well, but he was certainly a cut above the average merchant class in Moscow, on his way to affluence that would excite a pang of envy from his neighbors. When he finally retired from service to the state, there'd no doubt be an estate somewhere in the hinterlands, winters spent someplace where the sun was warm and bright.

Except that Chaliapin had no summers left. His very hours were numbered, and the Executioner was holding the stopwatch.

Bolan had watched the house for fifteen minutes, making up his mind that nobody was home. Pilkin had already told him that the major was unmarried, and a quick call to the home's unlisted number went unanswered.

It was time to move.

Ideally, Bolan would've liked to catch his quarry home alone, deal with him there and move along to other targets, but he wouldn't waste the drive. Maksim Chaliapin was about to join the ranks of Moscow's homeless.

Bolan left his Steyr and the MGL grenade launcher concealed in his rented car as he stepped out, locked the driver's door behind him and crossed the street diagonally to reach Chaliapin's property. He didn't know if any of the neighbors saw him, and he wasn't terribly concerned about it. Decked out in a stylish business suit, he fit the neighborhood and ought to trigger no alarms.

And by the time there was a reason for the neighbors to alert police, he would be on his way to other targets, other battlefields.

Beneath his tailored jacket, Bolan wore the Beretta 93-R with its sound suppressor attached, and carried two thermite grenades clipped to his belt in back. One should do, for a building this size, but why be stingy?

At the door, Bolan made a show of ringing the bell, then knocking, and finally picked the double locks in seconds flat. He half expected an alarm and security keypad, but none was in evidence. If he'd missed one, by chance, it made no great difference.

The place was coming down.

Without attempting any search, he crossed a smallish living room to scan the kitchen, then glanced down a hallway toward two bedrooms, both with their doors standing open. He palmed one of the thermite canisters, pulled its pin and pitched the grenade underhanded toward the far end of the corridor, retreating as it sizzled on the carpet.

Bolan was back in the living room when the grenade blew, igniting the back of the house, quickly filling the middle and front rooms with white, acrid smoke. He paused on the doorstep to toss the second grenade, saw it land on Chaliapin's sofa, then took himself out of range before the second whooshing detonation.

Mission accomplished.

Bolan couldn't know when word of the conflagration would reach Chaliapin, but he knew it would sting. The personal invasion would be doubly hard to take, for someone used to invading the privacy of others, turning their lives upside down for his own benefit.

It was a start. Call it a fair beginning of the end of Bolan's work in Moscow. By the time he finished, he would have removed the major players from Gennady Sokolov's team, leaving a power vacuum that would generate more chaos on its own account.

A final solution? Not even close.

But it might just be good enough for now.

"FIVE MEN! All dead!" Aldo Shishani fumed. And almost as an afterthought, he snarled, "The car was barely one year old!"

"I'll miss Zakhar," Magen Manaev said.

Zakhar Panin had been one of the five who went up with the limousine. Shishani scowled at mention of his name.

"Where are we with the Gypsy?" he demanded.

"Searching every corner of the city, turning over every stone. We'll find him, if he's here."

"They turned him, obviously. One day, he's with us. The next…"

"Dead meat," Manaev said, making a promise.

"I don't want him killed on sight," Shishani said. "If there's a way on Earth to bring him here alive, do it! I want to send him off myself, after we've had a chance to talk."

"You know Bezmel's responsible," Manaev said.

"Of course. Who else? You think this bitch from the FSB and her phony Canadian playmate met Danko in a bar and struck up conversation? 'Hey, you want to help us fuck Aldo Shishani for the hell of it?' I don't think so."

"No, Aldo."

"We used Danko, and then Bezmel turned the tables on us. *That* part's not in question."

"No."

Shishani *had* begun to question his own competence,

however. He had known the setup was a trap, prepared for it and still lost five good men, together with a year-old limousine. Some might have said it proved that he was getting soft, losing his touch.

Before he ripped their tongues out with a rusty pair of pliers.

Shishani's error, in this case, had been the simple act of *hoping*. Even in the face of logic, he had dared to hope that Matéo Danko, as corrupt as he was, would put Leonid Bezmel in the crosshairs for him. Hope had pressed him to continue, even as caution made him step out of the car before it reached ground zero.

"And Bezmel?" he demanded of Manaev. "Where is he?"

"We think he's at his place in Vidnoye. A neighbor tips us when he's there. It's ninety-five percent confirmed."

"With all his men?"

"Not all, but he's well covered."

"And can we crack the palace?"

It was what he always called Leonid Bezmel's mansion in the suburbs, usually spoken in a mocking tone. This day, his mien was deadly serious.

"We have the floor plans, as you know," Manaev said.

And they had cost a pretty ruble, too.

"That isn't what I asked you, is it?"

"No, sir. With the right equipment and enough men, any target can be cracked."

It was like talking to a child, sometimes.

"And do we *have* the right equipment, Magen? Do we *have* enough men left?"

"Equipment, certainly. We have Semtex and RPGs, more than we'll ever need, unless we have to fight NATO. As for the men, we've lost a number, as you know."

"Then tell me something I don't know."

"It may be possible, but I can't guarantee success. Of

course, the effort will create a serious disturbance in the neighborhood. Someone will call out the militia before we're finished."

"Have you any scruples against killing men in uniform?" Shishani asked.

"Scruples?"

"My point exactly. Send out the word. I want our men—*all* of our men—to drop whatever they are doing and report at once to the Kaminsky warehouse."

"As you say, Aldo."

"Have them bring any weapons they possess, and all their ammunition. When we hit the palace, it will be defended. I want no one killed for lack of shooting back."

"And the militia?"

"I'll call our man inside. Beyond that, God help any who get in our way."

MAJOR MAKSIM Chaliapin stood beside a captain of the Moscow fire department, scanning the blackened rubble of his former home. Houses on either side had suffered minor damage, but the firefighters had come in time to contain the worst of the blaze and prevent it from spreading. Only Chaliapin's house had been destroyed.

"It was a chemical, you say?" he asked the captain.

"Something like white phosphorus," the captain said. "I can't be sure until the testing is completed. It may take some time, with the reductions in our budget."

"I can have it tested at the Lubyanka," Chaliapin told him. "Send it over, will you?"

"Certainly. But we must still perform our own tests, Major, as I'm sure you understand. For the reports."

"Of course. You're confident that it was arson, though? Regardless of the medium?"

"Ninety percent," the captain said. "One hundred percent,

if you aren't in the habit of keeping such volatile items at home."

"You may take that for granted."

Of course, it was arson. What else? Chaliapin had known that as soon as he heard of the fire at his home, long before he had raced across town to stand before smoldering wreckage. He could likely name one of the fire-bugs responsible, too.

But tracking her down was another matter. When he laid hands on Anzhela Pilkin, the bitch would wish she had never been born. And when Chaliapin was through with her, it would be as if she never was.

His cell phone buzzed like an angry wasp in Chaliapin's pocket. He fished it out and answered curtly.

"Da."

"Major, it's Sergeant Argunov calling."

"Yes, Sergeant?"

"Sir, you asked to be informed at once of any news concerning Lieutenant Pilkin."

"You have news of her? Has she been found?"

"Yes, sir. And yes, again."

"Well, man, where is she?"

"In Veliky Novgorod, sir. We've received a call from the militia up there. They're holding her remains."

"I'll send a team to fetch her," Chaliapin said. "And…did you say *remains?*"

"Yes, sir. She's dead, sir."

"Dead! You say she's dead? Dead in Veliky Novgorod?"

"Yes, sir. Well, say a bit outside the city, sir. A call directed officers to Krechevitsy Airport, where they found her in a car she'd rented for herself. Oddly, they say she was belted into the passenger's seat."

She would be, Chaliapin thought, with that damned Cooper driving.

"How did she die?" he inquired.

"Gunshot wounds, sir. Or maybe *a* wound. They weren't

terribly clear on the phone, sir. There's been no autopsy as yet."

Chaliapin severed the connection, thinking furiously. If Lieutenant Pilkin had been shot in Novgorod, it had to mean she was involved in Sokolov's abduction. But if she hadn't returned to Moscow, who had torched Chaliapin's house?

Not Leonid Bezmel or his mob. They were Chaliapin's covert allies, if he dared admit it to himself. Aldo Shishani and his Obshina? The major couldn't make himself believe the Chechens were that foolish.

Who was left, in that case?

Matthew Cooper.

The man of mystery who had cost the FSB two agents so far, while jeopardizing Chaliapin's career and his very life itself. But if Cooper was sent to kidnap Sokolov, and his mission had now been accomplished, why would he come back to Moscow? Why burn Chaliapin's house down, except for some sort of revenge?

And would he now be satisfied?

Scowling, the major turned and stalked back to his car, leaving the fire-department captain staring after him.

It wasn't over yet. Chaliapin felt it in his aching bones.

"ANOTHER BLOCK. I see it now," Nikolai Tatlin said.

"On the left, there?" his driver inquired.

"That's the place."

One of Shishani's dives, the Foxfire Club, whatever that meant. Tatlin knew the place by reputation, though he'd never been inside. It featured second-rate strippers who tricked on the side, and bartenders who doubled as dealers. The Foxfire catered to a middle-aged, low-budget clientele including small-time hoodlums and the dregs of Muscovite nightlife.

Exactly what you would expect of the Obshina.

Chechens. Christ, what good were they to anyone?

Tatlin didn't expect to find Aldo Shishani at the Foxfire

Club, but he was bent on punishing the Chechen syndicate in any way he could for snatching Taras Morozov. There was no longer any hope of finding Taras still alive, in his opinion, and who else was there to blame for that, except Shishani and his savages?

The news wasn't all bad, of course. Morozov's disappearance had resulted in Tatlin's promotion to serve as second in command of the Brotherhood, an honor scarcely conceivable this time last year. Tatlin hadn't wished to advance by such means—well, not really—but who could refuse a golden opportunity when Fate presented it?

Not he.

Tatlin would never look a gift horse in the mouth, for fear of being bitten on the nose. It was his way to seize a chance and run with it for all that he was worth.

Now, having gained an elevation in the ranks by luck, he had to prove himself worthy. How better to accomplish that than by crushing the Chechens once and for all? In a single stroke, Tatlin could demonstrate both his grief at losing Taras and his worthiness as a successor to the vanished underboss.

"Stop here," he ordered. As his driver curbed the vehicle, Tatlin half turned, facing his soldiers in the backseat. "Who has the grenades?" he asked.

"I do," the middle gunner replied, and showed the dull green-painted orbs to prove it.

"One each," Tatlin said, then faced the soldier on his right. "And you're kicking the door?"

"Yes, sir."

"So do it. We don't have all day."

They scrambled from the car like clowns in a circus routine, or footballers spilling onto the field. Tatlin watched them go, the designated kicker needing two tries on the nightclub's door before he smashed the lock, then leaped aside. His comrades lobbed their hand grenades inside, then bolted for the car, leaving the kicker to follow with long, loping strides.

Six-second fuses were on the antipersonnel grenades, and Tatlin's car had barely pulled out from the curb when the first bomb exploded. He did not feel the shock wave, but he heard the muffled blast, saw the smoke and dust boiling out through the club's open doorway.

The second blast followed a heartbeat later, rattling windows on the street and thickening the cloud that fogged the sidewalk. Car alarms were shrilling now, like sirens wailing as the raiders sped away, northbound, to seek another target.

Tatlin hoped some of Shishani's men had been inside the club. He hoped that they were dead or mangled, wondering if he should have remained to check and finish off the wounded.

No.

He was the Brotherhood's second in command. As such, he dared not place himself at risk. His Family needed him.

And he was equal to the task.

Vidnoye, Moscow Oblast

"MORE VODKA, General?" asked Leonid Bezmel.

"Why not?" Ruslan Kozlov replied.

He had three glasses down, without showing a hint that he felt the liquor. These old soldiers were veteran boozers, as Bezmel knew well. But who in Russia today didn't seek consolation in vodka? Religious extremists and fitness fanatics who looked like animated corpses as they leaped around on television, contorting their stick figures into impossible shapes.

Bezmel watched with satisfaction as Nikolai Tatlin poured more vodka for Kozlov and himself. The young man was coming out of his first-day jitters, recovering from the surprise of the battlefield promotion that had plucked him from relative obscurity within the Family, ensconcing him as Taras Morozov's replacement.

If Tatlin was more assertive, and the past two days had been less chaotic, Bezmel might have suspected that his new number two had killed Taras himself, to clear space at the top. But Nikolai wasn't that clever.

Not yet.

Picking up their conversation where it had been interrupted by thirst, Bezmel said, "I share your concerns, of course, General. But Sokolov's removal is a temporary setback, nothing more. The world is still a vast market for surplus weapons of all kinds. That, I believe, will never change. We need another salesman, but one man—any man, anywhere—is easily replaced."

"You realize, I take it, that the buyers for this item were with Sokolov when he…evaporated? They've now been identified."

"Known terrorists, all dead," Bezmel said. "None of them a threat to us in any way. They can't be questioned, and there are no moles within the Sword of Allah. The militia and the Americans may speculate, but they have no supporting evidence of any crime but Sokolov's."

"So far. What if they still desire the item?"

"Then we sell…or not, as you prefer. They aren't the only bidders, General. I could name half a dozen countries that would pay more for our product than this ragtag gang of revolutionaries."

He sneered on the final word to make his point.

"Don't underestimate them, Leonid," Kozlov said. "What they lack in numbers, they make up for in obsessive concentration on their enemies. They don't forget. They don't forgive."

"I'm not afraid of raghead camel jockeys," Bezmel said.

"They want to blow themselves to bits outside my home, I'll send my gardener to hose the wall. Who cares?"

Kozlov allowed himself a smile at that. "I'm more concerned about Gennady," he admitted. "What he may decide to say when threatened with a life in prison."

"What's the difference?" Bezmel asked. "Neither one of us is extraditable."

"There is my rank and office to consider," Kozlov answered, somewhat stiffly.

"You've already reached retirement age, am I correct?" Bezmel inquired. Not waiting for the nod, he added, "So, you leave the army and become a businessman. You didn't plan to wear a uniform forever, did you? Drop dead on maneuvers, ten or fifteen years from now, the ancient warrior?"

Angry color tinged the general's cheeks. "I prefer not to leave in disgrace," he replied. "Or to lose the pension I've earned."

Bezmel smiled. "You've earned a great deal more than that, my friend. It's banked in Switzerland, if memory serves. But I take your point. Embarrassment is always best avoided. I suspect we can persuade Gennady not to implicate his partners in whatever crimes he stands accused of."

"How?"

"Appeal to reason and to friendship," Bezmel said. "If all else fails, he can be reached in prison just as easily as on the street. More so, in fact."

"To silence him?" the general asked.

"To do what must be done," Bezmel replied.

THE SOLDIER DIDN'T want to talk. He was a tough guy, born and raised, schooled at his mother's knee to hate informers with a passion normally reserved for child-killers. His father had been in the life, perhaps his grandfather before him, going back to Stalin's time. The odds were good that he expected to be murdered someday, in a gangland feud, before his hair turned white and thinned on top.

But not this way.

From the expression on his face, Bolan suspected that the soldier was experiencing problems with his short-term memory. A hard blow to the head could do that, sometimes. On the other hand, he might just be confused at suddenly regaining consciousness to find himself hog-tied and lying on a concrete floor, soaked through with gasoline from head to toe.

The chill of being doused had roused him from his stupor, and the gasoline smell, combined with the effects of pistol-whipping, probably made his head ache like there was no tomorrow. Which, in this one's case, could be true.

Bolan had snatched him from an alleyway behind a dive that catered to the Solntsevskaya Brotherhood, caught him chatting with a hooker, smiled and took him down before the soldier had a chance to reach his pistol in its shoulder rig. The hooker hadn't argued when a nod from Bolan sent her on her way.

It was a short drive to the warehouse where he'd questioned Taras Morozov. The underboss had been picked up by U.S. agents on station, and Bolan would call in with a request for a second haul.

He'd picked his latest prisoner after he heard the soldier chatting up a pair of lithesome British tourists in the bar. Call it a shopping expedition for them both. The girls had blown him off with giggles, but the mobster took it fairly well. His English wasn't great, but it would do for Bolan's purposes.

"You have one chance," Bolan said when his hostage finished blinking drops of gasoline out of his eyes. "Listen and think before you answer."

"I am not informer," the captive said.

"And you're not a French fry, yet. But that's your choice. Answer a simple question, or go up in smoke. Got it?"

"Better to die screaming than squeal like pig with treason."

"It's your call," said Bolan. He produced a lighter from his pocket, opened it and thumbed the friction wheel. "Any last words?"

A trembling moment's hesitation, then, "What is the question?"

"Leonid Bezmel. I need to find him, and there's no one home at his apartment. Where is he?"

"That's all?"

"That's all."

"You want an address, so you go and let him kill you? Why not say first thing you want to die. I help you, gladly."

"That's the spirit," Bolan said.

"You know where is Vidnoye? The Leninsky District? It is suburb of Moscow, to the southwest."

"I'll find it," Bolan told him. "Get to Bezmel."

"Is his place. Always there on weekends. Go out on Leninskiy Avenue to Troparevskiy Park. Then south on Teplostanskiy. See walls all around estate, with black iron gates. Maybe they let you in, if you ask nice."

"It's worth a try."

"You let me go now, eh?"

"Who said that?" Bolan asked him.

"You said!"

"Nope. I said I'd roast you if you didn't talk," Bolan replied. "You talked."

He drew the Beretta 93-R and rapped the heavy pistol against the man's temple.

"Someone will be along to take out the trash," he told the unconscious man.

CHAPTER TWENTY-ONE

Nikolai Tatlin was relieved when his boss ordered him to check in with the sentries patrolling the grounds. Their guest was nervous, although trying not to show it for his ego's sake, and Tatlin felt vaguely stifled in the study with two men of nearly equal power, eavesdropping as they debated an ex-partner's death.

He would have to get accustomed to such things, Tatlin knew, if he was going to survive and prosper in the role of Bezmel's underboss. More to the point, he had to absorb and emulate the chief's skill at manipulating others and controlling them, if he hoped to be boss himself someday.

It was a heady thought, once far beyond his wildest dreams but now within his grasp.

Almost. Assuming that he didn't disappear like Taras Morozov.

He moved among the guards with a familiarity that came from being one of them, until quite recently. They knew him, most of them respected him, and those who didn't were intelligent enough to fear him now that Tatlin had become Bezmel's right hand.

This night, a force of sixty-seven gunmen was assembled to protect Bezmel's estate and Colonel General Kozlov. All of them were armed with pistols, and the sentries roving the perimeter also had automatic weapons—submachine guns or Kalashnikovs—at the ready. In the house, spare rifles, SMGs and shotguns filled a spare room that had been converted to an arsenal when Bezmel bought the place.

Nikolai Tatlin hoped that it would be enough.

He didn't know exactly what was happening in Moscow, since the latest trouble started. Tatlin was accustomed to the skirmishes between his Solntsevskaya Brotherhood kinsmen and the Chechens, but the past two days had witnessed levels of unprecedented violence. From what he'd seen and heard, Tatlin knew the Obshina was responsible for part of that bloodshed, but not for all of it.

The Family had other enemies at large in Moscow, and beyond. Those other enemies had snatched Gennady Sokolov, whisked him away to God knew where, and Bezmel seemed to think the arms dealer wouldn't be coming back. Tatlin didn't pretend to understand it all, though agents of the FSB were certainly involved, and possibly Americans, as well. The only thing he knew for sure was that Bezmel expected him to stand against all adversaries, and to sacrifice himself, if need be, for the Family.

As Taras had. As any future boss would gladly do.

He moved among the sentries, joking with them, urging them to greater vigilance, making them feel that he was one of them despite his elevated rank. It was a quality of leadership that he admired in others, and was pleased to emulate.

It paid to have the soldiers on his side.

Relaxing, Tatlin told himself that no one, Chechen or American, would be so foolish as to challenge Leonid Bezmel in his own home. Aldo Shishani was a reckless mongrel, but he was no fool. As for the stranger Taras had been hunting when he vanished, the elusive Matthew Cooper, would he even know where Bezmel lived? And if so, would he dare to trespass there?

Tatlin hoped so. It would be quite a feather in his cap to bag the man his predecessor had pursued in vain. At one stroke, he could prove himself a worthy underboss *and* a potential leader of the pack.

One shot was all he needed. Just one—

When the crack of gunfire stung his ears, Tatlin was jerked out of his reverie, confused for just an instant by the synchronicity of thought and sound.

Then he was running, cursing silently, eager and frightened all at once, to see his wish come true.

THE SOLDIER hadn't lied about Bezmel's suburban hardsite. Bolan couldn't guess how many rubles it had set the mobster back, but if he had his way, the place would be a write-off soon enough.

It was full dark when Bolan parked his rental car on a tree-lined side street to the west of Bezmel's property and suited up for war. This time, he carried everything he'd purchased from the arms dealer his first night on the ground—or, rather, all that still remained after his other skirmishes in Moscow and Veliky Novgorod.

How many men had Bolan killed since touching down at Domodedovo International less than two days earlier?

Still not enough.

The only death that really counted for him so far had been Anzhela Pilkin's. There was nothing he could have done about it, short of ditching her before she got too deep into his mission, but the choice was hers. She'd hauled her weight, and then some, until Chance or Fate had brought her down.

Would she be living now if Bolan hadn't come to Moscow? Or would a different calamity have claimed her life, according to some cosmic timetable?

To hell with it.

The wall surrounding Leonid Bezmel's estate had one gate, on the street in front, but Bolan found his point of access at the rear, along the north side of the grounds. Back there, a pipe ran underneath the wall, presumably for draining during heavy rains or snow melt. It was broad enough for Bolan's body—barely—but before he could worm through it, he had to remove a stout metal grate bolted over its mouth.

He went to work with the Cold Steel Recon Tanto dagger, using its wedge-shaped tip as a screwdriver, putting every ounce of his strength and weight behind the effort to loosen screws that had rusted in place. It took Bolan the better part of half an hour to remove the grate, pausing each time one of the screws produced a high-pitched squeal, but finally the way was clear.

Bolan wedged himself into the pipe, pushing his Steyr AUG and the Mikor MGL launcher ahead of him, cursing the constant scraping of his gear that sounded as loud as thunder in the claustrophobic pipe. If there was grating at the other end, its screws beyond his reach, he'd have to wriggle backward to escape, then find another way inside.

There was no second grate.

Emerging into shrubbery that screened the pipe from view, Bolan wiped spiderwebs from his face with one hand and pushed up with the other, rising to his knees.

A startled sentry gaped at him, blurting something in Russian before Bolan's knife sank into his heart. The guy went rigid, dying on his feet—and triggered one round from his AK-47 as he fell into the shrubbery on Bolan's left.

A miss, but too damned loud to go unnoticed on the grounds, or in the neighborhood at large. As Bolan vaulted to his feet, he wondered if the guard had killed him, in effect, with that one shot.

"ONE MINUTE," said the limo driver, sounding the alert. Around Aldo Shishani, ten of his best soldiers double-checked their automatic weapons, putting on grim faces for the fight that lay ahead.

Two other limousines, both packed with gunmen, followed Shishani's tank in a curious convoy, looking more appropriate for a film premiere or a gala charity event than the climactic battle in a long-running gang war. The lead car, running well ahead of Shishani's limo, was a jet-black Lada Niva SUV with four men on board, all wearing crash helmets and padding for their role in the attack.

Shishani had to breach the gate somehow, and he assumed that Bezmel wouldn't open up to let him in. Hence, the SUV with its stout ramming grille on the nose, accelerating now into the run at Bezmel's gate, where sentries would have seen it coming and would now be wondering aloud over the driver's plan.

They knew a second later, when the Lada crashed head-on into the gate, delivering 2,600 pounds of irresistible force on target at something close to fifty miles per hour. The wrought iron buckled, heaved and swung aside, while sentries on the gate sprayed automatic fire along the Lada's armored flanks.

Before they had a chance to realize that their bullets were wasted, Shishani's limo followed the Lada inside, weapons chattering from gun ports on both sides, sweeping the lawn clear of defenders while the Lada charged on toward the great house ahead.

Bezmel's long driveway was flanked by globe lights along its hundred-yard length, and the windows of his mansion were illuminated from within. Still, it was dark enough outside to leave Shishani blinking in surprise as a rocket flared in the night, streaking from the southeast corner of the mansion toward the Lada Niva SUV.

"Watch out!" Shishani cried, a wasted reflex, since the soldiers in the Lada couldn't hear him, and it was too late for them already. The explosion turned their vehicle into a rolling funeral pyre, losing momentum as its blasted engine died and its fat, expensive tires began to melt.

"Son of a bitch!" he raged. "I want these pricks dead, you hear me? Every asshole you can find! All dead!"

A low collective snarl from his commandos told Shishani that they understood his order, shared his wishes. Their comrades would be avenged.

Ten paces from the house, already drawing fire, the limousine lurched to a halt, doors opening onto a view of Hell on Earth.

BOLAN WAS JOGGING toward the house before his first kill finished twitching in the flower bed. He'd snagged the soldier's AK-47 on the run, another ten pounds added to his load, but it might save him a second or so on reloading when he had used up the first magazine for his Steyr. Unless they weighed you down to the point of immobility, there was no such thing as too many weapons in battle.

The first shot, as expected, brought more gunners on the run. Two came around the northwest corner of the mansion as Bolan approached, a third appearing simultaneously to the northeast. All of them were packing automatic weapons, none more dangerous at first glance than the rest.

Bolan was diving through a shoulder roll when they began unloading at him, bullets of various calibers buzzing around him like giant mosquitoes thirsty for blood. Bolan returned fire on the roll, saw one of his targets stagger and clutch at his side, then the others were ducking and dodging, looking for cover.

The Executioner found it first, behind a set of lawn chairs. Nothing to them in terms of protection from incoming bullets, all nylon and aluminum tubing, but the chairs confused his target outline long enough for him to sight on the nearest shooter and tattoo his chest with a 3-round burst of 5.56 mm tumblers.

Then he was rolling again as fire from his right punctured one of the chairs, flipped it over completely and sawed off one arm of another. Bolan hugged the deck, angling to find his target through the Steyr AUG's Swarovski sight, framing a form in motion as the shooter tried to duck aside.

Too late.

At least one of the four rounds Bolan triggered found its

mark, drilling the sentry's shoulder, spinning him halfway around before he fell. There was no mercy in the midst of battle, when the stakes were life or death, and Bolan didn't let his adversary rise to fight again. A second burst ripped through the moving form downrange, and canceled further movement on the spot.

Time wasted double-killing any target was a loss no soldier could recoup, but Bolan did his best. Before the echo of his final shots could die away, he was up and running toward the house once more, closing the gap to fifty yards or so with loping strides. More soldiers would be on the scene in seconds flat, and then—

He broke stride, dropping to a crouch as gunfire crackled somewhere up ahead of him, beyond the house. Muffled by distance and the intervening bulk of Bezmel's mansion, Bolan knew it had to come from the front yard or thereabouts.

Now, what the hell?

Shouting was added to the mix, and then a loud explosion, reminiscent of an RPG warhead. The gunfire multiplied, became intensive, shattering whatever trace of peace and quiet still remained to the exclusive rich-man's neighborhood.

Bolan had no idea who had arrived to crash his party, but he wasn't fool enough to let the moment pass him by. Wishing the new arrivals well—but not *too* well—he rose and sprinted toward the house.

"MY GOD! What's happening?"

The color had drained from Colonel General Kozlov's ruddy face. His voice was on the verge of cracking, like a boy's in puberty.

"I'll need a moment to discover that," Bezmel replied, fighting an urge to punch the general squarely in his face.

Kozlov was pacing like a nervous lion in a cage, wringing his hands. Bezmel paused in the doorway to his study, shouting for Nikolai Tatlin, receiving no answer.

Turning on the general, Bezmel gripped an arm, noting the startled look on Kozlov's face with silent satisfaction, pulling him out of the room and along the hallway toward another door. Bezmel pushed through it, steering Kozlov toward what seemed to be a closet.

"Wha-what are you doing?" Kozlov stammered. "Have you lost your mind?"

"Only my patience, General." Bezmel threw back the door and shoved Kozlov across the threshold of his private panic room, a sanctuary fitted out to withstand any assault short of rockets or heavy artillery.

As Kozlov blinked at him, bewildered, Bezmel said, "You will be safe here, come what may. This door, when shut, may only open from the inside. Even I cannot reach you, unless you punch in the code."

Kozlov saw the keypad, swallowed hard and asked, "What *is* the code?"

"I'll tell you later," Bezmel said, and slammed the door. Retreating from the panic room, he smiled, adding, "If both of us are still alive."

Two of his men were waiting for him in the hallway, both holding Kalashnikovs against their chests. They looked confused and worried, with good reason. From the sound of things outside, the house was under attack from both front and rear. Bezmel had yet to glimpse a single enemy, but he assumed Aldo Shishani was responsible. Who else would dare attack his home like this, confronting Bezmel's guns while the militia came rushing in behind to close the trap?

He had a chance to finish it tonight. After long years of skirmishing with filthy Chechens for control of Moscow, Bezmel could conclude their struggle in a single stroke. But he wasn't invincible, and he'd gain nothing if a bullet brought him down before the final victory was his.

Before leading his men outside, Bezmel doubled back to his study, flung open a cupboard and snatched one of the

Kevlar vests hanging inside. He slipped it on, fastened its Velcro straps beneath his arms, then chose an AK-107 rifle from the rack of weapons. It was already loaded, but Bezmel grabbed spare magazines, stuffing his pockets as he moved back toward the hallway that would take him through the house and out to face his enemies.

The time had come to get his hands dirty.

ALDO SHISHANI CROUCHED beside his limousine, sheltered behind its open door. Despite the car's armor plating, he still felt exposed, squatting there in his enemy's driveway, with nothing but two stout soldiers shielding his back and right flank. He felt a great temptation to crawl back inside the limo, slam and lock the door behind him, but he couldn't bear the shame of being proved a coward.

They were pinned down within spitting distance of their goal, Shishani's limo and the others ranged behind it taking fire from half the mansion's southern-facing windows. Every time another bullet struck the car, scarring its paint and ricocheting into space, Shishani flinched and mouthed a silent curse. His knuckles ached from clutching his AKS-74U carbine in a numbing death grip.

So far, Shishani hadn't fired a shot. He felt a bit ridiculous, just crouching there, while his soldiers engaged their foes, but it was clear to him that if he raised his head, someone might shoot it off. For all his raging talk about settling old scores before they crashed the gate of Bezmel's property, Aldo Shishani found himself afraid to die.

He looked around for Magen Manaev, but couldn't see much past the soldiers who flanked him, could hear virtually nothing but the hammering reports from their weapons and those damned pinging, whining sounds of bullet impacts on the limousine.

How long before another RPG round sizzled through the darkness, this one with Shishani's name on it? The limo dealer had assured him that the cars he'd purchased were designed to drive through fire and shrapnel, shrugging off explosive charges, but that clearly didn't mean they could withstand direct hits from antitank weapons. One rocket was all it would take to ignite the car's fuel tank and bathe him in bright liquid fire.

That mental image quelled his urge to crawl inside the limousine. Better to take a bullet in the head than broil alive.

But better, still, to finish off his enemies and get away from there before the damned militia arrived.

"Where's Magen?" he demanded. The pair of gunners shrugged, more or less in unison, but offered no reply. Their focus was on killing, just where it belonged.

Shishani freed one hand from his carbine and whipped out his cell phone, speed-dialing Manaev's number. He couldn't be far off. It seemed to the mobster that he ought to hear his first lieutenant's phone ring, but the gunfire swamped all other sounds.

After what seemed a dozen rings, Manaev answered with a snarling, *"What?"*

"Where are you?" Shishani asked.

"Right behind you! By the second car!"

Shishani turned, but still saw nothing past the Kevlar-padded bulk of his protectors. Frustrated, he snapped, "Get your men together! We storm the house in one minute!"

"But—"

"Do it!" Shishani bellowed. "No fucking excuses!"

Snapping shut the cell phone, tossing it into the limousine so Manaev couldn't call him back and argue, Shishani felt that he was starting to regain control. Whatever happened in the next few minutes would become the stuff of gangland legends.

Win or lose, Aldo Shishani would be making history.

BOLAN HAD LEARNED from long and grim experience to seize any advantage in a firefight. Anything that granted him an edge over his enemies, be it a rainstorm, bolt of lightning from the heavens, or an unexpected raid by enemies he couldn't even see, Bolan would take that extra edge and gut his adversaries with it.

Puzzled as he was by the diversion, he was grateful when it drew most of Bezmel's soldiers away from the rear of his home, toward the front lawn and street. Only two stayed behind, huddled down near an outdoor spa, using its cedar housing for cover.

Bolan kept their heads down with a long burst from the AK-47 he'd appropriated, watched as the spa's tub sprang a dozen spouting leaks, then primed a frag grenade and lobbed it well over the hot tub, dropping it a pace or two behind the crouching shooters.

If they saw death coming, neither one of them was swift enough to dodge it. Bolan heard one of them screaming underneath the blast noise, paused for several beats to let survivors leap or scrabble clear, then left them to the work of bleeding out.

Before him, access to the house was blocked by sliding doors of tinted glass, not very different from those he'd crashed at Sokolov's villa in Veliky Novgorod...how many hours earlier? He emptied the remainder of the AK's magazine to clear the way, then dropped it, gripped his AUG and plunged into the house.

By chance, Bolan had dropped a shooter that he hadn't even seen behind the smoky glass. The guy was gut-shot, trying not to scream, and fumbling for a holstered pistol that he should've drawn before the party started. Bolan put a single round between his eyes, four grams of death tumbling through the soldier's brain and scattering his final thoughts into oblivion.

Being inside the house was one thing. Finding Leonid Bezmel in all the chaos that surrounded him was something else. For all Bolan knew, the mobster could have an escape hatch or tunnel, might pop up three houses downrange with a car waiting for him to whisk him away.

At least there'd been no helicopter on the grounds as he approached. He wouldn't need an antiaircraft gun, this time.

Small favors.

Bolan hurried through the spacious TV-game room, weaving through the thickly padded chairs and sofas. No one but the guy he'd left behind appeared to be responding to his blast-in, probably because the racket from the south—or front—side of the mansion had reached nearly deafening proportions.

This was no quick hit-and-git, no skirmish ranging half a dozen do-or-die raiders against the home team. It was sounding more and more like a pitched battle, verging on a siege. And while he knew it couldn't last, with the militia a quick phone call away, it still gave Bolan cause for hope.

If he couldn't eliminate Bezmel, perhaps the home invaders would. One bullet was as good as any other, if it did the job. But Bolan didn't want to let it go at that.

He wanted the godfather for himself.

With that in mind, he moved deeper into the vast, palatial house.

CHAPTER TWENTY-TWO

Nikolai Tatlin squeezed off two rounds from his Saiga 12K tactical shotgun, riding the weapon's heavy recoil. He saw the buckshot pellets strike a Chechen soldier who was charging toward the house and pitch him backward, tumbling head over heels.

The Saiga was built to mimic a Kalashnikov's appearance, down to its folding stock and detachable 10-round magazine. For some unknown reason, its designer had installed a mechanism that wouldn't allow the shotgun to fire with its stock folded, but a *Mafiya* gunsmith had overcome that obstacle with little effort. Now, with its 17-inch barrel, the 12K was an efficient semiautomatic killing machine.

Tatlin found another moving target, swung to lead it and did the job with a single round this time. The Chechen never knew what hit him—or, if he did, there was nothing the pig could do to save himself, Tatlin thought. The buckshot hurled him sideways, off the mansion's steps, and left him twitching in a flower bed, among the boss's roses.

Who said that life wasn't a rose garden?

As if in answer to that cocky thought, a burst of submachine gunfire ripped through the window frame, inches from Tatlin's face. The glass was gone already, but a storm of wooden splinters stung his cheek and scalp.

He cursed, ducking back from the window and dabbing fresh blood from his face. Tatlin glared at the soldiers beside him, daring one of them to smile at his discomfort. Anything at all to rate a swift kick in the head.

No smiles. They were too busy fighting for their lives and for the boss's home.

Tatlin had glimpsed Aldo Shishani near the closest of the limousines, but had missed his shot at the Obshina's warlord. Now he wished he had an RPG, but the only launcher they kept in the house had already fired off its lone rocket.

Tatlin wondered if he would be punished for that, or if Bezmel would place the blame where it rightly belonged, on his precious Taras Morozov. Either way, it wouldn't matter if he couldn't stay alive to face the boss, their enemies defeated on the field of victory.

A sudden storm of gunfire struck the mansion like a rain squall, pouring through the shattered windows, scarring walls and vaulted ceilings, chipping antique statuary, punching holes through furniture and men. One of his soldiers sprawled beside Tatlin, his brains spilling from a fist-size exit wound behind one ear.

Tatlin recoiled, though he'd seen worse, suddenly horrified at the prospect of standing in those brains. He risked a glance outside and saw the Chechens charging in a ragged skirmish line, taking their hits but moving forward. Near the center of the line, Shishani bawled commands and fired some kind of automatic carbine from the hip as he advanced.

Snarling a curse, Tatlin lined up his shot, was taking up the trigger slack when something struck his rib cage with the force of a sledgehammer blow. He toppled over backward, blasting plaster from the ceiling as he fell, then lost his shotgun as his fingers suddenly refused to hold their grip.

Tatlin had thought there'd be more pain. Instead, a kind of arctic numbness chilled him, took away all feeling as he lay there, heedless of the gunfire raging back and forth around him. It no longer mattered.

He wasn't sure if he believed in any kind of afterlife, but in the final conscious moments that remained to him, he realized that he would soon resolve the mystery.

When Bolan met the next small group of Bezmel's soldiers, they were in retreat, stampeding through a kitchen large enough to serve a five-star restaurant. They skidded to a halt at the sight of Bolan, spent a precious second verifying that he wasn't one of them, then raised their guns in unison.

Too late.

He dropped the nearest of them with a 3-round burst, then found cover behind a service island in the middle of the kitchen as the other three began to unload on him. Stainless steel and marble kept their rounds from reaching him, but ricochets around the gleaming room could prove as deadly as a well-aimed shot if Bolan lingered where he was without breaking the standoff.

First he tried a few grazing rounds of his own, stitching a burst across the room's stone floor but getting nowhere with it. Next he set down the Steyr, unslung the Mikor MGL and braced himself for what was bound to happen when he launched a 40 mm thunderclap at enemies no more than twenty feet away.

His ears would take a beating, certainly, but Bolan thought the service island would shield him from whatever shrapnel made its way around the room after the blast. The key was proper placement of his first round, putting it where it would spend most of its force against his enemies, when he had no real opportunity to aim.

And no more time to waste.

The twelve-pound weapon measured twenty-eight inches overall with its stock folded, and Bolan didn't need to aim it from his shoulder. Rising slightly from his crouch, he chose a mark against the wall directly opposite, behind his adversaries, and squeezed off a round before they glimpsed him and began to fire again.

The launcher's double-action mechanism made a clicking sound, immediately followed by the pop of firing, and Bolan was back in his crouch, hunkered low, before the impact fuse on his grenade made contact with the beige tiled wall. A heartbeat later, someone struck a giant gong and sent its echoes rolling through the house.

Accompanied by screams.

All three of Bolan's would-be killers were down and out as he rose to survey them. One was clearly dead or dying, while the other two writhed in pain from catastrophic shrapnel wounds. They might survive, if someone rushed them to a trauma ward within the next few minutes, but it wasn't in the cards.

Instead, each got a single round between the eyes.

The Executioner moved on.

MAGEN MANAEV watched his boss rally the troops that remained for a rush toward the house, and wondered if Shishani had lost his mind. The raid had never been a great idea, but now that it had clearly failed, shouldn't they be concerned with getting off the property alive, instead of giving Bezmel's soldiers one more chance to kill them all?

Manaev had a plan. Assuming that he was the only member of the raiding party still in full possession of his faculties, he meant to get out while he could and make his way back to Family headquarters, and begin the process of rebuilding the Obshina.

It wouldn't be easy, of course. But he knew Chechen gangsters all over Russia who would join his new band if he sweetened the terms a bit, made them believe he was stronger and smarter than Aldo. The *smarter* bit should be easy, when they heard about Shishani's half-baked scheme that climaxed with mass suicide. What decent boss would sacrifice his Family for ego, knowing that the fight was lost before it even started?

Manaev was working his way across the mansion's vast lawn, scuttling past decorative hedges and the leafy creatures in a topiary that would certainly have fascinated him under some other circumstances. As it was, all he could think about was getting through the shattered, twisted gate and sprinting down the street before the militia arrived.

Behind him, Magen heard explosions rattling the mansion's walls and windows from inside. He didn't know what that was all about—Shishani's soldiers hadn't brought grenades—but he experienced a moment's doubt about retreating.

What if Aldo pulled it off, somehow? What if he swept Bezmel and all his soldiers off the map, came out of it a hero, while Manaev was exposed as a cowardly traitor?

Impossible!

Half of the Chechen raiding force was dead before Manaev made his move to flee. Some of the rest were wounded, and they were outnumbered by Bezmel's defenders, fighting on familiar ground. The cause was lost.

Some forty yards of open lawn now lay between Manaev and his only exit from the battleground. Crawling across it on his belly would have been humiliating, and would take up too much precious time. No, he would have to run.

Magen Manaev ran. The last time he had run that fast, he had been twelve years old, fleeing a holdup scene with the militia pursuing him, one of them firing bullets past his head. That night had been like this one: he had everything to win—or lose.

And he made it!

Pausing at the gate, slumped against one of its stanchions to catch his breath, Manaev knew that he was only a half-dozen paces from safety. From freedom.

He stepped forward, toward the open street, was halfway there when a rough voice called out, "Hey, fuckhead!"

Now, who was calling him a fuckhead? Turning on his heel, Manaev saw one of Bezmel's gate sentries, kneeling gut-shot on the grass. One bloody hand clutched the front of his shirt. The other aimed a pistol at Manaev's face.

Well, shit! Magen Manaev thought—and died.

BOLAN STEPPED from the smoke-wreathed kitchen, moving deeper into Leonid Bezmel's palace. A silent stopwatch in his head kept track of passing time, reminding him that he was on thin ice already, edging toward a point where nothing but death lay before him.

Push the odds too far, and he was dead.

Wait for the cops to scoop him up, and he was dead—albeit with a brief delay for questioning.

The smart move would be to leave, but he couldn't do that. Not before he'd even glimpsed his primary target.

Bezmel was somewhere in the rambling house. Bolan knew it. And if he couldn't find the mobster, if his man had found some cubbyhole to hide in, there was only one way to achieve his goal.

Bring down the house.

The Mikor MGL would get him started, with its high-explosive 40 mm rounds. The mansion had been built to last, but who planned for a series of HE explosions when they drew blueprints? Bolan had already proved that Bezmel's windows weren't bulletproof. Neither was his palace in the burbs invincible.

The launcher's double-action trigger mechanism permitted a rapid-fire rate of two rounds per second, but Bolan didn't feel like rushing it. Despite the numbers running down inside his skull, he took his time to do it right.

The Mikor still had five HE rounds in its revolving cylinder when he started firing at doorjambs and load-bearing walls, ducking shrapnel and debris from each blast as he went. The racket drove soldiers before him, fleeing in lieu of attempting to stop the madman in their midst. Bolan let them go, as long as they were running in the opposite direction, and his Steyr AUG dealt with the few who stood to fight.

When he had spent the last five rounds, Bolan found himself crouched at the foot of a staircase curving upward to the second floor. Bedrooms up there, he reasoned, and who knew what else?

He released the Mikor's cylinder axis pin and swung the aluminum cylinder out to the left, then unlatched the rear plate of the cylinder to expose the spent casings. Dumping them out, Bolan inserted his fingers into the empty chambers and wound the internal spring mechanism that made it turn counterclockwise with each trigger pull. That done, he reloaded with a mix of HE and incendiary rounds, then closed the cylinder once more and reengaged the axis pin.

Ready to rock and roll.

His first round was incendiary, angled up the sweeping staircase for deflection off a wall and then along a corridor that was invisible from where he stood. A fire up there might flush some rats from hiding, even as he cut off their escape.

Was that a distant siren that he heard? Or more than one?

Move on.

The Executioner had enemies to kill.

ALDO SHISHANI didn't know which of the Brotherhood soldiers had shot him, but it hurt like hell. It might not be a mortal wound, despite the pain, but son of a bitch, it hurt! Slumped in a corner of the mansion's foyer, bleeding onto Bezmel's marble floor, Shishani felt like weeping from the savage pain.

The slug had bored between his ribs, on the left side, and he was having difficulty breathing now. Not quite a classic sucking chest wound, and he didn't think his lung was ruptured, but the blood spilling inside his abdomen was putting pressure on his lungs and heart. Shishani didn't need a medical degree to realize that he was dead unless he got some help.

But there was no help to be had.

He shifted, groaning, and rested his head on the hip of

a fallen soldier. Was it Mily or Tikhon? Shishani couldn't say, with the face blown off, since he'd paid no attention to clothing. Stone dead, either way, and now useless except as a pillow.

His new position eased the pressure in his chest a bit, but at a price. Blood ran more freely from his bullet wound, sapping Shishani's strength with each drop lost. He still had strength enough to crawl, perhaps even to stand, but walking would require assistance.

Shishani wondered what had become of Magen Manaev. His second in command wasn't among the latest dead, hadn't joined in the final charge on Bezmel's castle. The mob boss guessed that he was lying on the grounds somewhere, shot down before the last rally. There wouldn't be an opportunity for them to say goodbye. But, then again, what difference did it make?

Shishani looked around for his carbine and couldn't find it. He had paused to reload in the foyer, after killing one of Bezmel's men with his last rounds, and some prick had shot the weapon from his hands. Perhaps a fragment from the same bullet had torn into his side.

Shishani didn't know, and he no longer cared. What earthly difference did it make?

He reached his pistol, finally, and pulled it from its holster with an effort that left him gasping, drenched in sweat and blood. Shishani clutched the weapon with slippery fingers, hoping that he'd remembered to put a live round in its chamber.

Footsteps approached.

Shifting once again, hissing through clenched teeth at the pain, Shishani craned his neck and saw a figure drawing closer. From where he lay, the man seemed to defy all laws of gravity. Not walking upside down, exactly, but canting off at forty-odd degrees from the vertical. It took another moment to recognize the new arrival's face.

"You don't look well, Aldo," Leonid Bezmel said.

Shishani snorted. "I've been better."

"Well, you've wrecked my house at least. That must be some consolation."

As Bezmel spoke, explosions rocked the palace. Frowning, Bezmel said, "You brought the big guns, eh?"

Shishani didn't know what the asshole was talking about, but he would rather die than admit it. And that, he supposed, would come next.

"Anything to annoy you," he said.

"So, then, mission accomplished." Bezmel swung his weapon—some kind of Kalashnikov—downward, bringing the muzzle to rest on Shishani's forehead. "Any last words?"

"Only *fuck you!*" he spit, and squeezed his pistol's trigger once before the world exploded in his face and howling darkness swallowed him alive.

BEZMEL LIMPED back across his ravaged parlor, cursing the stupidity that had compelled him to bandy insults with a worthless Chechen. A worthless *armed* Chechen, whose last act had drilled Bezmel's left calf, six inches below the knee.

The slug had missed bone and vital arteries, cutting a clean through-and-through, but it still felt as if Bezmel had a red-hot poker thrust through his muscles and tendons. He hobbled along, trailing blood and curses, surveying the chaos around him.

The house was on fire. That was clear from the volume of smoke in the air, though he'd seen no flames yet. The explosions had done it, he guessed—and what kind of weapon was blasting his palace to pieces?

Whatever it was, Bezmel wanted a dozen.

The worst of it was over now, he thought, except for mopping up and dealing with the damned militia. Burying this mess would cost him a fortune, but it would be worth every ruble. With the Chechen gang out of his life forever—or at least until the next pack came along—Bezmel could concentrate on recouping his losses, expanding his empire.

But first, he had to get Colonel General Kozlov out of the panic room, before he baked like a potato in an oven with the house in flames around him.

The thought made Bezmel smile despite his pain. The look on Kozlov's face when he had slammed the door was priceless. He supposed the aging soldier might be itching for revenge, but then again, he should feel gratitude for still being alive when so many others were not.

And if he gave Bezmel any more problems, just now, perhaps he wouldn't live to see another sunrise, after all. It would be simple to arrange for one more death, blame the Obshina for assassinating Kozlov, while Bezmel took honors as his defender.

Then again, if he left Kozlov where he was and let him fry, no one would ever know the two of them had been together when Shishani's men attacked. Kozlov would simply disappear, consigned to ashes, and would be replaced by someone else. Perhaps someone more amiable, who charged lower fees for services rendered. And with Gennady Sokolov removed, there was no middleman to rake off a lion's share of the profits from the sale of Russian surplus weapons in a world obsessed with self-destruction.

Save the man, or let him burn?

Bezmel was still weighing his options when he turned a corner, halfway to the panic room, and found a stranger standing in his path.

"That's far enough," the stranger said in English.

"MATTHEW COOPER, I presume," Leonid Bezmel said.

"Looks like it's just you and me," Bolan answered.

"You think so?" the mobster asked. "I believe I still have soldiers here, somewhere."

"Not soldiers," Bolan said, watching the gun in Bezmel's hand as he replied. "Killers."

"Is there a difference?"

"A big one," Bolan told him. "Or, at least, there should be."

"Soldiers kill for God and country, eh?" Bezmel responded in a mocking tone. "Or, anyway, for country. Here in Russia, it is not so much for God."

"Soldiers have discipline," Bolan replied. "They follow orders."

"Mine obey. You may believe it," Bezmel said.

"From fear, not from commitment."

"You're American, I take it, not Canadian?"

Bolan moved one step closer to his adversary, nodding.

"So," Bezmel continued, "you have come a long way to discuss philosophy."

"I came for Sokolov," Bolan replied. "I've stayed for you."

"Should I be flattered?"

"Suit yourself."

"We have the shoot-out now? Like *High Noon,* in your films?"

Bezmel began his move, then, with the words still on his lips. It wasn't bad, but he'd been too long sitting in an office, telling others where to go and who to kill. He telegraphed the movement with a twitching at one corner of his mouth, and by the time he bent his knees to crouch and turn, Bolan had stroked the trigger of his Steyr AUG.

Five rounds left the weapon's muzzle at 3,100 feet per second, barely tasting smoky air at all before they ripped through Bezmel's chest, no more than fifteen feet downrange. They struck with 1,303 foot-pounds of force, lifting Bezmel a good six inches off his feet, tumbling erratically inside him as impact destabilized the full-metal-jacket projectiles, wreaking bloody havoc on his vitals.

Bolan stood above the dead man for a moment, nothing more to say. He thought of Anzhela in passing, knew that score was still unsettled and then turned his back on the dead.

Time to live.

Time to *go*.

Bezmel had been right about one thing. Whether you called them soldiers or thugs, he still had live men on the grounds. They'd soon be distracted by cops—there was no doubt he heard sirens now—but any one of them still might get lucky with a stranger, snipe him from a distance or from ambush as he fled.

Time to be careful, right, and get the hell away from there.

The best way, Bolan reckoned, was the way he had come in. The only other route meant stealing one of Bezmel's cars and driving through the front gate, where the militia would be arriving any second now. That virtually guaranteed that he would be arrested, if he wasn't simply shot on sight, and jail meant death for Bolan.

Someone—be it Bezmel's heir apparent, someone from the Chechen team, or Major Chaliapin from the FSB—would see to it that Bolan's hours were numbered in the lockup. He'd done jail in the States, and didn't plan to try it out in Russia.

Bolan retraced his steps and cleared the house, or what was left of it. Passing the grand staircase, he heard flames crackling on the second floor, and someone screaming up there, trapped. It was a man's voice, and he put it out of mind.

No rescue missions, here and now.

Sirens were at the distant gate and closing in as Bolan

wedged himself into the drainage pipe and started wriggling through. Moonlight at the end of the dark tunnel beckoned him on.

Toward more death.

CHAPTER TWENTY-THREE

Moscow

Kiril Astapkovich glanced at his Rolex watch, frowning at the time. He was a busy man, and waiting idly always made him nervous. Most particularly on this day, when fresh reports of carnage and chaos arrived by the hour.

The senator poured himself a glass of mint vodka from one of the complimentary bottles furnished by the Hotel Cosmos management. Astapkovich was well-known at the Cosmos, which was twenty minutes by car from the Kremlin, and he used it for some of his romantic trysts and for meetings like this day's, where discretion was critical.

The meeting itself wasn't due to start for another ten minutes. Astapkovich hoped that the man he'd come to meet would be on time, as usual. He knew better than to keep Astapkovich waiting—had felt the lash of the senator's tongue, the one time it happened—but things were unsettled in Moscow.

And beyond it.

Sipping his vodka, Astapkovich reflected on the mayhem of the past two days, incredible even by Russian standards. There'd been nothing like it since the Nord-Ost theater siege of 2002, and even that was different. The hostage crisis had been localized, contained. Despite three hundred dead and nearly seven hundred wounded, it could pass for entertainment. Muscovites had watched it on their television sets as if it were a bloody game show.

Not so with the bloodshed of the past forty-odd hours.

Death was everywhere and anywhere around Moscow, from downtown to the ritzy suburb where Astapkovich himself maintained an opulently understated home. And in Veliky Novgorod, as well.

Astapkovich cursed Gennady Sokolov in absentia. It was his fault, the senator thought, that this hell had descended upon them from out of a blue sky, wreaking havoc with business as usual. While Sokolov had put millions of rubles in his pocket, the senator felt no compunction about wishing him a life of ass-reamed misery in prison.

No, scratch that.

He wished Sokolov *dead*. Living, the man might start to feel aggrieved, abandoned, and decide to take some of his old friends with him on the one-way trip to some Western gulag. The impulse was understandable—Astapkovich might have done the same thing, himself, in Sokolov's place—but that didn't ease the senator's mind.

He had too much to lose at this point in his life.

That, of course, was one reason for his presence at the Hotel Cosmos. He would suggest, in no uncertain terms, that something had to be done to silence Sokolov—for his own sake, and to protect those even higher up the food chain.

The meeting's other purpose was to nominate Sokolov's successor, a new and improved Merchant of Death who would keep the wheels of commerce turning, possibly improve the profit margin, and ensure that customers around the world were satisfied with the products they received.

As long as wars continued and Astapkovich maintained his influence in Moscow, he would be a wealthy man. The first part of that formula was guaranteed by human nature. For the rest, he needed friends who both admired and feared him.

The warheads, now...that could be problematic. Sokolov had nearly closed a deal with one group of fanatics, but his kidnapping—and their demise—had evidently scuttled that.

Astapkovich didn't oppose selling off Russian nukes on principle, but he preferred a rather different clientele.

Given the choice—and he would have it, when Sokolov's heir was nominated and approved—he would prefer to see weapons of mass destruction sold only to governments. It was no guarantee of sanity, per se, but even the kleptocracies of Africa and Southeast Asia had some kind of checks and balances in place. Their rulers, crazed as some might seem when posturing for television cameras, still understood that life had to continue if they were to keep on receiving their perks.

Astapkovich wasn't concerned about expanding what the media referred to as the *nuclear fraternity.* At present, only nine sovereign states possessed nuclear weapons. Russia led the field, with a minimum of thirteen thousand warheads, trailed by the United States with less than ten thousand, while other fading powers ate their dust.

That left nearly two hundred nations worldwide, all eager to improve their self-image and influence.

Sometimes, Astapkovich missed the old "balance of terror," when great powers faced each other across frontiers and bargaining tables, deciding the fate of millions with one hand on the trigger and both eyes on the bottom line. He missed the days before "Western democracy" had turned Mother Russia into a weird, freakish hybrid of Manhattan and Las Vegas.

It might be too late to recapture Russia's lost glory, but Astapkovich was honor-bound to try. And if he got filthy rich in the process…well, what was wrong with that? He would take the best from both worlds, combine them and turn it all to his personal benefit.

What made a hero, after all, except initiative and courage?

Astapkovich was checking his watch again when he heard a muffled rapping on the door.

MAJOR MAKSIM Chaliapin was one minute early for his meeting with the senator. Red-eyed from lack of sleep, with stubble on his face resembling hoarfrost, wrinkles in the same suit he'd worn yesterday, the major ducked his head in deference while greeting Kiril Astapkovich.

"I must say that you look terrible," the senator informed him.

"My apologies. There's been no time for anything but counting bodies overnight."

"And is it true about Bezmel?"

"He's dead," Chaliapin confirmed. "And Aldo Shishani, as well."

"So, a housecleaning."

"Let's hope that it's finished."

"Why wouldn't it be?" the senator asked.

Chaliapin shrugged, even that effort leaving him weary. "Whoever kidnapped Sokolov is still out there," he said. "The damned Americans won't simply lock him up, you know. They'll want to know who helped him get the weapons he was selling."

"Kozlov," Astapkovich said.

"*Mostly* Kozlov."

"And where is the general? I tried to call him last night, and again this morning. His wife says he's out, and he hasn't been seen at his office."

Chaliapin frowned at that. "I called to tell him about Sokolov's abduction, but we haven't spoken since. Maybe he's got a girlfriend?"

"It would be a *boyfriend*," Astapkovich said, correcting him. "And those of the age he prefers should all be in school at this time of day."

The major's frown deepened, reflecting disgust.

"You don't approve, Maksim?"

"Do you, Senator?"

"We're all human. We all have our faults."

"Maybe so, but there used to be boundaries."

"And there still are. Wealth and influence, Maksim. They decide who's condemned for his foibles and who's excused."

Chaliapin nodded. Even under communism, it had been the same.

"If Kozlov's gone," Astapkovich said, "we'll need two new partners."

"I have files on Kozlov's aides," the major said.

"Of course you do."

"One or another of them will be pleased to take his place, but a promotion will be necessary."

"Not a problem. Friends help friends."

"As for replacing Sokolov…"

"We need someone of military background, separated from the service. Someone who knows weapons inside out, and who is free to travel widely."

"But a Russian, certainly?"

"Oh, yes. And this time, we must do a better job protecting him from kidnappers."

"Agreed."

"We can reduce the risk, to some extent, by choosing someone with a low profile. Less prone to courting journalists and film producers, eh?"

"More greed, less ego?"

"I believe we understand each other.

"And this business with the Arab rabble," Astapkovich said. "I would hate to see it repeated. Sell them small arms, of course, whatever they want. But we don't need them trying to blow up the world."

"If you have a candidate…"

"In fact, I have two," the senator said. "You probably know them already."

Chaliapin raised a wary eyebrow, waiting.

"First, Pavel Korovin," Astapkovich said.

"Ex-OMON," Chaliapin said, abbreviating Otryad Militsii Osobogo Naznacheniya, the special-purpose police unit that served as the militia's mobile SWAT team. "Cashiered after that business at the Minsk October Square four years ago."

"A good man, if an overzealous one."

"Your second choice?"

"Orest Losenko," Astapkovich replied.

"From SOBR," Chaliapin said, this time referring to Spetsial'nye Otryady Bystrogo Reagirovaniya, the Russian Interior Ministry's special rapid reaction unit. "A captain, if memory serves, when the unit dissolved in 2002."

"And employed since that time in private security," Astapkovich said.

"Either one could be suitable," Chaliapin stated.

"And you would have dossiers ready to keep them in line?"

"Certainly."

Korovin was a gambler, though that carried no real stigma in twenty-first-century Russia. The fact that he'd planned high-end burglaries to support his habit would be useful, though. Losenko was a family man, so perfect for it that he had neglected to divorce his first wife before wedding number two. Later, wife number one disappeared.

Chaliapin always knew where the bodies were buried.

"I'll consult with my superiors," Astapkovich said. "We shall decide who seems most suitable."

"You have superiors?"

Chaliapin meant it as a joke, but Astapkovich frowned in response. "We *all* have superiors, Major. It would be wise to remember that, always."

"Of course, sir."

"We can discuss the details over lunch, Maksim. You're hungry?"

Chaliapin thought about it and discovered that he was.

When had he eaten last? Had it been breakfast the previous day?

Before he had a chance to nod, a knock distracted him.

"Room service," Astapkovich said. "Go let him in, will you?"

THE BELLHOP'S JACKET wasn't Bolan's size, but it was close enough. The guy who'd started out the morning wearing it was smaller, but had drawn a coat too large for him. The end result turned out to be strained shoulder seams, but ample room beneath his left arm for the big Beretta in its fast-draw rig.

Bolan had left the bellhop in a service closet on the ground floor, bound with strips of plastic, gagged with his own tie. He'd have a headache when he came around, from Bolan's light tap on his skull with the Beretta, but no lasting damage should ensue.

The Executioner had pulled some strings at Stony Man, through Hal Brognola in Washington, in search of any information he could use to roll up the survivors of the network that Gennady Sokolov had run—or fronted—with connivance from the powers that be. The CIA was watching those presumed to be involved, including Major Maksim Chaliapin and a certain senator from Russia's Federation Council, Kiril Astapkovich.

And when Bolan learned the two were meeting for a quiet luncheon at the Hotel Cosmos, he'd decided to drop in.

One wheel on the room-service cart wobbled loosely, putting Bolan in mind of defective shopping carts. Thankful that the hotel's carpet kept the rattling noise down, he moved along the curving twelfth-floor corridor until he reached the door he sought. A soft knock, quiet and respectful, then he plastered on a smile and waited.

Maksim Chaliapin got the door, confirming Bolan's guess of who had to be in charge. He offered some gruff welcome

Bolan couldn't understand, and stood aside while the big American passed him with the cart. The door snicked shut behind them.

Kiril Astapkovich was a man of substance, literally. Heavyset, with every indication that he lived the good life, from his hairstyle to his double chins and custom-tailored suit. He glanced at Bolan, then half turned away, as if direct contact with service personnel might soil him.

Bolan pushed his cart into the middle of the room, let Chaliapin pass him, drifting toward the senator, then took a backward step.

"There's been a change of menu," he announced, letting them see the sound-suppressed Beretta 93-R in his hand.

Astapkovich answered him in nearly flawless English. "Who are you? What is the meaning of this?"

Chaliapin got it first. "Cooper!" he said.

"Today, at least," Bolan replied.

"You know this man?" the senator demanded, florid-faced.

"I've never met him in my life," Chaliapin said.

"Then, how—"

"The major may have told you he's been hunting me," Bolan said, interrupting. "Not much luck, although he's killed some people trying."

"You are the Canadian?" Astapkovich asked.

"Close enough," Bolan replied.

Keeping his eyes on Bolan, Chaliapin told the senator, "He took Gennady from the house in Novgorod, I think."

"You're catching up," Bolan allowed. "But you've run out of time."

"What now?" the senator demanded. "Are we hostages? Do you want ransom for our safe release?"

"Not even close," Bolan said.

As the senator started forward, Bolan cut loose. His first shot struck Astapkovich in the forehead, snapped his head back, sent him toppling over backward. Number two slipped in between his double chins and angled upward to the dying brain. A little cheap insurance.

Chaliapin stood gaping at the senator's corpse while the color drained from his face. His mouth worked like a fish's, but he made no sound. Bolan was curious to see if he would faint or have a coronary, but the major found his voice at last.

"Is this for the lieutenant?" he asked Bolan.

"And her friends. You're smarter than you look."

"You understand that this was not my fault?"

"You're just a cog in the machine. I get it," Bolan said.

"Is true! Why kill me, then?"

"Two reasons. First, I owe it to the lady. Second, you'll go out and do the same again—or worse, next time. I'm cleaning house."

"You think this ends it?" Desperation lit a spark of anger in the major's eyes. "You think this stops the sale of weapons? That it makes your world safe for *democracy?*"

"I'm not a politician," Bolan answered. "But it damn sure makes us safe from you."

Chaliapin clawed desperately at his holstered weapon.

Bolan fired twice more, dropped the major to his knees before the pull of gravity took over, and the man landed face-down on the carpet.

Bolan shed the bellhop's jacket, took his own from where he'd stashed it on the food cart's lower shelf and put it on. His fingerprints weren't on file, but Bolan used a linen napkin just the same, wiping the cart's handle and using it to turn the doorknob as he left.

Insurance.

Bolan had four hours, yet, before his flight took off from Domodedovo International. He wasn't flying out as Matthew Cooper, and wouldn't be using Canadian papers this time. "Joshua Burke" would show a valid U.S. passport at the ticket counter, and again when he passed through airport security. There would be no flags raised, no interruption of his flight to New York City.

And from there…

One bit of business still to finish, wrapping up the mission. Touching base with Hal Brognola.

Before the whole thing started once again.

The major had been right, on that score. Nothing ever truly ended but the lives of individuals.

But for this day, that was enough.

EPILOGUE

Arlington National Cemetery

Three hundred thousand heroes sleeping under grass. Their markers seem to stretch forever, row on row, and if a person listened closely, there was a whisper on the breeze.

What were they saying? Bolan couldn't tell.

He'd walked the cemetery grounds at least a dozen times before, and while he always heard the sound—or thought he heard it—Bolan never caught the words. It seemed almost as if the living spoke a different language, needed an interpreter.

Brognola's voice intruded on his reverie. "From what I gather, Sokolov is singing like Beyoncé, giving up the names of anyone he ever dealt with. Ranks and titles, chapter and verse."

"How's his dancing?" Bolan asked.

"He's covered the soft-shoe and two-step."

"Don't tell me he's skating."

"No, no. I'm assured by the highest authority that he'll do time. In light of his cooperative spirit, Justice is thinking two years, low security."

"Jesus!"

"I know. It means he'll go to camp somewhere, live in a dorm, likely without a fence."

"And hit the bricks within a year, when they count good time."

"Meanwhile, we indict a couple hundred other scumbags

on charges ranging from conspiracy to genocide. The AG thinks it's a pretty sweet deal."

"Since when did the attorney general try a case? Or meet a victim?"

"I don't have to tell you that you're preaching to the choir," Brognola said. "I'd like to see this guy dropped down a well."

"He could have been."

"But as it is, we staged a coup. Well, *you* did. In the media, I mean. One major fugitive arrested—brought to justice, more or less—and now we turn the spotlight on the problems he exemplifies. The global arms trade, loose nukes, terrorists with the capability to set a town like Washington on fire."

"And then what?" Bolan asked. "After the hearings and indictments, what comes next? Who extradites the generals and senators and ministers? Does anyone in Moscow even grant that there's a problem, now that it's been going on for twenty years?"

"We can't work miracles," the big Fed said. "Although sometimes you come damned close."

"Not close enough. Who's Sokolov's replacement?"

"Well…"

"He has a name, right?"

"There are several candidates. Right now, the front-runner appears to be some guy named Pavel Korovin. Some kind of former SWAT chief over there, with the militia."

"OMON," Bolan said.

"Nothing gets past you, eh?"

Bolan had to laugh at that. "You think not? Hal, it *all* gets past me. Set them up and knock them down. We change the names and faces, but we really don't change anything. Not where it counts."

"So, what? We just give up?"

"Did I say that?"

"Just wondering."

"We choose our battles and our targets. Fight because we can. Hold back the tide. Thin out the predators."

"Sounds like a plan," Brognola said, half smiling.

"And I'll make a note," said Bolan.

"Of…?"

"Sokolov's parole date. Throw him a little coming-out party."

"I didn't hear that."

"Just as well."

"Of course, they didn't put him into WITSEC. Would've had some trouble reaching out for cash reserves that way."

"Wages of sin," Bolan remarked.

"The last I checked, it's death."

"I'm not a televangelist," Bolan reminded him.

"Another reason why I trust you," Brognola replied. "Besides, a guy like Sokolov must have a world of enemies. How many thousands want him dead?"

"I've got a year or so to do the math," Bolan said.

"Easily. Meanwhile, the pot's still boiling, back in Moscow. Langley says they have a major dust-up going at the FSB."

"I won't expect a miracle," Bolan replied.

"Apparently, *Pravda* got hold of something and they're putting out a front-page series."

"Right beside the UFOs and sea serpents? That ought to be impressive."

"They tailor stories to their audience," Brognola said. "The standard bread and circuses."

"Sound and fury, signifying nothing."

"Faulkner?"

"Cribbed from Shakespeare," Bolan said. "The high school gig pays off."

"I can't remember back that far. Besides, we've got next week to think about."

"Next week? What's happening?"

"I don't know yet," Brognola answered, smiling with a

grim cast to it. "But I'll bet the farm that we'll have work to do."

"I never bet against sure things," Bolan replied.

"You ought to take a few days off. I'll call your cell if something breaks."

"You mean *when* something breaks."

"That, too."

Bolan had no idea where he'd be going next. It might be Africa or South America, maybe a job right in the old U.S. of A. Wherever it might be, he knew geography would be the least of his problems.

As always, the worst would be human.

Ancient mariners once navigated using maps marked with the legend "Here Be Monsters." Few people today spent much time seeking dragons or sea serpents, but there were monsters at large, just the same.

They walked on two legs and wore human faces.

They were everywhere.

And some, quite soon, would meet the Executioner.

* * * * *

The
Don Pendleton's
Executioner®
CARTEL CLASH

A Mexican drug dealer sends a deadly message to the U.S....

Tensions are high after a powerful Mexican drug cartel kills an undercover DEA agent in a declaration of war against the United States. A shipment of missiles is bound for the region, and Washington's hands are tied with red tape. With the border beyond American control, only Mack Bolan can stop the destruction before innocent blood is shed.

Available November wherever books are sold.

GOLD EAGLE®

www.readgoldeagle.blogspot.com

GEX384

Don Pendleton

UNIFIED ACTION

A greedy financier ignites a global powder keg....

The Stony Man teams are on seemingly separate operations in unstable regions. Able Team is following the blood trail of mysterious military contractors in Haiti while Phoenix Force stalks a group of dangerous extremists in Kyrgyzstan. But a stunning link between the two puts Stony Man on the hunt for a ruthless financier who is plotting a massive wave of terror—for profit.

STONY MAN®

Available December wherever books are sold.

TAKE 'EM FREE

2 action-packed novels plus a mystery bonus

NO RISK
NO OBLIGATION TO BUY

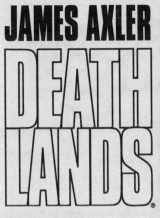